Fields of Gold

Fields of Gold

MARIE BOSTWICK

KENSINGTON BOOKS
http://www.kensingtonbooks.com

KENSINGTON BOOKS are published by

Kensington Publishing Corp.
850 Third Avenue
New York, NY 10022

All Kensington titles, imprints and distributed lines are available at special quantity discounts for bulk purchases for sales promotion, premiums, fund-raising, educational or institutional use.

Special book excerpts or customized printings can also be created to fit specific needs. For details, write or phone the office of the Kensington Special Sales Manager: Kensington Publishing Corp., 850 Third Avenue, New York, NY 10022. Attn. Special Sales Department. Phone: 1-800-221-2647.

ISBN 0-7582-0990-8

First Kensington Trade Paperback Printing: September 2005
10 9 8 7 6 5 4 3 2 1

Printed in the United States of America

To my husband, Brad, the finest man on the planet.

Prologue

This would be easier if I were writing about someone else. Then I could change it, fatten up the thin parts and leave out the dull ones, turning them like frayed collars and cuffs, making them over into something more romantic than they really were, but then the remembering would be neither so painful, nor so sweet. I suppose you can't have one without the other. A name seems as good a place to begin as any, maybe even better than most. I think we live many names in a lifetime. We take them on and off like new suits of clothes, donned or discarded according to the mood and moment.

Everyone calls me Eva. It's a name that makes sense in Dillon, plain and easy to pronounce, not too many syllables. My father always called me by my full name, Evangeline. He and Slim were the only ones who ever did. Papa named me, over Mama's objections, after Longfellow's Evangeline. When I was little he would hold me on his lap and recite from memory. I could feel the verses rumbling rich from his chest,

Fair was she to behold, that maiden of seventeen summers.
Black were her eyes as the berry that grows on the thorn by the
*   wayside,*

Black, yet how softly they gleamed beneath the brown shade of her tresses!

My eyes are green and my hair is auburn, nothing like the description of that poetic heroine, but Papa was never bothered much by details. He was given to taking the romantic view of life and always said exaggeration should never stand in the way of a good story. In Papa's stories it never did.

Mama thought Evangeline sounded pretentious. She wanted to call me Cora or Emma, something that wouldn't make my other differences so obvious, though there was never a prayer of that happening. People who are different draw a lot of attention in Dillon. Me more than most. After forty years, people still gawk when I walk through town. They can't help themselves. No disguise or name, no matter how bland, could camouflage me from the eyes of the curious as I thump and twist my way down Main Street.

I was born with a lame leg. My muscles are small and weak below the knee of my left leg, and my foot curls inward, looking like the gnarled root of the cottonwoods that grow near the river. I walk slowly with the help of a cane, bracing myself with one hand, contracting the muscles in my upper leg to drag my foot along the ground, and then swinging and dropping it forward for the next step—an uneven, rolling gait like a wagon with wheels of different sizes.

I never remember either of my parents talking to me about my leg. In Mama's case I think this was because she didn't want me to feel self-conscious, but Papa just didn't seem to notice. It never crossed his mind that I might not be as whole and capable as everyone else. He saw me from the inside out, full of possibilities, and assumed everyone else had the same view.

Until I started school I felt the same as Papa. I tried as hard as I could to fit in, which is to say too hard, but whenever I came into the schoolyard the girls would giggle and whisper behind their hands and I would feel ashamed, though I wasn't even sure what I was ashamed of.

In a sense, I came from a family of outcasts, yet we never left Dillon, even when it would have made a world of sense to go. When the storms came and the dust rolled, we fought with everything we had to stay on the land. Sometimes it seemed like the going price was . . . everything.

As I said, Papa wasn't from Dillon. He was born in a small seaside village in County Tipperary, Ireland. He emigrated when he was fourteen, settled in Boston, and became a lobsterman. He always loved the sea, and until he met Mama he never had a thought of living or working anywhere else than on the waves; but one rainy afternoon he went to the public library and happened to reach for a copy of the same book that had caught the eye of a twenty-five-year-old spinster who was on her one and only trip out of Oklahoma. Their fingers met on the spine of a worn copy of *Walden,* and, just that quick, they were in love.

When Mama climbed off the train in Dillon four months behind schedule, she was Mrs. Seamus Glennon. The folks back home were positively scandalized. In Dillon, Oklahoma, even a bride or groom who'd married into a family from only as far away as Liberal, ten miles north over the Kansas border, would be considered an alien for the first two or three decades after their wedding. Mama had brought home an actual foreigner, complete with a brogue and a handshake that wasn't nearly strange enough for a stranger. If that wasn't bad enough, he was a Roman Catholic to boot! For all the people in Dillon knew, the man might have horns.

When I was eight, Darla Simpson said her mother had said exactly that about us. I wanted to slap her for saying it, but I knew Mama would be mad if I did. Mama believed that whatever happened in life, good or bad, was God's will and had to be borne with humility or submission, as the occasion warranted.

I, on the other hand, figured that God's will could constitute any number of choices and it was up to us to choose the best among them, but whether we chose well or poorly, God still stood beside us. Secretly, I liked to think that sometimes God made little mistakes, like my leg. I just couldn't believe God would make me lame intentionally.

Mama would have disapproved of my theology. "God will be merciful unto whom He will be merciful," she would say. "Only He knows why he sends good fortune to some and bad to others. That's His business. Ours is to accept things as they come and bear them by His grace." To tell the truth, Mama seemed more at ease when things weren't going too well. Too much comfort could only mean calamity was around the corner. Mama was a farmer's daughter that way.

Papa, on the other hand, was a man who farmed and did it well, but he wasn't a farmer at heart. Eventually the people in town, especially the men, came to respect him, but they always held him at arm's length. He was just too different. For one thing, Papa read. In Dillon the only things a real farmer would be caught dead reading was the Almanac, seed advertisements, and the local newspaper. Papa read *books*, practically ate them, with an Irish love for language and lore that bordered on passion. He could recite scores of lines of poetry, and did, at the drop of a hat.

There was no one in Dillon, no one in the world, like Papa. The salt and romance of the ocean always clung to him. He always sat high on the seat of the combine, proudly above billows of golden bowing wheat stalks, looking for all the world as though he were scanning the horizon for a good port, a fisherman lost on the plains.

Papa came to Dillon because he loved Mama. I suppose he could have insisted they sell the farm and move. I could have done the same, but something changed in us. I don't know if Papa's transformation came over time or all in a day, like it did for me, but somehow that alien land became home. There were too many memories tilled into those furrows to just up and leave.

Before Slim came, I couldn't have understood how that was possible. No matter what came after, I shall always be thankful to him for that. The day I met him was the day my eyes started to open, though it took a long time to sharpen my sight. Up until then I saw things, Dillon especially, the same way other people did: a small, dusty farm town in the middle of nowhere that never bred anyone that mattered and likely never would, the sort of place that only looks good in a rearview mirror. But that's just the view from the ground.

From the air, Dillon is enchanted. The river cuts through the fields, carving them like sharp, silver thread. The cheap tin roofs shimmer and wink like gemstones in the sun. The colors of the dark earth bleed slowly into the yellow wheat, and the breathing air, burnt white as ash by the heat of the sun, melts into brilliant blue sky and pearly clouds. When you're airborne, the scales fall from your eyes, and suddenly you can see the full spectrum of quiet colors, inky black-brown to blinding white. So perfect and seamless, you can't feel where one color leaves off and the next begins. From above, the wheat crops are dressed in a thousand subtle shades of gold, each field just different enough to set it off from the others, showing colors you can't see from the ground: yellow and saffron and lemon and sand and a hundred other shades there aren't even words for. The fields make a tidy checkerboard of gold to the horizon, so square that you know they were made by man, cut and planted where they don't belong by sheer force of will. You can feel the sweat and muscle that went into each acre. And though you are so removed from it all, you can't help but feel a whisper of respect and pity for those left below, people of iron will who fight and inevitably die to bring order and plenty out of a hard, unyielding land.

From the air we see with the eyes of angels. I've only seen it that way once, but I remember it perfectly. For the first time in my life I felt sorry for anyone who wasn't me. I was the only one in the world who wasn't chained to the ground, forced to crawl and scratch along the earth, the taste of dirt sour in my mouth, pining without any real hope for one full, clear breath of air. Even when we landed and I was earthbound again, the feeling stayed with me. It is with me still. Slim described it better than I ever could. He said, "I lose all consciousness with the past. I live only in the moment, in strange unmortal space, crowded with beauty, pierced with danger." I guess that's why I stayed in Dillon, because that one memory we shared so long ago in my seventeenth summer is still stronger than all that came after. It changed everything.

Even when I'm on the ground, I see things as from above.

Chapter 1

1922

"Eva," Mama called from the kitchen window, "when you've finished picking the tomatoes, bring me in some of those cucumbers too. It's so hot I believe we'll just have salad and bread for supper. That sound all right to you? "

"Yes, Mama."

"Don't forget to get all the ripe ones. Pick up the vines so you can see the little red ones underneath. You don't want to waste them."

"No, Mama."

Actually, I didn't care if I wasted them or not, but there was no use arguing that we already had more tomatoes than we could eat in a month of Sundays. The tomatoes were ripe and had to be picked. It was part of Mama's creed. Just as Papa had been firm that naming me was his right, Mama was firm that she be in charge of my religious and moral training, which included those good Christian virtues, hard work and thrift. On that score, Mama was working toward sainthood.

She saved everything: bacon fat, paper sacks, bits of twine, and the smallest scraps of leftover fabric that she kept in a bag and used to make quilts. When I was young it seemed silly, saving every little thing, but now I'm glad she did. If not, I would never have started quilting. Trying to imagine my life today without a number ten needle clasped in the fingers of my right hand would be like trying to imagine myself mute.

My first quilt was a wobbly-seamed nine-patch in bright spring greens and yellows. Mama kept a sharp eye on me, making sure I didn't throw away even the tiniest patches of leftover fabric, urging me to experiment with my own patterns where smaller and smaller bits of cotton could be used. Eventually, all those scraps became the mosaic of my imagination, but in the beginning I was just trying to please Mama. "Economy is nothing to be ashamed of, Eva," she moralized. "I won't have you growing up to be a spendthrift."

For years I didn't even know what a spendthrift was, but the way Mama said it made me pretty sure it led down the path to hell, so I stitched tiny patches and picked the vegetable plot clean, both without complaining, at least not out loud.

It was so hot that day. Our farm was never a particularly beautiful place, not like those clean and green farms from out East like you saw on Currier & Ives cards, where the barns were painted to match the privies and the sheep never got mud splattered on their wool. Nobody would have ever thought of making a picture postcard of our farm. The house was small, just four rooms before Morgan was born and Papa added on a third bedroom. Except for those few dustbowl years when it was impossible to keep ahead of the dirt, it was always clean and neat, with crisp blue gingham curtains that Mama took down to wash, iron, and starch every spring. We had a few pictures on the wall, an average number of crocheted doilies and painted china figurines, and far more books than our neighbors, but we weren't exactly weighed down with ornaments.

We were too poor to think of wasting time and money painting fences and outhouses. All the farm outbuildings, except the barn, were weathered silver gray. The barn had been an honest mid-western red at one time, but the pigments had faded so much in the sun and the prairie winds had blown so hard that the boards now mostly matched the color of the barnyard, a deep, dull mahogany.

The barn itself was too close to the house, and there was no yard to speak of. Every inch of ground was used to grow crops; there was none that could be spared for decoration. Of course, Mama always planted a few petunias by the front porch each spring, about the same time the wildflowers came out and dotted the hills with specks of pink, blue, and gold for a few precious weeks, but by July the sun had burned all the wildflowers to straw and Mama's petunias had grown leggy and brown in the heat. August was worse. In August even the house looked dusty and oven-baked, as though if the tem-perature rose one degree higher the chipped white paint on the sid-ing would crackle and peel off like the skin of an onion and the little blinking windowpanes might shatter in the shimmering heat.

Normally I loved working in the diligently tended half acre that was our garden, the only green space for miles around. Working among the tender stalks and curling vines seemed to give rest to my eyes and soul, but that day it was too hot and the rows too long to think of gardening as anything but a chore. I wanted to lie down in the shade of our one big oak tree and ignore the vegetables; I knew I couldn't, so I picked up another vine and continued plucking at an epidemic of ripe tomatoes. At least I was outside, I thought a little guiltily. Mama was stuck in the house, standing over a mess of steaming canning jars, making sure every last one was filled with tomatoes against the coming winter. The shelves were already full of jars of stewed tomatoes, pickled beets, green beans, and yellow corn, but boxes and boxes of empty jars still sat on the kitchen floor waiting to be filled. How would we ever eat so many? And yet, come spring all those jars would be empty again, just like every year. I popped a tiny, fully ripened tomato into my mouth and crushed it against my teeth to feel the sweet, summery juice spill onto my tongue. Nothing ever changed, I thought with a sigh. Not in Dillon. Not to me. I wished it would.

With the taste of the wish and the summer still lingering in my mouth, I heard a faint, buzzing noise coming toward me, growing louder by the second. It was a sound I couldn't place, not like a bee or a locust, but more machine-like, though I knew it wasn't a car or a tractor.

The noise got louder, and I wondered if maybe I'd been in the sun too long and was going to faint. I'd heard of girls who fainted at school say their ears started buzzing just before everything went black, but I didn't feel dizzy. For an instant, a shadow shielded me from the sun, and I looked up to see a great sapphire bird soaring across the still, white sky—a flying machine! It moved so fast, faster than any car. I could see it clearly, right down to the riblike supports in each double wing and the cables that were strung between them. It was just like the planes I'd seen on the newsreels and in a book Papa had about the Wright brothers, but I'd never imagined them to be so loud and bright, vibrating like a living thing.

Mama stepped out onto the porch to see what all the noise was. We waved as the pilot dipped his wings and raised his arm to greet us. For a moment I could see him, his chin and the sharp line of his jaw jutting below a pair of goggles, like eyes on a grasshopper. In another moment he was gone, over the roof of our barn and toward the edge of the hill where Papa's fields lay. The humming grew fainter and fainter until it finally stopped and I remembered to breathe.

"Did you see that, Mama!" I marveled. "Did you ever see anything so fast?"

"I never did. That was something, wasn't it? Up in the air like that." We both stood and watched the sky for an expectant minute until Mama murmured distractedly, "Well, this isn't getting supper on the table, is it? I still need those cucumbers, Eva. It's nearly five o'clock."

"Yes, ma'am. Right away." But I didn't move. I stood very still in the middle of the garden, holding my breath and listening for the hum of a plane engine, wishing he'd come back.

Twice in a day my wish came true. Suddenly, there he was, wiping his feet on our front mat as Papa held the door and urged him to come in and make himself at home.

I knew him. I recognized the tanned curve of his face clearly, as though he'd been standing next to me and not soaring two hundred feet overhead, but in the plane I hadn't been able to see how tall and slender he was. He was a good head taller than Papa, thin but strong, like a tree you could cling to in a hard wind. Papa was grinning even wider than usual, bursting with the surprise.

"Look what dropped out of the sky and into our field! One minute I was alone, minding my own business, and the next minute a flying machine appears out of a cloud and lands on the wheat stubble, easy as you please, right where I'd been working not an hour before!"

The young man smiled shyly and pushed a blond curl off his forehead. He was the most beautiful thing I'd ever seen, tall and blond with serious gray-blue eyes and cheekbones so perfect they seemed chiseled out of marble and brushed over and over again with the scarlet feathers of some exotic, magical bird until they glowed pink and hearty. He smiled in my direction, showing teeth so white and straight they might have been crocheted in place, like one of Mama's lace doilies. My eyes clung to his face as though he were talking just to me. For a moment, I saw a spark of recognition in his eyes, like he remembered me from somewhere. I felt the same way. I'd known him for all my life, but I didn't realize it until just that moment. If only I could stand still and not move a muscle, maybe he'd leave thinking, "What a pretty girl." Maybe that night he'd dream about me, as I knew I would about him. He broke our gaze and turned to greet Mama.

"Well, the landing wasn't as easy as I'd have liked, Mrs. Glennon. I'm afraid I bent your fence a little in the process. Did a fair bit of damage to the Jenny, too."

"The Jenny?" Mama asked.

"That's my plane. She's a surplus trainer left from the war, a Curtiss JN4-D. Short name is Jenny."

"Don't you worry about the fence. It was due for some work anyway," Papa said offhandedly. "And if you need any tools to fix your plane, you're welcome to borrow anything I've got." Still grinning, Papa took off his hat and sat down at the table. "Clare, I told this young man we'd love to have him to supper, that is, if we've got anything to eat."

"I think we might come up with something. Eva?" Mama wiped her hands on her apron and shot me a look that said we'd need to scour the kitchen to find something suitable for a company supper. I didn't want to move. I didn't want him to see me walk, but I couldn't just stand there forever. Slowly, trying to be as quiet as possible, I limped to the pantry to see if there was any pie left from Sunday. I could feel his eyes following me, and I kept my head down, not wanting to see his reaction to my twisted gait. The thumping of my cane against the wooden floorboards seemed like a pounding drum in my ears. I was grateful when Mama spoke.

"Tomato salad and fresh bread and cold fried chicken sound all right to you, Mr . . . ?"

"That would be wonderful, ma'am. Thank you. You can skip the mister, though. Everybody calls me Slim."

He stayed at the farm, camping in our field next to his airplane for three nights. I didn't see much of him, but I thought about him all the time. Every hour it grew stronger, the feeling that I was being pulled toward him, inch by inch, and there was nothing I could do to stop it even if I'd wanted to. The breeze was full of sparks no one but I could feel. The night shimmered and crackled just because he was nearby, out of sight over the hill. I'd never talked to him, but I loved him. I knew it. I knew him. Better than anyone else ever could, ever would. It was real, like an electricity experiment we did in school showing how different things will or won't let a current pass through them. I was metal and copper wire, a perfect receptor for his every thought, dream, and longing.

He was full of ambition, I knew that, but it was the kind of ambition that didn't need an audience. He only cared to be tested against his own standard, because no other measure of merit could be as rigorous. He was a poet, saw music in the natural movements of life that other people missed, and wrote down his thoughts in a little book, transparent and completely honest because he thought no one else would ever see his words. I knew, too, that he was often afraid, but not of death or gravity. When he woke in the night, sweating and startled by the vapors of a bad dream, it wasn't twisted metal and flame that brushed across his memory, but a vision of a stretched white ribbon across his path, a finish line that he could never quite reach, no matter how hard he ran.

Oh yes, I knew him, every bit of him. Though I can't tell you how.

Two days later, the Jenny was fixed, and people started coming past our house, in trucks, wagons, on horseback, and on foot, to see Slim fly his airplane. If they were richer than we were and had five dollars to pay for the ride, they could even climb in beside him and see what Dillon looked like to the birds.

I watched the parade all day from behind the front-porch screen where I sat snapping the stems off a mountain of just picked pole beans. People waved as they went by, smiling and yoo-hooing like they were headed to a church picnic. I wished I could go too, but Mama had to get the beans into jars while they were still fresh. Of course, I wasn't missing all the fun. I'd seen Slim fly over five or six times that morning. Every time he did, my heart pounded with excitement and I craned my neck to see him soaring overhead like a proclaiming angel with a message just for me. Still, I longed to go out to the field with the rest of the crowd. Maybe just to see how an airplane got off the ground, to be where he was. Maybe to say hello.

Another cloud of dust rose on the road. It was Mr. Walden's ice truck bringing our order. My best and only friend, Ruby, was with him. I called to Mama that the ice was here and heard her shaking the baking-soda can she used for a bank, looking for a dime to pay for the ice. She came out onto the porch, smoothing her hair back, just as the truck pulled into our yard. Ruby leaped out of the cab and ran toward the house while Mr. Walden hoisted an ice block out of the back of his truck and onto his shoulder.

"Hello, Mrs. Glennon," Ruby said politely. "Hey, Eva! Mr. Walden gave me a ride out so I can go see the flying machine. You want to come?"

"I can't. I have to get these beans done." Mama opened the screen door to let Mr. Walden pass.

"Afternoon, Mrs. Glennon." Mr. Walden moved his hand toward his head, as though to tip his hat, but when he did, the bag of ice balanced on his shoulder shifted and threatened to fall, so he settled for a stiff nod of greeting instead. "I brought you a bag of extra chips, no charge. Thought they might be good for tea. It's been so hot."

"Thank you, Mr. Walden," Mama said with a smile. "That was thoughtful of you. Now I've got something cold to offer you. Can you sit and have a glass of tea? I've got a pound cake, too." Mr. Walden pretended to think about the idea and pronounced it a fine one, as he did every week. We were at the end of his Wednesday route, and his visits were a kind of tradition. He always stopped to eat something and visit before heading back to town, and we always got extra ice by way of thanks. Sometimes I'd tease Mama about it, calling Mr. Walden her secret admirer.

"Hmph," she'd grump, though I could see a smile play at her lips. "The only thing Cyrus Walden admires is a well-browned piecrust and there's no secret in that. He costs me more in flour and sugar than I save in ice with all those ice chips. I'm just being polite."

Still, I knew she looked forward to those Wednesday chats. Visiting nearly every farm in the county, Mr. Walden was a reliable source of news, and he wasn't shy about sharing it. Of course, Mama would never have actively engaged in gossip, but if the iceman wanted to talk while enjoying her hospitality, well, there was no help for that.

I got up from my chair to help Mama set out the tea glasses, but she shook her head at me. "That's all right, Eva. Why don't you go on with Ruby and see the airplane?"

"Are you sure?" I asked, not quite daring to hope she really meant it. "What about the beans?"

"They'll wait." She smiled and her eyes twinkled knowingly. "You don't want to be the only girl in town doesn't see that young Mr. Slim in action, do you? Besides, if I have to stand over that stove one more minute I'll probably steam all the wrinkles out of my face and your Papa wouldn't recognize me. That wouldn't do, would it?" She patted me on the shoulder. "Go on, you two. Have fun. Don't be too late."

I grabbed my cane and walked with Ruby across the yard toward the field where Slim's plane was.

Ruby and I became friends six years before when I was eleven and Clarence Parker, who was known as Clay, ran up to me on the playground and kissed me on the mouth. His lips felt stiff and chapped on mine, but I concentrated very hard so I would never forget what my first kiss felt like. When he let go of me, I took a step back, blushed to the tips of my ears, and looked up at him to smile, but he was turned around to face a group of boys who were watching near the swings. "There!" he shouted. "Y'all owe me a nickel! I told you I'd do it! For a dime I'll kiss your old man's pig!"

From then on I spent my recesses inside, reading books, traveling in my mind to places far away from Dillon. Ruby spent a lot of recesses inside as well, but not by choice. She was just my age, a freckled, redheaded girl with a father who drank and a mother who was too sickly to make sure her daughter's dresses were as clean and well-starched as they might have been. Ruby's red hair was no lie. Her short temper and general lack of interest in schoolwork meant the teacher frequently assigned her long punishments writing "I will nots" on the chalkboard. None of this curbed Ruby's behavior, but she did come to have the prettiest handwriting in school.

Not long after my humiliation with Clarence Parker, Ruby was in disgrace yet again and stood at the blackboard scratching out her latest penance while I read about Dorothy's trials in Oz. The teacher was distracted by some argument on the playground. While her back was turned, Ruby drew a caricature of Clay Parker puckered up to kiss a pig he held in his arms; the pig was squirming away with a face of chalky disgust. A balloon over its head read, "I wouldn't kiss ClareDUNCE for Five Dollars!!!!"

I covered my mouth to keep from laughing out loud. Ruby shushed me, but her eyes twinkled in fun. When the dismissal bell rang, she walked me home and we talked the whole way about what a fool Clarence Parker was. From that day and forever after we were fast friends, two outcasts united against the world.

That day, as she always did when we went walking, Ruby slowed her pace to mine. That was one of the things I liked about her. Normally, Ruby trotted everywhere, like she was hurrying home to a good meal, but the minute we were together she fell into my pace, meandering next to me as though it were her natural speed. I slipped my hand into hers, and we walked together in perfect rhythm.

When we were far enough away from the house so no one could hear, Ruby started peppering me with questions. "Tell me all about him! What's he like? Is he handsome? I heard he looks like a movie star. Were you scared when you rode in the plane? I would be! What did your mama say when he landed in your yard?"

"Landed in the yard? Ruby, you really are a goose. He landed in the field. I've never even seen his plane, let alone ridden in it. I barely know him at all. He came and had dinner once, but he spent the whole time talking with Papa about crops and engines. I've never even spoken to him." There was no use trying to explain to her how I really felt. She would insist on details and conversations and facts, things you could only feel with your skin on. I couldn't tell her that sometimes you can know a person inside and out without ever having passed a word between you. How could I explain? A week before I wouldn't have understood myself.

"Well, you're practically famous now." Ruby nodded sagely. "Everybody says he landed right in your front yard, almost hit the henhouse, and that he's been staying with your family and gave you all rides to pay for his keep. I was coming out of Garland's store yesterday and a bunch of the girls from school practically jumped on me asking me was it true that he was actually sleeping in the room next to you and that he took you flying every night. They were excited, but Mary Kay Munson was pea-green jealous! She said she didn't believe a word, that something like that could never happen to . . ."

Ruby blushed, embarrassed to have nearly blurted out whatever ugly name Mary Kay had called me. Poor Ruby. She was in such a rush she didn't always stop to think before she spoke. I pretended not to notice her stammering.

"I just can't stand Mary Kay," Ruby grumbled. "She thinks she's the queen of Dillon or something."

"Well, if I were going to be made queen I hope I'd be queen of someplace better than Dillon. What did you tell her?" I enjoyed the idea of the other girls being envious of me. If they were, it was surely a first.

Ruby smiled and opened her eyes wide with innocence. "I told her it was all true, of course."

"Ruby! You didn't!"

"Yes, I did!" she whispered excitedly, even though there was no one nearby to hear. "I told them he's staying in your house and the walls are so thin between your rooms that when he goes to bed at night you can hear him taking off his clothes and after he's done you hear the sound of water pouring into the basin so he can wash the sweat off his bare skin. I told them that he grabbed you and kissed you out behind the house and asked you to fly away with him, but you said no because you couldn't break your mama and papa's heart like that, but even though you'd probably never see each other again, you'd always love him."

"Ruby! That's terrible." I giggled with pleasure. "How could you tell such a lie?"

"Because it sounded so much better than the truth." She shrugged. "Besides, Mary Kay deserved it for being so nasty. She got so mad thinking about it she stamped her foot and dropped a perfectly good triple-scoop ice cream cone into the dust and ended up stepping on it and falling right on her behind."

I knew she was making that part up to please me, just like she made up my romance with the mysterious Slim to tease the other girl's imagination, but it was still a funny picture. We both laughed until tears came to our eyes thinking of Mary Kay and her ice cream lying, humiliated and melting in the dirt on Main Street.

When we finally calmed down Ruby looked at me with disappointed eyes. "So, you really never even talked to him? You don't know anything about him?"

"Well, maybe one thing. Everybody calls him Slim, and you're right, he *is* handsome," I whispered, which started us giggling all over again.

And there's a least one grain of truth in your fairy tale, I thought to myself as I squeezed Ruby's hand. *Though I'll probably never see him again, never talk to him, I will always love him.*

It was afternoon by the time we joined the small crowd of people, a few waiting to take a ride and many more just standing and watching the excitement. Slim saw me and waved as he helped boost a big backside that turned out to belong to Mr. Miller up into the cockpit. I was so surprised my heart jumped in my chest. Ruby dug her elbow into my ribs and hissed, "Wave back, you ninny! Ha! I thought you said he never even noticed you. I think he likes you. Look how he's smiling at you."

I could feel heat on my face and arms as I raised my hand shyly to acknowledge him. "Don't be stupid," I returned sharply. "You know it's nothing like that. He's just being polite, that's all. He ate dinner with us." Ruby didn't argue with me because she understood what I was really saying, that someone like him would never be more than just polite to someone like me.

We found a comfortable spot on a little knoll and sat rubbing heads of wheat in our hands and chewing on the kernels while Slim and the Jenny, loaded down with five-dollar copilots, landed and took off and landed again. I could have watched forever, the way the wings dipped and sliced through the sky, dancing on an invisible tide. I nearly did watch forever, or at least for hours and hours. Without my realizing it, the afternoon had passed and the crowd began thinning out, heading home to supper. Ruby stirred next to me, "Eva, I've got to go. Shall we catch a ride with someone?"

"No. You go on," I answered without looking at her, my eyes transfixed by the sapphire miracle soaring overhead. "I'm going to stay a little while longer. I can walk back. It's not far."

"You sure?" she asked uncertainly as she stood up and smoothed out the wrinkles in her skirt. "Won't your mama be worried?"

"No. It's hours until dark. You go on. I'll be fine." And I was. Ruby left reluctantly, but I felt fine and free sitting alone on the hill, a part of the late summer sky, at once warm and cool as a light afternoon wind blew across my face and the folds of my cotton dress while the heat of earth seeped into my body. The silky dance of the plane was even more beautiful silhouetted against a twilight sky, a poem not yet written, at least not by me. When the last rider climbed out of the cockpit, shook hands with Slim, and drove back toward town, it seemed like an instant had passed instead of an afternoon.

I rose to leave too, but Slim came bounding up the hill toward me. "Hey, there! Eva, isn't it? I was hoping you'd come out today."

"You were?" I asked without a hint of flirtation in my voice. I couldn't quite believe he'd actually remembered my name, let alone been looking for me.

"Yeah. I was wondering if you'd like to go for a ride. I wanted to ask you the other night, but your dad was so interested in talking about flying that I hardly got to say a word to you. And I thought"— he ducked his head and cleared his throat awkwardly, I could tell he was as unaccustomed to talking with girls as I was to talking with boys—"Well, I thought maybe you'd like to come for a ride with me. For free, I mean. My treat." He cleared his throat again and nervously reached up to push the normally disobedient curl off his forehead, forgetting it was tucked securely inside his aviator's cap.

My mind was so full that nothing came out of my mouth. Slim searched my face, and his smile faded a little, "Unless you're afraid. It really is safe, but some people are just scared of the idea. You don't—"

"No, it's not that," I rushed to explain. "Of course it's safe. Anybody can see that. I guess I was so surprised I didn't know what to say. I'd love to go."

We walked toward the plane without saying a word. My heart was beating so furiously in my chest I was certain the sound of it would drown out any conversation. He reached toward me tentatively, thinking, I suppose, that he'd have to lift me and my crippled leg into the plane, but I stopped him. "Just give me a boost like you did everyone else. I can do it. I like doing things for myself."

He looked at me seriously as he made his hands into a stair step. "I know what you mean."

Watching from the ground, I somehow never thought about being afraid, but now, as the propellor coughs and roars and the body of the plane shimmies, I am afraid, awfully afraid. Feeling my heart pound and almost hearing the blood coursing through my body, I realize that fear, some kinds of fear, are good. It makes me know I am alive in a way nothing else ever has. The plane is light and flimsy, made of wood and wire and cloth, nothing more. Somehow I thought it would be stronger, thicker, like a protecting cocoon. If anything goes wrong and we hit the ground, there is nothing to prevent injury or even death. I still want to go. I know somehow that there is something in the sky I'm meant to find. Maybe you have to risk death to find your life, your true life. I know if I stay on the ground I'll definitely stay alive and things will go on like they always have, but I know too that if I stay on the ground, my future will miss me.

It seems so long, so long that we run, weighted and clumsy, along the ground. It is as though gravity refuses to loosen her grip on us, and then, miraculously, speed and our defiant will, our refusal to stay pinned and helpless to the earth, breaks us free, and we rise on the fuel of our own thoughts, away from the heat of earth, up and over the fences and fields into the fresh and darkling sky.

Suddenly my heart isn't pounding anymore and I can breathe. For the first time in my life I can draw a full, greedy lungful of air into my body because I am part of the sky, in exactly the right place, exactly where and how I am meant to be. How perfect everything looks from an angel's perspective. There is nothing wrong with me. There is nothing wrong with anybody. There are no mistakes, only the beauty that comes from difference and surprise and the beauty that comes from sameness and order. How hard it is to see from sea level. How long it took me to understand this.

I lift my arm into the wind and feel it rushing, pushing, stretching past my open fingers, wanting to take me with it through clouds and stars to be part of the eternal, but today it leaves me behind. Today I am too heavy to join it. Someday I'll come. The winds tell me so, and I am sure of it. It's our destiny.

I never want to go back.

Chapter 2

I couldn't even wait for the propeller to quit spinning before I gushed forth a flash flood of words. I needed to find the right phrases to explain it all, right then, before one particle of it faded and I missed my chance to preserve it fresh and whole in a waxy casing of words.

I gasped for breath, trying to say everything at once. "Is it always that way? Is it? Ever since I first saw you, when you flew over the house and dipped your wings at us, I've tried to imagine what it would be like! I'd spent so much time at it that I almost convinced myself I'd gotten it right, that I'd already done it, but I was wrong! It's just so much . . . I don't know, bigger than I thought it would be. Not the world, or the sky, but the idea, the way your thoughts expand. Oh!" I screwed up my face in exasperation. "I'm not making any sense. You must think I'm crazy rattling on like this, but I'm so excited I'm tingling! I can't think of anything to compare it to. It's a new world up there! A new heaven and earth. Do you know what I'm saying?"

"Yes," he said, smiling, pulling off his goggles to reveal eyes that reflected mine. "I know. That's why I wanted you to come. I thought you'd know what you were seeing. Most people don't, you know."

"How is that possible?" I wondered.

He thought for a moment, then shrugged and hopped lightly out of the cockpit and onto the ground. "They just don't have the imagination, I suppose."

"Papa would understand. I know he would. I just wish I could find the right way to describe it to him."

Slim moved around the Jenny methodically, sliding wooden blocks under the wheels while my eyes followed his every move, memorizing him as if he were a vapor that might vanish into thin air if I turned my head even for a moment. "I've tried, a few times," he said, "but nothing ever quite hits the mark. The first time I flew I rushed right home to write it all down in my journal. I was so afraid I'd forget just how it felt."

I pushed myself up from my seat and swung my legs out and over onto the wing. "Yes! That's just what I was thinking."

"Don't worry," he said earnestly. "You'll never forget it. If it speaks to you, flight stays with you always. Sometimes I find myself talking to someone and I'll begin daydreaming about flying and realize the dream is more real to me than the person I'm talking to. Even though it's so real, you can't ever find the right way to tell people about it. At least, I can't. But there's something about you, Eva"—he nodded seriously—"you might have better luck."

He looked up, and I saw in his eyes the same expression he'd had the first night in our kitchen, a moment of recognition, as though he sensed we'd met somewhere before but couldn't quite remember where. For an instant, the doubt cleared away and he remembered my face and that we had been together from always. I waited for the perception to pass, for him to brush it away as a ridiculous fancy, but he didn't. When he spoke his voice was soft as the breeze, almost as though he were talking to himself.

"I bet there are words in you, Eva, poems and songs that could make sense of everything. I can see it in your face."

He reached up to me with both arms, and this time I let myself be helped off the wing. The touch of his hands was firm and comforting encircling my arms. My body slid steadily along his until my feet touched the ground, and I felt his hands resting too long between my shoulders and the small of my back. I knew I should pull away and say something awkward and blushing to cover my embarrassment, but I wasn't embarrassed. *How strange,* I thought. Stranger still that I felt so natural leaning my head onto his chest. Without pretense of accident or confusion I raised my face to meet the kiss I knew was waiting.

I didn't need to make myself concentrate on that kiss. It was like flying. There was no danger I'd forget how his lips felt, soft but solid, tentative and unapologetic all at once, or the gentle insistence of his fingers at the buttons of my blouse. If I had been thinking, maybe I would have told him to stop, but I wasn't thinking. I didn't want him to stop. If I were lying, maybe I'd say that I didn't understand what would happen next, but I did.

I could have said no, but instead I yielded to the pressure of his arms on my shoulders, pulling me down onto a bed of crackling wheat stalks, curling beneath the safety of his body sheltering mine, covering me like a blanket. Though it was my first time, my body responded to his without thought or instruction. Natural and familiar, like opening a thick, dusty book and finding you already know the story.

Afterward, we lay talking, encircled by a protecting wall of wheat that hid us from the world. He told me of his growing up in

Michigan and of the first time he saw a plane fly and how wonderful he thought it would be to have one of his own and be part of the sky. He told me how he had saved up to buy the Jenny and how he'd worked as a wing-walker with a flying circus before he'd started barnstorming on his own, but what he really wanted was something bigger, something to test himself against. He told me a million things about himself while I memorized the lovely flat vowels of his midwestern accent and practiced pacing my breathing to his, making my lungs expand and contract to his rhythm. Then he was quiet a long time, content as I was to stare up at a perfect elegant circle of evening sky. Finally he raised himself up on one elbow and turned toward me, resting his other arm on the flat of my belly.

"Now tell me about you. Tell me about that," he said simply, indicating my lame leg with his eyes. If someone else had asked me that question, I'd have felt ashamed, but with Slim it was different. I liked his honesty. He was genuinely interested in me and wise enough to know that my twisted leg was part of the story.

"Right after I was born, the doctor told Mama and Papa I'd never walk and they ought to take me to Texas to see a specialist. Mama asked if a specialist could make me walk, and the doctor said no, but they could brace my leg so at least it would be straight. Mama said she didn't see how a straight leg would do me much good if I couldn't walk on it, and besides, she wasn't going to travel four hundred miles to see a bunch of doctors who'd given up on me before they'd ever seen me anyway, so we never went."

"I like your mother." Slim laughed. "She doesn't let anyone get around her, does she?"

"Nobody except Papa, and I don't think that counts. Anyway, after that Mama started exercising my leg on her own, trying to make it stronger. She made a kind of bag that strapped on to my ankle, and she put a few washer rings in for weight. I'd kick my legs to hear the washers jingle. Gradually she added more and more weight, and my leg got stronger and stronger. By the time I was a year and a half old I could stand holding on to something. I could walk with a crutch before my third birthday. Later I just needed the cane."

"And after that you walked everywhere?"

"Not quite. I'm so slow they knew I'd never make it to school and back without help, so Papa taught me to ride, and when I turned five he gave me Ranger, our old plow horse, as a present. I loved riding. I used to gallop across the fields with my arms spread wide, pretending I was a bird. I'd imagine I was running a race and none of the other kids could catch me. But I couldn't have been going too fast," I said with a smile. "Even in his younger days, Ranger wasn't exactly a speed demon."

"You still have him?" Slim asked.

"Oh yes." I nodded. "I still ride him to school and town, but I never go to Dillon unless I have to."

"Don't like school? I don't blame you. I never saw the point of learning something out of a book that you could learn better if you just went out and experienced it for yourself. My mother is a teacher, and she's always on me for not taking my studies seriously, but I'm too restless to be much of a scholar. I went to college for a while, but I dropped out so I could learn to fly."

"You've been to college!" I marveled. "Really? Oh, I'd give anything to do that! I love books and learning things. Papa's just the same. He reads everything he can get his hands on. If there's nothing else available he'll read the Sears Roebuck out loud so Mama and I can hear all about the new advances in farm implements. You know, I actually like it." We laughed, and Slim reached over and wound a lock of my hair around his finger.

"So, you're a lot like your Papa, and you love school. Tell me more," he said and seemed so sincerely interested that I did.

"I don't love school. I love learning. School would be fine if it was just me and the teacher and a pile of books, but it's not. I hate going there."

"The kids tease you?"

"Not so much now as when I was little." I shrugged. "Now they mostly ignore me, all except Ruby. She's the girl I was with today. My best friend. My only friend."

"You don't have any beaus?" he asked. For a moment I thought he might be teasing me, but his question was genuine, and I was pleased to think he supposed anyone would be interested in me.

"No. Of course not." I blushed.

"Why not?" he asked incredulously. "You're beautiful, Eva. The most beautiful girl I ever met. Are all the fellows in this town blind or something?"

"Not blind. They just can't see past my leg. I'm the crippled girl, that's all." I sat up and started picking wheat stalks off my dress, suddenly wishing he'd change the subject.

Slim got up and kneeled in front of me, enfolding my hands in his. "I see you," he whispered looking square into my eyes. Then he leaned forward to kiss me again, softly, an endearment. "I see you just like in a looking glass, but better than that. I see you front to back and head to toe. I see you, crippled leg and all, and I'm glad for it."

I raised my eyebrows doubtfully. "You're glad I'm crippled?"

Slim bit his lip, searching for a better phrase. "Not exactly glad, but if you weren't you wouldn't be the same person, would you? From that first moment, in your parent's kitchen, I knew there was something different about you. I couldn't figure out what it was. Then, when you walked away and I saw how hard that was, something as simple as walking across the room, I thought maybe that was the difference. You know what it is to have to work for what you want. If not for that, you might be just as empty and twittering as any of those small-town girls that come hanging around my plane. But you're not. I never met anyone like you, Eva."

"I never thought about my leg that way." I couldn't help but smile at him. "That's the nicest thing anybody's ever said to me. But what about you? You must have lots of girlfriends."

"Not me," he said dismissively. "There are plenty of girls that come out to watch me fly, but they don't interest me. They flirt and bat their eyelashes at me, all painted up and squeaking. They remind me of a bunch of circus monkeys."

I laughed out loud at the picture he'd painted. The description fit Mary Kay Munson and her crowd to a tee.

"I mean it," he continued earnestly. "Most girls are just ridiculous, nothing in their heads but fluff, with no more interest or idea of how a plane works than a rabbit has of how the magician pulled it out of the hat. No," he said solemnly, almost to himself, "no girls for me. I've got plans. Aviation is going to change the world, and I'm going to be right in the middle of it. I don't have time to go and get myself tangled up with some girl."

I knew his words weren't intended for me, that he was only repeating his own resolutions to himself so he wouldn't forget, but they stung all the same. For a moment, I felt foolish sitting there with him, wondering what I'd gotten myself into, but then I remembered his ambition. It had been there from the beginning. Before he'd ever touched me, before we'd said a word, I'd known who he was. His pull toward me was strong, but the pull of a future he saw outlined only in shadow was stronger and always would be. I'd known that, and still I'd come to the field, flown with him, held him close instead of pushing him away. I told myself I had no right to feel hurt now.

"Anyway, I've never been much good at talking to girls." He

shrugged off his reverie. "My tongue sticks to the roof of my mouth whenever I meet one. It's different with you, though. I can't explain it. Right from the first moment I knew I could say anything to you and you'd understand. Isn't that strange?"

"I know just what you mean." I leaned over, kissed him, and pulled him down next to me as I lay back on the grass and nestled close to him, content for a time to say nothing, just watching the moon as it rose full overhead.

"Eva?"

"You know, my real name, my full name anyway, is Evangeline."

"Really? That's my mother's name, too, and that's what everyone calls her."

"Nobody calls me Evangeline except Papa. I think of it as almost a secret, like a pet name that only the people who really know me can use. I wish you'd call me by it."

"All right, I will. Evangeline, I . . ." He lowered his eyes to look where his hand rested stroking the soft fabric of my dress. "What I mean is . . . did I hurt you? I didn't mean to. I didn't plan any of this." Finding the courage to look at me, his eyes were anxious and sincere. "I wouldn't want you to think this was what I was planning when I invited you to ride with me. I wanted to share the sky with you, that's all."

I reached up and pulled a strand of golden grass from his hair, "Shush. You don't need to explain. I didn't feel tricked, if that's what you're thinking. I felt . . . oh, I don't know . . . alive! All my veins were running hot and cold at the same time, and there was nothing I could do to stop it. The truth is, I didn't want to stop it. It would have been wrong to try, like standing against a force of nature. If we'd have fought it we would have been altering our destiny somehow."

He smiled and rolled onto his back, sliding his arms under my shoulders and pulling me close, "I'm glad. I'd never do anything to hurt you, Evangeline."

"I believe you, Slim, but some kinds of hurts you can't help. Sometimes hurt and happiness are all part of the same package, so you'll always know it really happened. You know how when something wonderful happens people say, 'Pinch me so I'll know I'm not dreaming'? Life is like that sometimes, a little pain thrown in so we know we aren't imagining the whole thing. The pain will help me to remember it all after you've gone." I took a deep breath and tried to sound light and brave. "I guess that will be pretty soon, won't it?"

It made me feel better to say it first and give voice to the thought I knew was worrying him, how to tell me that even after what had happened he would have to leave. It would have been nice to lie there and imagine a life together, to pretend for a little while that we would never part, but there's too much of my practical mama in me to give in to daydreams. He shifted away from me ever so slightly, and I felt his breathing find a new rhythm, separate from mine.

"I'll go tomorrow morning. I'm supposed to fly down to Texas to do some stunts in a flying circus." He sat up and looked me in the eye, and I knew it was because he wanted me to believe his words. At that moment, he believed them himself.

"I'll be back, Evangeline. I promise. Just as soon as I can, I'll come back, and then we'll . . ." He hesitated for a moment trying to think how the sentence ended, but I could see him struggling with the choices before him. Whatever he said next would either be a lie or alter everything he'd ever envisioned for himself. I interrupted him before he was forced to choose.

"Slim, my papa and mama love each other as much as two people can. They don't talk about it, of course, but what they've got is real special. Every once in a while, though, I see Papa standing on the porch watching the horizon, and there is a lonely look comes into his eye and I know he's thinking of the sea. He misses it. He loves us, but there is this silent part of him that wonders what he might have done if only." I sat up taller and smoothed the wrinkles out of my skirt. "I'd never want that to happen to anyone I loved. If someone I care about is going to dream about something, I'd rather it was of one more hour with me rather than one hour away so they could find out how the story might have turned out 'if only.' Wouldn't you?"

He took my hand and pressed his lips to my palm. "I barely know you, but I love you, Evangeline. Is that possible? I don't want to go."

"I know." I didn't tell him that he had to go. There was no need to pretend to discuss what we both knew had been decided.

Papa was furious when I got home. I'd figured Mama would be the one who would want to skin me and Papa would be the one trying to talk her out of it, but nothing that day happened the way I thought it would. When I arrived, well after nine o'clock, Papa was pacing the floor and Mama was sitting calm in her chair, rocking and knitting as though nothing out of the ordinary had happened. She told Papa to shush, that I was home now and that was the important thing. I explained about the airplane ride and that Slim and I had gotten to talking and lost track of the time. It wasn't a total lie. I figured they didn't really want to know the rest anyway.

"You won't let it happen again, will you, Eva?" Mama asked, more to reassure to Papa than to exact any promise from me.

"No, Mama," I replied contritely. "I'm sorry I worried you."

"Worried us!" Papa barked. "I was half out of my mind with worry! You try a stunt like that again, miss, and I'll take my strap to you! I swear I will!"

"Now, Seamus," Mama soothed, "that's enough of that. You've

never laid a hand on her and you know you never would, for all your bluster. There's no harm done. It's late. We'd better get to bed. Eva, we'll want to get started on those pickles early tomorrow, before the heat sets in."

Alone in my room, I took off my shoes, dress, and slip, and poured water into the flowered basin. I lifted the sponge out of the washbasin and squeezed tiny streams of water over my skin before putting on my lightest nightdress, enjoying the feeling of the damp cotton against my body, a cool, caressing hand against my tingling new breasts and thighs. Would it last, I wondered, this burning, enlivening sensation that spilled, inside and out, over every part of me that he'd touched? Did it happen that way to everyone? Had Mama felt like this? Had stout Mrs. Dwyer who sold aspirin and cough syrup behind the counter of the drugstore? Or Corinna Leslie, Ruby's cousin who'd gotten married last April? Picturing them each in turn—canning pickles, making change, hanging laundry—I couldn't remember seeing a shadow of anything as wonderful as the awakening that surged through me. *It couldn't have been the same,* I thought. *Surely if they'd felt it, even half as strong as I did, they'd never be able to hide it.*

I was glad to be alone, not because I wanted to escape Papa's anger, but because I was afraid they'd be able to read what had happened on my face. I wanted to think, to hold it all close without trying to explain it, willing myself not to remember that in the morning Slim would be gone.

I opened the window and lay down on top of the quilt Mama had helped me patch when I was only ten years old, a blue and red Ohio Star pattern. As I lay there, looking at the moon and wishing for a bit of breeze to stir the hot night air, I could hear Mama and Papa getting ready for bed in the next room. The hinges of their door squeaked in a familiar pitch, and the drawer on their chifforobe scraped against the frame just like every night. Papa always swore he was going to oil the hinges and plane the drawers, but he somehow never got around to it. I was glad. Those night sounds were like a lullaby to me. I don't suppose I'd have been able to sleep without them.

Papa's boots thumped on the wooden floor, and I could hear the sound of his voice murmuring something to Mama as he walked to the window and struggled to open the sticky sash. Then I could hear his voice as clear as if he and Mama were addressing me face to face, but of course they weren't. They'd have never shared with me the things they told each other that night.

"Just for tonight, Clare. The night air won't kill us this once. It's so hot, and I feel so restless. I'm suffocating."

"All right, Seamus, but don't blame me if you catch pleurisy. At least come away from the window and get into bed."

"I won't be able to sleep. I keep thinking about Evangeline, out with that boy, so late, in our field. In *our* field! I let him park his plane there, fed him at our table, lent him my tools, and he has the nerve to take my daughter up in his plane without even asking my permission. She could have been killed up there in that contraption of his!"

"But she wasn't, and everything is fine," Mama replied factually, "so come to bed and forget about it."

Papa grumbled as he paced. "She was so late! What could they have been doing out there that time of night?"

I could hear my mother shift under the covers and roll over to face Papa. Her voice was quiet and more patient than it had been. "Seamus, you know what they were doing. You *know*," she urged.

"Clare! What are you talking about? Evangeline hardly knows him. Never even spoke to him when he came to dinner. Besides, she wouldn't, she—"

"Why not? Why wouldn't she? I did, Seamus. We did."

"That was different. We were in love and we couldn't . . . Well, it wasn't like this. Some stranger passing through town. We were in love. It was for life, you and me."

"Yes, I'd known you for three days and it was for life. What makes you think it isn't just like that for Eva? Oh, Seamus." Mama sighed, and I heard a rustling of bedclothes and then footsteps as she got out of bed and crossed the room to stand near him. I could see her in my mind's eye, her arms wrapped around Papa as he stood looking out the window, frowning at the full moon.

"Did you see her when she came in?" Mama asked. "Did you see her face and how her eyes shone? It's love for her, and for *her* it is for life, even though for them it may not be more than a night. She's your daughter, Seamus. She wouldn't have settled for less than the real thing."

"The real thing," he scoffed. "What would she know about that? She's a child. The real thing is with someone who'll stick around for more than a week; someone who'll be there when the crop fails, or your sight grows weak, or the baby gets sick. There's nothing fancy to real love, but you can count on it, like the earth under your feet. You don't get that with some clown in a flying circus! Oh, leave it," Papa huffed. "I don't know why I'm letting you get me so tied up in knots over this, anyway. This is my Evangeline. She'd never waste herself on someone like that. Nothing happened," he stated with finality. "I know it. She'll wait for the right one. I know she will."

"The right one? Just who do you think that will be?" Mama's voice sparked with impatience the way it sometimes did when she'd burned the bread or broke a dish, but I'd never heard her speak that way to Papa before. "Seamus, Eva is all the things you imagine her to be. She's bright and beautiful, *and* she's crippled. That's part of the package. It's part of what makes her special. Why won't you see that?"

Mama's voice was cold and hard as she continued. "Her leg is twisted like a corkscrew, and no one around here is going to make her their wife, not ever. Even if they did, who would she find here? Clarence Parker? Harold Jessup or some other illiterate dolt with no imagination and no plans? It would suffocate her. No, I'm glad she was out in our field with that exciting, handsome boy with the big dreams. She deserves someone like that, someone as remarkable as she is." She choked, and her voice lowered until it was almost a whisper. "I hope it was wonderful, Seamus. Lord, I hope it was, because it's going to have to last her a lifetime."

Then I heard the muffled sound of Mama crying, and I knew that she was in Papa's arms, her face against his chest, wetting his shirtfront with her tears. I buried my head into the mean comfort of my pillow and wept quietly by myself. I cried because I'd never known before how much Mama loved me—not just doing her duty, but really loved me—and how love forced her to see me sharper and deeper than she'd have liked. I cried because I'd always known what she said about my being crippled was true, but like her, I'd never said it out loud because that would have made it too real, solid and visible and hard, like words on a page. Once true words are released into the air you can't ever take them back. I cried because the truth cuts so deep. Most of all, I cried because the night was nearly over and in the morning Slim would be gone.

I dreamed of Slim that night. We were back in Papa's field, hidden in a den of sweet-smelling wheat, our arms around each other. Then, without any warning, the Jenny's propellor spit and sputtered and spun all by itself, and the plane started taxiing across the field without her pilot. Slim had to run alongside and climb onto the wing to get hold of her, a rider racing after a renegade horse, before she took off without him.

I ran as best I could, limping behind them, but it was no use. I was too slow. Slim never reached his hand back to grab mine. I could see as I ran that the Jenny, which had formerly been a two-seater, now only had a cockpit for one. There was simply no room for me. I gave up the chase and stood where the little sapphire plane had rested a moment before, waving halfheartedly at its retreating shadow, my legs so heavy I couldn't move another step.

Then, just when the plane was so far away it looked like a dot on the horizon, Slim turned back and flew straight toward me, dipping his wings and waving, like the first time I'd seen him. He sailed overhead, stirring the air the way a fountain troubles still water. Reaching skyward, I caught the breeze in my hand and felt Slim in it. His power and life, the cool familiarity of his skin, the rhythm of his heart, the pull and pain of his destiny were physical reality in my hand. I had eyes in my fingertips and knew everything that was coming, though I knew I would forget it all before waking. None of that mattered.

"All right," I consented and let him disappear into a cloud, content to wait below, remembering how it was going to be. Then in an instant he was gone, and I was alone with only the hum of the Jenny's engine to remind me that he'd ever been there at all.

The engine noise woke me. It took a moment to separate myself from the dream, though I knew for certain, sleeping and waking, the buzz overhead was real. Slim was leaving.

I could hear Mama in the kitchen, clanging skillets and making coffee. The smell of my favorite breakfast, pancakes and Virginia ham, wafted in from the kitchen, and I knew Mama had heard the plane leave too and was cooking comfort into my meal, whisking the unspoken words of understanding into the silky batter, knowing I wouldn't miss her meaning.

I stood at the window until the engine sounds died away completely, until I was certain he wasn't turning back, and a little longer than that. Finally I left off waiting and got dressed. There was nothing else to do.

Chapter 3

Life in Dillon plodded on. It was as if Slim and I were pebbles dropped into a pond, creating a brief, transparent disturbance on the surface, and when it was over everything returned to flat calm.

It didn't seem right. The most important thing that had ever happened in my life, that probably would ever happen in my life, had come and gone, yet nothing had changed. I wished I had asked Slim for something, a lock of his hair, or one of his shirts, some physical evidence of our little time together, but it was too late for that. Resolved not to feel sorry for myself, I determined not to be surprised at how little effect Slim's unheralded entrance and exit would have on the steady march of days and weeks in Dillon. *What did you expect,* I thought, *that the sun would set a different shade of red because you love someone? Be satisfied with your moment.*

Oddly, most of the time I was. In some ways, he was still very much with me, or, at least, I was with him. I can't explain it, and I don't expect anyone to understand it because I don't understand it myself, but sometimes, at unexpected and cherished moments, I could see him, talking, resting, working, on city streets, in empty darkened hangars, in places I didn't know. Not confused or cloudy like a dream, but bright, clear scenes, like a picture show, but in color and more true, as though I were actually standing next to him.

I can't say that he saw me, or even sensed my presence, but that didn't worry me. I didn't ask myself those questions, not then. It was enough to wrap myself in his life and make it my own. His curiosity and excitement and ambition were always present, his driving, propelling need for something bigger passing through the atmosphere to me like a magnet until it became part of me. That summer and fall I clung to the smallest glimpse of his life and wore it as a disguise over my own, which marched on as predictably as every year.

The county fair was in September after the harvest was in. Mama won prizes for her pickles and for a Baltimore Album style quilt she'd made out of my old dresses the previous winter. Papa went to watch the cattle judging, at least that's what he told Mama, but I'm pretty sure he snuck off to place a bet or two on the horse races. I'd wager Mama knew that too, though she wouldn't admit it. Gambling was something she simply could not condone, at least not right out in the open, so she pretended not to know, and he pretended she didn't know, and somehow that made it all right.

While Papa was off on his own, Mama and I went over to the poultry barn. The moment we walked in, the smell washed over me like a wave and I felt sick at my stomach. Mama had met a friend and was busy congratulating her on winning a blue ribbon in the pie judging, so I didn't say anything. It seemed ridiculous after so many years of living on a farm that a little whiff of chicken manure should leave me feeling nauseous. I scolded myself for a being a weakling and willed the feeling to pass.

Mama turned around to include me in the conversation, "Eva, you remember Mrs. Stanley, don't you?" When she saw my face her eyes opened wide in alarm. I thought I must look pretty bad off to see her look so worried, or not exactly worried, more like shocked. Her hand flew up to her cheek, and she said, "Oh my goodness, look at the time! Eva," she lied, "we were supposed to meet Papa almost a half hour ago. We'd better run. Nice to see you again, Vera." Then, quick as a shot, she grabbed me by the elbow and propelled me out of the barn.

Mama steered me over to the nearest bench and sat me down. "Breathe in, now, Eva. Breathe deep, and it will pass in just a minute. Put your head down between your knees if that helps. There you go. Feel better now? That's my girl."

"I'm sorry, Mama," I said, fanning myself with a brochure for chicken feed. "I don't know what came over me. I must be coming down with something. The smell! It just made me so sick, but it's better out here in the fresh air. I'm fine now."

Mama sat down next to me on the bench and took my hand in hers. "Eva," she said, then hesitated. "You are fine. I want you to know that, you're going to be just fine. I'm not going to be angry with you, but when were you going to tell me?"

I didn't understand what she was talking about—until a frightening thought popped into my mind that maybe I did. Suddenly I felt butterflies in my stomach again, not from any strange smell, but because I knew that if Mama was talking to me so patiently, so serious, then something really must be wrong. I didn't want to believe it. "Tell you what, Mama?" I asked softly.

She took in a deep breath and let it out slowly, "About the baby, Eva."

I looked at her blankly, still not completely understanding, not wanting to believe what she was trying to tell me. "Didn't you know?" she questioned incredulously. I shook my head, and tears started to well in my eyes.

"I'm not sure, Mama," I choked out. "Maybe I did. Remember when Ruby and I took a picnic down by the pond? I got sick after. For a moment, maybe I knew, but then I told myself it was the heat or maybe the mayonnaise had turned. I didn't want to think about it.

"Oh, Mama!" I sobbed. "I didn't mean for this to happen! That night, we weren't either of us thinking. It was just that . . . We found each other, Mama. We were the only two people in the world that night and we had be together! We didn't stop to think if it was right." I fell into a fresh wave of weeping, and Mama held me, murmuring sounds of comfort that weren't even words, but meant much more. She was so patient and calm, as though she were nursing a child with a cut finger that would soon heal, but I knew that inside she had to be churning, and with good reason.

Mona Gilroy's parents had sent her away to visit an aunt three years before, and she'd never come back. Word in town was they'd shipped her off because Mona was going to have a baby and the boy wouldn't marry her. Ruby's mother said that she didn't blame the boy one bit and that a girl who would give in to one boy might as easily give in to a dozen, so who was to say who the father was. The scandal was whispered around town for months. Mrs. Gilroy was so embarrassed that she never came to town anymore, and finally they sold their place and moved.

I started crying for real, thinking how I'd shamed my parents. "Mama! What are people going to say? What am I going to do? You can't send me away, please, Mama!"

Mama's look of patience suddenly turned hard. She grabbed me by the shoulders and held me still, her expression more serious than I'd ever seen it, and made me look at her. "Eva, stop that nonsense! Right now! What do you mean, what are you going to do? You're going to have a baby, and then you'll go on and live your life, that's what you'll do." She shook me firmly, the way you shake someone out of a bad dream. "Listen to me! We're not sending you away! The very idea . . ."

"But Papa will be so angry!" I sniffed, trying to get hold of myself and failing. "I've disgraced him! I won't be able to make him understand . . ." I choked on my thoughts and buried my head in Mama's shoulder, unable to put words to my fear, terrified that my father could never love me again. Somehow discovering so suddenly that I was to be two instead of one made me feel smaller, more alone, and more in need of my father's love than ever.

"Nonsense!" Mama clucked in reproach. "Your papa could never be ashamed of you. This won't be easy, not for you—or us, either—but whatever we have to get through, we will. We'll manage, as a family, just like we always have. I'm not saying he'll be happy or that it will be easy to tell him, but you'll see, he understands, oh . . . a lot more than you think."

Mama fished around in her handbag for a handkerchief. Her tone softened a bit, but she kept her eyes downcast, searching inside her bag while she spoke. It was hard for her to speak plainly about such things. "Your papa and I . . . we were . . . we got married in a hurry, Eva. You understand what I'm saying? We were engaged anyway, and I've never for one instant regretted a thing, but when we moved the wedding up, well . . . there was a lot of talk. You understand?"

I nodded as I dried my eyes with the hankie she held out to me. Suddenly a lot of things about my parents, but especially about Mama, made more sense than it ever had.

"Oh, Eva, people can be awfully cruel, but loose talk is the least of your problems. You're so young! It's going to take all your courage, but, like it or not, you're going to be a mother and you have to be strong. Life is hard for a woman and even harder for a woman alone, but you'll see, in the end it will all have been worth it."

She put her arm around me and stroked my hair. I could feel the sadness in her fingertips and knew that it was the last time she would touch me like that and the last time I could cry on her shoulder. From now on I would be too big for that kind of comfort. "You'll see, Eva. Children are always worth it."

I believed her, everything she said.

It took several days before I worked up enough courage to tell Papa about the baby. He was known for his ready grin and Irish humor, but when he was finally pushed to anger it was something to behold. His thick brows would draw together to a single, immovable line, and a stream of language would spill forth from him that was part English, part Gaelic, part gutter, and pure fury. His wrath had almost never been directed at me, but I was sure I was in for it this time. A part of me actually wanted to face the anger I felt he was entitled to. However small a penance it might be, enduring his righteous fury might remove some of the shame I'd brought on him.

But he didn't yell, or bluster, or even slam his fist into his hand. He didn't allow himself the smallest gesture of ire. Instead he just stared at me hard, then looked at Mama, who confirmed the news with a nod of her head. Silence clouded and filled the room for a long moment before Papa spoke.

"Will you be finishing school, then?"

I shook my head no. Even if such a thing would have been possible, a ruined girl allowed to go to school with the rest of the students, I wouldn't have returned to class. All my life, people had stared at me and whispered behind my back. I wouldn't have them doing the same to my baby.

"And, that fella. That . . . Slim," Papa said, a curl of derision playing at his lip as he spoke the name we both knew was no name at all, "will he be coming back, do you suppose?"

"I don't know, Papa." Heat rose on my cheeks and the back of my neck when I realized how cheap he would think I'd held myself not even to have exacted a promise of return from my baby's father. "I don't think so," I whispered and hung my head, too ashamed to look him in the eye.

Surely it would come now, I thought. Surely all the anger and hot words he held back would finally spill out and soak me through to the bone. I wouldn't have blamed him. Instead, he just rocked back on his heels and stared at a corner of the ceiling as though something important were written there. "I see," he said, without looking at me, then turned and went to the barn, mumbling something about being late feeding the stock.

He didn't come in for supper. When the clock struck nine, Mama said we'd better be getting to bed. I wanted to go out and get him, but Mama said he needed some time alone. "Best let him come back when he's ready. He's got to think things through. Now go to sleep and quit brooding."

I went to bed, but didn't sleep. I lay awake, ticking off the hours by tracking the moon's progress across my window and waiting for the sound of a footfall on the porch and the squeak of the screen door opening. The moon had set, and I was half-dozing, waiting for day, when I heard the sound of someone trying to be quiet and a whispered shuffling of papers. Papa stood in his stocking feet, his boots removed to keep from waking anyone, bent over the kitchen table and poring over a stack of books he'd pulled out of a trunk where he stored them. He jerked in surprise when I asked him what he was doing.

"Evangeline, why are you up? You should be getting your rest, especially now." He gestured awkwardly in the direction of my still flat belly.

"I was waiting for you. I . . . I thought, maybe . . ." I didn't know what I'd thought, just that if I could think of something to say, maybe it would prime the pump and end his silence. That silence was more painful to me than a slap on the face.

"Look here," he said, pointing to one of the books on the table. He opened it and began flipping the pages, "I've got out my collected works of Shakespeare. He wasn't a bad writer for an Englishman." He winked. "Here's my Hume's history, and a book on French painters, and another by Saint Augustine. What I was thinking," he continued excitedly, "is that you can keep studying here at home, even if you can't go to school. I've got more books in here than you could read in a year. You finish these and you'll know more than they'd ever teach you in high school anyway."

"That's a good idea," I agreed. It was such a relief to know he was still speaking to me, I'd have endorsed any plan he'd proposed, but I was genuinely interested. The sight of a new book always piqued my interest, and the idea of passing the time until the baby arrived wrapped in study of places and ideas far removed from Dillon was appealing.

"Good!" he enthused. "I won't have it said that the mother of my grandchild was dull-witted. We Glennons have never had much formal education, but we could never be called ignorant. Most of these books were my mother's. Before she married, she was a cook for a rich family. When the old woman died, she left these books as a legacy to my mother. They were her most treasured possessions. She couldn't read them herself, so she made me read them to her. We both got quite an education that way."

He was quiet for a moment, still with remembering. "My mother put a great store by learning. She wanted me to go to university, Trinity College in Dublin." He spoke the name reverently, and I could almost see what a magical place it had become in his mind, a fairy tale of heaven whispered from mother to son. He smiled and brushed back the memory and longing. "We were so poor, I'm sure it never would have happened in any case, but when Ma died and there were so many mouths to feed, university couldn't be thought of. My father buried his sorrows in the bottom of a bottle, and I caught a boat for Boston. That was that. I wanted better for you.

"I've never spoken to you about this, Evangeline, but I'd thought, when you were done with the high school, you might go on to be a teacher before you settled down and got married. I'd put over two hundred dollars by already. If I could've gotten two or three more good crops, we might have managed it," he said wistfully.

"Oh, Papa!" I cried. "I'm so sorry, Papa. Not about Slim. I won't ever say I'm sorry about him. I love him, and, heaven help me, if he were here today I don't think I'd have done a thing differently, but I am sorry I ruined all your plans. I never meant to disappoint you or embarrass you."

"There, now. That's enough." He dismissed my apology with a wave of his hand. "Sometimes the fates blow our plans to dust and something better comes out of it. If my mother'd had her plan for me, I'd be the most educated potato farmer ever to scratch an existence out of the rockiest five acres in County Tipperary. Instead, I've got a fine farm, a fine wife, and a fine daughter that I'm proud to call my own, no matter what her queer ideas on love, and a fine grandchild on the way that'll probably be born with wings sproutin' out of his back like Pegasus."

"You mean Hermes, Papa," I corrected gently. "Pegasus was a horse."

"There now, you see? You've not even read my books and already you're smarter than me. This baby's bound to be a genius!"

I laughed and put my arms around him. "I love you."

"I love you too, Evangeline." We held each other, squeezing tight for a long moment before he spoke again.

"You're sure, then, that he won't be coming back?" he asked, the hope that he was wrong showing plainly in his voice and face.

"I'm sure, Papa."

He sighed. "Then I suppose this child will be needing a grandfather, won't he?"

"Or she," I corrected him with a smile. *We'll both be needing you,* I thought. *I can't even imagine how I could go on without you.*

I squeezed him again, even tighter.

"Whooo-ah! Eva! Hey there!" I saw Ruby come loping across our yard, carrying a lumpy-looking gunnysack, waving her arm high and wide like she was signaling a train. Usually I was glad to see her, but today I bit my lip and sighed as I watched her hustle toward me. *Well,* I thought, *no use putting it off.* I put down the feed pail I'd been carrying and waited until she was near before opening the porch screen to let us both pass.

"Hey, Ruby. How are you?"

"How are you!" She made an exasperated face at me. "You drop off the face of the earth for over a month and all you can say is, 'How are you?' Eva Glennon, if you weren't my best friend I swear I'd—" She lowered her voice and composed her face when she saw Mama coming up from the cellar, carrying a basket of potatoes. "Oh, hello, Mrs. Glennon."

"Good morning, Ruby."

Ruby stood awkwardly for a moment, wanting to continue with her interrogation, but knowing she couldn't as long as Mama was in the room. "Oh, I almost forgot!" Ruby dug into the depths of the gunnysack she was carrying and pulled out a pint-sized Ball jar capped with red gingham and tied with green yarn. "My ma asked me to bring you this jar of strawberry preserves. Early Christmas present."

"How kind. Your mother's preserves are always so much more delicious than mine. She's quite a cook. Is she teaching you all her secrets, Ruby?"

Ruby smiled and shook her head no, embarrassed by the question. It was well known in Dillon that Ruby couldn't boil water. Once she'd made an apple pie for her papa's birthday and mistook the salt for sugar. Mr. Carter told the story often, and each time he told it, his show of spitting and sputtering, pretending to taste the pie, became longer and more exaggerated. Ruby always laughed good-naturedly along with his audience, but I could see the color rise in her face each time he repeated the tale. After that she kind of lost interest in the kitchen.

"Don't you worry, Ruby," Mama said reassuringly. "It takes years of practice and mistakes to make a good cook. You'll learn how yet. Thank your mother for me. I've got something for her, too. Make sure I give it to you before you leave."

"Thank you, ma'am," Ruby answered automatically. I could see in her eyes that though she knew Mama was trying to be kind, she'd just as soon be spared such painful encouragement. When Mama turned, Ruby raised her eyebrows at me and twitched her head in the direction of my room. There would be no avoiding the list of questions I knew was coming. We excused ourselves and went into my room, where we could talk privately.

Ruby flopped stomach-first onto my bed like a rag doll and propped her head up on her hands, staring at me as I settled myself next to her on the patchwork quilt.

"Well," she pressed, "where have you been? At first I thought you were sick. I came over three times to see you, but your mother said you weren't feeling well and I should come back another day. About a week after school started, Mrs. Carmondy assigned Carla Winslow to sit beside me in your old seat because she said you weren't coming back to school, so I thought you must be dying or something. Now I come out here and you're fine, feeding the chickens and looking at me like *I'm* the odd one for asking where you've been!"

I sat calmly watching her face, working hard to keep myself from smiling and enjoying the mounting frustration my flat expression was causing my impatient and dear friend.

"So?" Ruby huffed impatiently.

"So what?" I asked innocently. Ruby heaved a down pillow at me and let out a growl of irritation as the pillow thunked me softly on the head and a stray feather floated calmly to the floor.

"So, are you dying or what?" she demanded. A stricken look passed over her face, and she put her palm over her mouth the way she always did when she realized she'd said something she shouldn't, which was pretty often. "You're not, are you? I mean, you look fine, but . . . Oh, Eva! You don't have some rare disease that makes you look like always but eats up your insides and turns them black, do you?" Ruby clapped her hand over her mouth again and then thumped herself on the forehead with a fist, "Oh no. There I go again. I'm so stupid! I always say the wrong thing. What I meant was—"

"I know what you meant, you goose." *Poor Ruby,* I thought. *I should have told her before.* She was my best friend. It was wrong to have kept her in the dark. "I'm fine. Really." I took a deep breath and plunged ahead, determined to sound casual and brave and normal. "It's just that I'm going to have a baby, that's all. That's why I can't come to school anymore. I'm studying at home instead. Papa is helping me."

Ruby stared at me, her mouth gaping in a perfect round O of shock. "A baby! A real baby?" She was surprised into silence for a long moment, and then her expression boiled and clouded into anger. I felt my heart sink. *She is scandalized,* I thought. All my worst, secret fears about telling her were going to come true. She would stomp out of my room and slam the door. I'd never see her again, except in town on the arm of Mary Kay Munson, in whose ear she'd be whispering, telling her all my confidences and laughing at me. I really was alone.

I steeled myself for her exit. Ruby eyes sparked, and a deluge of words poured from her. "Eva Glennon, you're going to have a baby and you didn't tell me? I've never kept a secret from you in my whole life. I even told you about my drunken Uncle Dwight grabbing me and kissing me in the barn. I thought we were friends! I thought we were always supposed to depend on each other, no matter what!" she spat accusingly. "How could you keep a thing like that from me?"

"Ruby, I'm sorry," I said, genuinely bothered to think I'd hurt her feelings. "I was going to tell you eventually. I just thought it would be best to keep it to myself for a while. I was afraid you'd be mad at me or . . . I don't know what I thought. I was just afraid you wouldn't want to be my friend anymore."

She calmed down some, but I could see that she wasn't entirely ready to forgive me. "Well," she said, "I can see not telling the whole world, but I'd think you'd fill in your best friend, at least to let me know why you weren't coming back to school. You had me scared to death. You should know me better than that. We're friends forever. Nothing could change that."

"Oh, Ruby, do you mean that?" She nodded an affirmation, and I reached over and squeezed her so tight I'm sure she couldn't have drawn a breath if she'd wanted to. "I'm so glad! Nothing could ever be as good anymore if I didn't have you to talk to. And I'm going to need you, you know." My eyes started to fill with tears of relief. "I don't have any blood sisters, and the baby's going to need an aunt. I guess after all we've been through together that makes us practically related, doesn't it?"

"'Course it does." Ruby nodded firmly, then broke into a wide grin of surprise. "Aunt Ruby! Think of that! We'll be great together. We'll sew baby kimonos and blankets, and when she's older . . . Oh, I hope it's a girl! When she's older we'll take her riding on Ranger and go on picnics and everything! I'll be just like a real aunt. Except for one thing. I'm not changing diapers, Eva; that's your job." She chuckled at the thought and started to laugh, but stopped when she noticed the tears streaming down my face.

"Now, don't go crying, Eva. I'm sorry. I was only joking about the diapers. I'll change them too, I swear I will!"

"It's not that." I wiped tears from my face. "I'm just happy, and everything makes me cry these days. Ruby, you're such a good friend. I'm so lucky! I should have told you before." We both grinned, me through my tears and Ruby with all her teeth showing. We hugged once more and promised never to keep secrets from each other again. She swore she forgave me, though I knew a part of her was still miffed that I'd kept her in the dark for so long.

Ruby spoke soothingly. "I 'spect it was your mama's idea to keep things quiet anyway. Old-fashioned. Like you read in those English novels, a girl gets in trouble and then disappears, never to be seen again. A lot of married ladies still hide out when they're expecting, as though no one will notice and folks will think babies just pop out of the air like magic."

"No, it wasn't Mama's fault," I protested. "*I* wanted to keep it to myself for a while. I wanted time to think about the baby, you understand?" But I could see from the look on her face that she didn't, and I didn't blame her. How could I explain it to her?

Confinement sounded like a punishment, something that people came up with because they were embarrassed that other people might look at a woman's swelling belly and know what she'd been doing, but I didn't think so. I thought it was something women had invented as an excuse to be alone, sit very still, and treasure every little sensation and change going on inside, to quiet their minds in preparation to meet the most important person in the world.

"Eva? Eva, hello." I was startled out of my daydream by Ruby waving her hand in front of my eyes. "Even though I forgive you for leaving me hanging for so long, you aren't getting off that easy. As punishment," she tittered excitedly, "you have to tell me *every-thing.*"

She cracked off questions like bullets from a gun, and mostly I answered them, even the ones that made me blush. Why should that be, I wondered. Why should I be embarrassed to talk about something that had seemed so natural to do? Words stripped and shrunk all my feelings, reduced them to a list of actions, like trying to learn ride a horse by reading a book. The instructions never took into account the power and gentleness of hundreds of pounds of silken muscles, or how it felt to gallop across the field, or how you and the horse became one animal instead of two, or how soft and sweet it was to bury your head in his mane and drink in the feel and smell of sweat and newly cut wheat and damp earth. There was no describing it; it was too fast and fluid, like trying to catch quicksilver in your fingers.

But to please Ruby I tried. I owed her that at least. Ruby sat spellbound, her mouth slightly open as she hung on my every word, trying to imagine each detail and not quite being able to put together the pictures in her head. Every once in a while she'd shiver and say, "Yewww. That's disgusting!" and put her hands over her ears as though she couldn't bear to hear more. Then, a moment later, her eyes would spark, and she'd ask another six questions, each more personal than the last.

She also wanted to know about the father. I didn't want anyone to know about that, ever. I couldn't bear to think of people imagining Slim and me together. It would have made it all so sticky and cheap. Instead I invented a boy I'd met when we went to visit Mama's cousins in Kansas. I said he couldn't marry me because he'd been engaged and gotten married before I knew about the baby.

"He was engaged?" Ruby piped, scandalized and intrigued. "Eva, how could you!"

"Well, I didn't know it at the time or I'd have never gone out riding with him."

Ruby clucked her tongue and sighed a sigh of sympathy and delicious shock. At least if I had to tell her a lie I was glad it was one she could enjoy.

"Gosh, that's so awful—how he took advantage of you." Ruby sighed again and shook her head as curiosity overcame concern. "Was he handsome, though? What color were his eyes?"

I made up more stories. I marveled at how easily she believed my lies, much more easily than she'd have believed the truth. For once I was thankful that I'd been made so imperfect and twisted that it would never occur to people that someone as straight and beautiful as Slim could want me.

"I can't believe it. I still just can't believe it," Ruby mused. "You don't even look fat or anything."

"I had to put a safety pin in the waistbands of my skirts last week. Guess I'll be big as a house soon." I pulled up my blouse to show her how my secret child was pushing, taut and swelling, under the coarse fabric of my skirt.

Ruby smiled and instinctively, without thinking to ask permission, reached out her hand to lay it on the tiny bulge. Reverently, as though not to wake the baby, she whispered, "What is it, do you think? A boy or girl?"

"I don't know. I guess there's no way to tell for sure."

"My mama says there's a way," Ruby reported solemnly. "You

take your wedding ring, put it on a chain, hold it over your stomach, and if it swings in a circle it's a girl, but it swings in a line it's a boy. 'Course," she faltered, "you don't have a wedding ring, so I guess we'll just have to wait."

"I guess so."

But, I did know. I was sure of it. I *knew* I was carrying a son. The same way I'd known Slim when he walked into our house, though we'd never spoken a word, I knew our son. He was inside me, part of me, and when I closed my eyes I could see him, tiny and translucent, curled inside the watery protection I'd instinctively made for him, cushioned and cradled so completely that the blows of the world would seem only a buoyant swell to him. How was it that other women didn't know who it was they carried inside?

Lying in bed that night I felt him move for the first time. A ripple, not a push. A silky spool of bubbles unwound inside me, rising and skating along the skin of my stomach. I lay my hand over the bulge of my abdomen and felt him swim, knotting himself under the heat of my hand, the way a cat searches out a sunbeam on a cold winter morning.

The life in him was pulsing and unmistakable. My strong, beautiful boy—as restless as his father, as faithful as his mother, as helpless as a kitten and too unwise yet to realize it. Our destinies were connected in a way that was entirely new to me, but strong and right. At that moment I realized protecting him and raising him would be the focus of my life. The cold winter would never touch him, capricious life never scar him. Everything I'd ever wanted for myself dimmed to a vague memory, a dream barely remembered upon waking from a dark night.

I smiled to myself and moved my hand to another spot on my stomach just to feel him flutter and glide as he swam and balled himself under a new fountain of my warmth. I whispered to Slim in the darkness: "Feel our boy, he's floating already; nothing will weigh him down. He's the best of us both."

But the words bounced back to me, empty in the cold, slicing darkness. Slim was too far off to hear me. As weeks stretched to months he moved just a bit farther off every time I reached for him. Now, when I wanted him more than ever, he was just a stretched fingertip beyond my grasp. It wasn't forgetting or distance of time that set him back; it was fear. The pull of memory was more compelling than he could bear, and so he had wiped it away in a full, absolute sweep that sometimes haunted him, an amazed observer of his own self-absorption. I could see him, though, in that strange new compartment of my mind that hadn't seemed to exist before I knew Slim. I saw him there like a reflection in a glass, clear and sharp in one untouchable dimension. He crouched, shivering in the cold night under the wing of a plane, staring at the stars, too thickly engulfed and tortured by ungratified ambition to remember the sound of my voice because that's how he had decided it had to be. The choice to burn brightly was a straight, seldom used path that left no room for regret or divergent routes.

Looking back on it, I wonder that I didn't feel angry, deserted, betrayed. I suppose I'd have hated him if I'd been able to convince myself he had deceived me. As it was, I remember only a deep sense of regret, more for him than for me. He was going to have so much and miss so much. The things we want have to be paid for. The price he'd paid was peace. Mine? My price was to stand on the dark side of the one-way mirror, seeing, anticipating, suffering, and knowing, but invisible and ineffectual—like a witness to a car accident shouting warnings that can't be heard over the roar of the motor and the sound of wheels skidding on gravel. It was too painful a scene to return to daily.

Mama had said, "You go on, and you live your life," so I did. I dropped a gauzy curtain over the glass to obscure the view, though I knew that nothing in my lifetime would make the reflection go black. Forgetting was not to be one of my gifts. That would have been too easy and too hard.

"We're all together, baby," I whispered to my unborn son. "You won't see him, but he'll be there, a part of you, the part that longs for and believes in something golden beyond the horizon. That's the thing we share. It makes us a family, connected, you see? You and me and him, now and for always." I pulled the quilt high over my nose and mouth and pulled in gulps of cold, silent air and gave it back again, my breath an incubating warmth in the cocoon of blankets covering us.

"There now," Mama crooned, "he's all clean and dry and ready to meet his mother." Gently, as though the slightest tap would shatter him, she handed me a soft nest of flannel that protected my son.

I pulled back the blanket to see his face. Two dark blue jewel eyes stared solemnly up at mine, searching, as though he were as curious about me as I was about him. Looking at him warmed me straight through. Suddenly, a place in my heart I'd never known existed opened, filled, and spilled over, soothing all the sharp points of my life and answering, for that moment at least, all the questions I'd never even known to ask.

"Oh!" I whispered in wonder, "Look at you! You're perfect!"

"He is that." Dr. Townsend snapped his black bag shut with a flourish that spoke of a job well done. "He's big and strong and about as alert as any newborn I've ever seen. You won't need to make up any tonics for this boy, Miss Eva. If every child in town were as healthy as this, I'd probably be out of business." He leaned down to take another look at the baby before turning to me with a wink. "Not bad for homemade, young lady. Not bad at all. Almost as pretty a baby as you were when I delivered you."

Mama stood at the end of the bed and beamed. "You did fine, Eva, just fine. Never saw such a beautiful baby, and you were so brave. You'll see, he'll be a good baby because of it."

"He's good already," I breathed. "Look at those beautiful eyes. He's the one I've been waiting for all my life, but I didn't know it until just now."

We all stood for a minute more admiring my son until a tentative knock broke the silence and Papa spoke in a stage whisper from the other side of the door, "Is everything all right? Can't I come in yet?"

"Of course you can, Seamus. I was just leaving," said Dr. Townsend, picking up his bag and opening the door to reveal Papa's anxious face. "Sorry to keep you waiting so long, Seamus. Another hour and I swear you'd have worn a hole in the floor pacing, but, I think you'll find it was worth the wait." He shook Papa's hand. "You have a beautiful grandson."

Mama showed Dr. Townsend to the door, and Papa sat next to me on the bed. I handed him the tiny bundle, and Papa held his grandson tight in his arms. His eyes shone bright and wet as he examined the angelic face and hands and arms, murmuring wonderment over the baby's perfect, tiny form. Beaming with delighted wonder, he crooned, more to the baby than to me, "Oh, he's lucky, is this one. You can see that just by looking at him. He's like a magic charm that will rub off good luck to everyone he touches." Papa looked up at me and nodded profoundly. "You see if I'm not right, Evangeline. I know these things, just like I knew about you the day you were born, how you were meant for something special, and now look what you've gone and done. Here he is, my darling girl: our lucky star."

Chapter 4

May 1927

"Are you sure you'll be all right, Papa?" I asked uncertainly. "I'm not all that set on going. You and Mama could go instead and I could stay with Morgan." I stood in front of the mirror fiddling with a hat pin, accidentally stabbing myself in the finger while studying Papa's reflection instead of my own.

"Go on, go on," he said, waving me off impatiently. "We'll be fine. Won't we, Morgan?"

Morgan nodded, shaking his blond curls over his forehead and pulling his finger out of his mouth to give me a wide grin. "We'll be fine, Mama. Papaw's goin' to show me how to play mumbley-peg, ain't you, Papaw?" Papa gave Morgan a little nudge with his knee to remind him that this had been a secret.

"Papa!" I scolded. "He's too young to be throwing mumbley-peg. He'll cut off his fingers."

Papa made an exasperated face. "Bah! He'll be four in just a few more days."

"May nineteenth," Morgan piped in.

"That's right," Papa affirmed. "So, don't get your dander up, Mother Hen. Besides, I wasn't going to let him throw it. I was just going to show him how." He turned to Morgan with his eyes gleaming and his brogue thickening like it did whenever he was telling a story. "Sure now, me boy, when I was your age, I already had a knife of me own, and me brothers and I, we'd use them to hunt snakes in the old country. Huge, slithering serpents they were, as long as my arm."

"Papa," I said reprovingly, "you know there aren't any snakes in Ireland."

"Not *now* there aren't," he said solemnly and nodded to the knife held in his hand. I grinned at the joke I'd heard a million times before, then we broke into loud laughter, and Morgan joined in, more from fellowship than understanding.

Mama came out of the bedroom wearing her good Sunday dress and coat. "Goodness! What a racket. Eva, you ready to go?"

"Ready," I knelt down and planted a kiss on Morgan's smooth forehead. "Be good, now. And"—I shot a warning glance at Papa—"remember, absolutely no mumbley-peg. No knives. No shotguns. Nothing dangerous. I mean it."

"Fine, have it your way, then. No knives," he huffed, his eyebrows drawing into a single, bushy line before a new idea brightened his expression. "Say, Morgan! You ever chew tobacco?"

"Seamus, that's not funny," Mama accused good-naturedly as she opened the door. I laughed at Morgan's bemused expression and turned back to give him still another good-bye kiss.

Mama drove our Ford like an expert, with superb control and a little faster than you might have supposed if you judged her by the fussy bunch of false cherries she'd pinned to her coat collar.

Our new used car was a great source of pride to us all and a measure of how well things had gone on the farm the last few years.

Crops had been so good we'd been able to make improvements on the farm and buy some modern conveniences for ourselves, though I suspect some of our newfound riches came from the savings Papa had earmarked for my education; there was no need to hoard pennies anymore. We could finally afford to get hooked up to the power lines that ran down the county road, and, first thing, Papa bought Mama an electric mangle. It ironed everything so quick and neat, we got the laundry done in half the time. But the car was the most exciting purchase we'd ever made. I'll never forget the day Papa chugged up to the house, shouting and honking the news that he'd bought Mr. McCurdle's Ford at a bargain price. He couldn't have been any happier if his name had been Rockefeller. It seemed like the twenties were indeed roaring, even in Dillon.

Though Papa bought the car, Mama was the better driver. He was always too busy looking out the window and exclaiming over the beautiful day or the freshly plowed fields to bother much with keeping his eyes on the road. I was more like him. The passenger seat suited me fine.

I leaned my head out the window and took in the endless mural of clear, black sky, pricked with stars, felt the spring wind on my face, and smelled the loamy freshness of the newly turned earth and sprouting wheat. I breathed the perfect night deep into my lungs and sighed contentedly.

"What are you thinking, Eva?"

"About how lucky we are. The night Morgan was born, Papa said he'd bring us luck, and he was right."

"Well, I think we might give the good Lord some credit, too," Mama said piously, "but, yes, I think you're right. We have everything we need and then some."

"Yes," I agreed, "just about everything." To myself I thought, *There is no point in asking for more.* If I sometimes stood outside on a summer afternoon and searched the hot, empty sky for a glint of sun on a sapphire wingspan, or if I woke from a dream crying, my hands clutching the air for something that had seemed so solid the moment before, if the sight of young couples walking hand in hand through town made me cross to the other side of the street where I wouldn't have to watch, then the sound of Morgan's chortling laughter as he roughhoused with Papa, or the feel of his soft, cunning hand wrapped in mine pulled my heart back from the heavens and filled the empty places. Most of them.

Slim had said he'd come back, and he meant it at the time, but I'd always known he wouldn't. From the first day, I'd prepared myself to be alone forever. Most of the time I succeeded, but the reality of loneliness was a harder road to walk than it had seemed when I'd released Slim to his future. At unpredictable times he would still appear in my mind, waking or sleeping. I could see him, hear him, but that was all. In a way, that was sadder than not seeing him at all. Sometimes, at the oddest moments, moments when I should have been happy, I was suddenly pierced through with loneliness, because, at those times, being happy didn't seem to make much sense if I couldn't share it with Slim.

I berated myself for wanting too much, especially on such a beautiful night, when things were going so well. Times were good. The crop was in, and my son was healthy, happy and smarter than any four-year-old I knew. Slim had popped into my life for an instant and disappeared, but at least I'd had an instant. Some people never even got that. I had my beautiful boy, loving parents, and a good home for us all. And as if that wasn't enough, now it seemed that my quilting hobby was about to become a real little business.

One day, while I was studying some photographs of Monet's paintings in one of Papa's books, I got the idea you might make a quilt the same way, blending small splashes of color into a larger, richer scene.

I dug though dozens of scraps of blue, aqua, turquoise, sapphire, cobalt, and teal until I had enough cloth to design and piece together a watercolor lily pond of my own. Morgan and I gave it to Ruby for Christmas.

When Ruby's rich Aunt Cora came visiting from Dallas, she made the biggest fuss over the quilt and wanted to buy it. Ruby explained it was a gift and not for sale, but she introduced us, and Aunt Cora ordered another one "just like it." The fussy old lady said she'd pay me fifty dollars! I accepted her offer but explained I couldn't make it exactly the same as Ruby's.

"Quilts are like names, Miss Cora. It's important they match the personality of the person they belong to. Otherwise, they'll never quite fit, no matter how pretty they are. You let me think on it a bit. I'll make a quilt just with you in mind, and if you don't like it, you don't have to take it." She agreed, and I worked hard and finished the quilt in two months.

It was a garden scene, with bougainvillea and gardenias and hibiscus, flowers I'd never seen except in books, but as I cut and stitched and pricked my fingers I could smell a sweetness in the air that seemed to float in from far-off trade winds. When it was finished I embroidered my name and the date on the back in purple thread and shipped it off in the mail.

About two weeks later, I received a manila envelope from Dallas, fat with checks and a letter from Ruby's aunt.

Dear Miss Glennon;

    I can't tell you how happy I am to have received my quilt at long last. It is more beautiful than I could have imagined. You were right to insist on designing one just for me even though I pressed you so to make a copy of dear Ruby's. I have always loved gardens and flowers. There is nothing that brings me as much peace as kneeling in my flower beds, working the earth and finally seeing the fruits of my labor in full bloom. How did you know I raise gardenias? How beautifully you've captured them in color and cloth! Now I shall sleep surrounded by elegant white blossoms even in winter. Thank you so much.

I have enclosed letters from three of my friends, Mrs. Pryor, Mrs. Byrd and Miss Shelton, who would also like to commission quilts from you. Please find enclosed three checks for $25 (as a deposit) along with a $50 payment for my own quilt. At my suggestion, the ladies have sent photos of themselves and letters to give you a bit of information about their backgrounds so you can "think on" the type of quilt you want to design for them. I told them not to expect the finished product for at least six months as I know how many hours you put into each creation. Several other friends have also expressed interest, but I have suggested they wait until these first three are finished so you are not overwhelmed by the work.

Please give my regards to dear Ruby and to your family. Thank you again, Miss Glennon, for your beautiful work. You wield your needle like an artist's brush.

> *Affectionately,*
> *Mrs. Cora Shaw Daniels*

Personally, I thought she went a bit overboard with the "artist's brush" comment, but I was flattered by her praise and only too happy to make some money of my own. Most of the money went into a bank account I'd started for Morgan. I tried to give some to Papa and Mama to help with expenses, but they wouldn't accept a dime. Instead, I was doing some little things to treat them. I'd bought a new pair of boots for Papa, and now I was taking Mama to town for an ice-cream sundae and a movie. It wasn't much, but I wanted them to know how much I appreciated all they'd done for me and Morgan.

It was pleasant sitting at the drugstore counter with Mama and watching her eat ice cream, delicately spooning the last swirls of chocolate out of her parfait dish without even a clink of spoon on glass. I thought of how she'd lived all her life without any little luxuries, and now here we were, fine as anybody in town. Two months before I hadn't had five dollars to call my own and now, all at once, I was practically rich.

"Eva," Mama said, interrupting my daydream, "it's almost time for the picture to start and you've hardly touched your sundae. Better hurry up before we're late." She relished a last dribble of chocolate syrup. "My, that was delicious! Thank you, Eva."

"Mama, out of my next quilt money I'm going to buy you a dress. I bet you never had a store-bought dress in your whole life."

"No, I haven't," she confessed, "but then again, I never really needed one—still don't. You save your money for little Morgan; you might need it someday. Things look fine now, but that can change in a moment; crops fail, doctors' bills come due. You've got to be ready for everything."

"Oh, Mama. Don't be so pessimistic! I saw in the paper where Oklahoma and Kansas are some of the best areas in the country for business," I lectured between gulps of strawberry ice cream. "New people moving in all the time, and more and more land being bought up for farms. There's four hundred times more wheat being produced here than there was just ten years ago."

"I'm not a pessimist, Eva. I'm a realist. Are you finished? Let's go. I don't want to be late for the picture show."

We hustled over to the theater, and I bought a bag of popcorn for us to share. The theater was small and lacked the elegance of the movie house I'd seen on our trip to Oklahoma City years before. There was no balcony, no gilt angels peering down from the proscenium, but it was pretty fancy for Dillon, with seats upholstered in red plush and armrests of polished oak. As it was Saturday night, the theater was full, and we saw several people we knew. One or two acknowledged Mama with a surreptitious incline of the head, though most pointedly ignored us. I was still considered a disgrace by most people in town. Their obvious contempt made me feel ashamed, and I sank a bit lower in my seat. However, for every inch I retreated, Mama rose up two, her face looking as determinedly proud as I'd ever seen it. I was relieved when it was time for the show to start, the red velvet curtain pulling back to reveal a gauzy white scrim. As usual, the projector started playing while the scrim was still closed, showing images behind that looked slightly fuzzy and dreamlike.

The cartoon and the newsreel were shown before the feature. Mrs. Poole, whose husband owned the theater, sat at a nearly in-tune upright piano, banging out marches, or rags, or dirges depending on the mood of what was being projected on the screen. Mama and I sat in the darkness munching on popcorn and laughing at the cartoon. When the newsreel began, I couldn't help but lean forward in my seat. It seemed like all the news was about aviation that day, at least that's all that I remember of it.

The first story was about two Frenchmen, Nungesser and Colli, who had set off for New York from Paris, attempting to be the first men to fly across the Atlantic nonstop to win fame and the $25,000 Orteig prize being offered to whoever broke the record. Everybody knew about the Orteig prize. Many planes had crashed and several pilots had disappeared making the attempt to win it. The same had happened to the two Frenchmen. They'd taken off on May 8th, and no one had heard from them since. They were assumed lost and dead at sea. Reaching for some more popcorn, Mama leaned over to me and whispered, "I think they're crazy even trying. You can't fly across a whole ocean!"

She was probably right, but wouldn't it be wonderful, I thought, if you could fly across the sea. Imagine rising up into the clouds and over the waves one day, and the next day touching down next to the Eiffel Tower, or Big Ben, or even the pyramids of Egypt. The screen flickered, and the next story headline appeared in bold white letters: NEW AVIATION RECORD SET. CHARLES LINDBERGH FLEW SOLO FROM SAN DIEGO TO NEW YORK, BREAKING RECORD FOR TRANS-CONTINENTAL FLIGHT.

The screen showed a sleek little plane flying low over a field thronged with reporters. She had only one wing, a closed cockpit, and, as near as I could tell from the film, no real window. I wondered how the pilot could see out of a plane like that. It seemed a shame to fly closed in like that, cocooned from light and sound and all the things that made flying so wonderful. The plane landed shakily while Mrs. Poole pounded out a triumphant, tinny march before the picture on the screen changed to these words:

> Fresh from his new record breaking flight, Lindbergh waits at New York's Roosevelt Field for a break in the weather to try his chance at winning the Orteig prize. Some call him "Daredevil Lindbergh," others call him "The Flying Fool." Small wonder. Young Lindbergh will make his flight alone and with only a single engine!

The screen flashed to reveal a handsome young man in a leather flight jacket standing next to the strange-looking plane I'd seen earlier. The pilot turned to face the camera, grinned, and pushed his curly hair off his forehead in a gesture that was engraved on my heart. My hand flew to cover my mouth and for a moment I forgot to breathe.

"My Lord!" whispered Mama, "It's Slim!"

Chapter 5

If I hadn't seen it for myself, I wouldn't have believed it. He seemed the same and yet not. The grainy black-and-white film image made him look older, but, of course, I reminded myself, he was older. Nearly five years had passed since I'd seen him last. We were neither of us as young, naive, or trusting as we'd been.

It was his eyes, though, that helped me know for sure it was my Slim. They were harder and more cautious, but unmistakably his. I could see the same hunger, the need for something more that pulsed though him as he lay next to me scanning the sky for something he knew existed only by faith. The pull was so strong it blocked out every other source of light and compelled him to drop all the baggage of life, excess or essential, to make himself light enough the journey he had to take alone.

Outwardly, he was changed, but the most important part of him wasn't diluted. He stood tall, a celluloid image stopped in time, young and strong and sure, ready to face whatever it was that had woken him on so many nights, be it dream or demon, or one and the same. One thing I understood, though I still can't understand how, was that no matter what he met over the dark and seamless ocean, he had to meet it alone, and it would change him; he would be drawn into a tide over which he had no control and from which there was no possibility of retreat.

All the while, as this cloudy vision circled in my mind and an indefinable sense of dread rose within me, the one-dimensional image of Slim smiled, waved, and patted the plane with deceptive confidence. No one but me realized there were more angles in this picture than the screen could possibly reveal.

"God help you," I whispered to the shadow. "God protect you."

Mama was as transfixed as I. Her mind was filled with thoughts of her own, but when she heard me speak she leaned closer and patted my arm. "Eva, don't worry. He'll be all right. It's a wide ocean, but if it *can* be crossed I'd bet on Slim. He'll make it."

"Oh, Mama," I moaned as the screen went black and the end of reel slapped a circular clack. "I'm so afraid for him. It's not the flight that threatens him, but what lies on the other side, something that stretches out much farther."

"What do you mean?" Mama asked uncomprehendingly.

I shook my head, trying to force everything into focus, "I don't know exactly, but it is stronger than the ocean and more powerful. He's prepared for that. What's ahead is unknown and more dangerous, something that can kill your soul, not just your body. I can't tell you how I know that or exactly what it is, but he's not ready for it."

We drove home in silence. I lay my head back on the seat and stared out at the black night sky, the same sky that blanketed Slim, and wondered if the stars shone as brightly over New York as they did over the prairie and if he would sleep this night. I knew I wouldn't.

For the next few days it seemed people everywhere were talking about him: Charles Lindbergh, who was standing by on a lonely field somewhere in New York, watching the skies and hoping that they'd clear just long enough to welcome him inside before closing behind him so the long awaited match could commence in private, as it was meant to be.

Charles Augustus Lindbergh. How strange his name sounded. Colder and more closed than the man I knew. "Slim" seemed more human and real to me than "Charles Lindbergh."

People in town remembered his visit. Now it seemed everyone had a story to tell about the time they flew with Lindbergh, even the ones who'd never in their lives had five dollars to spend all at one time and couldn't possibly have made the trip, but I couldn't blame them. Nobody famous had ever been born in Dillon or even passed through before. It didn't hurt anything for them to take a little slice of the fame for themselves and keep it in their pockets.

Papa and I walked into Dwyer's drugstore just in time to hear one of the many debates about Slim's chances. "Well, if you ask me," Mr. Dwyer drawled, "I think the papers are right. They're callin' this Lindbergh fellow the 'Flyin' Fool' and that's about the size of it. Here he is, getting ready to fly across the ocean all by himself and with only one engine in a skinny little plane that looks like a tin can and is probably just about as safe. I don't call that bright."

The other men standing around the counter guffawed at Mr. Dwyer's description of the plane, which the papers had told us was named *The Spirit of St. Louis.*" Dwyer grinned and went on, encouraged by his audience. "Is there a Saint Louis? For Lindbergh's sake, I hope so. That boy's gonna need a whole choir loft full of saints on his side to make it to Paris—two on each wing, two on the propeller, and one real big one, Gabriel maybe, holdin' up the tail." Mr. Dwyer howled and slapped his knee in appreciation of his own joke, and the rest of the crowd joined in.

I smiled inwardly to think of the men of Dillon suddenly becoming aviation experts. Mr. Dwyer was a big man. Not big the way some farmers are, with wide, muscled shoulders and spreading mid-sections hard as rocks; he was just fat from a life of eating well and working indoors. Looking at his stomach bulging under his white work apron, it was hard to imagine a man of such girth squeezing into the cockpit of a plane.

"Morning, Glennon." The storekeeper smiled at Papa and nodded to me. "What can I get for you today?"

"I need some alum," Papa said, "and what have you got that'll help this foot of mine. It keeps swelling up on me ever since Ranger stepped on it last month."

Mr. Dwyer squinted in thought. "Well, stayin' off it'd be the best thing, but it being time to plant I don't suppose that's a possibility. Let's see if soaking it in Epsom salts does the trick."

I walked to the candy counter and eyed the sweets, considering which kind to take home to Morgan for his birthday the next day while Mr. Dwyer gathered up the rest of our order.

"Say, Glennon," Mr. Parker, Clarence's father, called to my father across the crowded shop. "What do you think about this Lindbergh boy? Seems I recall he stayed with you folks when he was here, didn't he? You think he's got a chance in the world of seeing Paris?"

Papa rubbed his chin thoughtfully. "He's going on only one engine, it's true, and it seems that all the other, more experienced flyers have thought that backup engines and teams of pilots are the way to go. Maybe they're right. Admiral Byrd's team is using the same strategy, and he's quite a pilot. On the other hand, so far all those boys with all that experience have failed. Young Lindbergh seems to think the thing is to fly lighter and faster. He might be on to something. I don't know him well. He camped out in the field and only ate one meal with us, but I'll tell you one thing, that young man is awfully smart and determined. I went out with him one day to help him work on his engine, and he sure knew the inside of the plane." Picking up the box of alum Mr. Dwyer had set down on the glass counter, Papa continued: "He might crash, and he might die, but no matter what the papers say, the boy's no fool. Whatever his plan is, he's thought it through. I guess he's got as good a chance as anybody."

The men were quiet for a moment before Mr. Dwyer spoke. "You might be right at that, Glennon. I suppose you might. It'll sure be something if he does make it." Papa paid him for the medicines and the striped paper bag full of lemon drops for Morgan. We nodded our good-byes. As we left I could see that, despite their dire predictions, every man in that store was rooting for Slim. Every pair of eyes reflected a touch of jealousy and admiration for the young man with courage enough to live large. Being farmers and naturally pessimistic, they were sure it was impossible, practically impossible anyway, but if he did make it all the way to France, wouldn't that be something? They'd be able to say they'd seen him in person, so they'd live a little larger too, just by virtue of having known him.

It wasn't just people in Dillon who were excited about Lindbergh's flight. The whole country waited to see what would happen to the good-looking young flyer in the tiny, lonely plane. The newspaper reports did everything they could to foster the image of a wholesome, midwestern boy fresh off the farm. They had him perpetually grinning and affable, simple and humble, and nothing like he really was: an ambitious and serious young man, much more complex and interesting than a cheerful boy-next-door.

"Listen to this, Mama," I said, opening the paper. "After a test flight the reporter has him patting the plane and saying, 'Boys, she's ready and rarin' to go!' He'd never say that," I scoffed, "especially not to a bunch of strange reporters. He doesn't talk like that at all! Why are they doing this? Making him into someone he's not."

Mama shrugged her shoulders as she stirred the batter for

Morgan's birthday cake. "Eva, people expect a lot from their heroes. On the one hand, they want them to be like their sons and brothers, not too educated, not too proud, not too smart. Probably because if people really do have to be remarkable to accomplish remarkable things it means most of us never will. If you have to be *born* with a great destiny it might mean the rest of us are here just taking up space. Nobody wants to read that in their morning paper, even if it's true.

"On the other hand, people want heroes to be without human flaws—unfailingly honest, immune to temptation, fearless. And if they aren't, the same crowd that was so quick to put them up on a pedestal will pull them down even quicker."

"But that's crazy, Mama." I tossed the newspaper aside in disgust. "If heroes aren't just as flawed as the rest of us, where is the bravery in that? I would think that heroism means overcoming your fears and failures long enough to do something great. Isn't that more difficult than not having fears in the first place?"

Mama shrugged her shoulders again. "Eva, if you haven't already, you'll find out soon enough that just because something is true doesn't mean it gets reported that way in the paper."

"Well, it ought to be," I answered irritably. Then I picked up the paper and began reading again, because no matter how annoyed I might be, when it came to hearing about Slim, even shallow or badly written news was better than none at all.

We made a red velvet cake with chocolate icing and chicken-fried steak for Morgan's birthday supper. Morgan ate three slices of cake and, ignoring Mama's raised eyebrows, I let him, even though I wondered if I'd be up half the night tending a child with a belly-ache. I was. Ruby joined us for the party and gave Morgan a counting picture book. Mama gave him a new cap with earflaps that buttoned down. Papa had carved a little wooden biplane with a bright red propeller that wound up with a rubber band and spun so fast it melted into a scarlet blur.

My present was the lemon drops I'd bought at Dwyer's, along with a quilt for his new bed in the room Papa had added on to the house the month before. It was one of the prettiest quilts I'd ever made and so right for Morgan. It was like a painting of fabric just for him. The setting cotton sun shone rays of light across the plains and spilled a spectrum of color over the clouds, gold blending to vermilion, creeping upward to the deep night sky until it joined the border of midnight blue I'd embroidered with golden-white stars.

Morgan's eyes shone as he unwrapped the soft folds of cotton and brushed the little starpoints with his fingers. "Oh, Mama!" he whispered in wonderment without taking his eyes off the quilt. "It's just like my dream! You stitched my dreams right out of your fingers! How'd you do that?" he marveled, turning his gray-blue eyes to me, amazed, as though discovering the woman before him was more magician than mother.

That night I tucked him into bed with his new toy plane right next to him. He was still fingering the quilt, tracing the outlines of the clouds as he sucked on a lemon drop. I leaned down to kiss him on the head, then settled myself comfortably on the edge of the bed.

"Do you like your quilt, baby?"

"It's the whole sky on my bed! Look," he said soaring the wooden biplane over the quilted landscape, "I can fly my plane over Papaw's fields and over here to the hills, all the way to Kansas! 'Bout a million miles!"

"Kansas isn't quite a million miles away, but almost," I said with a smile. "And what about here?" I pointed to the starlit border. "Where do you end up when you fly over there?"

He shook his head solemnly. "Oh, you can't fly there. That's heaven over there, where my papa is."

"Where your papa is?" I frowned. "Who told you that?"

Morgan wound the propeller of his plane with his finger absent-mindedly. "Nobody 'zactly. I just been thinking about it. Johnny McCurdle said I didn't have a pa. I said I did too, that Papaw was my pa, but Johnny said that wasn't right. He said Papaw was your pa, and I didn't have one."

I sucked in my breath, searching his little face for signs of worry, my mind speeding ahead trying to anticipate his questions and come up with a story true enough to help him know who he was and vague enough to preserve his pride.

"But that can't be right," he continued wisely. "Everybody has a pa, so I thought about it a long time and I decided if my pa isn't here that means he must be in heaven." He left off playing with the plane and looked up at me trustingly. "That's right, isn't it?"

"Yes," I breathed, releasing the air that crowded my lungs. "That's right. Your papa was a brave man—an airplane pilot. He was an airmail flier. One day his plane crashed, and so he went to heaven."

Morgan nodded his agreement. "And he's there now"—he pointed to a starred corner of his quilt—"watching me. And some-day I'm going to fly an airplane just like him, and when I'm big I'll go to heaven and see him. Then later you'll come too, won't you, Mama?"

"Oh yes," I said. "But, I'll go first, long before you do. You won't go to heaven for a long, long time."

"Why not?" he asked innocently.

"Because mamas and papas go first, that's why. So they can get everything ready for their children."

"Oh." He yawned and snuggled under the covers, satisfied with my explanation. I sat by his bed for a long time, watching him, warm and safe under the quilt. His steady breathing stirred the covers, making the sun rise and set under the heavens I'd created for him with my own hands.

I dreamed of Slim that night, but it was clearer than dreaming and sharper than life. I could see him in the flesh and feel his thoughts, and I could pull, from a well of knowledge that he could not tap, the outlines of the road that lay ahead for him.

It was cold and cloudy. Slim stood alone on the field, but there were dozens of people standing nearby watching him, making it hard to concentrate. He knew they were waiting for him, hoping he'd try and believing he'd fail. A wave of fear washed over him, fear of failure, fear of waiting too long and missing his window, fear of being afraid.

For an instant, just a breath, I knew he felt I was there. He looked straight into my eyes as though I'd just walked in a room, the same look of recognition his face that had been there the first time I'd seen him in our kitchen. I wanted to take him in my arms, tell him I'd always love him, no matter what happened, and then, as quickly as it had lifted, the curtain fell between us and I was invisible once more.

"God hates a coward," he whispered to himself. Straightening his shoulders, he turned to face the waiting group of hangers on and said simply, "Let's go." He turned his back to me and walked toward the silvery plane, waiting, ghostly and expectant, at the end of the runway. I lost sight of him as a cloudy dawn obscured him from me and the world.

I woke instantly, the dream complete and intact in my mind. I had no doubt that everything had happened just I'd seen it in the dream. I couldn't sleep anymore. There was nothing to do but wait.

I sat at my quilting frame, stitching thread clouds on a field of monotonous blue, passing the eternal hours of night. When morning came I was distracted and unsettled. Any moment when I wasn't needed by Mama, Papa, or Morgan found me back at the quilt frame sewing piercing tracks across the cotton sky, keeping my hands busy and my mind blank until the confirmation came in bold, black newsprint. On the twenty-first of May, 1927, Charles A. Lindbergh landed safely at LeBourget Field in Paris.

The headlines screamed his victory as though it were theirs. The photos showed him being greeted by jubilant throngs, surrounded by a mass of rapturous faces. There were so many thousands that I could hardly see Slim's face for the crush of these strangers who suddenly owned the rights to him, who heard without listening and touched without feeling. I finally understood my apprehension in the theater. These were the ones to fear. They were the undertow I'd sensed, waiting on the other side of the sea and around the world to submerge him under their weight as a drowning man climbs onto his savior and shoves him under, killing them both in a desperate fight to breathe. The crowd was strong and hungry and terrible beyond imagining. There had never been anything like it before, the consuming worldwide adulation of one lone individual shaped and remade and poured into a mold heroic and inhuman—poured out so wide and thin that sooner or later it was bound to break.

The camera showed Slim smiling a tired, slightly confounded grin, bemused, determined to tolerate this temporary madness for the sake of aviation, a passion he was determined to share with the world.

He doesn't understand, I thought, *that it isn't temporary. He has fulfilled his destiny more completely than he could have ever envisioned. He has sparked their imaginations so brilliantly it won't fade tomorrow or next year. Just look at their faces; they're smiling and cheering, but they could eat him alive with the same smile on their faces. They'll never get enough of him. He doesn't realize just how much he will grow to hate them.*

Chapter 6

September 1927

I stood at the cutting table Papa had made for me, tracing dozens of delicate reeds onto a piece of bottle green fabric that would be appliquéd onto a swamp I'd created out of hundreds of inch-wide squares of fabric—a lush, rich everglade with an elegant, stately crane hidden in the rushes. It was monotonous and tiring, laying my sharpened pencil sideways and painstakingly outlining the same template over and over on the same piece of cloth. My shoulders were knotted with tension. It was the part of quiltmaking I usually enjoyed least, but that day I found pleasure in the thoughtless routine this warm Indian summer morning, with a shaft of sunlight angling through the window, illuminating ordinary specks of floating dust and making them look like something magical and fine. I gave myself up to the rhythmic purposefulness of the job.

My little room had been turned into a kind of studio. After Morgan had moved into his own room, Papa put in a bigger window for me and placed my quilt frame under it where the light was best. In the corner, where my rocking chair sat, he'd built tall columns of shelves to hold my fabrics and notions. The cutting table was in the middle of the room, so I could walk around it easily without having to turn the fabric. Papa had made use of every inch of space, but it was still pretty tight, so I'd gotten rid of my big bed, bought a single, and shoved it up against the wall as an afterthought. I didn't suppose I'd ever have need of a double bed again, but I missed sleeping with Morgan next to me, burrowing in the covers to be nearer, instinctively seeking out my warmth. I slept less than I had before. Now, when I woke up in the night with a new idea or a new color pressed into my memory, it was easy to stir myself to work, no matter what the hour, knowing I wouldn't be waking the rest of the family.

Outside my window I could hear Morgan playing and talking to himself, lost in his imaginary world. Papa knocked lightly on the open door of my room and peeked around the corner to see if he was disturbing me. "Hello, Papa." I greeted him, looking up from my work. "Come on in. I'm not doing anything that I actually have to think about."

Papa peered over my shoulder at the piles of fabric. "That's a nice green. Almost like dragonflies' wings."

"Hmm." I nodded, searching for a pin to hold the pattern in place. "It is pretty, isn't it?" I secured the template just where I wanted it and looked up to see Papa shifting uncomfortably from one foot to another. "Well," I said cheerfully, "what brings you here? You must want to talk to me about something important to have come in from the fields so early."

Papa pulled on his nose like he was trying to squash a sneeze, the way he always did when he was thinking out how to explain something. "Well . . . yes," he began hesitantly. "I saw Mr. Walden this morning. He drove by the field I was working in, on his way to deliver the ice like usual, you know. We stopped to chat and he told me that he's coming to Oklahoma City on the thirtieth."

The uncertain, hopeful look on Papa's face spoke volumes, but I kept on working, feigning intense interest in placing the pattern just so. "Mr. Walden is going to Oklahoma City?" I asked innocently.

"No!" Papa frowned. "Not Walden. Slim! He's been flying all over the country, visiting all forty-eight states in *The Spirit of St. Louis*. It's kind of a victory tour, you see. Getting people all fired up about aviation. Anyway, he's coming to Oklahoma City on the thirtieth. Walden said it was in the paper, and I thought that we could drive over there, you see, and—"

"And what, Papa?" I spoke sharply, cutting him off before he could spell out his plan. He stood awkwardly next to me, hooking and unhooking his thumbs through the straps of his overalls. I felt badly for speaking to him so sharply and continued on more gently. "And what do we do then, standing in a crowd of ten thousand people? Do I climb up on your shoulders and hold Morgan up above the crowd, hollering and waving, 'Mr. Lindbergh, it's me, Eva! You remember me? The crippled girl from Dillon, a thousand years ago? One night in a field? This is your son, Morgan. I'd have named him after you if only I'd known what your name was.'" Try as I might, I couldn't keep the sarcastic edge out of my voice. "Is that what you think I should do, Papa? Because that's how it would be."

Papa hung his head and looked at the floor, as though the words he needed might be lying there near his shoes. "I just thought maybe, if he met Morgan. He'd, you know . . ."

"Make an honest woman of me? Oh, Papa," I said with a sigh. "I know you mean well. If you want to take Morgan, go ahead. He's as wild about Lindbergh as all the other kids. Nobody would think anything strange in that, but I can't go. It would just hurt too much.

"I know you want the best for Morgan and me, but it can't happen like you imagine. Even if I could get to Slim, talk to him or write, and he actually read *my* letter, out of the thousands of pieces of mail he gets every week, he *couldn't* marry me. He's the biggest hero in the country, in the world. Everybody thinks he's without a flaw, brave, strong, pure and selfless. If people found out that he'd gotten some poor crippled girl from Oklahoma in a family way and then left her, they'd hate him. I won't be the cause of that, because even though he isn't flawless, he *is* honorable. If Slim knew about Morgan, he probably would want to 'do the right thing' and marry me, and that would crush him and me. I won't be responsible for his destruction."

Papa lifted his eyes to mine, his mouth a flat line of resignation. "I just want you to have a proper life, Evangeline. I want Morgan to have a father."

"He does," I said. "There's not a man in this town who cares more for his son than you do for Morgan."

Papa scooped me into his big, muscled arms and held me close. "Evangeline," he murmured. "My darling girl. I hope he deserves a woman like you, this Slim Lindbergh of yours."

"Papa, I wouldn't have done anything differently."

They went to Oklahoma City without me. I insisted, though Mama didn't want to leave me behind. I won the argument, saying it might be Morgan's only chance to see his father. Someday, when he was older, I intended to tell Morgan the truth about his father, but not yet. Now it seemed important that he see Slim in the flesh, if only for a moment above the heads of a thousand people. Later he would have at least one memory of him, even though, for now, he wouldn't know they were connected.

I tried to help Morgan put on his coat, but it wasn't easy because of the toy airplane he held clutched in his fist. "Let go, Morgan. I can't get your arm through the sleeve. Here, I'll give it right back." He gave up the plane, reluctantly.

"Mama, why can't you go, too?" Morgan asked, frowning.

"Don't you want to see him? The plane will be there. *Spirit of Saint Louis*! Just like mine, but bigger! Ain't that right, Papaw?" He looked anxiously to Papa for confirmation.

Papa nodded and assured him it would all be there, just as he imagined.

"See, Mama?" he insisted. "Don't you want to come?" He tugged on my sleeve to make sure he had my attention.

"Of course I'd like to, Morgan, but I can't. Somebody's got to stay here and watch the place and feed the animals. You wouldn't want Ranger to go hungry now, would you?"

"Well," he whispered so as not to offend his grandparents, "what about you come and Papaw or Mamaw stays here?"

"Papaw has to drive the car, and Mamaw . . . well, she's got to go and take care of Papaw."

Morgan's brow furrowed as he thought about my reasoning. "But who takes care of you?" he asked after a moment's consideration.

I smiled at him and began doing up his coat buttons. "Oh, I'm young and strong. I'll miss you, but it's only two days, and you can tell me all about it when you get back. I can take care of myself. I always do, don't I?"

"Yes." He scratched his nose and turned my logic around in his mind. "Papaw *is* pretty old, isn't he? I guess he needs more help." I nodded in agreement. Morgan's eyes were solemn and innocent as he spoke. "Don't you worry, Mama. When you're old I'll take care of you."

"Thank you, baby." I ruffled his blond curls with my hand and smiled. "That's nice to know." Morgan beamed, satisfied he'd said the right thing.

I waved good-bye from the front porch as the Ford chugged down the road trailing a cloud of dust. Morgan turned around in the backseat and waved his whole arm back and forth like a semaphore flag until I couldn't see him anymore.

It was so quiet when they were gone. Even the prairie wind that constantly whistled around the house and through the trees, that high-pitched score that had been the accompaniment of my whole life, suddenly seemed to shush itself into silence. I'd never been in the house alone before. I wondered if I'd be lonely once night fell. Even so, I was glad I'd made them go.

I did the chores like always, both mine and Papa's too. They went more quickly without Morgan dogging my steps, asking a thousand whys and insisting on "helping." By late afternoon I'd finished everything.

My quilt frame was waiting in my room. There was plenty of work I needed to finish, but the quietness made me feel awkward about working. So I pulled Mama's rocker onto the porch and sat doing nothing at all. Looking down at my idle hands, I felt guilty for a moment, but the sunset was so pretty, orange and coral and pink spun sugar, it seemed right that someone sit very still and admire the day's end.

I sat for a long while in the fading light and then in the darkness, sorting out my feelings. It made me happy to think of Morgan and Slim together, even though they'd be lost to one another in the crowds. At least Morgan would know who Slim was, how he looked and sounded and walked. It was important. Someday Morgan would be able to look at parts of himself and know where they'd come from. He was only four, but it was such a big event. First overnight trip, first restaurant meal, first hero. Surely he'd remember it always. I hoped so. There was no knowing if he'd get another chance to see his father.

Five years had gone by and Slim had never returned to Oklahoma. For the first two or three I'd half-waited, half-hoped he'd turn up, even though I'd told him he mustn't. After a while I forced myself to quit waiting and think of him as gone for good. It was better that way, I told myself. Cleaner for everyone. But that didn't lessen the ache that crept over me at odd moments.

Finding out who he was and what he'd been doing helped lessen the pain, but it left me with questions. Certainly he had reasons enough to stay away. The boy I'd known was just Slim, a simple name for a boy with a simple life. Now he was Colonel Charles Augustus Lindbergh and his life wasn't his own anymore. He belonged to the country more than to me—even more than he belonged to himself.

Yet there was always a part of me that kept waiting and wondering why he never came back. My thoughts spiraled and chased each other like a dog trying to gnaw on its own tail. He hadn't been able to find the time to come. Maybe he didn't want to come. Maybe he was afraid I'd demand an explanation. Maybe he'd just forgotten, as simple as that. No, I wouldn't let myself think that. Much easier to never see or talk with him again than to think I'd been a . . . a what? Mama would have said conquest, but that wasn't what bothered me. That was all tied up with pride and image. I just couldn't bear to think that I was nothing to him. It was all right with me, not to be everything to him, but to be nothing would be more than I could bear. That's why I hadn't gone to Oklahoma City. Not to protect him, though that was partly it, but more to protect myself. "What a coward you are, Evangeline Glennon," I said to the empty evening air. "What a chicken-hearted coward."

"Well, now, I don't know about that," a voice rumbled in through the darkness. "I've thought of you a lot. A lot. I've remembered you and described you to myself with so many phrases it got to be like reciting poetry by heart, but never once in all that pretty prose did the word coward come to mind."

I closed my eyes for a moment before I turned, just to measure the weight of the words, see if the sound was real or imaginary. When I opened them, there he was, standing tall and lean and so alive that I realized how small and flat my memory was. "Hello, Evangeline," he said softly.

"Hello." I paused awkwardly, trying to think what I should say after so long. Nothing came to mind. "I . . . I didn't hear a plane. Didn't see it."

"Didn't want you to. Didn't want anyone to know I was here. That's why I waited until it was dark. Where are your folks?"

"Gone. They'll be back in a couple of days." A hint of a smile played on his lips, and I could see in his eyes it was the answer he'd been hoping for. Embarrassed and elated at once, I couldn't look him straight in the eye, but focused on his hands, lean and strong and tan. I wanted to reach out and hold them in mine, but I couldn't bring myself to be so bold. "I didn't know you were coming. I mean, how—"

He brushed aside clumsy small talk. "Come here." His voice was deeper and more certain than that of the boy I'd known five years before, but it was still his. I could have picked it out in a crowd of one hundred people all talking at once.

Somehow I stood up and crossed the porch to meet him. Perhaps I even said something more, but I don't remember any of that. I just remember the deep, warm solace of his arms and how right and complete it felt to be there, how simple and authentic. When we walked together to my room there was no need to ask why or if we should. We already knew everything that mattered, that we could not have gone on one more minute without each other. We came together more instinctively, more urgently than the first time, so long before. We breathed each other in like oxygen, as though our survival depended upon it. We'd have crawled inside each other and stayed cocooned there, safe and complete until we became something whole and new, until the danger had passed and the strangers moved on, if only we could have managed it.

I couldn't sleep after, just lay awake and watched him, wanting to sculpt and chisel him perfectly in my mind in dimensions that had shape and depth and wouldn't erode when morning came. He slept and woke and slept again, keeping me close through the whole night, so that if I stirred even an inch he reached out and gathered me back in close. My whole body ached for him, though we were already as near as breathing. I surprised myself by reaching for him. When we came together again it was sweet and slow and peaceful, as though our lives together lay stretched out before us far, far into the distance and there was no need to hurry. I found myself stirred in a new way, electric and deep and wide, so surprising that I wanted to turn my mind to examine it, but I had no strength left to think, the tide of need pulled me along so completely. Before it was over I cried out with Slim, as he alone had before, and we collapsed and held each other tight, exhausted and gasping like slippery newborns. We slept, nested together, close as felt-wrapped silver spoons, waiting in a dark, musty drawer, hidden away for safekeeping.

I had never been that happy before. So brief.

In the morning we got up together and smiled natural sunrise smiles at each other like an old married couple, pleased to see each other, the way I'd seen Mama and Papa do. We talked quietly about small things at first, family and crops and gossip, testing the water and exercising our voices and nerve for the bigger questions that waited to be voiced. The morning was too fine and we felt too good to risk conversations with unpredictable outcomes just then. Better to pretend for a few minutes, play house, and imagine our lives as they might have been, dull and ordinary and complete as anyone else's.

I fixed eggs and ham and hotcakes and coffee, and he ate as though he hadn't had a meal in a long, long time. He sighed and patted his stomach contentedly after he'd scraped his plate clean the second time. "I was right. I knew you'd be a good cook. Too good. I'm stuffed."

With a groan, he got up from his chair and stretched his arms up high, nearly brushing the ceiling with his fists. Then he smiled and glanced around the kitchen as though looking for someone. "So, where did your folks go off to? I'd hoped to find you alone, but I can't believe I was lucky enough to get you to myself for two whole days."

"They drove to Oklahoma City. To see you."

He laughed, and I treasured the sound of it. It was the first time I'd heard him laugh out loud, bright and strong like thick brass bells. "Well, isn't that something! I never thought about that. Here I thought I'd sketched out every detail so nothing could go wrong, but I never figured I might miss you because you'd gone to see me." His voice softened, and he touched my cheek with an outstretched fingertip. "Good thing you didn't go too. If I'd shown up and you hadn't been here I think I'd have lost my mind." He reached over and pulled me onto his lap, and we kissed for a long moment, a maple sweet breakfast kiss. Then he grasped both my shoulders, pushed me to arm's length, and examined me sternly, "Hey, how come you *didn't* go?" he teased. "Don't you like me anymore?"

"Somebody had to stay here and feed the stock and watch the place," I said, shrugging.

"A practical answer," he agreed. "Thank heaven you're so practical, Evangeline. It would have broken my heart to fly all this way and not find you home. If you only knew." He sighed a tired sigh, like an old man, and rested with his arms about me, content to let it go for now. There was more to the story, I could tell, but he didn't trust himself to give it out all at once. It would come in small pieces, secrets he could share only with me, but not right away. The years apart had taught us both how precious a few moments of pure happiness could be; he didn't want to contaminate them with painful memories. I understood completely. I had secrets of my own to tell, but they would wait. He squeezed me tight and kissed me again.

"It's taken me months to work out how to disappear for twenty-four hours and not have a pack of reporters chase after me. I was supposed to have an unpublicized stop in Kansas last night, but I flew in the dark so no one'd see me and landed in your father's field. I covered the *Spirit* with canvas and hay. Looks just like a haystack. They'll be worried that I didn't show up, but it would take them days to figure out where I'd gone. When I arrive in Oklahoma City right on schedule tomorrow morning, I'll tell 'em I had engine trouble and no one will be the wiser. Simple as that."

"Good plan," I agreed and laid my head on his shoulder.

He twined his fingers in my hair. "Oh, Evangeline. I've missed you. You have no idea how much. If I could sit in this chair and keep this moment, just like this for another day, a week, a month, it would be enough. I'd die happy. Look at me," he said ruefully. "On the front page of every paper. I've got money, fame, and all that comes with it, but what I'd like most is to freeze this moment and keep it forever. Sitting in a chair in Oklahoma with you on my lap and the sun outside, that would be enough. Nobody'd believe it."

"I would," I murmured and rubbed my cheek on his shoulder. "It is enough, just for this moment. But then the moment passes and something catches your sight, just out of the corner of your eye, and you have to get up and see what it is. Then you're gone." I hadn't meant it to sound like a rebuke, but even listening to myself I knew it was there. The moment had passed. Pretending was over; it was time for explanations and truth.

"Evangeline, I'm sorry I didn't come back before. I don't know exactly why I didn't. As much as I love you, as much as I dreamed about you day and night, I just *had* to keep flying. I couldn't have supported you," he spoke evenly, as though his absence had everything to do with rationality. "Even if I could, you wouldn't have had the attention you deserve, and the real truth is, I just wasn't ready.

Flying took everything that was in me. I couldn't afford any distractions." He was silent for a moment, and it seemed like that last phrase echoed around the room. Then he spoke more softly, almost pleadingly. "Do you understand?"

"It's all right now." I slid off his lap and knelt in front of him, so he'd know whatever things he'd done were loosed. I wasn't a fool about this. I didn't believe his reasons were as simple as he made them sound, but I knew he believed them, so there was no point in pushing him. The world was so demanding of him, I wanted there to be one place that was easy, where his words were taken at face value. That is my understanding of love. I comforted and released him like I did Morgan when he felt guilty over something he'd broken. "I always understood. You don't need to say more."

"Yes I do," he protested. "After Paris, I wanted to come right away, but I couldn't. I had to keep you from them. They'd have turned our lives into a sideshow. You have no idea what it's like. Never a moment to myself. They tear at me like dogs at a piece of beef. It's the loneliest feeling in the world, standing pressed on all sides by a throng of strangers. None of them knows me, but they all want a piece of me. All of them *want* something, like I'm supposed to touch them or say something and that will make everything all right." His forehead furrowed in deep lines of concentration, as though still trying to puzzle out just what was expected of him. "I can't stand it alone anymore, not one more second, so I came as soon as I could."

My heart broke for him. I had known, even before he did, how it would be and how he would hate it. There was no way I could have helped him, no way in the world, and yet I was overcome by feelings of having failed him terribly.

He took both my hands in his and looked me with a mixture of relief and longing. "But it's all right now. I'm here, and everything is going to be better, for both of us. Evangeline, please marry me. I need someone that understands me. Someone I can be myself with. I need you. I can't stand it alone anymore, not for one more day."

In my mind, over the long years, I'd imagined him saying just those words, just that way a hundred times, but in my dreams everything had been so much easier. I wanted to say yes. It should have been so simple and made us so happy, but it wasn't. Nothing about Slim was simple. An image flickered across my mind, the one I'd seen in the newsreel where he was standing in the throng of people, his lips stretched tight and unnaturally across his teeth while flashbulbs popped in his face and strangers grabbed his hands. If it was only Slim and me in the picture, I'd say yes first and tell him about Morgan after, and we'd work it all out later. We'd move away and start over where no one knew us. But it wasn't that easy.

There was no way to erase the slate and start over now. He wasn't Slim anymore, he was Charles Augustus Lindbergh, national hero, household word. National heroes marry prom princesses with rows of straight white teeth and clean-smelling hair. They don't stop over in fields in the middle of nowhere and leave pregnant girls behind and five years later parade them in front of the flashbulbs with bastard sons in tow, not if they want to stay heroes, they don't. I feared that as much as Slim hated the press, the lights, the crowds, he needed them, too. There was no way to know for sure but to tell him. What happened after would be up to him.

I took a deep breath. "Slim, I had a baby."

His eyebrows jumped in surprise and then lowered slightly as the meaning of those words sunk in, understanding what I was saying, but hoping he'd heard me wrong. "You mean"—he hesitated, searching for a delicate way to ask the question—"you met someone . . . or do you mean, after I left . . ."

"*We* had a baby," I said, an edge of irritation in my voice. "A little boy. I named him Morgan. He's four years old. Nobody knows he's yours but me and my folks, if that's what you're worried about."

His face was blank with shock, and he buried his head in his hands for a moment. For once, I couldn't tell what he was thinking. I shouldn't have spoken to him so harshly, but I was angry with him. It was too much to expect that he'd be overjoyed by the news, especially when I'd laid it out so suddenly, I knew. Still, it made me mad to think that even though by a measure of time we were practically strangers, I knew him inside out while he seemed to know me scarcely at all. How he could possibly think, even for an instant, that there was someone else?

When I was a little girl, I used to read the Bible, and when it talked about two people getting together it always said "and so and so went into so and so and he knew her." He *knew* her! I'd always thought that was so beautiful; that was love to me, and when I grew up it all came true. I saw Slim, and he became a part of me, waking and sleeping. The thought that he hardly recognized me stung like a slap on the face. For a moment I just wished he would leave, though even in my anger, I knew I could never push him away. A mile away or ten thousand miles away, I'd given up a place in my soul to him, and it couldn't be taken back.

He lifted his face to mine. Regret was written on every inch of it.

"Oh, Evangeline! God, I'm sorry! I'm so sorry. What you must have been through, and all alone. I should have come back right away." He berated himself, rubbing his brow hard with his fist like trying to scrub away a stain. "If I'd only known then, we could have gotten married before I'd flown to Paris. Before the press . . ." his voice trailed off in regret. "I should have known."

He was speaking of our life together in the past tense, a path we'd missed. Something hopeful in me sank. That was that. There would be no more talk of marriage. Hadn't I always known that? I'd sent him away in the first place. There were a dozen good reasons I should have been furious with him, thrown him out of my life forever, but I looked in his eyes and I saw love, so I couldn't speak of what should be. His love was different from mine, I realized. His love left room for others, other people, other things, for himself. It was all he had to offer me, and it was that hook I'd hung my life on. I'd either have to accept it for what it was or go without. I couldn't go without. I loved him. Why did I feel so numb inside?

I reached out to him and breathed forgiveness on him like a cloud of incense. He was so tender, so human and imperfect, and that was part of what I loved about him—this flawed, anxious part of him, searching for the right thing, that was the side only I got to see, and I cherished it. The world didn't know him, but they expected perfection of him. For a moment, I had been expecting it too, just as grasping and selfish as the crowds in the newsreel. I couldn't stay angry with him.

"Don't do that, Slim. Don't punish yourself for what you should have done." I reached out and stroked his hair. It was unruly and full of waves, just like Morgan's. "There's plenty of guilt to go around on that score. If we talk about what we should have done, we could say that we should never have made love. Maybe we shouldn't have gone flying, or shared our dreams, or even looked at each other. Maybe we shouldn't have, but I wouldn't take back anything." I pulled his hands away from his face, placed my palms flat against his, and leaned in to kiss him. He pulled me closer and responded deeply and gently, making an apology with his kiss for all that he'd missed and all the things he couldn't be.

Then he said the words that seemed to heal everything, that made me believe we'd always be one, though only in secret.

"Tell me about Morgan," he whispered into the tangle of my hair. "Tell me everything about our son."

* * *

The dusky afternoon cast long shadows through the front-room windows. We sat on the sofa, his arm draped over my shoulders while I showed him the small stack of photos taken with the camera Papa had bought when Morgan was born, a black-and-white biography. Baby, toddler, little boy. Morgan's eyes were hopeful and bright, always looking forward. We lingered over the most recent snapshot, one of Morgan sitting on Ranger's back, beaming from ear to ear and leaning down to wrap his arms around the horse's dusty mane.

"This one was at Fourth of July," I narrated. "See there? He's got a little flag stuck in his back pocket. He ran around all day waving that flag. He and Papa set off a million firecrackers and made a terrible racket. The cow wouldn't milk for three days after."

Slim laughed. "Wasn't he afraid of the noise?"

"No, Morgan's fearless," I reported with pride. "More than he ought to be. I have to keep an eye on him every minute. One day I caught him piling up crates so he could climb up on the ridgepole of the tool shed. He had two big elm branches with him and he said he was going to strap them to his arms for wings so he could fly."

Slim grinned. "Chip off the old block."

"I'd say." We sat together a moment longer, admiring our son. "Here. Keep this one." I pressed the picture into his hands.

"Thank you." He held the photo studying it throughly before putting it carefully in his shirt pocket. "What did you tell him about me?"

I hesitated a moment, knowing how cruel it would sound. "That you were dead. An airmail pilot who crashed."

"Oh," he said flatly and then was silent for a long moment. "I'd like to meet him, Evangeline. I know you said what you thought was right at the time, but I'm here now. Don't you think that would be better for him to know he's got a father and that I didn't run out on him?" He gave me a searching look. "I don't want him to think he was abandoned."

"He doesn't," I assured him. "Morgan thinks you were a brave, handsome pilot who died and flew higher than anybody has ever dreamed about, and now you're in heaven looking down on him, watching over him and me to make sure we're both all right. That makes sense to him right now. I don't think it would be fair to confuse him by suddenly resurrecting you, especially when you can't stay and he can't tell anyone about you."

Slim flinched just a bit, stung by my unintended rebuke, but he knew what I said made sense. Longing and reason did battle in his eyes. Reason won out. "I just wish I could meet him somehow, without letting him know I'm his father. When he's older and can understand, I'd like him to know the whole truth. For now, I'd like at least to see him."

Then it dawned on me, "You can! He's in Oklahoma City right now," I exclaimed, "probably too excited to sleep because tomorrow, he's going to see his hero, Charles Lindbergh, the Lone Eagle."

"You're right." Slim's face brightened. "I could look for him tomorrow. He'll be with your folks, right? Do you think that would be all right if I talked to him, just for a minute?"

"That would be just great!" I enthused, thrilled to think of Slim and Morgan together even for a moment. "He'd love it."

"Me too," Slim answered, clearly pleased with the idea. We held each other close for a long quiet moment as the shadows became night and the clock ticked. "Evangeline, I don't know how long it will be before . . . I mean, when I can write or something without . . ."

"I won't go anywhere," I answered his question before he had to ask it. "I'll be here, and Morgan will, too." I laid my hand on his shirt pocket and felt his heart warm and beating through the layers of fabric and photograph paper. "You'll never be alone. None of us will." I said it convincingly, like a prayer, willing it to be true.

* * *

I didn't cry when he left. I stood in the barnyard away from the house where the trees didn't obstruct the view, and I could see clearly in the dark night sky. Slim was just a flash of silver above me, impossible to tell if it was a plane or a bird or a balloon, it was so dark. His departure went exactly as planned, in darkness and secret so, even if they heard the engine, no one would know it was the *Spirit*. Everything about us was always done in secret; it always would be. Things seemed so simple for other people. Why should my life be different, I thought, joy rationed out in mean, stingy portions? It seemed so cruel.

A few days before, I'd told Papa that I had more than I could have ever imagined, and it was true, but now everything was different. The trouble with small bites of happiness is that they stretch you, teach you to imagine what it would be like to have a full plate. Now I would have to start all over again, learning to live without him. Still, I was glad he'd come. Why?

In my mind, mama's voice answered, *Don't ask so many questions, Eva. Be grateful for what you have.*

"I'm trying, Mama. I'm trying my best." Slim circled above one last time and then headed southeast toward his meeting with our son.

"I'll be here," I called to the fading sound of the engine. "I'll be right here."

Funny, I didn't think of it until later; he never said where he would be.

Chapter 7

If I were telling a story, those next years after Slim left, after having him so close and then watching him slip out of my grasp again, would have been the saddest, but they weren't. They were some of the best. When Morgan came back from Oklahoma City beaming from ear to ear, hollering out the window of the Ford before Papa even had a chance to turn off the motor, all my self-pity fled. Suddenly it seemed like things would be all right in the end.

"Mama, look! He signed it himself, a picture just for me!" Morgan leapt out of the back seat, almost crushing Mama in the process and forgetting even to say excuse me, but I could see she didn't mind. Morgan ran to me and flung himself around my waist, hugging me tight as he could.

"Look what he wrote! It says, 'To the World's Best Co-Pilot, Morgan: The sky's the limit! Sincerely, Colonel Charles Lindbergh.' I'm going to hang it on my wall in a real frame. Ain't it something!"

"It's beautiful, Morgan! Just beautiful."

"And he let me sit in the cockpit of the *Spirit* and told me all 'bout how it works, and he said I could be his navigator anytime!"

Seeing the pure joy on his face wiped away the feeling of loss that had weighed me down just moments before. Morgan would always remember that day and feel special because of it. He and Slim were connected, tied with invisible cords, father and son. Nothing could change that.

Brief as it had been, Slim's visit authenticated everything: my life and his and Morgan's. Of course, in a perfect world, I would have had Slim stay, and we'd have lived happily ever after, but I was too old to believe in perfection. If I had doubts, I pushed them to the back of my mind. Life was always a struggle, I reasoned. Mine had been from the moment of my birth, I needed only to look down at my hand clutching my cane to see that. But life was nevertheless rich and real. And that would have to be enough.

Surprisingly, it was. Slim was somewhere out there, pushing himself, greeting the crowds, opening up the skies as Columbus had opened up the seas and, in the midst of all that, thinking of me, as I thought of him. If I couldn't share his life completely, at least I was part of his life, however secret that part might be. Knowing this was enough for me. I would make it so.

Soon after Slim had left, Mr. Ashton, of the First State Bank of Liberal, appeared on my doorstep. His name suited him well. He had a face so white and expressionless it reminded me of a pile of cinders, as though his whole head might crumble and blow away if he smiled or drew a deep breath. It was the sort of face that a person would have distrusted in a lover, but for a banker it was perfect; it spoke of confidentiality and discretion. Mr. Ashton handed me a bankbook with my name on it that showed a balance of one thousand five hundred dollars. "Where did this come from?" I asked.

"It was wired by a Mr. Lawrence Martin of the firm of Reilly, McCormick and Martin, Attorneys at Law of New York City, New

York," Ashton said blandly. "Mr. Martin sent a letter saying he represented an anonymous party, and that if the funds ran out I could contact the firm for replenishment annually."

"But, I don't need all this," I protested.

"Nonetheless, there it is. You may draw upon it whenever you wish, or leave it be and let the interest accumulate. Good afternoon, Miss Glennon." He tipped his hat and twitched his lips in what I supposed was meant to be a smile. "If I can be of any assistance, please contact me at the bank."

And just like that, I was rich, or richer than I'd ever thought I'd be. I didn't tell anyone, not even Mama and Papa. I resolved to keep the money where it was and save it for Morgan, so he could go to college. He was smart as a whip, had started reading the funny papers out loud, doing all the voices, even before he went to school. Now, in first grade, he brought home stacks of papers with shiny gold stars perched proudly in the upper right-hand corners. I had thought about him going to college once or twice in a dreamy sort of way but knew I couldn't afford it. Now everything had changed.

My little quilting business brought me a lot of satisfaction as well as a good income. We didn't need Slim's money to live on. Even before Mr. Ashton knocked on my door we had everything we needed. Though I suppose the female population of Dillon thought of me as an utter failure, I was proud that I could provide for my son on my own.

It seemed like every girl I'd gone to school with was in a rush to find and marry a good man, or any man, for that matter. Failing to marry would have been the worst kind disgrace imaginable to most of them. Ruby was one of the last brides in our class. She asked me to stand up for her at the wedding. I guess I was less enthusiastic than she'd hoped.

"Clarence Parker!" I hissed. "You must be joking!. We used to make fun of him. Remember? We called him Clare-Dunce behind his back." I knew Clarence only too well. He was the boy who had kissed me on a nickel dare, the most humiliating and painful moment of my childhood, and now Ruby was going to marry him! It seemed like the worst kind of disloyalty.

"Eva," Ruby reasoned, "that was a long time ago. I know he was terrible then, but he's grown up. We all have, haven't we? Clay isn't so bad, really. He's real nice to me. He's going to rent us a place not half a mile from here with a sweet little house and a quarter section that we can plant. The owner says we can buy it gradual if we want. Just think! I can see you and Morgan every day!"

She smiled at me convincingly, but I just shook my head. "I just can't believe you're going to marry Clarence."

"Eva, I know he doesn't have a lot of imagination," she said with a sigh, "but he's solid. He doesn't drink much, and he doesn't chew, and besides," she added practically, "nobody else has asked. I don't want to be an old maid. You *know* I'm not smart enough to teach school." She winked at me mischievously, but I refused to play along.

"Do you love him?" I asked.

"Oh, come on now, Eva," she huffed. "Don't be like that. Hardly anybody gets to marry for love. At least if I marry Clay I'll *be* somebody! I can't live with my folks forever. Who knows? Maybe I'll even have a baby boy as cute as Morgan." She smiled at the thought, and then her face clouded with a new concern. "You don't think I'm too old, do you? I'm already twenty-three . . ."

"Don't be silly." I dismissed the idea with a wave of my hand. I still wasn't thrilled with her choice, but the sight of Ruby's hopeful face made me put aside my misgivings. Besides, she was right. We'd all grown up. "You're fertile as a field. You and old Clarence will have a dozen babies. He'll probably have to hang an extra washing line just to keep up with diapers that'll need drying."

Ruby brightened at the idea. "That'd be wonderful, wouldn't

it," she cooed. "A houseful of babies of my own." She looked at me pleadingly. "So you'll do it, won't you, Eva? You'll stand up for me?"

"Yes," I said, taking her two hands in mine and grinning. "I will stand up for you, Mrs. Parker. And as a wedding present I'll make you a big double wedding-ring quilt for your bed, and I will be happy for you. How's that?"

I was as good as my word, because if Ruby wasn't deliriously happy, she was at least content. *Heaven knows,* I thought, *that's more than a lot of people ever get.* But I told myself I didn't envy her the constraints of hearth and husband. After the wedding our lazy afternoon coffee visits were more hurried. The moment the clock struck three, Ruby would drop her teaspoon on the saucer with a clatter and rush out the door, afraid of being late to get Clarence's supper on the table. I did not feel at all sorry to be unmarried.

"You're lucky, Eva, not to have to answer to a man," Ruby clucked in a knowing, matronly voice as she pulled on her coat. "If he don't eat within fifteen minutes of walking in the door he blesses me out something awful."

Yes, I thought as I stood on the porch waving to her jogging up the road to the little house she shared with Clarence. *I'm lucky not to have a man to answer to. It's better this way. Just me and Morgan and Papa and Mama. I don't miss being married a bit.*

My life ran in pleasant, settled patterns, each separate activity a rivulet that flowed steadily and surely forward, emptying finally into a wide, flat river of days. The happy, monotonous rhythm of it was as sure and even as the stitches that made up my quilts, each one seeming exactly like the one before until you stood back and saw the tiny curves and curls that made pretty, satisfying patterns, a dozen gratifying little bits of business in a day that, one after another, made up a year.

Actually, next to taking care of Morgan and thinking about Slim, doing business was the most enjoyable part of my life. I loved imagining and planning a new quilt and then going to the dry goods store to finger the fabrics and make my choice, seeing the colors in my mind the way a painter designs his picture with mental brushes before laying a single dot of paint on canvas. Of course, the storekeepers' wives still avoided talking to me directly and were scandalized and disappointed that I didn't carry shame in my hands like an extra piece of baggage, but their husbands looked at me straight with the kind of friendly solemnity they reserved for other men. We were doing *business,* all of us sharp and fair, looking for as good as we got. The dignity of the transactions was right and proper for the occasion.

Working and saving brought me an inner satisfaction and self-respect. Gazing out over the ten acres of land I'd bought in Morgan's name, right next to Papa's, and seeing my bankbook growing to the point where I could almost buy another ten without touching a dime of Slim's money, filled me with a degree of pleasure that more than made up for the distance between the wives of Dillon and myself. Everything about my life felt fortunate.

For Slim it was another story. Fame was a chain that held him captive. His every move and word were noted and reported by a press and public that couldn't seem to get enough of him. Whether they were maddened by the opportunities opened by the world of aviation, maddened by admiration of their very own hero, or just plain mad, I never really knew. Probably some of each.

I didn't hear from him much. We had agreed that with reporters dogging his every step, even to the point of paying hotel maids to let them sift through his wastepaper baskets, it would be too dangerous for us to write. Any reporter who got to me would be only a step away from finding out about Morgan, and neither of us wanted our son exposed to that kind of attention. But every few weeks I'd get a postcard from some far-off town with a colored picture on the front and a few lines on the back, often nothing more than, "Thinking of you both. Miss you. S." Never more than a dozen words, but they were like poetry to me. I kept them all, few and far between as they were. And even though the news he sent me of himself was non-existent, I was still able to keep up with his every move. Lindbergh mania kept the papers full of Slim's exploits. It was almost as if he were there with me. I could pretend we really were man and wife, that he was away on an extended and important business trip, and each news story was a personal letter home keeping me up-to-date on his progress. It was easy, when he was away, to imagine him as I wished he was.

The illusion I invented became my own story. His picture was everywhere, and sometimes, without realizing it, I drew myself into the shots. The photos became stamped on my brain as though they were actual memories, the way parents show a child pictures of family reunion they were far too young to really recollect, but after seeing the pictures and hearing stories a hundred times you think you really do remember the exact shade of yellow dress you wore and the smooth sweetness of Aunt Martha's famous creamed onions on your tongue.

That was my secret life with Slim. In it he was always young, strong, calm, and as devoted, in his own way, to the memory of our love as I was devoted to supporting him in his life mission and holding down the home front in his stead. It felt noble and fine, this fidelity that asked nothing in return. I never had to learn of his imperfections—if he got grouchy when dinner was late, or rolled over to go to sleep without kissing me good night, or was mean about money or in-laws. We were the perfect couple, and I was content to share him with the world, knowing there was a secret part of him that belonged to Morgan and me alone.

I didn't think of that ever changing. In my mind Slim and I were frozen and constant as images in a photograph, and I liked it that way. But nothing is ever as steady as it seems. Life swirls and eddies around us like the infinite prairie sky in summer when the days are stifling and endless. Then suddenly, you smell something new in the air, and when you look up from weeding the garden to study the horizon you notice a little gathering of vapor. Before you can get to the end of the next row of beans the haze becomes a cloud, and then a black thunderstorm, and you run under cover to watch the pelting, angry sky in awe, wondering where it all came from. When the storm passes, you walk outside to see the plants are beaten down and nothing is like it was just moments before.

Chapter 8

I remember Valentine's Day, 1929, perfectly. My birthday had fallen two days before. I was twenty-three. Morgan made me a card decorated with flowers he'd gathered and pressed all by himself. Seeing his face, so proud of his work, was present enough.

When I opened my eyes that day the house was quiet. I thought it must be very early. I stretched my toes to the end of the bed and sighed, enjoying the feeling of cool sheets on my skin and the luxury of empty time before getting up to start the day's work. I threw back the covers and got out of bed. Pulling back the curtain, I was surprised at how high the sun sat on the horizon. It was late, probably past seven, but I hadn't been wakened by the usual morning sounds of water running and doors closing.

I berated myself for laziness and rushed to dress and help Mama with breakfast, but everyone had already eaten and Morgan had left for school. Mama and Papa were sitting at the table, finishing their coffee and talking to each other in hushed tones. Papa's face was stormy, and I heard him grumbling something like, "The bastard might at least have told us before." Then Mama said it was bound to happen sooner or later and it was best just to face up to it and move on, which struck me as a phrase that summed up Mama's entire philosophy of life. The conversation halted awkwardly when I entered the room.

Papa didn't respond when I said good morning and kissed him on top of the head. He slurped up a last taste of coffee before springing to his feet, grabbing his barn jacket, and heading out the door after kissing Mama and mumbling something about the sow being off her feed.

Mama smiled brightly at me and said, "Good morning, Eva. Did you sleep well?"

"Too well. I guess I must have been tired. I didn't hear a thing this morning. I'm sorry, Mama. Here, let me get the dishes for you."

"No, no," she waved me off and stood up to clear the plates. "Sit down and I'll fry you an egg and some bacon. Here, Eva," she scolded as I poured my coffee, "take a new cup. You don't have to drink out of Papa's. We've got plenty of clean ones."

"It doesn't make any difference," I protested as Mama took away my cup and thumped a new one down on the table. "Clean cup or dirty, the coffee tastes the same."

Normally this would have roused Mama to launch into a lecture on cleanliness. Instead she just cracked two eggs into the iron skillet and busied herself slicing bacon.

"Too bad I missed Morgan," I said. "I had a chocolate bar for him. Valentine's present." Mama didn't respond, just stared into the pan like she could make the eggs cook faster if she looked at them hard enough. She was so quiet I thought she must be angry with me. I sipped my coffee as quietly as possible trying to think back on what I could have done wrong. Maybe she was still upset because I'd overslept. Finally she set the plate of eggs down in front of me and handed me the salt shaker. "I've got to go out and hang the wash," she said.

"Oh," I mumbled, my mouth full of bacon, "Let me help you. It won't take me a minute to finish."

"No, I can do it." She picked up the morning paper that had been lying on Papa's chair and gave it to me. "Finish your breakfast, Eva. Then you need to read this. There's a letter, too." She drew a clean white envelope out of her apron pocket and handed it to me with a little frown before she walked out the back door, balancing the laundry basket on her hip.

I started to rip open the envelope first, but the picture on the front page caught my eye. It was a picture of Slim and a young woman. The eggs got cold on the plate while I picked up the paper and read, finally understanding what had made Mama act so strangely. The story was set off by a fancy border edged with Valentine hearts. The headline was bold and big enough that if I hadn't been so distracted trying to figure out what was wrong with Mama, I'd have surely noticed it first thing.

ST. VALENTINE'S DAY SURPRISE: LUCKY LINDY LANDS LOVE!!

Ambassador Dwight Morrow issued a surprise statement to reporters in Mexico City on February 12th announcing the engagement of his daughter, Anne Spencer Morrow, to Colonel Charles Lindbergh. No date was given for the wedding, and the happy couple were unavailable for comment.

Lindbergh is an aviator and 1927 winner of the Orteig Prize awarded to the first man to cross the Atlantic in a heavier than aircraft. Beloved by millions throughout the world, "Lucky Lindy" is the most recognized and idolized celebrity in the world, as well as the most reticent. Famously shy of the press and publicity regarding his private life, Lindbergh denied rumors of a romance between himself and one of the Morrow's three daughters. As early as November of last year the famous flyer told reporters his only reason for returning to Mexico City so soon after his previous visit in December, 1927, was that his first visit had so favorably impressed him that he had "determined to come back as soon as possible."

Colonel Lindbergh had never been seen in the company of any young women since his record-breaking flight and indeed, had never been photographed in public with Miss Morrow before the release of the engagement photo shown below which was given to reporters on the day of the announcement.

The bride elect is 23 years old. She is a graduate of Smith College and the second of Ambassador and Mrs. Morrow's three daughters. The Morrows are well-known members of New York Society and own a large estate in Englewood, New Jersey. A former senior partner in J.P. Morgan and Company, Ambassador Morrow held many important positions for the U.S. government in both Washington, D.C. and Europe before being appointed ambassador to Mexico.

Miss Morrow, a popular debutante, was noted for her engaging manner as well as her shy grace and fresh, pretty good looks. She distinguished herself at college, receiving excellent marks and many prizes for essays and literature . . .

I didn't need to read anymore. I already knew what they would say, that she was pretty and petite and smart and educated, of good family and good fortune, an appropriate bride for the man who was the nearest thing we Americans had to royalty, a fitting and proper princess-in-waiting. Everything I wasn't. Her picture told the whole story.

She stood next to Slim (a sleek little plane served as background, as though it were one of the bridal party), dressed in a modest but fashionable suit, smiling peacefully for the camera, already having the gaze of a calm and settled young wife. Her face was pretty rather than beautiful, and her eyes were bright with a depth and intelligence that matched Slim's. She would be his equal, I could see, in intellect and wit. They were properly matched, and their faces dared anyone to say otherwise. Only her hands, a slight nervous gesture betrayed by the way her left hand clutched at the right thumb, gave away anything of what she was really feeling, her doubts of keeping up with his ambition and restlessness.

She'd needn't have worried. She was up to the task. Anyone with eyes in their head could see that just by looking at her picture. She would dedicate her life to keeping up with him. She would be the steadying foundation for his life of relentless action. She would be his safe haven and his constant supporter. She would be to him all the things I wanted to be but couldn't.

She loved him completely. It was there in her eyes. She could have lived her whole life on the warmth of just one of his smiles, and now they were to be one forever. The magnitude of her good fortune was still just a bit beyond her grasp, wonderful and overwhelming; they were to be joined until death, for better or worse, though the idea that there might be any worse involved was beyond her imagining just then.

I put down the paper with the picture turned facedown and stared out the window to the bright morning sky, so even and blue; nothing had changed.

She was perfect for him. Wasn't that what I wanted for Slim? Hadn't I told Papa just that? I was the one who had refused to go looking for Slim in Oklahoma City because I said he deserved more than I could give him and I was willing to sacrifice my own happiness for his. Had I meant it? At the time, I did. Back then it had felt so selfless and heroic. But the truth was, I'd never really believed that anyone *would* be better for him than I would. So easy to be noble when you think there's nothing to lose.

Over and over I told myself I had no right be feel betrayed, and yet I did. "Damn you to hell, Charles Lindbergh!" I cried to the empty air. "I *know* you. Why can't that be enough for you?"

As though in answer, the letter Mama left for me slid off the table and into my lap. I recognized Slim's large, looped handwriting on the face of the envelope. The script on the inside was smaller and neater, but still Slim's, as though he'd been ashamed to lay the words out on paper where anyone might see them.

> *Dear Evangeline,*
>
> *I hope this letter reaches you before you see it in the papers, but I wanted to tell you myself. I am getting married. Anne is a lovely girl and I think you would like her. You have a lot in common; intelligence, imagination, wisdom and strength. I need that in my life. I would have sought it in you if circumstances had not stood in the way but, as you said yourself, that was impossible.*
>
> *For a time, I thought the furor that surrounds me would die down and I could come back and claim you and Morgan and no one would notice much. But now I realize that will not happen. I hope you won't hate me for my weakness, but I can't stand the loneliness anymore. In Anne I think I have found someone I can feel completely at ease with, as I did with you.*
>
> *I won't say that I am marrying Anne merely as a substitute for you. That would be disloyal and untrue. You are each unique, but you each possess that same core of strength I so admire. If you'd asked me a few months ago, I'd have said it wasn't possible for me to care for more than one person at the*

same time, but the world is so much more complicated than I thought it was.

When I was a boy, I only ever wanted to be a farmer. What a peaceful life that might have been. You and Morgan and I together on the farm. Morgan. I only saw him once and yet I miss him. You've done a good job, Eva. He's such a bright, quick little lad. I think of him every day and it makes me happy. "I have a son!" But then I remember that I can't touch him, or talk to him. I can't teach him to read or throw a ball, and it depresses me, eats away at me.

Shall I be completely truthful with you? The life of a farmer would have been enough for me, if I'd never seen a plane, or if I'd failed and never touched down in Paris, but I did. Since then it seems as though I'm never at home in my own skin except when I'm flying. Nothing can compete with that, not even you, not even Anne. I think she knows that already, as you have had to learn only too well, or maybe you knew from the start. In any case, I'm sorry for it. I have given you so little and it pains me terribly. Perhaps when you read this you will feel relieved that I'm out of your life after all. I surely wouldn't blame you.

I feel torn apart. With Anne, I think I can finally patch the pieces together and find some peace in my life. Anne understands me and accepts all my flaws, but is strong and loyal enough to help me present the brave face the public demands.

I will not be able to write as I used to. To continue to do so wouldn't be fair to Anne or to you, but know that I love you and I love Morgan and I always will.

Of course, I will continue to support you financially. It concerns me that you have not asked to have another deposit made to your account. Please, don't feel shy about doing so. I don't like to think of you wanting for anything. It's the only thing I can do for my son and it's so little. If you or Morgan are ever in trouble, please contact my attorneys in New York. They have instructions to help with whatever you might need.

I wish I could think of something more to say. I'd like to say that I hope this won't hurt you, but I know it will. It hurts me too, even as it brings something I want so much. I wish, for your sake, I was as brave and wise as my press clippings, but they've got me all wrong. I'm just a man. No matter what I do it seems I hurt those I care about. Please forgive me.

Love,
Slim

If you love someone, you want the best for them even if it hurts. That's what Mama would have said. I could almost hear her voice in my mind. God, it did hurt. Like a physical blow, a breathless sharp pain like giving birth. How could he throw us off like that? Talking about the money as though money would make up for all that Morgan could never have. As though he were some minor god and raining down money on us would absolve him of any guilt so he could forget us and move on—new wife, new sons, while Morgan and I, the hushed and pliant skeletons, were locked away in a closet, paid to forget. How did everything change from one moment to the next? And yet, how could it not? I was foolish to think things could stay as they were, to expect him to live out happily the story I'd written for us both.

He had told me, that day, "I can't stand it out there alone any-more, not one more minute." But he had endured being alone for two whole years more because he loved me and didn't want to hurt me. I could have pushed for marriage, but I'd released him because I was afraid of what would happen to him if we'd married and the public had turned on him. All that pain and loneliness, and we both ended up hurt anyway. But at least we'd tried. There was something in that.

Mama was right. The pain was part of it, maybe the most important part. I had to bear it, or all we'd been to each other would be worthless.

My place at Slim's side had been filled, but until then it *had* been my place. I had not imagined it or wished it into being. He was part of me—then, now, and long before. Nothing could change that. At least I could find peace in that.

My eggs sat cold and untouched on the plate. Outside, I could hear the chickens clucking and scratching in the dirt and Mama's voice humming a worried little tune as she hung the wash. I knew I should go outside and stand beside her and pin shirts on the line so she'd know I was going to be all right. Instead I sat by myself a moment longer. There was nothing else to do. I said a little prayer for their happiness and mine too. I wished them well.

Chapter 9

The 1930s

"Dirt, dust, grime, powder, sand. Just plain filth, that's what it is," Mama muttered as she swept the floor, a gray mound accumulating after just a few swipes of the broom. It was the third time she'd swept that morning, and the wood of the floor looked no cleaner for her efforts. "I hate it." She grimaced and smashed the bristles even harder against the floorboards.

The storm had come the afternoon before, a howling black cloud of dust that surrounded the house and worked its way inside through the cracks and crannies. Our attempts to block the invasion by stuffing rags in the windowsills and doorjambs were fruitless. Wet sheets and croaker sacks hung over every door and window. They were our only protection against the dust that had become a living enemy to us. Yet, no matter what we did, or how often we swept, the dust overcame our lines of defense, sticking in our throats, creeping into piles of freshly laundered bedding, covering our lives with a fine gray grit that never washed away.

The year 1931 brought a bumper crop. Unfortunately, there was too much wheat on the market, so prices dropped like a stone. Everyone counted their losses and hoped for better times. After that the rains stopped falling, and any seeds that sprouted thirsted and died in the fields. With no moisture in the ground, what topsoil there was kicked up with the winds and created black-brown clouds that rained dust instead of water. Everyone in Dillon had endured dust storms from time to time, but this was different. The storms just kept coming, day after day, for months that stretched into years. Everyone said it had to end sooner or later, but after a while I wasn't so sure.

We stayed in the small protection of the house as much as possible whenever the storms roiled. Even Morgan, who always complained when he was cooped up inside the house for long, was content to sit quietly and read when the dust winds howled and scratched at the house like a cat trying to break into a mouse hole. Papa was the only one who went out in the storms. No matter the weather, he had stock to feed and crops to plant. He was driven out in spite of the odds against him, as much from the belief that it simply had to end soon as from the conviction that a man couldn't simply leave his life to lie fallow for lack of knowing the day and hour when the barrage would cease and the rains would come. Perhaps this crop would be the one to take, or if not this one, then the next. Surely it would all be over soon. Papa had waited out droughts before, and he was determined to wait out this one too, but it was too much for a lot of people.

Ruby's mama, who'd always been sickly, passed on soon after the dust storms came. Mr. Carter packed up and moved to Florida the day after the funeral. He sent Ruby a Christmas card every year until 1936, but after that she never got another one and all her letters came back stamped "Return to Sender." The prairie winds blew away a lot more than dust. They blew away people, too. Some never found their way home.

Clarence and Ruby were among the first to go. They rented their place, working the land on shares. Clarence tried his best, but after working the land and proudly bringing in his first bountiful crop only to lose money on it because of the overburdened wheat market, he hadn't enough money left to try again. They didn't own the land, so they couldn't even get credit against their house as so many others were doing. There was nothing for them to do but pick up and try somewhere else. Clarence decided to go out to California and send for Ruby once he'd found some work.

We had a farewell supper for Clarence. It was meant to be a party, but no one was in the mood to celebrate. Clarence was quiet. He already wore the shamefaced expression of a drifter, a look I had come to recognize on the ragged, hollow-eyed men who knocked on our door looking for a plate of food to sustain them as they traveled westward to someplace greener and kinder. Even Ruby, who normally talked and laughed at a typewriter-paced clip, was silent and barely touched her food. Mama had cooked the sort of feast we had taken for granted in better times, two whole chickens and a chocolate cake made with the last of the white sugar. Papa told some funny Will Rogers jokes he'd heard on the radio and everyone chuckled politely, but only Morgan's laughter was genuine.

The next morning, I got up before the sun to wish Clarence farewell and bring him a boxed lunch Mama had made from the cold chicken and leftover cake. She even put in a little bottle of spirits thinly disguised as cough medicine that Mr. Dwyer sold by prescription in his store. In these days of Prohibition it seemed every man in town had developed a cough that required liquid medical attention. Dr. Townsend wrote prescriptions for a dollar apiece with the speed and ease of a bartender pouring glasses of neat whisky, but in Papa's case the need was legitimate. Sometimes he would come in from the fields gasping for breath, choked wordless by dust and discouragement, to stand over the washbasin and spit out streams of swallowed black earth that looked like tobacco juice and smelled like defeat. Mama dosed him with whiskey nearly every day to ease the chronic sore throat Papa had developed from swallowing so much dust, but it didn't seem to help much.

While packing Clarence's lunch, Mama climbed onto a chair to retrieve the little flask from the high shelf where she kept it hidden. "You know I normally don't approve of a man who carries a bottle," she answered as though reading the surprise on my face, "but a fellow so far from home and comfort is entitled to carry a little of his own on the road. Just don't tell your papa about this, will you?" She tucked the whisky under a napkin where it wouldn't be readily seen and returned to her work without looking me in the eye.

Papa met me as I walked across the yard toward the road. "Going to see Clarence off? Here," he muttered, drawing a creased and much handled five-dollar note from his pocket and smoothing it flat. "Hide this in there somewhere he won't find it until he's too far out of town to think of turning around to bring it back. Put it under the napkin. Clarence doesn't use napkins much, I noticed. Likes his sleeve better. He won't find it until he's out of the county."

Papa reached for the box, but I took the bill out of his hand before he could open the lid and find Mama's secret bottle. "Don't worry," I assured him, " I know just where to hide it."

"Just let's not mention this to your mama," he whispered conspiratorially. "We're short ourselves. But five dollars one way or another won't ward off a sheriff's sale if it comes down to it." He winked.

I smiled at the little charades of married people. "It'll be our secret, Papa. Do you want to come with me to say good-bye to Clarence?"

"No. Better not. I think he'd rather not have an audience, but tell him I said good luck and not to worry about Ruby. Morgan and I'll be over every day to make sure there's wood cut and the place is kept up."

"I'll tell him. Papa," I asked, "Is it going to get that bad? Sheriff's auctions and such?"

"No, nothing like that." He waved off my question with practiced unconcern. "Of course, it's tough on young couples like Ruby and Clarence. They didn't have any time to get a nest egg before the storms hit. It's too bad. But things will get better soon. Maybe not like they were, but once we get some rain we'll be all right. It's just hard coming up with cash right now. Speaking of which"—Papa shoved his hands in his overall pockets and sighed—"I hate to ask you, but I'm a little short for the taxes, sixty dollars, but I was wondering if, maybe . . ."

"I've got some money in the bank, Papa. Why don't you let me pay the taxes this year?"

Papa's face broke into a relieved grin. "Oh no. Not all of them, but if you could lend me that extra sixty, it would sure help. It's just a loan, you understand. I'll pay you back as soon as the wheat comes in, don't you worry."

"I'm not worried, Papa."

"Good," he said, smiling. "You'll see. It's bound to rain soon. It's bound to. Nobody ever heard of a five-year drought now, did they?"

By the time I got to Ruby's, Clarence was already a good piece down the road, though the sun had been up barely half an hour. I ran after him as best I could, raising a cloud of dust as my foot and cane stirred up the grainy dirt of the road.

"Clay!" I hollered. "Wait up a minute!" He turned and walked back toward me until we met in the gray morning light. "Whew," I puffed, "a hundred feet more and I'd have kicked up enough dust to start a storm of my own." He smiled at my poor joke.

"Here, " I said handing him the battered shoebox. "Some food for the road. Mama thought you'd need something to keep up your strength. Hope you can carry it. I think she must have packed half a steer in there. You know Mama, 'Feed a cold, feed a fever, feed the neighbors.'" I rattled on awkwardly, feeling a perfect fool but helpless to stop the flow of useless words that spilled from me.

Clarence cleared his throat. "That's nice. Tell your mama I said thanks." He looked down at his feet for a moment before expending the effort to lift his head and settle his gaze somewhere between my nose and my chin. "Eva . . . I . . . I don't know when I'll see you again," he stammered, "and I just wanted to say that . . . I did something awful mean to you a long time back. That kiss, I mean. I shouldn't have done that, and I wanted to tell you I'm sorry. It was so stupid of me. Partly, I was just a dumb kid showing off for my friends, and partly, I wanted to kiss you. You were so pretty and smart. I figured you'd never notice a clod like me, so I made it into a joke. Here you been so good to Ruby and me, even after I was so mean to you." He paused, and his forehead wrinkled as he worked to find the right words. "Well, I'm sorry. I really am, and I just wanted you to know. In case I don't see you again."

I felt my eyes tearing up but forced the tears back, knowing any display of emotion would hurt and embarrass poor Clarence. "Don't be silly. 'Course you'll see me again," I declared. "And don't worry about the other. That was all so long ago, I'd practically forgotten about it."

He stubbed his toe in the dirt, then hitched his rucksack up to a more comfortable spot on his shoulders. "I told Ruby to stay in the house," he mumbled. "She's pretty broken up, and I didn't want her standing in the road crying while I walked away. Don't think I could leave if she did. Would you check up on her? Make sure she's all right?"

"Of course I will. She's my best friend, isn't she? I'll take good care of her. Papa said to tell you that he and Morgan will keep an eye on the place." Clarence nodded his head and looked down the road, fresh out of words. We'd said everything that needed saying.

"Well, you'd better be on your way before the heat's on. Good luck. Write when you can." I touched his shoulder for a moment before stepping back, then walked back to their little house and stood on the porch, watching Clarence walk down the dirt road until he was nothing but a dust devil and a spot of blue work shirt in the distance.

Ruby's cottage was as neat and tidy as ever, but somehow it already wore a scent of neglect, the kind of air you sense in houses that are just houses, not homes, and whose occupants are just passing through. Ruby sat on the sofa staring off into space with red-rimmed eyes, holding a pillow close, the way a mother clutches her child in moments of loss. I didn't say anything to her, just walked over and stroked her hair for a moment to announce myself and then, thinking it was what Mama would do if she were there, I went in the kitchen to put some coffee on the stove.

Ruby sipped at it without really seeing or tasting. I sat down in a chair across from her and tried to think of what I should say, but nothing came to mind.

Ruby spoke first, but without looking at me, just staring off into the distance as though she could see farther than other people. "You remember when I told you I was getting married and you asked me if I loved him? I told you not to be so sentimental, that hardly anybody gets to marry for love. Do you remember?"

I answered yes, and Ruby continued on as though she hadn't heard me. "I was right about that. Most people marry and get dishes and a house and some kind of life. It's expected. But if you get love, that's something extra, a gift. You can't count on it as part of the deal. You marry somebody and feel lucky not to be an old maid, just grateful not to be left out of life. You wash his shirts and fix his meals and at night you lie under him and hope for babies that never come, and in all this you never ask for love because it would be too much to expect. Then one day he walks in the door, hot and tired, and you realize, my Lord! You love him! You love the way he smiles as he eats his food, eats without saying a word, but his smile lets you know better than any words how happy he is to be home with you after a long day. You love how when he goes to town he thinks to bring back a little bottle of cologne, though he can't really afford it, and leaves it on the dressing table where you'll be sure to find it. And when he holds you in his arms at night, so gentle, it's the safest place in the world to be."

She looked up from her reverie, as though noticing me there for the first time. "I love him, Eva. I was one of the lucky few, and now he's gone and I never even got a baby so I can remember him. Lord, Eva. I miss him so much already, it feels like I'll die."

"Oh, Ruby!" I sprang out of the chair and went to wrap my arms around her. "I know it hurts. I know all about that, but it's not forever. He'll send for you soon, you'll see. You'll take a train out to California, and he'll be there when you arrive. You'll live in a house with a green yard, and your children will pick oranges and eat them, right off the trees."

"No," she whispered. She looked away from me again and stared off into space at a place only she could see. "No, we won't. He's not coming back. I'm never going to see him again."

I shushed her for talking such foolishness, but a chill ran through me as I tried to comfort her. Looking at her face, I wondered where she was, maybe in that place where I had been with Slim, where you can see the one you love as sharp and full as life and how everything will be, a cruel preview of things you cannot change.

Chapter 10

The Depression was when everyone in America learned they were alone.

Most people will tell you it started in October of 1929 when the stock market crashed, but that didn't matter in Dillon. We couldn't have located Wall Street on a map if we'd wanted to, and I didn't know anyone who owned a single share of stock. The Depression started and ended on different days in different ways for everyone, but rich or poor, no one was untouched by it.

For most people in Dillon, the Depression started when the dust whirled and crops died and they realized it wasn't going to stop anytime soon. My hard times began when I opened Slim's letter. His began on March 1, 1932, and, in a way, would never really end.

After his marriage to Anne, the everyday details and emotions of Slim's life were no longer entwined with my own. Of course, I heard about the wedding and the birth of their son, Charles Jr.—the papers were full of both stories. But in general I willed myself to forget him. Still, every now and then I noticed the connection that was there, whether I wanted it to be or not. Sometimes the air would seem to crackle with his essence, and I knew something was happening, something so big that Slim couldn't force himself to stay completely inside his own skin.

That's what it felt like that first night of March. I woke up in the night and knew something was wrong. I got out of bed and went to the window, looking to see what it might be, but the house was quiet. I couldn't shake the feeling that something awful was happening to Slim. Worry chased me as I paced the floor, my arms wrapped around myself to ward off the cold that suddenly seemed to chill the night air. I couldn't think what to do, so I prayed through the night, not knowing the reason or the effect of my petitions, but pleading with the spirit of God to do the things that were needful.

The next morning, right after Morgan left for school, I heard Ruby yoo-hooing outside, running across the yard and waving a sheet of paper over her head like a white flag of surrender.

The letter from Clarence she'd been waiting for so long had finally come. Mama, Papa, and I gathered in the kitchen to hear the news. I forced myself to put Slim out of my mind for the moment and concentrate on Ruby's news.

Clarence hadn't gone to California after all. He'd tried, but a band of thugs, actually policeman from Los Angeles, were waiting at the state line to "persuade" immigrants from the dust bowl— Okies, they called us—not to invade their own personal paradise.

"Some persuasion." Ruby curled her lip in disgust. "They beat him so bad he couldn't see out of one eye. Listen, he says, 'They hit me till my face looked like hamburger meat. One of them wore brass knuckles. After they was finished, lying in the dirt on the Nevada side of the border, I decided they was right. If that's what California people was like, I didn't want no part of them.'" Ruby smiled at Clarence's dry humor even as her brow gathered with worry about his wounds, and she clucked her tongue and sighed, wondering aloud if he'd had any witch hazel to put on the cuts.

I assured her that Clarence was a big boy. "Don't worry," I soothed, "he can't be too bad off or he wouldn't have been able to write you such a long letter. What happened next? Did he stay in Nevada?"

"No, he says that he caught a freight to Oregon. Heard that there was work in the logging camps up there. Here"—she squinted at the paper—"this part is for you. 'Tell Eva and her folks thank you for the five dollars. I was going to send it back when I got to California, but I had to use it for eating money to get to Oregon. I don't know what I would have done otherways. I still have a dollar fourteen cents left, but it will have to last me till I get paid. Tell them I will pay them back when I get some money ahead.'"

"No need," Papa piped in as he sat in Mama's chair rocking and listening. "When you write, Ruby, you tell him it was a gift."

Mama stood next to him, listening, and laid her hand on his shoulder to signal her approval of Papa's generosity. "That's right. You tell him we're just happy everything worked out. He said something about getting paid," Mama prodded. "He's got a job, then?"

"Yes, ma'am," Ruby said. "He got a job as a high climber for a logging company. He shinnies forty or fifty feet up to the top of these trees and cuts off the highest part so they'll be easier to fell."

"Sounds dangerous," said Mama.

"It is," Ruby admitted. "That's how he got the job. The man that did it before fell and broke his leg. Clarence was in the right place at the right time, and there wasn't any other work, so he took it. He says I shouldn't worry because he's real careful, and work is work. The pay is pretty fair. Of course, he's so far up on the mountain. There's no place for me, only men in the camp. I'll have to stay here until we get some savings. He gets paid in three weeks. I've got to figure out how to get by until then," she mused. "The next month's rent's due, and I don't have more than three dollars left myself."

Mama interrupted Ruby's worried reverie and looked at Papa. "You know, we've been talking about that very thing, Ruby. Why don't you come here and live with us until you can go out to join Clarence. We've got plenty of room. There's no sense paying rent on a house that's too big for one and land that you're not working."

Ruby protested that it was too much, but Mama and Papa were insistent, pointing out how nice it would be having an extra pair of hands around the place and generally making it sound as though she'd be doing them the biggest favor in the world by moving in. Finally she accepted. When she did, the relief that spread across her face was obvious, and it wasn't just about not having enough money. I realized how lonely she must have been these past couple of months.

It was decided that an extra bed could be moved into my room. Ruby would give notice and pack up her things that very day. It would be wonderful having her so close, but I'll confess to a moment's hesitation about giving up my privacy. Ruby must have read my thoughts, because she leaned over and said, "Don't worry, Eva. It's your room. I'll just sleep there at night and keep to the kitchen during the day."

I scolded myself for being so selfish and told Ruby not be silly, that I'd be glad to have her there, it'd be just like the old sleepovers we had when we were girls. I squeezed her hand and she squeezed mine back. Then we went back to her house to pack up her things, few as they were.

She and Clarence didn't have much in the way of worldly goods, just some dishes and a little furniture that we stored in one of the empty horse stalls. There was nothing of real value except an almost new Philco radio set Ruby's folks had given her as a wedding present. We didn't have a radio of our own. At Ruby's insistence, Papa lugged the radio, shining wood and glass and big as a good-sized pie safe, into the parlor.

"Oh my, won't this be wonderful," Mama murmured, and I could see by her eyes that she truly was almost as excited as Morgan, who was already leaning up against the speaker while Papa turned the dials to pick up crackling radio waves. He finally tuned in on a strong signal from a station out of Tulsa.

The voice of the announcer interrupted the program to bring us an important news bulletin. That's how I heard that Slim's other son, his pink and sturdy baby boy, whom Anne called the "fat lamb," had been stolen. Someone took him, warm and drowsy from his bed, and no one knew where he was.

"Oh my Lord!" gasped Mama. "How could they?" We stood, silent and disbelieving, as the announcer droned on.

My knees were suddenly weak, and I carefully lowered myself into a chair, my mind echoing Mama: *How could they? How could they sneak into a home and steal an innocent child from his bed, for the sake of greed?*

That was the pain that had woken me in the night, Slim's pain. His world was turned upside down. They'd stolen his child, his heart, and his last grain of trust. I knew that no matter what happened, Slim would be never be the same. He would be maimed by hatred, not just for the kidnappers but for the entire carnivorous world that consumed his life as though it were their own. In his way, he would be just as crippled as I was, but it would be worse, because his deformity would be invisible. No one would make allowances for a wound they couldn't see, a thick but imperceptible scar tissue of suspicion. I could not think what he had done to deserve this.

The papers and radio stories continued full of recycled accounts of the kidnapping, with lurid headlines about ransoms paid and rescues attempted or achieved. People were horrified and sickened by the story, even as they demanded more of it, factual or invented. I heard where the sales of newspapers increased twenty percent during the kidnapping. I couldn't blame people; I followed the story with the same addictive devotion as the rest of the country.

Morgan, who was only nine years old, seemed more upset than any of us. He would stop work on his latest balsa-wood airplane and listen with furrowed-brow concentration when his radio program was interrupted to announce some new development or other. He scoured the paper for updates about the kidnapping, and at night, when I tucked him in bed, he prayed fervently for the safe return of Baby Charles. It was the first time I'd heard him pray out loud for something. Usually he kept his head bowed as I voiced petitions for him while he affirmed the requests with a sleepy and disconnected "Amen" before I pulled the quilt up and he dropped off to sleep.

Maybe I was imagining it, but Morgan's concern was so deep and genuine it seemed like more than just sympathy for a cherished hero. Then again, perhaps it wasn't anything more complicated than that. He was mad about planes and the men who flew them and dreamed of flying on his own one day. Maybe it was just the Lindbergh name that drew him. Or could he be picking up on my own distraction and worry? As I watched him kneeling on the cold floor night after night, begging God for a happy ending, eyes and hands clenched so tightly you couldn't have pried them open, I couldn't help but wonder. Maybe he knew, in some deep recess of his soul, that they were connected, he and his curly-headed half-brother. The Lindbergh babies. I dared not ask him.

Finally, we learned the truth. Our prayers had been fruitless from the beginning. The baby was dead. He had been from the first night and for all the drawn-out days and nights that came after. They found him with his skull crushed in, lying in a shallow grave so near his home that if he'd been alive, Slim and Anne could have gone outside and called for him and he'd have run, laughing and wobbling on stubby toddler legs, back home where it was safe.

During all that time, the killers called Slim and cruelly acted it all out, played on his hopes and fears and desperation, when all along hope was dead and had been from the first moment they'd stolen it away.

The world was in shock. It was so unbelievable, like some horrific fairy tale of witches and lost children, but without a redeeming moral or the small comfort that the tragedy had been caused by some mistake on the parents' part or some flaw in their character. Therefore, there was nothing in this story to assure the public that their lives, their children, would be secure as long as they never made a similar mistake or developed a similar flaw. There was no such comfort. Nothing made sense. People everywhere, women and men, shed tears of sympathy. They knew exactly how they would feel if one of their own children were lost, cold and alone, bleeding and dying among strangers. The thought was too painful to be borne. So they held their own children close and wept, because it was the only thing they could do. Everyone had learned a little more about how cruel life could be.

Morgan wanted an explanation. He looked at me with accusing eyes. "Mama, why would God allow something so awful to happen to a baby? Colonel Lindbergh is the bravest man alive, and his wife is so pretty and smart. They can't have done anything wrong. I just don't understand how bad things can happen to people like that."

"I know, Morgan. It's all so sad. The only thing we can do is pray for them."

Morgan shook his head, and I could see that he wasn't satisfied. Some of his trust had been stripped away. Simple answers couldn't erase the doubts. He looked at me with eyes like his father's and dared me to find an explanation.

"I already did that," he insisted, "and nothing happened. If God is out there, wouldn't He hear my prayers? And if He heard them, why wouldn't He answer them?"

I began to tell him that God knows best. That there's always a reason, even in something as senseless as this, but we just can't see it. But as the words took shape in my mind, I didn't believe them myself, so I told him the truth.

"Morgan, I could tell you the things mothers are supposed to say, but you're too old now to believe what I say just because you're my son, so I'm going to tell you plain." I took a deep breath and searched once more for some elegant collection of words that would make sense of everything, but none came to mind. "I don't know," I finally admitted. "There's a lot of things I just don't understand. But I feel sure deep inside myself that God is out there and He cares. So many things just don't make sense to me. I can't fathom why such terrible things are allowed to happen to people. I don't expect I ever will."

"Then why even go to church?" he shot back in anger. "Why pray if nobody hears?" His brows pulled together in an impatient line that again dared me to answer.

"Because I have to. There are some things you have to decide for yourself, Morgan, and you may choose to accept it or not, but I sincerely believe that God hears my prayers, even when He doesn't answer them the way I'd like. I have to believe. If I didn't, I'm not sure I'd be able to get up in the morning. That's just the best I can do."

Morgan pushed a curl out of his eye to see me better and bit his lip thoughtfully, his expression a mixture of surprise at seeing my lack of confidence unmasked and gravity as he realized that adults don't have all the answers. He ground his fist into his hand and said, in voice that seemed wiser and deeper than it had a moment before, "It doesn't seem right, does it?"

"No," I agreed, "it surely doesn't."

That night, after everyone had gone to bed and Ruby's breathing sounded deep and regular on the other side of our room, I buried my head in my pillow and sobbed. I mourned that dead child as though he had been my own. In a way, he was. He was my family. I grieved for Baby Charles and for Slim and Anne and the people they would never be again. They were dead, too. The golden, untouchable couple had melted to dross, never to shine as brightly again, and the hope of the whole world was a bit dimmer than it had been the day before. We were all wiser and sadder.

I felt like Morgan. I wanted to run to the highest peak and stand on it, shake my fist to heaven, scream "Why?" and refuse to move until I got an answer, though I knew none would come.

I didn't hear Ruby creep across the cold wooden floor to perch on the edge of my bed. She patted my back and shushed me, told me it was all right, that everything would be all right. I choked back the tears and apologized for waking her.

"No need to be sorry," she said, patting my arm. "No need at all. You feel better now?"

"Oh yes," I muttered, wiping tears off my cheeks. "I shouldn't get myself so upset. I just can't get over that poor baby. And the parents. I'll be all right now." I sniffed. "I can't think what's come over me."

"You don't have to explain. Cry all you want to," Ruby soothed. "Get it all out. I understand. You love him, Eva, and when he suffers, you suffer. It all comes too close to home, but you can thank God that Morgan's safe and you'll keep him that way. Nobody knows about him. Nobody even suspects, though I can't think why."

Panic rose in my throat as I realized what she was saying. I made my voice flat and unemotional, not wanting to give anything away in case she knew less than she pretended to. "Ruby, I don't know what you're talking about." I sniffed again and wiped my eyes on the sleeve of my nightdress.

Ruby pulled a cigarette out of the pack she kept on the nightstand, lit a match, and drew a deep breath through the filter. The tip glowed red in the darkness, and she blew smoke out through her mouth in a long, impatient sigh. "I am talking about Morgan Glennon, your son and Lindbergh's," she said simply.

Words of denial bubbled up in my throat, but she interrupted before I could get them out.

"Oh, Eva!" Her eyes twinkled at me, like they used to when we were children and shared our whispered and terrible secrets. "Don't look at me that way! I won't tell a soul. I'm just so happy I finally put it all together."

She grinned as wide as her mouth would allow and threw her arms around me. "Eva, you were in love. I'm glad for you!"

I pushed her away, then held her by the shoulders. "Listen to me, Ruby." Glaring into her eyes, I spoke more sharply than I'd intended to, but it was important she realize I was serious. "You can't tell anyone about Morgan. Not ever."

"Of course I won't," she answered a little indignantly. "How could you even think such a thing? Look," she said, crossing her heart solemnly with her index finger, the signal from our youth that meant we'd take each other's secrets to the grave, "I swear. Are you satisfied?"

I was. Ruby would never go back on her word. Still, if she could figure it out, who else would? "Do you think anyone else knows?" I asked in a worried voice.

"No." She dismissed the thought along with another puff of her Lucky Strike. "They ought to, of course. Morgan looks so much like him, especially around the eyes, and has that same half-smile, like he's embarrassed to show his teeth, and he's so crazy about airplanes. But, shoot, every kid in town is nuts for fliers. They all think they're goin' to grow up and break records instead of grow wheat. "Still"—she shrugged—"You'd think they would have figured it out. Maybe if Lindbergh had already been famous when he came to town instead of after, they'd have paid more attention."

"Of course," I answered wryly, "it helps some that it's me. They might have put two and two together if we were talking about Mary Kay Munson or Edith Hopkins or one of the other local beauties, but nobody would expect the handsomest, most famous man in the world to take up with the town cripple."

"Oh, Eva," Ruby clucked in an offended voice. "I never said that."

"I know you didn't," I said, laughing. "I did. Believe me, I've thanked God a million times He made me so twisted and people so blind. How else would I have been able to keep Morgan to myself all these years? They'd be hunting him, too, if they knew. But what made you so smart? Did you figure it out, or did you always know?"

"I didn't realize it until the night of the kidnapping. The look on your face was like death, like it was your baby they'd taken. I knew then that you and Slim shared something more than you'd told me. The next day I watched Morgan, his gestures, his face, everything. It was like a map leading to treasure. All the clues were there, I'd just never looked for them before."

A treasure. She was right, Morgan was my treasure and Slim's, too. Until Ruby mentioned it, I hadn't really thought about Morgan being in danger. If someone was crazy enough to steal one Lindbergh child, they might be crazy enough to try for two. I had to be more careful than ever, and not just to preserve Slim's reputation. I would keep Morgan hidden, safe here in Dillon, growing tall and strong and golden like wheat ripening to harvest, a promise that someday things would be better.

Morgan couldn't take his half-brother's place, I knew. Each child is irreplaceable. But I hoped it would comfort Slim to know that Morgan was protected, a small secret piece of himself that lived and thrived, untouched in the prairie. He would grow to be as we had been on that one perfect afternoon, lying on the warm earth, gazing upward at an incomparable piece of sky. He was the firstborn of the flock, flawless and without blemish. I would keep him that way for both of us and for what we had been on that day, as a matter of trust.

Ruby interrupted my thoughts. "Seems like Slim got everything in the world except what matters most. If you think about it, that's everybody's story, isn't it? Sometimes life seems almost too sad to live, but what else are you gonna do?"

"I don't feel sad," I said sincerely, "Not anymore. I've got Morgan."

"That's a better reason to get up in the morning than most people have," she agreed.

Ruby took another long drag on her cigarette and held it out to me. I took it, and she lit up another for herself. We sat on my bed, our backs to the wall in the half-darkness, smoking, not thinking, not talking. We didn't need to say anything, just be together, inhaling deeply of the same acrid, widowed air, lighting the day to come with twin tips of ash glow.

Chapter 11

1935

"Evangeline!" Papa called, striding into the kitchen, tapping a clean white envelope against the palm of his hand. "Got a letter here. Looks like it's from that Mrs. Clemson in Houston."

"Thank heaven," Mama said with relief.

Ruby glanced up from the bowl of beans she was sorting for supper. "About time," she grumbled. "Now maybe we can afford to buy some ham to go with these beans."

My spirits were buoyed by the sight of the long awaited letter. "Ruby," I said, grinning, "after we pay the taxes, we'll buy ham and some beefsteaks and ribbons for our hair." I laughed with relief and took the letter from Papa's outstretched hand. *Thank God it got here in time,* I thought as I ripped open the envelope and searched for the check I'd been expecting for weeks, payment on five quilts that I'd made for Mrs. Clemson's daughters. It was eight months' work I'd compressed into five so we'd have the money we needed to pay the taxes. After that I didn't know what we'd do. There were no new orders coming in, but I'd been counting on the Clemson payment to get us through tax time. There was a check and a note written out in careful, copperplate script, but it wasn't the check or the letter I'd expected. My face must have told the story.

"What's wrong?" Mama asked. "Didn't she like the quilts? She doesn't want to send them back, does she?"

"She loves them," I said quietly. "Says they are even more beautiful than she could have imagined."

"Of course she does," Papa said stoutly. "It's your work she's buying. It's art, not just something to throw on the bed. How could she not love them? What's the problem?"

"It's her husband. He's a banker, and his bank closed. She can't pay me, not all of it, anyway. She's sent me ten dollars now and says she will send me five dollars a month until she's paid up the whole amount."

"That'll take years!" Papa bellowed. "And you're just supposed to sit by and let her pay on time without even a bit of interest attached? That check doesn't even come close to covering the cost of your material and the postage, let alone your time. Write her back, Evangeline! Write her back and demand she send back the quilts. You can sell them to someone else and get a good price for them with money you can put in your pocket."

"No, she can't," Ruby said flatly.

"And why not?" Papa blustered irritably. "It's beautiful work."

"Ruby's right," I said, rubbing my brow with my hand, trying to soothe the headache I could feel coming on. "It may be fine work, but no one can afford it. I use the best fabrics, and each quilt takes me hours and hours of handstitching. No one around here can pay enough to make it worth the time, or even the cost of materials. I'm better off to leave them with Mrs. Clemson. I might get the money back eventually, and we need every penny just now."

Papa jammed his fists into the pockets of his overalls and

frowned at the floor. I wished I hadn't said that last part. Even though he worked every day, as hard as he ever had, he couldn't coax a crop out the ground to save his soul. Time and time again, though it pained him terribly, he'd borrowed money from me for seed and sown it only to watch his work blow away in a cloud of dust and bitterness. He was ashamed, and nothing I could say would soothe his wounded pride. Papa worked as hard as he could, but it wasn't enough. He'd been reduced to living off his daughter. Now even that thin stream of sustenance was drying up.

"It's all right, Papa," I said hopefully. "Maybe you're right. Maybe we should ask Mrs. Clemson to return the quilts and look for a buyer. If I cut the price in half I could still make a little money on them."

"Nobody around here has twenty-five dollars for a quilt, Eva. Not even one of yours," Ruby remarked practically. Out of the corner of my eye I could see Mama throwing an irritated glance in Ruby's direction, but she didn't correct her, probably because she'd been thinking the same thing herself.

We all thought about what to do for a long moment. Ruby broke the silence. "You've got enough for the taxes?" she asked seriously.

I hesitated a moment before answering. "Yes." It wasn't a lie. I did have enough, if I dipped into Morgan's college fund. Something in me had always resisted spending that money. At first it was just a desire to hold on to it for Morgan, but then something deeper was involved. Pride, I suppose. After Slim married, I was more determined than ever to prove I could stand on my own two feet—not that he'd ever know about it, but it was important to me. I'd tried my best to release him, forgive him, and mostly I had, but there was still some resentment there. A tiny part of me felt that taking his money would somehow turn me into nothing more than his youthful indiscretion, a mistake bought and paid for and forgotten.

That was my worst fear, that he'd forget us. Some debts can't ever be paid. I didn't want him to have the escape of thinking he'd "settled up" with me and Morgan.

Now it seemed there was no choice. Morgan needed a home, and everyone was depending on me, and it wasn't the first time. The money I'd saved from quilting before the crops started to fail had been winnowed away until only eighty-five dollars and sixty cents were left. "Yes," I said. "I've got the money."

Ruby thought for a moment more. "Have you got any extra?" she asked. "Because if you do, if you could scrape up even twenty or thirty dollars more, I think we might be able to come up with a plan that would save your quilting business. We'd just need a little seed money to get started."

"What are you talking about, Ruby?" I asked in exasperation. "I can't see the sense in putting the last of my savings into a business that's losing money as it is."

"Just hear me out for a moment," she insisted, holding up her hand to interrupt my objections. "I saw a sign in Dwyer's store that somebody was wanting to sell an old sewing machine real cheap. If you could buy it, then invest in some inexpensive yard goods, nothing fancy, just the ends of the bolts that get marked down, and sew them into real simple, quickly made, nine-patch quilts, we could do it assembly-line style, like Ford makes cars. You could probably make them fast and cheap enough so you'd have something you could sell at a price people could afford. We could drive around and sell them, maybe go up into Kansas even. We could even trade them for food if people didn't have cash." She paused and studied my face to see what I thought of the idea.

I was uncertain about the whole thing but had to admit I didn't have a better idea. "Do you really think it could work?" I asked.

"I think so." Ruby nodded convincingly. "What do you think,

Mr. and Mrs. Glennon?" Mama and Papa agreed it was worth a try. "Good!" Ruby said. "Eva, I've got an extra ten saved up that I can give you toward the price of the machine."

"No," I protested, "you need to save up so you can go out to Oregon and join Clarence." She had insisted on paying three dollars a week for her board, though Papa had told her she should keep the money. Clarence had already been gone close to three years. His letters home still assured Ruby that they'd be together again as soon as it could be managed, but he no longer made predictions about when that might be. His paycheck was so small they were lucky to put away five dollars in a month. "You keep giving away your savings and you two will never be able to afford a place of your own," I said.

"Well, seems like the Depression has already licked us," Ruby said with resignation. "I won't stand by and watch it beat you down, too. Not after all you've done for us. Besides, you've got to do something."

She was right. I had to try something. Even the money Slim had sent wouldn't last us forever, and I'd die before I'd write and ask him for more. I had to find a way out of this myself. Despite Papa's faith that he'd get a good crop any time now, day after day the winds kept blowing and the dust piled against the house as though it intended to bury us all alive. The Depression stretched out in front of me like a road to the top of a hill. You couldn't see what was on the other side, but you sensed it was simply more of the same.

I didn't like the idea of giving up my other quilts. Wielding needle and thread like a soft sable brush, I created the world as I wished it to be and wrapped it around myself and those I loved like truth. It seemed wrong to put aside something that mattered so much to me. Those quilts were my voice, my heart. How was I to still my voice and turn out piecework, just for money? But I had a son, and he had to be housed and clothed and fed. That would be voice enough.

"All right," I said. "I'll give it a try. But I'm not taking your money, Ruby. You keep that for your trip." She started arguing with me, reaching in her apron pocket to fish out a wad of dollar bills. I put my hand over hers. "No, I mean it. I have enough money on my own. If you want to help, you can do the cutting while I do the sewing. It'll go faster that way."

Ruby agreed, and Mama piped in that she could help, too. Papa started to say something, thought better of it, and walked to the window. He stared out to see if the dust was still flying, as though he could still the winds if he just concentrated hard enough. He frowned in frustration at the sky, still brown and blowing with wasted soil.

Ruby and Mama actually seemed excited over the idea of the new project and began discussing patterns and color choices, but I was too worn out to join in the conversation.

We would survive, all of us, in some condition or other, yet I couldn't help but wonder what would be left of our souls when it was done. It was a decade of compromise.

I read in the paper that Slim and Anne and their new son, Jon, left the country to live in Europe, where the boy would be safe from kidnappers and the relentless pursuit of the press and public. The arrest and trial of Bruno Hauptmann, the alleged kidnapper of Baby Charles, had been an even bigger circus than the Paris flight. Day after day the newsprint beasts were fed a diet of Slim and Anne's anguish, anguish that would have been devastating enough in private; illuminated by the macabre glow of flashbulbs it seemed to be eating them alive. Every photo showed them older, sadder, more distant from the world and one another. I couldn't blame Slim for running away. Even so, I waited a week, then two, hoping for a letter from him or even just a note of farewell, though I wasn't really surprised when none appeared. I didn't expect good news on the doorstep anymore. Nobody did.

Not long after, a telegram came saying that Clarence had died. Ruby's reaction was surprisingly resigned, more angry than grieved, not really shocked. It was as if she'd been expecting this all along. I couldn't help but remember her premonition on the day he'd left. I tried my best to comfort her. She'd always known just what to say when I was grieving, but my efforts were clumsy, and only platitudes seemed to fall from my lips, heavy and false and tasteless as the cups of weak tea I urged her to drink.

The teacup was hot when I placed it in her empty hands; she didn't seem to notice. "At least he didn't suffer, Ruby. The telegram says the fall broke his neck and killed him instantly. He didn't feel any pain."

"Don't be such a simpleton, Eva," Ruby snapped, her voice sharp with irritation. "If he'd been in terrible pain and lingered for hours, you don't suppose they'd tell me that, do you? Not in a telegram. It would take too many words. Think how much something like that would cost to send!" I was flabbergasted. I couldn't think how to respond to her outburst. I shot a questioning look to Mama, thinking she would know what to say, but Ruby carried on with her tirade before anyone could get a word in.

"You don't suppose I believe anything they say, do you? They didn't even spend the money on a harness to secure him to the tree so he wouldn't fall in the first place. He wrote me that he'd told the foreman to get some harnesses or someone would get hurt, and the man said, 'Mind your own business, Parker. Equipment costs money, but you Okies come a dime to the dozen.' You don't guess a cheap chiseler like that's gonna pay extra to tell me the truth about how my husband died, do you? "

For a moment I truly thought she'd lost her mind. It was such a crazy thing to say under the circumstances, and I'd never heard her use language like that. Mama shot me a look that said not to worry. She took the telegram from me and read it over herself, then spoke calmly to Ruby.

"You're right, Ruby. Probably they'd never tell you a thing like that in a telegram, but I'm sure money didn't enter into it. They'd want to spare you thinking of him in pain." She pulled a chair up next to Ruby's and looked at her thoughtfully, as though they were having a serious but completely normal conversation. I stood watching in confusion, uncertain what to make of the entire scene.

Mama continued in a low, even voice, "From how Clarence described his work, I'm inclined to believe the telegram. He must have fallen at least forty or fifty feet, maybe more. A fall like that would have killed him instantly. You can be sure of it." She nodded confidently.

"Do you think so?" Ruby eyes searched Mama's, and she hung on to every word as though they held a special importance only she and Mama could appreciate.

"Oh yes," Mama affirmed confidently. "Old James Tetley, you remember him, he lived over in Hooker? Fell roofing his barn and was dead the second he hit the ground, and that barn wasn't near as high as Clarence said these trees were. Really, he'd have never felt a thing."

"Tell me more," Ruby demanded, and so Mama did, recounting the stories of every man who'd fallen to his death from a height of more than fifteen feet for the previous twenty years. Down and down they tumbled, over and over, from grain elevators, ridgepoles, and church steeples, all of them meeting the ground stone dead and past their pain. The way Mama described it, it sounded like *the* way to meet your end. Ruby listened intently to each story until, seemingly satisfied, she said she'd better go pack if she was to make the westbound train.

When she left the room I whispered urgently to Mama, who was ironing a stack of handkerchiefs to include in Ruby's luggage, "What in the world was that all about? Have you both lost your minds? Worrying about the price of telegrams and a bunch of farmers who were pitched to their deaths when it's *her* husband who's gone? What kind of questions were those?"

"Eva, people act strange in strange situations. There is really no way to predict what someone will do in a time of loss. Weak people become strong and strong people become weak. It doesn't get any stranger than this; a man comes to the door and hands you a piece of paper, and because he does, your husband is dead. Now you tell me, how does your mind make room for something like that?"

I shrugged helplessly. It was impossible to understand. Clarence had been dead for hours? Days? And yet, until she read the telegram, he'd been alive for Ruby and for all of us. Shouldn't we have known?

"I don't know," I admitted. "How can you make any sense of it?"

"Well, unless you're crazy as a bedbug, you hang on to whatever little shreds of good news you can salvage from the situation, like being absolutely certain that people who fall from great heights don't suffer. It's not much, but it's something to hold on to. Ruby's not crazy, she's just trying to hang on to what little comfort is left to her. Under the circumstances, it may have been the only sane question for her to ask."

The money Clarence had sent to Ruby over the years, hoarded in dollars and quarters and dimes, hidden in thick white envelopes of letters, was just enough to pay for Ruby's fare to Oregon to bring the body home and for the funeral. The logging company offered to pay for a burial in Oregon, but Ruby refused.

"He went without new shoes and lunches to save up money so we could be together again someday," Ruby said. "That's what I'm going to use it for, to bring him home."

She traveled alone because no one could afford to make the trip with her. At the train station in Portland, Oregon, she was met by two men from the logging company who took her to a room where a rough pine coffin was waiting. One of the men lifted the lid so Ruby could confirm that the man inside was her husband, though she told me later that the body inside didn't look anything like the Clarence she remembered. "I only recognized him by the scar just under his right ear where he got cut on some barbed-wire when he was little, a jagged white mark, like a lightning bolt. We were married close to six years, and I loved him, but that's the only part of him I knew by sight. How could that be?"

After the coffin was closed, some porters helped load it into the baggage car of the train that had just brought Ruby west. The men from the logging company tipped the porters a quarter each, shook hands with Ruby, and said they were real sorry about Clarence, that he was a good worker and a good man. "The taller man, I guess he was the boss," Ruby said later, "he handed me an envelope with the last of Clay's pay plus some money he said the fellows had collected to give me. Forty-two dollars and thirty-five cents. Then they said they had to be getting back up the mountain to the job site.

"I went and sat in the coffee shop and waited for six hours while they got the train ready to turn around and head east. I spent the thirty-five cents on coffee and a ham sandwich, but I wasn't really hungry. Just figured I had to buy something so I could sit in the restaurant and kill time before it was time to leave. That's all I ever saw of Oregon, the coffee shop in Union Station."

Papa and I hitched Ranger up to the old hay wagon, and we all went to meet Ruby's train, which had actually come in a few minutes early. Ruby was calmly supervising the unloading of the coffin when we arrived. We loaded the casket into the wagonbed and drove directly to the cemetery. Papa had arranged everything while Ruby was gone. Pastor Wilder met us there to say a short service next to the open grave. After he was done, the coffin was lowered into the ground while Ruby stood by, tearless and steady, to make sure the hole was filled in properly. The next day she asked Papa to drive her into town to order a marker.

Papa told me she spent almost the whole forty-two dollars on the headstone. "Nothing fancy, but she insisted that it be granite. 'The best you can get,' she told the stonemason, 'and engrave the letters extra deep. I want it to last.'"

I was amazed by her strength. We sat on the porch steps after supper that night, Ruby watching fireflies and me watching Ruby smoke cigarettes one after another. "How can you be holding up so well?" I wondered. "It's all right to grieve, you know. No one will think the worse of you."

She looked at me sadly and said, "I grieved when he left, remember? Something told me then he wasn't coming back, even though I tried to pretend I was wrong. Sometimes I even came near to believing it, but deep down the truth was always there."

She twined a lock of hair absentmindedly around her finger and stared off in the distance, remembering that day so long ago. "When he walked down the road, I cried and waited to die, but nothing happened, so I got up and went on with life. Funny, that's what people always say you should do when someone you love dies, that the dear departed wouldn't want you to grieve, and then, when you take their advice, they look at you like you've lost your mind."

"Oh no, Ruby!" I cried putting my arm around her, "I didn't mean it like that."

"I know. You're worried about me, that's all. It's just that I think it makes good sense. Clarence wouldn't want me to sit around pining and sobbing." She tossed her cigarette butt into the dirt and ground it out with the toe of her shoe, then leaned forward and hugged her legs with both arms, resting her chin on her knees and staring out at evening sky. It was such an unconscious and childlike pose, I was suddenly reminded of how young she really was; we both were. "Besides," she continued, "I don't think I have any tears left; I used them up so long ago. It must look odd to you."

"No," I assured her. "Not at all. I've never had a husband. How could I pretend to know how you should feel? I just want to make sure you're not trying to be tough and hold it all in. You don't have to go around being brave on my account."

"Or you for me, Eva," she said, looking at me pointedly. "Husband or no, we've been in the same boat for a long time, two women who loved their men and got left behind with just a few mementos to remind us that any of it was real in the first place. You've got a son with a face like his father's, and that seems pretty concrete, but all I've got is a shoebox full of letters and a ring I can see whenever I look down at my hands." She was quiet for a long moment, studying the plain gold band on her left hand as though trying to remember just what it had to do with her.

"Eva," she asked, finally breaking the silence, "do you even remember what it was like when Slim was here? Doesn't it all seem like a dream sometimes? He was here for a day or two and everything changed. It must have been like blinking in daylight and opening your eyes to find that the sun had set. Now we're both alone. Clarence has gone to his reward, and Slim's gone to Europe.

That's an awful long way," she murmured thoughtfully. "Did he ever write to say good-bye?"

I shook my head no. Ruby exhaled a cloud of disgust. "And you're worried about how I'm holding up? I might ask you the same question."

I shrugged at her concern. "I'm fine. Nothing has really changed. He left me behind a long time ago. Europe is just geography. If he lived in the next county, we'd be just as far apart. When you think about it, this shouldn't bother me any more than the rest of it."

Ruby searched my face, and without meaning to, I shifted my gaze away from hers. "But it does," she said.

"Yes," I admitted. "For all the difference it makes."

Ruby sighed. "We are some sorry pair, aren't we? Guess that's what makes us such good friends." She laughed sarcastically. "Wouldn't it be awful to be this miserable all by yourself?"

Chapter 12

It was ironic that the only faint ray of hope we had that year came while Ruby had gone to bring home Clarence's body.

Papa got a job. He was hired by an absent landowner to list his fields for him, cutting deep furrows that were theoretically supposed to keep the soil from blowing away, though I couldn't see that they helped much. The pay was poor and the work was hard, but it was a job. At the time, it seemed like Papa's salvation had come just in the nick of time.

Before Papa got work, the wind seemed to be sucking away slivers of his spirit day by day every bit as ferociously as it consumed our fields, steadily and methodically, as though it wouldn't be satisfied until Papa was eroded completely, powdered fine and scattered across the plains. His shoulders stooped, and he never whistled anymore. He'd stopped reading to Morgan in the evenings and spent more time alone in the barn. He said he was working, but he just puttered, honing the blade of his scythe over and over again, making it sharper than ever before and every day a bit thinner and smaller, just like Papa himself. It was hard to mark the difference from one day to the next; you sensed rather than saw a gradual diminishing.

Then he got work. Overnight he was one of the luckiest men in town, and he looked it. I could hear him padding around the kitchen before dawn, humming to himself as he ground coffee and clanked the lid of the donut jar optimistically. Though he coughed more than before, I didn't worry. He was actually plowing those drought-stricken fields, stirring up the dust and swallowing it in every breath, but he looked so well and beamed with such purpose that I never questioned what it might be doing to him. None of us did.

Things were going so well, no one wanted to speculate on how long it would last. Every Saturday for two months, Papa brought home a plain manila envelope containing his pay minus whatever he'd spent to bring home a few groceries from Dwyer's. It wasn't much, but it meant everything to Papa, and we were all thrilled to see him acting like himself again. When he brought home something extra one Saturday, it seemed like the clock was actually turning backward and Papa was younger than ever.

A section of the land Papa was working had some old train cars sitting abandoned on the property. Mr. Ashton, the bank manager who was serving as trustee for the owner, wanted them moved off and gave Papa permission to have them hauled over to our place, anywhere as long as they weren't on his client's property. Before the week was out they were parked out next to our barn, a rusted freight car and a caboose scoured so hard by the winds and dust that the paint had been stripped off as clean as if somebody had used sandpaper.

"And just what do you think we need with some old, filthy train cars?" Mama asked, obviously less than pleased with Papa's new acquisitions. "Look at them cluttering up the yard! People will think we're living on a scrap heap."

"You'll see," he said with a grin. "When I'm done you'll be so surprised that you'll apologize for doubting me. Morgan!" he shouted heartily. "Get my toolbox and get over here. The men in this family have work to do."

"Yes, sir!" Morgan replied and ran off to find the tools while Papa rolled up his sleeves and strode, whistling, to inspect the cars.

"The men of the family. Hmmph." Mama shook her head and chuckled tolerantly.

For weeks on end the sound of scraping, hammering, and sawing filled our ears. Morgan and Papa spent all their spare time on the project, only coming inside to sleep and eat before they were back at it again. It was a happy, purposeful time; three months passed quicker than three weeks used to before Papa had started working. Using part of his small salary and whatever they could salvage from abandoned farms around the county, Papa and Morgan worked magic.

One day they made us close our eyes while they led us by our hands to see what all that hammering and sawing had wrought.

"One, two, three," Papa and Morgan counted together. Morgan shouted out the final command: "Open your eyes!"

It was amazing. The caboose had been turned into a private and cozy little apartment all its own. It was really nothing more than a tiny sitting room connected by a hallway to an alcove for the bedroom and closet, but it was just as cunning and complete as it could be.

"It's for you, Ruby," Papa said, smiling. "It's small, but it's yours."

Ruby was speechless, not daring to believe, I suppose, that such a perfect little space was really meant for her alone. Somehow Papa and Morgan had managed to sneak into our room and spirit Ruby's own quilt off her bed and into the caboose without anyone noticing. It looked clean and crisp on the new bed. The bedroom had just enough space for the bed, Ruby's rocker, and a shiny black wood-stove that would keep everything warm as toast in winter. The walls were a warm brick color, mounted with two gleaming brass oil lamps that gave off a clear, bright light. Everything was so tidy and clever. Ruby, who had been stoic and strong throughout the after-math of Clarence's death, suddenly burst into tears.

"Now don't go doing that, Aunt Ruby," Morgan squeezed her arm while Papa fished in his pocket for a clean handkerchief to offer the sobbing Ruby. "We can paint it a different color if you don't like this one." Morgan laughed. "You just say the word and we'll break out the paintbrushes, but there's no need to cry about it."

"I'm sorry," Ruby wailed. "It's just so beautiful. You've all been so good to me, and now that Clarence is gone I'm more of a burden than ever. I can't even pay you the three dollars a week for my keep anymore, and you all go and do this!" She broke into a fresh stream of tears, bawling louder than before and trumpeting her nose into Papa's handkerchief.

"Don't be silly," I said, patting her on the back. "You saved my quilting business. We couldn't manage without you."

"That's right," Mama agreed. "If you didn't help with all the cut-ting, we'd never be able to make quilts up fast enough to make any money. With the arthritis in my hands, I'm not as much help as I used to be. Anyway, you're family now."

That only made Ruby cry harder, but we could all tell they were the good kind of tears, the sort of release you just have to have now and then if for no other reason than to know that some things can still touch you down deep.

"That's enough of that, Aunt Ruby," Morgan said gamely. "You haven't even seen the best part yet." He led the way toward the old freight car and pushed open the door with a strength and enthusiasm that reminded me he wasn't a little boy anymore. Thirteen years old, practically grown up. We all followed him inside. The freight car had been cleaned and shelved with row upon row of chicken coops and roosts. Papa grinned from ear to ear as Morgan gave the tour. We all admired their handiwork. Everything was planned out so cleverly. I told Morgan it looked beautiful and wondered how he ever thought of raising chickens.

"It was all his idea." Papa beamed, winking and pointing to Morgan. "And he did almost all the carpentry by himself, too."

"I read about what you need to farm chickens in my Four-H handbook," Morgan said proudly. "Once we got a place to keep them, the rest was easy. I've even figured out a design for an incubator for baby chicks. Works with a light bulb. Now all we need are the chickens!"

Ruby sniffed away the last of her tears. "I'll take care of that," she said. "How many do you need to start?"

"Oh no, Ruby," Papa holding up his hands in protest. "We couldn't let you do that."

"Mr. Glennon, I've got a little money left over from Clay's funeral and I'm buying chickens with it," she said in a voice that would brook no argument, the stream of tears suddenly blocked. "You've given me a home here with you, and now you've even built a place I can call my own. It's little enough for me to do by way of thanking you. I'm sure if Clay were here he'd agree with me. Besides, if I really am family, why shouldn't I help?"

And so it was agreed. Morgan and Ruby would go into town the next day and buy enough baby chicks to start a real flock. Though it would be months before we had hens laying and eggs to sell, when we sat down to our small supper that night it was like old times, with everyone laughing and talking at once. Papa was himself again, presiding over the table with the confidence of a man who is sure of his usefulness in the world. Morgan kept chattering excitedly about pullets and cockerels and even drew out a diagram of his new incubator invention. Mama, Ruby, and I studied it with genuine admiration.

I couldn't help but think that Slim would be so very proud of his son, a chip off the old block, his mechanical mind already seeing things that other people missed and turning his ambitions into plans. I resolved to start writing him about Morgan, forwarding the letters to his lawyers in the hope that he'd read them. I wouldn't mention anything about myself, just about our boy. He had a right to know about his own son. His son had a right to be known. The idea warmed me inside.

For myself, I was through with love, through with Slim Lindbergh, but where Morgan was concerned things were different. They were still father and son. Surely there was a happily ever after for Morgan.

Morgan felt my eyes on him, admiring him, and got up from his place at the dinner table to come and kiss me on the cheek. It was a good day. The best we'd had in a long, long time and the best we would have for a long time after. For a moment, we really believed the worst had passed. Is it better sometimes not to know what's coming?

Chapter 13

Iused to believe that if I lived my life a certain way and didn't make mistakes, I could make things come out the way I wanted. If I planted the right seed, it would grow; if I said the right thing, he would love me; if I ate the right food, I could ward off death. It's all foolishness, of course, but you've got to hang hope on something. The older I get the more I see our struggles for what they are, but still I think our efforts have a certain brave, tender optimism that must touch the heart of God. We mean so well and we try so hard, and in the end, we are at the end.

I never asked to know what was coming. No one had ever read my palm or tried to see my future in the bottom of a teacup, and I wouldn't have wanted them to. Yet, oftentimes, I knew more about Slim's life than he did. I could almost smell the trials around the corner, though I was unable to change any of it. What good did it do, for me or for him? I never did understand it. How often I tried to wish away that strange gift, even to the point of closing my eyes and refusing to see. I didn't seem to have the same sensitivity for anyone but Slim. It might have been of some use for someone else, but my sight failed me when it came to those who were near enough that I might actually have helped them. If I had known what was coming, the day and hour, I would have done something differently. Don't ask me what, but something.

When Papa came in from work early that day in September, complaining of the heat and coughing more than usual, I didn't know it was the last day. He said he wanted to lie down and rest awhile. Mama brought him a glass of cool water and dosed him with two tablespoons of amber-colored whiskey before he fell into a fitful, troubled sleep.

During the night his breathing got raspy and irregular. Mama came into my room to wake me, but I was already sitting up in bed, listening to Papa struggle for air. The rattling sound scared me so much I didn't even stop to look at Papa before running out the door, my only thought to call for the doctor. I never said good-bye.

The nearest house with a phone was Thompson's. I drove there as fast as I could and called Dr. Townsend to come right away, but it was too late. Papa died before he arrived.

When I returned Mama was stretched out across the bed, covering Papa's feet like a blanket, screaming, just screaming, as though someone was tearing away parts of her flesh while she was still alive. That was more shocking than anything. I could never have imagined her losing herself that way. Ruby tried to comfort her, but it didn't do any good. Morgan stood holding on to the doorjamb of Mama and Papa's room with both hands, tears running down his face at the sight of the only father he'd ever really known lying so still and white on the bed, a stillness that can't be mistaken for anything but death. I didn't know what to do, so I just waited, paralyzed, until the doctor came and brushed past us all, ordering Ruby to take Mama out. Ruby half-walked, half-carried Mama into the next room, but I could still hear Mama's sobs coming from behind the closed door. Dr. Townsend examined Papa quickly, listening to his chest and lifting up each eyelid perfunctorily before he spoke.

"It's dust-bowl pneumonia," he said with finality. "This isn't the first time I've seen it, Eva. Your father's swallowed so much dust it gradually clogged up his lungs, probably his stomach, too. One of my own hogs up and died last week. When we butchered it there was over two inches of dirt blocking the stomach."

I could not put Dr. Townsend's words into a picture that made sense. I wanted him to keep quiet while I figured things out. Talking about butchered hogs and blocked entrails and my papa all in the same breath. I didn't understand what he was saying. What did any of that have to do with Papa lying still, looking pale and small in the big bed and Mama in the next room sobbing like she'd lost her mind. When was he going to shut up and do something?

"Eva . . . Miz Eva? Did you hear me?" I looked up to see the doctor's face, tired and patient, peering into mine.

"I'm sorry," I whispered. "What did you say?"

"Had he been eating well lately?" he said each word slowly, as though talking to a child.

"No. He said he wasn't hungry. Said it made his stomach hurt to eat too much. He put most of his food on Morgan's plate. I thought he was worried about Morgan getting enough to eat."

"Well, it was likely some of both. Glennon doted on that boy and you." The doctor patted me on the arm awkwardly. "I'm sorry, Eva. I'm real sorry. He was a good man. Don't go blaming yourself, now. Even if I'd gotten here earlier, I probably couldn't have done anything. He was too far gone. You'd best pull yourself together and help your mama. Be better if you left the room while I finish my examination and fill out the death certificate." I stood still as a statue, trying to believe what the doctor said.

"G'on now, Eva," he prompted. "Tend to your mama. She needs you."

"Yes," I started as though waking from a bad dream, "I have to take care of Mama now."

As quick as saying the words, I was head of the family. I'd never thought about Papa dying. He was young, years from sixty. If I had thought about a time when he wouldn't be there, I would have supposed that Mama would rise up, strong and straight-necked, practical as always, and taken over, pushing me and Morgan, getting us through it all somehow. I never realized, until Papa was gone, that any strength Mama had she drew from him. It was like she had said, death changes the balance of things somehow, the weak become strong and the strong become weak. Maybe they were never all that strong to begin with. Whatever the reason, Mama was overcome by grief, and the funeral arrangements were left up to me. It was just as well—having something to do saved me from thinking too much.

Pastor Wilder, who had spent thirty years in the pulpit, had retired only the month before, so I called the new minister, the Reverend Paul Van Dyver, to say the service. I had never even met him until the morning of the funeral. His face was serious and not especially handsome, though it had some interesting angles, as if it were composed entirely of triangles. He was well over six feet tall and very, very thin, reminding me of an illustration of Ichabod Crane I'd seen as a child. He wasn't quite thirty at the time, but the expression of a much older man was written upon his face. His manner was sincere; even in my grief, I felt there was something about him I liked. Maybe it was the way he looked at me straight on, in a manner that was so frank and plain it might have been mistaken for rudeness if his blue eyes had not been so kind. He spoke with an accent, enunciating each word carefully to make sure he was understood properly.

"I did not know your father, Miss Glennon. Normally, as his pastor, I would want to say a few words about him. However, in this case, I feel it would be improper and, coming from a stranger, insincere. It is clear that your father was very much loved by his family. It would do him more honor and be more meaningful if one of you would speak of him."

I appreciated him stepping aside. Many a new minister trying to make an impression on the community wouldn't have wanted to miss the opportunity to give a sermon. On the other hand, maybe he wasn't much of a speaker and was merely afraid he'd embarrass himself. Either way, Pastor Van Dyver was right. It wouldn't do to have a stranger eulogizing Papa. But who would speak? Mama certainly was in no condition to do so, and I wasn't sure I could carry it off without dissolving into tears.

"I can do it." Morgan stepped into the conversation. "I'd like to," he told the young minister. "That is, if it's all right with you, Mama."

"Oh, Morgan. It's going to be such a hard day for all of us. Are you sure you want to? I could ask Mr. Dwyer. He liked Papa, and he's a good speaker. "

"He's too good," Morgan said seriously. "You've heard him give the announcements at church, haven't you, Mama? Hooks his thumbs in his vest and booms on and on as though he were giving the Gettysburg Address instead of letting people know the time of the deacons' meeting had been changed." The minister's eyes twinkled, and he suppressed a chuckle by suddenly needing to clear his throat.

"I'm sorry, Pastor," Morgan apologized sheepishly. "Guess I shouldn't say something like that about one of the deacons. Don't get me wrong. I like Mr. Dwyer; he's a nice man and a real good deacon; it's just that . . . Well, I think someone from the family should talk about Grandpa. That's all."

Van Dyver nodded to Morgan and assured him he understood entirely, then he turned to me with a trace of a smile still on his lips. "Miss Glennon, I hope you will forgive me for interjecting myself into family business, but I think young Morgan is right. For a boy his age he shows not only intelligence, but remarkable insight." He smiled at Morgan and then turned to me again. "Though I did not have the privilege of knowing your father personally, I am sure he would be honored to have Morgan say his eulogy."

I had to agree. Papa would have been proud to have Morgan speak of him and pleased that doing so obviously meant so much to the boy.

"It's decided then," the minister said. "I will return at one o'clock tomorrow, an hour before the service." He said good-bye and shook my hand, locking my eyes again with his compassionate, concerned gaze. "If there is anything I can do to help you, I want you to feel certain you may call on me at any time."

As many times and as many people as had said those exact words in the previous forty-eight hours, it was the first time I felt that they were spoken with utter sincerity.

Mama cried and cried, but not at the funeral. Just before the service she pulled me and Morgan aside and said, "If you have any crying to do, do it now. I won't have us shame your papa by blubbering in front of the neighbors, do you hear?"

For one wonderful moment, I thought the old Mama was back, ordering us around like always, but guarding her grief from outsiders was as far as it went. That was the last reserve of her force. She took my arm as we walked out to the front porch to greet the ar-

riving mourners, leaning on me for balance, suddenly becoming ancient.

The day was hot. The house was filled to bursting with sweating,
sober-faced neighbors. Farmers and merchants Papa knew from
town twisted their hat brims nervously in their hands and looked
pitifully at their shoes as they told me of a hundred little kindnesses
Papa had done them, secret loans of money or tools, and well remembered words of encouragement given in moments of despair.

Women who would not have spoken to me on the street before
suddenly called me by my first name, all my past sins apparently
paid for by my loss, at least for this one day. They wrung my hand
and told me how sorry they were and asked me to tell Mama to let
them know if there was anything they could do, though she was
standing right next to me and they could easily have told her themselves. Somehow they sensed that I was in charge now, the conveyor
of condolences and maker of plans.

Mr. Ashton, from the bank, tipped his hat to Mama as he came
in and shook my hand more firmly than I expected. He murmured
his sympathies and asked in a soft, discreet voice, "Miss Glennon,
would it be convenient for you to meet me at the bank tomorrow
afternoon? If you're feeling up to it, that is." I just had time to answer yes before Morgan came up and whispered in my ear that it
was time to start.

Everyone filed into the parlor where Papa was laid out in his best
suit in front of rows of straight-backed chairs, some ours, some borrowed from neighbors. If I had not known it really was Papa, had
not helped wash him and dress him with my own hands, I would
not have recognized him, so small, so shrunken, so still he was.
Strangely, that was a comfort to me. It seemed the part of him that I
knew, the part that was truly Papa, was simply gone, leaving behind
a shell that had nothing to do with him or where he was now. I

squeezed Mama's hand as she sat next to me, a black veil shading eyes that seemed to see but not understand what was happening around her.

Pastor Van Dyver gave a short, simple sermon about hope and eternal life. There was nothing fancy to it, but I liked it because it affirmed my belief that Papa was in heaven and past his pain. At the same time, I couldn't help but wonder and worry about our pain and how we were going to manage without him—and what Mr. Ashton wanted to see me about.

After the hymn was sung, Morgan stepped up to the front of the room. He stood tall and gangly in last year's suit, his wrists showing a good two inches of white shirt cuff. I had not noticed how tall he had become, almost overnight. His voice was firm and steady, stronger and more grown up than that of the little boy he'd been just three days before.

Morgan had chosen to read from Psalm 112, "A good man sheweth favor and lendeth; he will guide his affairs with discretion. Surely he shall not be moved for ever: the righteous shall be in everlasting remembrance." He stood a long moment before he spoke again, looking into the eyes of everyone present, his face at once innocent and wise.

"Just about every Saturday, my grandpa gave me a nickel for the picture show. I like the serials best. When I'd get home, I'd always tell Grandpa about what happened, how the hero had saved the day, and the girl, and how I couldn't wait to see what happened next week. Grandpa always sat and listened to whatever I had to say, like it was something important. Then when I'd finished he'd whistle and wink his eye and say something like, 'That Tarzan, he's a brave fellow, all right.' Then we'd go back to feeding the chickens or cleaning the barn just like we did every day.

"Sometimes I'd wonder to myself if I'd ever have the chance to do something brave, but somehow, when you're doing chores it's hard to imagine you'll ever be a hero or even meet one face to face. Mucking out the stable on a Saturday afternoon, all I wished was that time would go more quickly so I could get back to the pictures and see what happened to my heros. A week felt like a million years, and our farm felt like the end of the earth.

"But now my grandpa is gone, and the time I had with him seems like a minute. I'd give up every Saturday picture show for the rest of my life to have one more talk with him. See, I know something about heroes that I didn't know before, something I wish I'd realized when he was still alive so I could have told him about it to his face.

"Grandpa was the real hero in my life. He didn't rescue the girl or sink the pirate fleet, but he was a hero just the same. These last years on the farm haven't been easy, as all of you know. Year after year the crops dry up and blow away, and some days it seems like things will never get better. Sometimes it's enough to make a fellow want to give up. A lot of people have. But not Grandpa. He kept working, even when there was no work to be had. He kept hoping, even when things seemed hopeless. He kept trying, even when there was no reason to think he'd win.

"If you think about it, that's what heros are: people who try to save the day, though the odds are against them. At the picture show, the hero always wins. In real life, it doesn't always work that way, but it doesn't mean my grandpa was any less courageous than Tom Mix. I think Grandpa was more courageous. Serial heros only have to be brave for twenty minutes every Saturday. Grandpa did it every day of his life.

"I'll always remember him. I hope you will too."

Despite mama's warning, a tear rolled down my cheek. I wiped it away quickly before anyone could see.

The strangest part of Papa's funeral was the day after. My eyes opened just before dawn. I pulled myself to a sitting position on the edge of the bed, my leg feeling even stiffer and heavier than usual, and combed through my hair with my fingers. Already the hens were scratching around in the yard and a young cockerel was cock-a-doodling a pitiful imitation of a full-fledged rooster. The floorboards were cold on my feet as always, and the sounds of morning on the farm ticked off dully and reliably like minutes on a clock— and, *yet,* I thought, *Papa isn't here.* Suddenly, I was too sad to get dressed. I sat for a long time thinking nothing until Ruby cracked open the door and said it was time for breakfast.

Sitting at the sewing machine later that morning, I found myself adding up bills for coffin and headstone and labor to dig the grave, trying to figure how many more quilts I would have to make and sell that month to see us through, and wondering what Mr. Ashton wanted to see me about.

While I was picking out a bad seam, the needle pierced my finger deeply. Three perfect drops of blood fell onto the quilt like tears that wouldn't wash out. I finished the sewing and found myself wondering who would buy that quilt and lie under it nights. Would they notice the bloodstains and be curious as to how they got there, or would their eyes be drawn to the overblown roses and silly daisies instead, completely overlooking the signature I'd left for someone to find?

Mr. Ashton stood up as I entered his office and motioned me the chair nearest his desk. After reiterating his sorrow at our untimely loss, completing the proper inquiries after myself and my mother, and offering me a glass of water, he cleared his throat. Briefly, a flicker of uncertainty in his eyes made me think that despite his appearance of infallibility, Mr. Ashton might be human after all. I liked him better for it.

He cleared his throat a second time before squaring his shoulders and plunging ahead with the assurance that I was more accustomed to hearing in his voice, as though all of his nouns started with capital letters.

"Miss Glennon, as you will remember, some years ago I informed you of the existence of an Account which was opened in your name and to which you were entitled to request Annual Deposits, though you have never availed yourself of the Opportunity. Over the years I have received instructions, through the law firm of the Anonymous Party, to keep an eye on your Financial Situation so they might inform their client of any needs you might have, but might be, shall we say . . . hesitant to inform me of directly."

His face was so implacable that I didn't know if he had wanted to use "proud" or "ashamed" in place of "hesitant," but as he took off his perfectly clean glasses and rubbed them with his spotless handkerchief, I saw a whisper of a smile crinkle his eyes and felt he'd meant the former.

"I have been pleased to report to the Anonymous Party"—he said it with such emphasis that I was sure the party wasn't anonymous to him, but felt just as certain my secret was safe with Mr. Ashton—"of your industriousness and ingenuity and that you have not only refrained from spending the funds in your account, you have added to it from time to time. Of course, in these last few years, you have drawn down the account to meet your expenses, but still, in spite of your difficulties, you have never withdrawn the principle."

"It's not mine to spend," I explained. "I promised myself I never would. That money is for Morgan. For his future."

"I ascertained as much," said the banker, balancing his glasses on the end of his nose and peering at me over the shining clean lenses. "You should be congratulated, Miss Glennon. Very few young women would have been able to live up to such a principle in such challenging times."

"Thank you, Mr. Ashton, but any mother would have tried to do the same in my situation," I demurred.

"I very much doubt that, Miss Glennon." He shook his head gravely and raised his eyebrows so his forehead wrinkled, revealing just how many layers there were to his doubts. I couldn't help but wonder that a man as skinny as Mr. Ashton had enough spare skin on his frame to leave room for wrinkles. "Most women in your situation would have been in my office every year, asking for more and larger deposits." (Mr. Ashton never seemed to use the word "money," as though it would have been coarse and not quite polite to do so.) "Some would have had good intentions of saving the funds, but there are none that I can think of by name who would have been able to follow through with their resolution in the face of this terrible economic crisis. Your endurance has won my sincere admiration. I say again, Miss Glennon, you are to be congratulated." Then, to my surprise, he actually stood up, leaned across the desk, and shook my hand with all the vigor of an aspiring politician.

Smiling politely to mask my confusion, I thanked him again before retrieving my hand. "But, surely, Mr. Ashton, that's not why you asked me to come see you?"

The expression of cheer fled from his face. "No, Miss Glennon, I'm afraid not." He cleared his throat again, as though to give himself time to formulate his next sentence. "You have done well, with your finances, very well indeed. Your father, however, was not as fortunate. Two years ago, he took out a second mortgage on your farm to pay back taxes as well as meet living expenses and purchase seed to plant crops, which, as you know, failed."

My stomach dropped. How much did we owe? Would the bank foreclose and leave us without a home if I couldn't find the money?

A thousand questions assailed my mind, and then I thought of Papa. Poor Papa had carried this load all alone. It broke my heart to think how desperate and alone he must have felt.

"In these economic conditions, Miss Glennon, it's doubtful I would have made that loan to another man, but I felt your father would do whatever it took to meet his obligations. When he fell behind on the payments I gave him more time, still believing him to be a good risk. Indeed, since beginning his new job he'd made good progress toward bringing his loan up to date. Had he lived, I believe he would have done just that, but given the circumstances . . ."

"How much do we owe?" I asked weakly.

"In addition to the loan itself there are back taxes and penalties for the last two years, amounting to well over three thousand dollars," he said softly, almost apologetically.

Three thousand dollars! The figure rang in my mind like a bell. Even if I emptied out Morgan's account it wouldn't be enough. I couldn't even begin to think how many quilts that added up to, but somehow I had to try. I had to buy some time first, and then I had to find a way to hold on to the farm. After that, I'd figure out how to earn Morgan's money back.

My hands were shaking, but I willed my voice to sound strong, "Mr. Ashton, if I could give you the money in Morgan's account now, surely a system of monthly payments could be worked out. I don't earn much with my quilts, but I'm sure there is a way to make good on the loan over time. You can't take the farm." I tried to keep my voice firm and emphatic, but it was impossible to keep out the note of pleading. "At least not without giving me a chance to pay the money back."

For a moment the banker looked a bit startled, "Miss Glennon, I didn't bring you here to threaten foreclosure! I merely wanted you to know—that is, I felt you had the right to know . . . Miss Glennon, I took the liberty of cabling the Attorneys of the Anonymous Party on the day of your father's death and informing them of the situation." He cleared his throat again.

"It has all been paid, Miss Glennon. All of it, and next year's taxes in addition."

Suddenly the reason for Mr. Ashton's discomfort was clear. He had called Slim's lawyers without my permission because he knew if he had asked I would have said no. I would have told him we would manage without the help of the Anonymous Party. My feelings of warmth toward the banker gave way to irritation mixed with an underlying sense of relief.

Mr. Ashton removed his glasses again and leaned toward me urgently. "There simply was no other way, my dear, or I would never have done it," he said gently. "You want to fulfill your obligations to your son, I know, and you have done so, very ably. But you must consider, you are not the only one with a duty to the boy, are you?" He raised his eyebrows questioningly, and the layers of wrinkles creased his forehead again. "Sometimes our responsibilities to our children extend even to admitting the need for help. For you I suspect that may be the most difficult debt to pay. It certainly was for your father."

The thought of Papa all alone with that terrible burden threatened to bring me to tears. If he had told me, wouldn't I have done anything I could to help? Wouldn't we have found a way, together? And, if there was no other way, wouldn't I have gone out and plowed those barren, blowing fields by his side, swallowed half the dust that was meant for him? Yes. I'd have done anything if it had meant we might be together. If only he had let me help him.

"All right, Mr. Ashton," I conceded. "I understand. It's hard for me to admit, but you did the right thing. Thank you for your help. I truly appreciate all you have done for my family." I swallowed hard, and Mr. Ashton reached into his pocket to offer me his handkerchief.

"No, that won't be necessary," I said. As I got up to leave, Mr. Ashton rose from his chair.

"Oh, Miss Glennon, there is one more thing." He picked up a plain white envelope from his desk. "Your father asked me to give this to you in case anything ever happened to him." He put the envelope in my outstretched hand, then patted me gently on my shoulder. "It is a delivery I am genuinely sorry to make."

I held the envelope for a moment before opening it. The letter inside was written in Papa's bold sloped handwriting, each word leaning forward as though anxious for the one that came after. It was hard to believe that the hand that wrote them—the hand that had always been so warm and vibrant and alive—was now cold and still forever. Blinking back the threat of tears, I began to read.

My darling Evangeline,

If you are reading this it is because I have gone and, I am afraid, left you with a terrible burden to carry. It is my hope you never will see this letter, that the rains will come again and the wheat will sprout and thrive and I will be able to pay off the loans I have been forced to take out. When that happens, I'll ask Ashton to give me back this letter, I'll burn it, and we'll all live to a ripe old age with you none the wiser about this whole thing. That is my hope, but I've lived too long on this earth to think that things always turn out as we hope.

So, if I've left you and you do read this, I'm sorry. I have tried my best to protect you and Morgan and your mother. I hope you'll not be too hard on me, or on yourself, if my best turns out not to be enough.

I know I don't have to tell you to work hard and be a good girl. I know I don't have to tell you to take care of your mother for me and do your best for Morgan. But there is one thing I must tell you. Be happy, my girl. Enjoy life and I don't just mean in your life with Morgan. He is a wonderful son, but he can't be your whole life. That's too big a pair of shoes for one boy to fill. If you are willing to risk being hurt, you'll find love in all kinds of places. Look at me, broken-down old Irish lobsterman that I am, if I hadn't taken the risk of getting hurt and asked your mother to marry me and moved halfway across the country to get her to do it, I would have missed nearly thirty years of wonderful times with her and the best daughter and grandson a man could hope for. It was all worth it.

I know I don't have to tell you that I want the world for you, and I know I don't have to tell you how much I love you, but I will.

I love you with all my heart.

Papa

Chapter 14

The following week I had an unexpected visitor.

"Miss Glennon?" Pastor Van Dyver tipped his hat respectfully before he set a foot on the porch step, as though he needed my permission to come up to the door.

"Hello, Pastor. It's nice to see you again," I opened the screen door and reached out to take his hat. "Please, come inside. Can I make you a glass of tea?"

"No, thank you. Water would be nice, though." He sat down at the kitchen table, took a clean white handkerchief from his coat pocket, and carefully mopped his brow. It was terribly hot that day, and when I brought his glass of water he drained it in one gulp. Thank you," he said. "I just wanted to come by and see your mother. I was concerned about her after the service. Is she at home?"

"She's asleep. I was hoping that in a few days she would perk up a bit, but she seems to be about the same. It's like she's in a world of her own, somewhere off with Papa."

"Ah," he sympathized, "I have seen this before in couples whose love for each other runs very deeply. After so many years together they seem to truly become one, and when one of them passes on, the one remaining is unable to go on alone. They become less than half of themselves somehow. It is very tragic and at the same time, very touching."

Again, I was struck by how plainly he spoke. For all his careful phrasing and clear enunciation, he was so very so frank—indelicate even—in speaking about what he knew and saw, that it was shocking in a way. I might have found it upsetting, if I hadn't already been thinking the same thing myself.

In Dillon, people didn't speak of death or illness or sorrow bluntly. People in Dillon weren't sick, they were "under the weather." They didn't die, they "passed on" or, if they were Baptists, they "went home." It was all very careful and polite and unnatural. I found Paul's direct approach something of a relief. It gave me permission to voice my own worries.

"I was thinking about that just now, Pastor, wondering if she is going to get better in time or if she will always be this way. What do you think?"

He tipped his head to one side and thought for a moment. "If she were alone, with no children," he reasoned, "I would say she might never recover from losing your father, but she loves you and Morgan. It has been less than two weeks since your father's death. She has so many reasons to become involved in life again. She needs time."

We left it at that. I took comfort in his words because I knew he meant what he said. I could tell it was not in him to tell me something just because I wanted to hear it, and, besides, he made sense. Mama did have so much to live for. We still needed her.

"Thank you." I smiled. "I hope you are right."

He glanced furtively at his wristwatch as though he had remembered something more important and was anxious to leave. I felt suddenly embarrassed for taking up his time. "Well, I won't keep you any longer." I said, starting to rise from my chair. "I'm sure you have so many other things you must be doing this morning. When Mama wakes up I'll tell her you called. She'll be sorry to have missed you." I stood up stiffly and busied myself picking up the empty water glasses.

The young minister looked surprised and stammered an apology, "Oh, forgive me, Miss Glennon. You must have so many things to do. I didn't mean to keep you from them. I'll come back another time." I detected the barest pink blush of embarrassment on his cheeks. Somehow I had misread him, and now he thought I wanted him to leave. It was my turn to apologize.

"No, Pastor," I started clumsily, "I don't have anything to do! Nothing important, I mean. You can stay. I just saw you looking at your watch and felt like a fool sitting here taking up your time when you really came to talk to Mama, but you can stay if you want to." I silently cursed myself again for my awkwardness. "I mean, I'm enjoying talking with you. Please, I'd like you to stay longer, if you can."

His face broke into a grin, and he laughed a short, rumbling laugh. I realized it was the first time anyone had laughed in our house since Papa died. "Miss Glennon, please forgive me. Glancing at my watch is a bad habit of mine. I don't even realize I'm doing it. Someone gave me this as a gift when I came to America. Whenever I look at it I calculate what time it is in Holland and wonder what everyone is doing there. I must think of a way to stop myself." He smiled genuinely.

"If I'm not keeping you from your work," he continued, "I'd like to stay longer and talk with you. I did come to see your mother, but I wanted to see you as well. I had hoped we could talk and perhaps become friends. You see"—he looked at me earnestly—"I feel so much like an outsider, so *foreign*, and not just because of my accent."

I nodded encouragement, and he went on. "I have lived in America for five years now, but never have I felt so out of place as I do in this little town. Of all the people I have met since I came, I hope you'll forgive me for saying so, you seemed most like myself." I thought I saw him glance in the direction of my twisted leg, and I pulled it more closely under my skirt. "As though you don't quite belong, either. Perhaps you can help me understand these people a little better."

"Well, I don't know about that," I said wryly. "I've lived here all my life, and I don't know that I understand them now any better than I ever did. If you want to be accepted by the town, being seen spending much time with me won't help your cause much." Despite their recent sympathy and acceptance of my new role as head of the Glennon family, filling the space left by Papa and abdicated by Mama, I still felt bitter toward the nice women of Dillon. I had cut through their sea of accusing stares and wakes of whispering for too many years to believe they'd forgiven and forgotten my past sins. No, it wouldn't do a new pastor any good at all to be seen with me.

"Oh yes," he said, nodding seriously, "your boy, Morgan. I wanted to ask you about him. Who is his father? Does he ever see him? I also wanted to ask about your leg. Were you born with it this way, or did you injure yourself?"

My mouth dropped open. I couldn't believe he was asking me these things. I had admired his candor, but to ask such personal questions of someone he had just met! People who had known me all my life would never have asked me such things. They'd have talked about them, certainly, speculated, and asked the neighbors what they thought and then heard the story third-hand, but to come right out and ask, "So, who fathered your bastard son and why are you a cripple?" These were not things you said to someone's face. Not in Dillon. The young minister was right. He was not going to fit in here.

"Pastor, you don't just ask questions like that! Not of someone you barely know. Besides," I murmured, embarrassed, "you probably have already heard all kinds of stories about me."

"No," he said simply. "And even if I had, I wouldn't have paid attention. Gossip is not only sinful, it's usually inaccurate. What people say about themselves is so much more interesting."

"But, Pastor," I protested.

"Look here." He frowned impatiently. "I want to get to know you, not what others whisper about you, but what you believe about yourself. I need a friend here, and from what I can see, so do you. Now, how are we to be friends if I can't ask you questions? Unless I am mistaken and you don't need a friend." He looked at me quizzically and waited for my answer. I could not help but grin at his abrupt manner and indelicately logical reasoning.

"No, you're not mistaken," I said. "I'd like to have you as a friend, Pastor, it's just that—"

"Good!" he said, beaming. His face, which, like his body, was long and angular, every part of him so loosely hung together that he might have been strung on wire like a puppet, seemed to grow fuller and softer when he smiled. He had a way of looking at people square on, as though there was something fascinating written in the depths of their eyes. I had been wrong in my first assessment, I realized; he was handsome, even more so when he smiled.

"Now, is there some way we can get around this 'pastor' business? It makes me feel very ancient. Why don't you call me Paul, and I can call you . . . ? What is your first name, Miss Glennon?"

"Everyone calls me Eva, but my given name is Evangeline."

"Evangeline," he mulled it over it carefully. "No, that doesn't seem right on you. Too stylized. Evangeline is the person I see before me, but clouded by a dream, unfocused. Eva suits you better. Like Eve, the first woman. She mothered the world; she was strong and adventurous."

"But what good did that do her?" I said. "That adventurous streak got her thrown out of the garden."

"That's why your name is even better," he said with a nod. "Eva, a distillation of that first Eve, more refined by time and experience. Though in the end, I think you will prove wiser." His eyes twinkled, and I couldn't help but laugh out loud.

"There now," he said with satisfaction. "I've made you laugh. Surely that clinches the deal. We'll be friends, yes?" He extended his hand, and I shook it.

"We'll be friends," I said, and I meant it, but even as I took his hand I thought, *But that doesn't mean I'm going to tell you everything about myself.*

"As a friend, Paul"—his name stuck a bit uncomfortably in my throat at first—"my advice is to remember where you are. Here time is measured in seasons, not minutes. We plant seeds and water them and wait. If enough time passes and conditions are perfect, things grow. When the time is right and if the sun is hot enough, they ripen—not before and sometimes not at all. That's the way things are. All right?"

"All right." Paul smiled as he accepted the bargain. "I see. Now, we can talk, but nothing too personal. . . ." He rubbed his chin thoughtfully, searching his mind for a topic. "I know! How about the weather? Do you think it looks good for the harvest?"

He looked so pleased with himself, I couldn't help but laugh again. "Oh no! Anything but that! You'll forgive me for saying so, Paul, but you're fitting into Dillon a little too well.

"Let's talk about something more interesting," I said, pointing to his wristwatch. "Tell me about that. Who gave it to you?"

The watch was a gift from his brother, Nils. Their mother died in childbirth when Paul was four and Nils was nine. Their infant sister survived their mother by only a week. Paul's father, who was not in good health himself, was often overwhelmed by the demands of raising his motherless boys, but he never remarried. When Nils was away at university and Paul was only fifteen, their father succumbed to diabetes. The two boys had always been close, but after their father's death Nils became even more important to Paul as he took on the role of parent and provider to his younger brother. As Paul spoke, his love for Nils shone on his face.

"My father was also a minister, a poor one, and left no estate. We didn't even own the house we lived in. Father's sister said I should come live with her, but Nils wouldn't hear of it. He left the university and came home to take a job as a painter. One of the members of my father's old congregation gave us a place to live at a very cheap rent. Nils's plan was that he would go back to university when I did, but there wasn't enough money for two students in the family. He insisted I go first, and he said he would finish his education later."

"And did he?"

"Well, yes and no. By the time I got my degree, I already knew I wanted to go on to the seminary, but I said nothing to Nils, knowing that if I did he would insist on supporting me until I entered the pastorate. Instead, I went home to begin looking for a job. Nils had begun helping at a school for retarded children in his free time, and just about the time I returned he was offered a full-time teaching position.

"I tried to talk him out of accepting, saying that he finally had a chance to go back to school and he should take it. I wanted to repay him for caring for me all those years, but when I told him so he just brushed me aside. 'I *am* back in school,' he said. Then he leaned over and whispered, as though letting me in on a secret, 'Only it's so much better now because I get to draw on the chalkboard and no one can stop me!'"

Paul was so animated as he imitated his brother's mischievous confession that I couldn't help but laugh.

"Nils loves what he does," Paul continued proudly. "You should see how the children respond to him. When he takes his class on outings to the park, people stare at his students and pull their own children away, as though retardation were something catching. Nils doesn't see any of that."

"He sounds like Papa," I recalled.

"To Nils, every child in his class is a genius. When one of them learns to button his coat or write his name, he picks them up on his shoulders and carries them around the room, whooping as though they had just discovered a cure for polio. He truly loves them. My brother is a good man. I miss him very much."

"It must have been so hard for you to leave him," I said. "Why did you come to America? Why not just stay in Holland?"

"Money. I couldn't ask Nils for help on a teacher's salary, and if I had to work while I was finishing my education it would have taken me twice as long. There was a scholarship being offered for Dutch students to attend seminary in New York, so I applied and was accepted."

"Didn't you want to go back home after you graduated?"

"Oh yes," he answered earnestly, "more than anything. I did go back for a time, but there were hardly any positions open in Holland. I was offered an associate position in Germany; an old friend of my father's was the pastor at that church. I almost took it so as to be closer to Nils, but after I visited, I knew I could never live there."

"Why not?" I asked. "It's so close to Holland. Surely it can't be all that different."

"Oh, but it is!" he exclaimed. "The language, the food, the culture, everything. Holland and Germany are two entirely different countries, but that is not what bothered me. Hitler is what I didn't like about Germany."

"I've read about him." I tried to remember what the newspaper articles had said. "He's their president, isn't he?"

"Chancellor," Paul corrected. "But, he's much more powerful than a president could ever be and much, much more ambitious. There is really no one who can stop him, and the thing that bothers me is, no one even seems to want to try. Today in Germany the people don't worship God, they worship all things German. Hitler is the high priest of their religion. He decides who does and doesn't belong in the congregation, and they love him for it. And if a few outsiders are hurt by that, what does it matter as long as there are bread and jobs."

His eyes went flat for a moment and he was silent, lost in thought. Then he murmured to himself, "No one seems to care that he is a very dangerous man."

Paul became my friend. Not just my friend, but a friend of the entire family. We all liked him. Even Mama, who had always been so wary of strangers and private about her personal life, looked forward to Paul's frequent visits and spent hours talking with him. Partly it was because Paul was such a good listener, but partly I think it was her way of coming to grips with Papa's death.

She told Paul how she and Papa had met, and how Papa had

sprained his back on their honeymoon when he'd tried to carry her over the threshold. She recited a thousand chapters of their life together as though she were living it all over again, emotion by emotion. Some of them were stories even I had never heard. Sometimes I was a little jealous that she could share so much with him so easily, but mostly I was grateful, because, bit by bit, Mama seemed to be coming back to life.

True, she was living in the past, but at least she was living. She always referred to Papa in the present tense and talked to him when she thought no one was in the room. Once, thinking it would be better for her to face the truth, I reminded her that Papa was dead. She looked at me clearly, perfectly lucid, and said, "No. It's too soon for that." I saw her point. It was comforting thinking of Papa as being just in the next room, still around to watch over us all. Besides, Mama was happy. I was grateful to Paul for helping revive her spirit.

He was kind to all of us. Paul always had a smile for Ruby and praised her as the best cook in Dillon. Ruby did almost all the cooking now to give me more time for sewing the quilts that, along with Morgan's egg business, had become our main source of income. She'd come a long way from our youth when she couldn't tell salt from sugar, and she was justifiably proud of her skill in the kitchen. Paul's appetite was a compliment to her achievements. He could eat an entire half of one of her apple pies in a single sitting, though he never seemed to gain an ounce.

"I'm lucky," he would quip. "The ladies of the church always seem bent on fattening up the minister. But gluttony is never such a pleasure as when I am sitting in Ruby's kitchen." He would sigh with pleasure, and Ruby would tell him to stop his foolish flattery, then fill up another plate for him.

Morgan and Paul became great friends, and I was glad. Morgan badly needed the companionship of a man since Papa's death. Whenever Paul came visiting he had a new book tucked under his arm that he thought Morgan might be interested in. It might be any-thing from a Dickens novel to a book on the inner workings of the internal combustion engine. When the weather was fine, they would go fishing together.

Usually, after his visit with Mama and hearing all about Morgan's day at school over one of Ruby's huge suppers, Paul and I would sit on the porch and chat while we sipped tea, hot or iced depending on the weather. Over time, I heard all about his life and he heard all about mine—almost all. I still didn't feel comfortable talking about Slim, even to Paul. His clerical collar made it even harder than it might have been otherwise. No matter how much I liked him, no matter how easygoing and accepting he seemed, I didn't think a minister could understand. He saw me, I was sure, as a quiet, sensi-ble mother and daughter who patiently bore her physical handicap by reading books and sewing straight seams. How could he possibly comprehend the kind of overpowering passion that I had known with Slim when I didn't understand it myself? If I had told Paul about Slim, I supposed that, as a pastor, he'd want to offer forgive-ness. That's what held me back. I didn't want to be forgiven. In the logical part of my mind, I knew that what I'd had with Slim was sin, but I wasn't sorry for it. I would never be sorry for having Morgan or for saying yes to the brief, rapturous passion I'd shared with Slim. After all that had happened, I loved him still. He was an ocean away, but a part of me was always waiting for him to walk though the door. My hope survived, dormant, stored in darkness against the chance the skies might open and stir it to growth again. Other than the monthly letters I wrote updating him on Morgan, I willed my-self not to think of Slim, but the memory of him was etched upon my soul. I didn't want to alter that image by examining it too closely.

Paul, on the other hand, was easy to get close to. And he was easy to trust. I liked him very much. Ruby would tease me about him, but it wasn't like that. I felt none of that crippling passion I'd had for Slim, and that was a relief. We were just friends. Not that our friendship was a small thing—not at all. It made me realize how lonely I had been. I wasn't about to risk that friendship by telling Paul too much of my past. Thankfully, after that first day he never asked, and I never offered. Nor did I ever write Slim about Paul. Of course, I never talked about myself at all in the letters I forwarded to Slim's lawyers, anyway. He wasn't interested in me, I was sure, and even if he had been, I doubted he read those letters or even received them. He never answered a single one.

June 20, 1937
Dear Slim,

Congratulations on the birth of baby Land. Another son! Boys seem to be your specialty. I read about it in the papers, but not until recently. News travels slowly from London. I saw too, where they reported your plane as missing over the Alps a few months back, but you turned up safe and sound once again. Sometimes I think you like disappearing just to confound the reporters. About the time they finish their big story that your plane is lost and you've undoubtedly perished, you turn up again, grinning and healthy, just to prove them wrong.

Morgan is doing fine and is a greater help than ever now that Papa is gone. We don't have as much stock as we used to, except for the chickens I told you about, but he takes care of what there is before going to school. On Saturdays he drives into town with me to sell or trade the eggs and chickens for what we need in the way of groceries. Sales of the new quilts I'm making, you remember the ones that Ruby helps me with, are steady enough so between quilts and eggs, we are making out all right.

Morgan has your talent for the mechanical. A friend of ours lent him a book on engines. Morgan read it and was able to figure out how to fix our broken tractor all by himself. Of course, we don't really need a tractor at the moment. There is still no rain so I haven't bothered trying to put in a crop. Maybe next year. But it is nice to have all those engine parts up off the barn floor. Morgan's grades continue to be among the best in his class, though he and two other boys got into trouble for smoking a cigarette last week. The teacher was pretty hard on him and so was I, though I don't think he really smokes. He was trying to impress the other boys.

Hope you are well. I won't ask if you are coming back to the states since I know you wouldn't tell me anyway. You have been over there so long now, I don't suppose you're ever planning on coming back. Europe must agree with you.

Best wishes,
Evangeline

Over the years I wrote dozens of similar letters. I made copies, thinking they would serve as a kind of chronicle of Morgan's growing up and our lives together. After a while I wrote them more for my benefit than Slim's, though I mailed them just the same. Very newsy and cheerful they were, but I didn't record everything.

When Morgan came home with a split lip and refused to tell me what the fight was about, I didn't write that down. He was so dark and silent for the rest of the week that there was no doubt in my mind as to what had happened and that I was the cause of it, but I never wrote about that. Bastard is such an ugly word on paper. My pen was too heavy to form such painful words. No mention was made about the chicks dying of pullorum disease and how Morgan and I both cried as we raised and lowered our axes over the necks of the infected birds until there was not one left and the chicken yard was eerily silent and awash in wasted blood. The words doubt, longing, hunger, fear, abandonment, tears, aging, sickness, foreclosure, or war never stained the picture I painted in those letters. They were all part of the landscape, but it was a part I would not allow myself to dwell upon. I wanted no unhappy memories weighing us down, and now, as I write that word "us," I can be honest about who that included: me, Morgan, Slim.

By refusing to put the uncomfortable questions out where they can be read and reflected on, you can fool yourself into thinking none of it matters. Pain can be concealed for a long time—but not forever. Eventually the tanks come rolling over the border, the bodies are exhumed, the masks are removed, and words cannot be misconstrued or minced any finer. We are what we are.

Chapter 15

"Ruby, listen to this." I squinted to force the newsprint into focus and mentally scolded the editors for making the type so tiny.

"You need to get some glasses," Ruby mumbled through a mouthful of toast. "Your face is all squashed up like a prune." She said the same thing every morning when I read the paper over breakfast; I was starting to think she might be right.

"Oh, hush up and listen," I growled as I held the paper farther away and read it to her.

> *With the permission of its readers, the Daily Times today moves the war.*
>
> *It can't be moved out of Europe and off the face of the earth, of course, pleasant a thing as that would be. But the editors feel news of the war can and should be moved off page one.*
>
> *For some time, they have felt that what has been reaching*

us, and through the Daily Times has been reaching you, has been a spoon feeding of propaganda in its most vicious form: propaganda designed to sway our sympathies, even to move us to action. Given a free rein, sooner or later such propaganda would drag the United States into the European mess, just as it did in 1918. We don't care to be a party to high treason.

On the other hand, people are interested in war news therefrom, it seems, regardless of how inaccurate and highly colored available reports may be. We can't toss out bodily the thousands of words of purchased war "news" that comes over the wires to us daily. So we are giving over the back page of the Daily Times to the war. You'll find the war news there—but not here. If editorially possible, the word "war" will be eliminated from this and subsequent issues of the Daily Times, with the exception, of course, of this editorial today.

Each day, the war reports have been so directly contradictory that it was actually surprising yesterday when a bulletin from Paris said the leading story from Berlin could not be contradicted. Each day's quota of "news" has carried stories from Allied capitals that denied every gain reported from Berlin, and laid claims to Allied gains which Berlin, in turn, denied.

Censors of all belligerent nations have clamped down with iron fists on all reports being sent from their countries. The best reporters in the world are forced to file the news the high commands want them to file—or nothing at all. Careful study will give convincing evidence that many purported "war" pictures are posed, "set up" publicity stills and nothing more.

So, the Times is moving the hokum—some of it may amount to more than that, but you can't be sure—to the back page. If you are interested, you may find it there.

"Can you believe it?" I marveled. "They're moving the entire war to the back page."

"'Bout time." Ruby blew on her coffee to cool it. "I'm sick to death of hearing about it."

"Ruby, really! This is ridiculous. Only in Dillon could they put hog prices and church picnics on the front page while all of Europe is at war. I know the reports might not be one hundred percent reliable, but it is news. Pretending it isn't happening won't make it go away."

"But what if they're right?" Ruby mused. "What if this is just a lot of hokum shoveled out by a bunch of foreigners who want to drag us into their war? You don't want us to go to war, do you?"

"Of course I don't want war. Nobody does. Morgan's already sixteen. I wouldn't want him going off to fight, but it doesn't seem right to just shove it all on the back page like none of it matters."

Ruby held a platter out to me, offering me the last piece of bacon, but I was too distracted to eat. "Suit yourself," she said, grabbing the bacon with her fingers and finishing it off while she listened, halfheartedly, as I talked.

"These newspaper editors complain about Allied censorship and at the same time they're acting like censors themselves. We can't just ignore what is happening, can we?" Ruby's mouth was too full to answer, so she shrugged as though she was at least willing to give it a try. I continued on even more stridently, determined to make her understand my point.

"Paul got another letter from his brother Nils last week. You can't imagine the terrible things that are happening over there! Whole neighborhoods of Jews rounded up and sent away to labor camps, but they never come back. No one ever hears from them again. All kinds of awful rumors. Nils is afraid of what will happen

184 • Marie Bostwick

to his little students if the Nazis were to invade Holland. Hitler has made it clear there is no room for the feebleminded in his master race."

Ruby shifted in her chair uncomfortably, "Well, of course, it's terrible what's going on in Germany, but I don't know what it has to do with us. I'm not the only one who feels that way. Your Mr. Lindbergh seems to think we ought to stay out of it no matter what. Listen to this," she said, leafing through the back section of the paper until she found the article she wanted. "It says right here, 'Colonel Charles A. Lindbergh, who resigned from his voluntary army service only the day before, addressed the nation in a radio broadcast from Washington D.C. last night, urging America to 'keep carefully out of Europe's war,' asserting that 'if we enter fighting for democracy abroad, we may end by losing it here at home. We must not be misguided by this foreign propaganda to the effect that our frontiers lie in Europe.'"

"There!" She thumped the paper for emphasis. "Your hero is on my side. It's not our war."

"But how can we just ignore what's happening over there? From everything that Paul hears and says—"

Ruby cut me off. "Eva, even if those rumors are true, what good would it do us to fight if it's a war we can't win? Slim seems to think it's impossible."

"Well," I said quietly, "maybe that's the difference between them. Slim worries about what's possible, and Paul worries about what's right." Though I remembered a time when Slim didn't believe in the existence of the impossible. How do people change so much?

Still, I thought, perhaps Ruby had a point. Could Paul be giving Nils's stories more credence than they deserved? And if the Germans were really so strong, what good would it do to fight them? Slim had seen their planes and pilots and factories firsthand. Ever since he'd come home from Europe five months before, he'd been subtly making his point. Now that he'd left the army, he clearly didn't intend to be subtle anymore. Well, Slim had seen a lot more of the world than I had. Maybe he was right. Maybe we couldn't beat the Germans, but if someone didn't put a stop to Hitler soon, where would it all end?

"All I know is," said Ruby as she rose to clear the table, "we didn't survive the Depression just so we could turn around and get mixed up in another war."

"Hmm." I nodded, acknowledging her point. "Things are looking better, but I don't know that we've survived yet. It wasn't much of a crop."

"No," she said with a grin, piling the dirty silverware onto the bacon platter with a cheery clatter, "but it's a start." I couldn't help but grin back, remembering how we'd sweated to bring in the crop, working like madmen to cut and stack the wheat before any hail or wind or insects could destroy our little harvest. It didn't matter that the yield was only ten bushels an acre, we were so happy it might as well have been fifty.

"Well, I don't want to jinx things, but I think you're right. We may have lived through the worst of it." I raised my coffee cup in a self-congratulatory toast. "Good-bye, desperation, drought, and dust! We have survived you and lived to tell about it; scarred and bruised, but all in one piece!"

Ruby raised her own cup and clinked it against mine, "Happy days!" she crowed and we laughed together, content to forget Europe, and the war, and the world away from Dillon. It was so wonderful, for a change, to consider our troubles behind us.

The rains had returned, and so had Slim. Surely, I thought, it was an omen of better times.

* * *

The *Aquitania* docked in New York harbor on April 14, 1939, and Charles Lindbergh walked down the gangplank, come home to America. I read the newspaper story over and over, trying to picture what he must have looked like and what he must have felt, returning to the country he had left, or rather fled, for the safety of his surviving son more than three years before. I could see it in my mind—the white steel of the ship's hull dotted by portholes, the gray New York sky, the noise of reporters, and the jarring pop of flashbulbs, startling, like rifle shots—but no matter how hard I concentrated, I could not imagine his eyes, his smile, his thoughts. The man who stepped off that ship was a stranger to me.

I put the paper down next to me and went looking for my scissors, remembering I'd left them in the mending basket. They were at the very bottom, lying on top of an old white shirt of Morgan's, long outgrown and missing some buttons. I picked up the scissors and shirt and brought them back to my chair. Without really thinking, I cut a long, thin strip off the fabric and then snipped pieces off the strip into perfect little squares. I still remembered how to make the tiny blocks come out even, exactly one inch square. I cut until there was nothing left over and stack after stack of white squares sat bravely on the table like miniature flags of truce.

Then I picked up the newspaper and, just as carefully as I had with the fabric, making sure all the corners were sharp, cut out the article about Slim's homecoming. I folded it reverently and put it in the largest envelope I could find, so there would be room for more. It turned out to be the first of many envelopes full of clippings on Slim. He had opinions on what America should do about the war in Europe, and he wasted no time or opportunity in voicing them.

Ruby's attitude was pretty typical of people in Dillon and probably in the rest of the country. We were just putting the Depression behind us. The last thing anybody wanted to do was go off and fight a war, especially one so far from American shores. I, too, felt torn between the desire for safety and peace, and the pleading faces and frightened eyes that seemed so vivid when Paul read Nils's letters aloud. It was a confusing time.

Slim's voice was one of the loudest and most fervent of the many beseeching Americans to stay out of the war in Europe. He seemed to be everywhere at once, appearing at rallies, making speeches, and writing articles. I read every word, clipped the articles out, and filed them away. Sometimes I'd take out all the clippings and read them over again one by one, trying to stitch this newsprint character together with the man I'd known, the man who'd left his eyes in my son's face, but none of it held together.

The article I most remember was one he wrote for *Reader's Digest* magazine called "Aviation, Geography and Race." It had Slim's name on it, but it might as well have been a stranger writing, it sounded so unlike the man I knew. He talked about "alien hordes" and said we needed to "build our White ramparts again" and that we should protect ourselves by relying on "an English fleet, a German air force, a French army, an American nation." This while Hitler stormtroopers were already marching through Europe, crushing everything in their paths like some maniacal steamroller! I just couldn't reconcile my knowledge of Slim with whoever was writing those words. My bewilderment was so complete that more than once I promised myself to give up trying to figure things out. None of it concerned us, I reasoned; time to quit reading so much and just let Slim be Slim. Then Morgan would bound into the room, all youth and energy and good intentions, smiling his father's smile, and my resolve would melt. It did concern us, so I would pore over the articles again, compelled to search for and find the thread that linked us all.

In the beginning, of course, a lot of people agreed with Slim. They wanted to ignore Hitler. They discounted the stories of aggression and cruelty because they just didn't want to believe them. If I hadn't known Paul, I suppose I would have been as blissfully ignorant as anyone else, but month after month he read me letters from Nils filled with rumors of disappearing people, and broken glass, and yellow stars, and new edicts. There were so many accounts of such ugliness and hate, I knew at least some of it had to be true. Even then, I was torn. Germany was so far away from Dillon, the town where my son and the sons of everyone I knew studied and worked and played in safety. Hitler needed to be stopped, but surely it was the job of the European powers to stop evil in Europe. We had problems of our own.

Then, in May of 1940, neutrality about the war became impossible. In a single day the Nazis invaded France, Belgium, Luxembourg, and Holland. No one could believe it. In less than two months' time, every nation had surrendered. Holland capitulated only five days after the first German tanks rolled across the border.

When I heard the news, I jumped into the car and drove to town as fast as I could, looking for Paul. He sat at his desk while the radio reports droned on and on, sitting up straight and silent in his chair while tears rolled down his face and I looked on helplessly. Finally, I pulled a chair up next to his and listened with him, hoping my presence would help.

The surrender of France changed people's minds. Farmers, thick in the middle of crop worries, started to talk about war and to realize that Hitler wouldn't be satisfied until he controlled all of Europe. The *Daily Times* put the war back on the front page. Not long after the French defeat, Slim made a speech on the radio.

Paul came over for supper that night. After the pie was eaten and the dishes cleared, I took out another piece of Morgan's old clothing, a pair of black pants worn out in the seat and started cutting them into one-inch blocks while we listened to the radio. At one point in the broadcast Slim said people shouldn't pay attention to "this hysterical chatter of calamity and invasion which has been running rife these last few days."

Paul actually leaped to his feet, eyes blazing, put his face in front of the Philco as though Slim were sitting right in front of him, and shouted in frustration, "Good Lord, man! They're marching around the Eiffel Tower and eating in the cafés! It's not like people have made this up! What's the matter with you, Lindbergh? Are you blind or a coward or both?"

Words of defense bubbled up in my mind as I searched for some excuse or explanation for Slim's attitude, but there was none. I blushed red with shame, so red that Ruby asked if I was feeling all right. I just said the fire was too warm and went back to my cutting, concentrating on making each black square as perfect as possible.

After the broadcast Paul said he'd better be going, then cleared his throat and asked if I'd mind walking out to his car with him, "There's a book I just finished reading that was very good. I thought you might want to borrow it."

The night was chilly. I pulled my sweater closer around me. Paul, usually so ready to chat or joke after spending an evening with us, was silent. He had been pensive lately. No word had yet come from Nils since the invasion, and I knew his mind must be tied up in knots of worry for his brother's safety. We walked toward the car in perfect time. Our feet crunching the gravel in unison sounded brave and out of place in the wide stillness of night. Paul reached in the backseat to fish out the book.

"Here," he said holding it out to me. "It's not new at all. It's just an old copy of *The Great Gatsby*. I know you've already read it, but I needed an excuse to get you alone, and I remembered I had a copy in the car, so . . . here. Take it anyway. You might like reading it again."

I accepted the book and wrapped my arms around it, holding it protectively against my chest, schoolgirl fashion. "Have you heard anything from Nils?" I asked.

"No," he murmured, "not yet. I suppose the mails are completely disrupted." He held the back of his hand to his face, as though shielding his eyes from the sun, and for a moment I thought he might cry. "Oh, Eva! This horrible war . . . being cut off from my brother and not knowing when I might see him again, it's got me thinking about families and the people we love. We mustn't take them for granted. It's important to say the things you want to say, while you have the chance. Do you understand what I mean?"

"I do," I agreed. "When Papa died, I was so filled with regret for all the things I felt and never got a chance to say to him. I think he knew it all anyway, but still . . . You always think there will be time enough for everything."

"Yes." Paul nodded earnestly. "Times like these make you realize it's important not to waste a moment." He rubbed his face with his hand and sighed impatiently to himself the way he did on those rare occasions when he couldn't remember the exact word he was looking for in English. "I know you said, when we first became friends, that I shouldn't ask too many personal questions, that it takes time to build trust, even among friends, but we have known each other a long time now."

It was a long time, I thought to myself, and we were friends, good friends. Surely after all that time he had earned the right to ask whatever he wanted, but I said nothing. I knew what the question was. We had been through too much for me to forbid him asking—but I hoped he wouldn't.

"What I want to know is"—he raised his head and looked me

steadily in the eye—"about Morgan's father. Is he someone from around here? Do you still see him? Do you still love him? Will there ever be room in your heart for anyone else?"

Paul had buried my father, and through his patience and care he had resurrected my mother. He had befriended my son and challenged the boy's mind. He had braved the clucking tongues of disapproval to forge a relationship with an unmarried woman of questionable reputation. *Yes,* I thought, looking into his solemn eyes, *you've earned the right to ask the question. I can trust you with the answer.*

I told him the truth, all of it, how Slim and I met and loved and parted. How I'd loved Slim from the first moment. How I loved him still.

Paul's eyes grew even more solemn as I told him the story. I could see him struggling to don the neutral mask of a confessor, but he failed. He shook his head in bewilderment. "Eva, if it were anyone, anyone else but you, I would say they were lying or ..." He stumbled to find the right word. "Or delusional. But I know you wouldn't lie. Yet what you are saying is just ... Well, it's just so hard to believe!"

"Why?" I shot back defensively, the color rising in my face, "Because of who I am?"

"No!" he exclaimed vehemently. "Not because of you, but because of who that man is." He spat out the last words contemptuously; then his expression softened. He reached out and pulled back a strand of my hair that had fallen out of place and moved closer, the lock of hair still clasped between his fingers. "I don't doubt that Charles Lindbergh landed in your father's field and fell in love with you the moment he saw you," he whispered. "I don't doubt that for one second. Seeing you, your sweetness, the way I do now, how could he not have loved you?" His hand dropped from my face to my shoulder down to the small of my back, lighting just on the swell of my hip. The naturalness of his touch surprised me, as though the curve of his palm had been carved to fit that particular spot. I remember feeling, not relieved, but tired, so very tired. I wanted to lean into his chest and rest there. For a moment, I did.

"He loved you," Paul murmured into the tangle of my hair, "and maybe, at that moment, you loved him. But that you love him still? No, that I can't believe."

I took a step back and let his hand fell away from my waist. I pulled myself up tall again and blinked hard, determined not to let Paul see me cry. "What's so hard to understand? We have a child, a beautiful child. Have you looked at Morgan?" I frowned, irritated by the blank, patient look on Paul's face. "He looks exactly like him. He's perfect. He's Slim."

"No, Eva. He is you. His face may belong to Lindbergh, but his heart is yours. Thank God." Paul groaned. "Eva, I don't know what Lindbergh was like when he was young. Maybe he really was the hero you say he was, but don't you see what he's become? Did you hear him tonight? It's not possible that you could love such a man as that."

"Be quiet, Paul!" I snapped. "You don't know anything about it. I want us to stay friends, so just don't talk about it, ever again!" As I started back toward the house, Paul reached out and held me tight by the wrist.

"I have to, Eva. Because we are friends, I have ask. You really love him? Even after what you heard tonight?" His eyes searched my mine anxiously.

"Yes," I answered with finality, not wanting to explain more. I knew Slim was changed, or rather, he was lost. When I searched through my clippings of cutout, newspaper-gray photographs, I couldn't find him hidden behind the thin, hard gaze of Charles

Lindbergh, but I had to believe he was there, because if he had disappeared, I might too.

Paul continued carefully and less emotionally, as if he were filling
in information on some blank, white form, but he couldn't keep an
edge of contempt from stealing into his voice. "And he loves you?"

I nodded with more conviction than I felt.

"Then where is he, Eva? Why isn't he here?"

Unbidden tears sparked, angry and hot in my eyes, and I inhaled
deeply before finding breath to answer. "He couldn't be. He was
meant for big things, things you can't strike at tied down to someone like me. I knew that, even then. I sent him away myself because
I wanted everything for him. Because I loved him."

"But he never came back," he said flatly.

"No, you're wrong," I retorted. "He came back. He wanted us
to be together, but he couldn't stay. See, he didn't know about
Morgan. If anyone had found out it would have . . ." Tears were
filming in my eyes, and it was hard to see Paul's face, hard to remember why Slim had left, why he'd never returned. "It was just
impossible, don't you see? It would have ruined everything for him!
You just wouldn't understand."

"You're right, I wouldn't. I don't." He encircled my wrist with
his hand and drew me closer to him, our bodies only an inch apart.
I could see the tiny crows-feet near his eyes and the cloud of his
breath in the cold night air. His words spilled out, brisk and whispered, almost mechanically, like a prayer memorized and repeated
so many times that you don't need to think about it anymore.

"If you were mine, I'd never leave you alone. I wouldn't share
you with anyone or anything. No ambition, or hope, or mistake
could keep me from you, and the night would be so full of you and
me, there wouldn't even be room for the stars. Now explain to me,

Eva, about love. Because if that isn't it, then you're right. I don't understand."

He took one step, hardly moving, closing the bare space between us and circled his arms around my shoulders and waist, leaning into me and putting his lips to mine for a moment, just a moment, before I pushed him away.

"Stop that," I said, wiping tears from my cheeks. "Don't do that again." He wasn't listening.

"I am here, and I always will be, no matter what you do. Even if you told me to leave, I'd stay. Where is Lindbergh?" he asked accusingly.

Without thinking, I pulled my arm back and swung at Paul's cheek, slapping him as hard as I could. The sound of it rang out like a gunshot in the night, and the second it did, my tears stopped flowing.

"Don't you ever ask me that again! Ever! It's none of your business, Paul!"

I fled to the house before he could speak. I wouldn't have heard him, anyway. The echo of his question pounded in my brain and drowned out everything else.

The morning paper carried an article about Slim's radio address. I read it over eggs and coffee the next morning.

The "hysterical chatter" is the talk now heard on every side in the democracies if France and Britain stand in danger of defeat by Germany. Colonel Lindbergh is a peculiar young man if he can contemplate this possibility in any other light than as a calamity for the American people. He is an ignorant young man if he trusts his own premise that it makes no difference to us whether we are deprived of the historic defense of British seapower in the Atlantic Ocean. He is a blind young man if he really believes we can live on terms of equal peace and happiness "regardless of which side wins this war" in Europe. Colonel Lindbergh remains a great flier."

I cut out the article with short, careful snips of the scissors. Before putting it in the envelope, I smoothed it out and laid it on the table alongside all the other clippings. I read them yet again, trying to add up the equation in my head, pieces of a puzzle that didn't match the picture on the box they'd arrived in. Finally, I gave up and put them all back in the envelope, out of sight, knowing there were still pieces missing.

Chapter 16

"Well," Morgan quipped, "now that you three got me all tied up good and tight in this straight jacket, how do I look?" He stretched out his arms and turned around in a circle so we could see him from all sides.

"Oh, Morgan," I sighed. "You look fine. Just fine. You *look* like a valedictorian in that suit. So grown up." He did, too. The thick wool of the jacket made his shoulders seem broader and more substantial and gave his lanky frame an aura of maturity that he didn't possess when dressed in dungarees. He seemed so much older than eighteen. For a moment I wanted to tell him to take off the jacket and put his childhood back on. It was too soon for him to be so old, but the pride and expectation on his face were contagious. His future couldn't be postponed.

"Is Paul coming?" Morgan asked. "I haven't seen him for ages. Did you and he have a fight or something? You'd better patch it up quick if you did. I want my fishing buddy sitting with the family at graduation." He twisted around to look at me quizzically. Ruby clucked and told him to quit moving while she was trying to mark the hem of his pants.

I answered without looking at him, concentrating hard to see that the suit lay smooth across his shoulders. "We didn't have a fight. We're just busy, that's all. He's got a whole congregation that wants him at their dinner table. It wasn't fair of us to keep monopolizing the pastor's time that way." I pushed in pins to ease the seam I was going to take in. "Of course he'll come to the graduation; he's got to give the prayer. I imagine he'll be sitting up on the stage, not in the bleachers with the rest of the audience." I stuck a last pin into the puckering seam and stood back to examine my work.

"Those sleeves need to be let out," Mama noted practically. "His wrists are showing at least three inches."

"Oh, we can fix that," said Ruby. "It's not his fault he's so tall."

"Still," Mama said begrudgingly to Morgan, "you do look nice. Real nice. Just make sure you've got your speech memorized, in case you lose your place. I hate it when people get up on a stage and read to me. It's like they're afraid to look me in the eye. Grandpa always says you can never trust anybody who doesn't look you in the eye."

"Don't worry, Mamaw. I'll look at you. I know the whole thing by heart. Listen. 'Ladies and gentlemen,' he boomed, planting his feet apart and hooking his thumbs under his lapels in a mocking, elocutionary stance, 'It is said that great floods flow from simple sources, and as I look upon my fellow graduates of the class of 1940, as I gaze into your blank and vacuous faces, I see some of the simplest sources imaginable—'"

"Morgan!" Ruby clapped her hand over her mouth in horror. "You're not going to say that, are you?"

"Oh, Aunt Ruby! You're too easy," he said, laughing. "Of course I won't say that."

"That's a relief, anyway," said Ruby with a sigh. "But, what are you going to talk about?"

"Don't worry." Morgan winked knowingly and tapped his head

with his forefinger. "I've got it all up here, and if you to want hear it, you'll just have to show up at graduation in a week's time, park yourself on the bleachers, listen, and be amazed, just like all the rest of the paying customers. Won't she, Mama?"

"That's right." I smiled. "And I, for one, can wait. I don't mind being surprised." *Maybe we'll all be surprised,* I thought. I hadn't been able to stop myself from dropping a graduation invitation in the mail addressed to Slim, care of Reilly, McCormick and Martin, Attorneys. He'd never answered before, but maybe, just this one time.

"In the meantime, Morgan, we've got to have you looking your best," I said, picking up my pincushion again. "Hand me the scissors, would you please, Mama? Let's see what we can do about these sleeves."

That night, after everyone else had gone to bed, there was a tentative knock on my door. It was Morgan.

"That was good timing," I said. "I just finished hemming the lining on those jacket cuffs. Why don't you try it on and see if the length is better."

"No, Mama," he said distractedly. "I mean, I will later. Can I ask you something?" I laid the jacket over the arm of the chair and gave him my full attention. He took a deep breath and plunged in. "I know how excited you are about me going to college in the fall."

"What do you mean me? You're the first college man in the family." I knew I was beaming. "Your grandmother's so proud she's about ready to bust, and folks in town are starting to walk to the other side of the street when they see Ruby coming because they're afraid she'll corner them again while she tells them all your marks since grade school. We're all just as proud as can be, Morgan. Me especially." I reached over, took his hand, and squeezed it.

Morgan chuckled halfheartedly and started to pick at his fingernails, the way he did when he was nervous. "Well, I'm glad you're
all proud, but I've been thinking, Mama. Maybe it would be better
if I didn't go to college. There's an awful lot of work around the
farm, more than you can do by yourself."

"Now, Morgan, that's all settled," I reminded him. "I told you
before, I talked with Luther Krebs. He lost his place for taxes and is
willing to work for a share of the harvest. He's all set to move into
the old implement shed in September, do all your old chores, and
the planting as well. And I've got Ruby, too. She's stronger than
most men. We'll manage. You'll see."

Morgan kept his head ducked down and didn't say anything, just
tapped the toe of his foot in rhythm with his own thoughts.

"What is it?" I asked. His sudden change of heart was genuinely
confusing. "Are you scared to go away? Morgan, you're as smart as
anybody else. You'll do fine," I reassured him.

"It's not that." He raised his head and looked at me seriously.
"I'm just worried about you. I really think I should stay here."

"And do what?" I asked, truly perplexed. For as long as I could
remember Morgan had talked about going to exotic places and seeing new things. He cut photographs of islands and rickshas and
deserts out of magazines and pinned them up on his wall next to his
autographed picture of Slim. He'd tacked up a map of the world
next to the pictures and, with bright red Xs, marked all the places
he'd visit someday. His walls were fairly papered with all those daring dreams, and now he didn't even want to go as far as Oklahoma
City? It didn't make any sense. His concern for me was genuine, I
was certain. Ever since he'd been a little boy he'd tried to take care
of me, sensing in his too-grown-up way that no one else was going
to do it, but there was something more to this than simple feelings
of obligation.

"Morgan, of course I want you to take over the farm someday, but you need to see some of the world first. Then, after you've got your agriculture degree, you'll be able to run this place better than ever. You're a young man! Go see the world!" I urged. "You'd be bored to death spending your days with three old women."

"No, I wouldn't," he promised brightly, his scheme finally suddenly spilling out in a fervent, convincing-sounding flow of words. "See, I was thinking I could take care of the farm and start my own business on the side. I could take the money for college and buy a little plane, get my license, and in a few months I could start a business crop dusting."

"Crop dusting?" I asked doubtfully.

"It's the latest thing!" he enthused. "You can fly over a field and fertilize or drop chemicals to kill pests quick as a wink. I've already picked up so much from Whitey Henderson over at the airfield, I can practically fly a plane already. I could have my pilot's license in just a few weeks."

"That idiot Whitey Henderson hasn't let you go up in that rattle-trap plane of his, has he?" I growled. Whitey, who was in charge of the tiny airfield in Liberal, owned a World War I surplus trainer so old and rusted it looked like it was held together with baling wire. Ever since he'd learned to drive, Morgan had spent most of his free afternoons at the airstrip, watching the few planes that landed in Liberal and running errands for Whitey. "You listen to me, Morgan. I will not have you flying in that death trap," I scolded, shaking my finger at him for emphasis. "I told Whitey that."

"I know, Mama. I know," Morgan huffed impatiently, like a dog pulling against his lead. "Whitey's so scared of you, he won't let me near his plane. He's just been showing me stuff you learn in ground school—navigating and how the engine works. Things like that. I could pass the ground-school exam today. I've read every book about aviation I can get my hands on. I *know* that's what I want to do with my life. I just need a plane. There's a fellow in Tulsa Whitey knows who's got a used Stearman trainer he's willing to sell real cheap—a little over a thousand dollars—and it's in good shape. The college money would cover it plus some extra for flight school. I could have my pilot's license in six months and start earning money right away instead of waiting four whole years."

Four years. I had forgotten how eternal four years can seem when you're eighteen and so impatient for life to begin that time drags you down like a pocketful of stones. I looked at my son's handsome, unlined face, so fervent and anxious to find his purpose.

"Morgan, I know you want to fly. It's something that goes deep in you, but four years go so much faster than you can imagine right now. Flying will be there always. You can go back to it, but a college education will stay with you for life, and now is the time to do it, while you're young and energetic, free of responsibilities. When you've finished you'll know so much about agriculture you'll make this farm as fine a place as any in the county. Then you can get any plane you want and fly in your free time."

Morgan shook his head and frowned as if I were speaking a language whose words made no sense to him. "No, Mama. That's not for me. You said yourself, flying goes deep in me. I haven't even piloted on my own yet, but I know it's part of me, like an extra heart beating inside me, a rhythm that's different from what everybody else is walking to. I don't want to farm, Mama. I want to fly. I want to get myself up off the ground and never come back down." He took my hands in his own and peered into my eyes, begging me to understand.

"Look at me, Mama. Look hard. Can you really imagine me spending the rest of my life being a farmer? Because I just can't see it. Can you?"

He was right. Everyone I knew was either a farmer or a merchant, and so I'd thought that's what Morgan would be, too. Actually, I hadn't thought, not at all. Just going to college seemed so fine and elevated to me, I hadn't ever thought what it would lead to, whether or not it would make him happy. No, I couldn't see him as a farmer. But a crop duster? That didn't seem right, either. It didn't seem big enough somehow.

Maybe that was the problem, I didn't know how to think big and I hadn't taught Morgan how to, either. Some of us are so timid and uncertain when we're young that even the crumbs from the table can seem like a banquet. That's the way I was. Morgan didn't know yet about how dreams that seemed so rich and unattainable today could shrink and leave him hungry once he actually held them in his grasp. Some late night, years from now, he would furrow his brow and puzzle: why wasn't he happier? Then he'd chide himself for ingratitude.

No, I vowed, it wouldn't be that way for Morgan. Not if I could help it. I needed money. I could write Slim's lawyers and get it that way, but that was a last resort. It had been hard for me to accept Slim paying off the farm mortgage. I just couldn't bring myself to write and beg for more money, not even for Morgan, unless there was no other way on earth. *But there is a way,* a voice that wasn't mine spoke in my mind. *You know there is.*

All at once I knew what to do. For the first time in a long time, I felt Papa was very near to me, giving his blessing to a plan that would have seemed inconceivable only a few minutes before.

"All right," I said, nodding decisively.

"All right what?" Morgan asked softly, searching my face for a clue to my thoughts, barely daring to hope that "all right" might mean yes.

"You can have your plane, and you can learn to fly."

"Yeow!!" Morgan yelped in exultation and lunged forward to scoop me up in his arms.

"But!" I shouted over the noise, making him halt in mid-whoop, "You are still going to college." Morgan's face fell, but I continued before he could begin arguing. "You don't have to study agriculture. You can study something that will help you with your flying. I don't know what that would be, but at such a big school there's bound to be something. We'll buy the plane. You can keep it near school and take lessons on the weekends. I'm sure we can work it out."

Morgan started to interrupt, but I stopped his protestations with a firm shake of my head. "Morgan, right now crop dusting sounds like a fine profession, but as you get older you'll want something more exciting. Something where you'll be breaking new ground every day. I don't know what that is, but you'll figure it out. I'd bet the farm on it."

"Mama! Didn't you hear what I said?" he nearly wailed in despair. "The plane costs over a thousand dollars; there won't be enough for it *and* college."

"Yes there will, if you're really serious about not wanting to farm. Are you absolutely sure?" I asked. He solemnly nodded his resolve. I took a deep breath and went on. "In that case we won't be needing nearly so much land. We'll sell that quarter I bought for you when you were little and one more next to it. That ought bring in enough to buy the plane with a little left over."

For a moment, Morgan was dumbstruck. "Sell off part of the farm? Papaw's land? We can't do that. You've said yourself, a hundred times, that you'd die before you'd sell one acre of Papaw's land."

"Well, that was before. I didn't have a good enough reason then." Morgan began to protest again, but I quieted him before he could go on.

"Sweetheart, listen. Years ago when I saved up to buy you that land, it was for a reason. I wanted you to have a future. Back then I figured that meant farmland. Nothing else ever crossed my mind, but now I can see so much more ahead of you. I bought the land for you. Your grandpa and I kept the farm together for *you*. All we ever wanted was for you to be happy and live a life that would make us all proud, so if selling off a couple of pieces of property can make that happen, so be it."

"But, you'd have fewer crops then, less money, and me not bringing in anything . . ." he sputtered. "Mama, I want to help you, not be a burden to you."

"I know you do, and it makes me proud to hear you say it. When the time comes, I'll let you, but for now I'm just fine. Morgan, I know I seem ancient to you, but I'm not even forty. My fingers are still pretty fast with a quilting needle, and I like doing it. Now that money's loosening up, I can go back to making the pretty quilts, the watercolor ones like I used to, and there will be people to buy them."

Morgan looked at me curiously. "I've seen you cutting up all those little squares out of my old clothes, just like you used to, but is that what you are going to sell? Quilts made up of our worn-out shirts and pants?

"No," I said, laughing. "Those little squares are for a special one, for a friend. But starting on that one quilt has kind of primed the pump, if you know what I mean." I locked eyes with him so he'd know I was serious as I spun out my plan, trying to convince him that I was sincere in my desire to get back to work that meant something. As I talked I realized it was true. I couldn't wait to start creating again.

"I've got a dozen designs floating around in my brain, Morgan. I want to stitch them together with my own hands and wrap them around a complete stranger who thinks I must have read their thoughts and patched them whole. I can't wait to start, so you needn't sit there with that guilty look on your face. I've always managed. I don't see how not having a little bit of ground that barely produced anything in the past ten years is going to propel me into the poorhouse."

"Still," he said dubiously, "Papaw's land. I just wouldn't feel right about it." Morgan's face looked so solemn and culpable that I couldn't help but laugh.

"They're just fields, Morgan, not holy ground!" He was unconvinced by my levity. Talking about selling off part of the farm was serious business to him, and he was right, I thought. It was more serious than he could imagine. "Morgan," I said in what I hoped was an authoritative tone, "I know that right now you think there will always be time to backtrack and fix up the mistakes you made, or explore the paths you missed, but you're wrong. I want everything for you, the things I never had and the things I never had the courage to imagine having. That's what I want, and that's what your Papaw would want."

A shy little smile started at the corner of Morgan's mouth and spread across his face. "Do you really think so?"

"I know it as sure as anything," I said with finality and joy as I watched the relief flood my son's face and felt myself swept up into his grateful embrace.

And, I thought to myself, *if your father were here, he'd want it too.* Thinking of Slim chilled me for a moment. It ought to be Slim having this conversation with Morgan, not me. Just this once, he ought to be here for his son. Why wasn't he?

That simple, silent question opened the door to a bigger one. Paul had been right; I should have asked it years before.

All the next week, whenever I could spare a moment, I sat in my room sewing the tiny squares I'd cut and collected from our cast-off clothes: mine, Morgan's, Mama's, Ruby's, and even some of Papa's old shirts I'd found wrapped in paper and stored in a chest. Years had passed since Papa worn them, but they still seemed to carry the faintest scent of him. I stitched them together with the rest, laying them out, rearranging the colors and patterns, sewing them and ripping them apart and sewing them together again, trying to piece all those separate scraps together into a whole cloth that would explain everything. A still life that was life, or at least a frozen moment of it. As I stitched and snipped and thought, Paul's voice played louder in my mind, until I wasn't afraid to hear it or think about what he'd said anymore.

Why isn't he here? It was the first question. Once I allowed myself that one, the others weren't far behind.

Watching Morgan's valedictory speech was the proudest moment of my life. I sat wedged between Mama and Ruby. We applauded until our hands stung. We clapped when Morgan received his diploma, when he won the science award for designing a new windmill so light that it spun circles on just a breath of air, and again when he was announced as the "Graduate Most Likely To" and walked across the stage one more time to accept the $75 Grange scholarship.

It was one of the best days of my life. Even so, I kept finding myself glancing at the door of the musty gymnasium, waiting for Slim to walk through. Late, or in disguise, or without saying a word, I didn't care. I just wanted him to come for a moment, to see his son and what he had become and how what we had started together in ignorance and love had become, finally, a happy ending to share. But the door stayed closed.

After the ceremony Paul came over to shake Morgan's hand and congratulate all of us. Morgan asked him to join us for ice cream. Paul threw me a quick, questioning glance before saying he had an appointment. I didn't urge him to change it. We went for pie and ice cream at the café without him, and I told Morgan that my tears were only from happiness and pride. He believed me. It was so easy to make him believe the lie. Easier than it would have been to explain I was crying over closed doors.

The acreage sold quickly, and the plane was purchased and delivered to Liberal. Morgan began taking short flights under Whitey Henderson's direction. He wanted to take me up, too, but it was a two-seater. I'd have to wait until Morgan earned his license and could take up passengers alone.

"As soon as I can solo, Mama, I'm going to swoop down from the sky, land in one of the fields, and take you for a ride. I don't care if it's day or night or in the middle of exams. You're going to be my very first passenger," he declared emphatically

"I'd be honored, Morgan, but if it is during your examinations, maybe you'd just better stay grounded until you finish. I'll be waiting right here when you're done."

The weeks flew—flashed in front of my eyes like the blinding blast of a summer storm, a series of still photo-poems I collected in my mind: "This was the last time he ate my fried chicken, the last time he cranked the Ford, fed the stock, slept in his bed." Then it was time to go. September came, and Morgan and Whitey stuffed the plane to bursting with Morgan's clothes and books. They flew off at dawn, a red streak of metal across the morning sky as I waved good-bye . . . just like I'd waved good-bye to his father.

But this good-bye was different in that I understood exactly why I was staying behind, why the one I loved was going. Ever since Paul had dared me to ask the question, reasons for those partings, or at least the finality and persisting silence of them, had become less and less clear in my mind. I guess that's how everything starts. It's the unanswered questions that push us out the door and into the world.

Morgan didn't know what he could be, what lay round the bend or inside a cloud, and so he was off into the world to find out. I didn't know why, after so many years of silent compliance, I should still be waiting for the sound of an engine in the dusk, still waiting for him to walk into a room, shake Morgan's hand, and say, "We've met before, but it's time we got to know each other."

I packed a bag, went to the train station, and bought a ticket to Des Moines, Iowa, where Slim was scheduled to speak. I wanted some answers. I wanted to stop waiting for the footsteps that never came.

Chapter 17

For some reason, my decision to go to Iowa cleared the clouds from Mama's mind and roused her to action. She seemed more herself than she had in years, industrious and commanding. The lunch basket she packed for my trip was an embarrassment. Big enough to carry a week's laundry, it was loaded with cold chicken, ham sandwiches, dried apples, cookies, cake, bread and butter, and an amber jar of cold, sweet tea. You'd have thought to look at me that I was taking the train all the way to the north pole instead of Iowa. Under all those provisions, on the very bottom of the hamper, was a flat, soft package. I'd wrapped it myself in three layers of brown paper to make sure the contents arrived in Des Moines undamaged.

Balancing the load on my lap, I felt self-conscious, figuring the other passengers must be wondering about the size of my appetite, but I knew that enormous lunch was Mama's way of saying, "I love you. I'm worried about you."

I was worried myself, but a lifetime of carefully engineered avoidance of pain was exhausting. I was tired of being afraid. Mama knew that, so she came to the station and leaned on Ruby's arm, waving a tiny white handkerchief. It seemed I could see it through the dust and grime of the coach window, clean and fluttering like a flag of surrender, long after the silhouette of the station had faded in the distance.

After an hour or two I started to feel more at home with the rocking motion of the cars. The steady thunk of steel wheels against steel rail became familiar, even comforting, like the tuneless, constant song a mother hums to quiet a child.

The landscape changed quickly as we headed farther north. The dunes of sand that still nestled against buildings and fences got smaller and smaller until I realized that just a few hours away from Dillon there had been no dust bowl. If I'd stopped in that town and told the folks there that my papa had died from swallowing a small mountain of dust, or described storms of dirt so thick and black they blocked the sun and made noon seem like night, they would have looked at me with wide eyes, wondering if I was telling stories. In a way, I suppose they would have been right.

Looking around the coach at the other passengers, one eating an apple, another reading a newspaper folded in half, still another sleeping with head lolled back, breathing heavily through an open mouth, I realized they all had stories. We were all human, born of mothers, but beyond that there were so many differences among us that it was a wonder we recognized each other as the same species. Their lives were nothing like mine. Their Depression was theirs alone. Some were easier, some harder.

I had lived in Dillon all my life, surrounded by people I'd known since the day I was born. Yet it seemed I knew more about these strangers I was traveling with than the folks I knew by name. People in Dillon had become such a part of the landscape that I'd forgotten to notice what was special about them. It seemed odd that my fellow passengers seemed so much less guarded than my friends and neighbors. Maybe it was because when you're on a train, surrounded by people you know you'll never see again, you forget to keep up appearances, so you reveal more of yourself than you'd intended.

If I looked at the faces around me long enough, I could just make out, in the web of worry wrinkles and smile lines, the outlines of who they were, where they'd been, and how it had changed them. Not a single person was like the one sitting next to him, but I could see in their eyes, whether darting and suspicious or steady and stoic, the one thing they all had in common: they didn't know what was coming next or if they were up to handling it.

Even the bravest among them flashed expressions showing little seeds of doubt at unguarded moments, like stray thread ends I found in my quilts sometimes. I always shoved them back under the fabric so everything looked smooth and planned, but though the stitches looked perfect to others, I knew where every little thread was tucked, a hidden weakness that might unravel the entire seam. A whole train, a long, narrow world full of complete strangers seated side by side, a thousand different stories, and the only thing we really shared was uncertainty. It comforted me in a way I still can't explain.

I let my head drop back and slept like the others, not concerned about how I'd look if my jaw relaxed and dropped open onto my chest, or if people stared, wondering why my leg was so twisted, or if the woman sitting in the next seat could read my life in the lines near my eyes. Why shouldn't she? I was what I was. What could it hurt for people to know?

The hall was like the city, loud and smoke-filled, everybody talking and nobody listening, everybody knowing somebody, except me. I left my suitcase and basket at a hotel and carried only the package I'd wrapped to give to Slim when I found him. If I found him. The green velveteen dress was my very best, but compared to the tailored suits and cunning little hats I saw on the women sitting on folding chairs, murmuring and smoking cigarettes while waiting for the program to start, I felt like just what I was, a country girl come to town. I sat down on the far left of the auditorium, near two double doors where a group of serious-looking men in gray suits stood, visually assessing the crowd and talking to each other knowingly out of the sides of their mouths. They looked official and tense. I figured they were waiting to escort Slim and the others to the platform.

Eventually, the doors opened slightly, but Slim didn't enter. Instead a carefully dressed man with glasses and a receding hairline approached the microphone and announced that, as promised and in the interest of fairness, the America First Committee had decided to broadcast President Roosevelt's speech to the nation before beginning its own program. He thanked the audience for their attendance, and almost before he finished speaking, the warm, familiar, nasal voice of the president came over the loudspeaker, and the crowd grew quiet as they strained to hear the broadcast.

The president lashed out against the Nazis. He announced that he had given the navy permission to clear the sea of enemy warships whenever it was necessary to protect American interests. The crowd was supposed to be made up of isolationists, dedicated to keeping America out of the war, so I was surprised at how many times they cheered the president's words, especially when he verbally attacked Hitler as a despot. Apparently, the people of Des Moines were as torn between the desire for peace and the hatred of evil as the rest of the country. Between the reaction of the crowd and the president's announcement that the navy was authorized to attack "enemy" ships, before we'd even officially declared an enemy, I could see our entry into the war wasn't far off. There was no stopping it now.

When the address ended, the audience applauded warmly, then laughed and covered their ears when the loudspeaker squealed as the microphones were adjusted for the America First speakers. They'd set them too high for Slim, I could see that. He was tall, tall as anyone I knew, but the stagehand set the microphone so high he must have thought Slim was some fantastic giant of Nordic legend and not a man at all. I knew better.

The double doors burst open as the band struck up a patriotic tune. The committee came striding in, some grinning and pointing to people they recognized in the crowd, others looking nervous and pulling at tight collar buttons. Slim looked calm, serious, and re-signed, like a doctor coming to give bad news to a terminally ill pa-tient. He was so alone. Despite the questions that had driven me to be there, I couldn't help but feel compassion toward him.

For one ridiculous moment I thought that if I could push through the crowd somehow and reach him, I could tell him that war was inevitable and he should just thank everyone for coming and go home, before it was too late. The crowd that heard his words today might believe him for a moment, might even cheer him, but tomorrow they were going to war, and they'd forget. Once the declaration was made, all these people, everyone who'd been against fighting, would deny they'd ever said such a thing, and no one would remember if it was true or not, but Charles was too famous and his campaign too fervent for people to forget his words. They'd think he was a coward, a traitor to a just cause. I was afraid for him. What could be so worth hating as a hero made unheroic?

Flashbulbs exploded in his face, but he didn't look at the cam-eras. I leapt from my seat as he passed near me and tried to grab his sleeve, but one of the stern-looking men I'd seen guarding the door pushed me back. "Slim!" I called. He couldn't hear me above the din of the crowd and the band. I yelled once more, so loudly it made my ears ring. "Slim!"

He turned for a moment and searched the mob, trying to pinpoint the voice that must have sounded faintly familiar in his ears. When his eyes found me I saw recognition there, but nothing else. In fact, he seemed embarrassed and slightly annoyed, as though my appearance was an unwelcome development, designed to break his concentration. I knew then that nothing I could say to him would stop him from making his speech. He frowned at me and whispered something to the man in a pinstripe suit who was standing next to him. Frowning again, he shook his head at me in warning before continuing to the stage. He walked up the steps heavily, like a man ascending a gallows scaffold.

Though the whole thing had taken a second, it seemed longer, and all I could think was, "He's ashamed of me." Ever since I'd decided to come to Des Moines, I'd imagined how his face would look when he saw me; I'd pictured many different reactions, possibly joy, anger, even denial. Somehow shame had never occurred to me.

Well, it should have, I scolded myself. *It should have. What did you expect? You should have left things alone.* The room seemed even hotter and louder than before. I started to gather up my things and leave. I couldn't wait to get out of there.

But as I stood up, a hand reached out and gently pushed me back down into my chair. The man in the pinstripe suit laid his hand on my shoulder and spoke into my ear. "Stay right here until the speech is over and the crowd has left. I'll come back for you, but it may take a while. If anyone asks, you're waiting for me, Ben Hodges. You're my cousin Edith, and I promised to introduce you to Colonel Lindbergh. You understand?"

I nodded dumbly and murmured an awkward thanks, but I don't suppose he heard me. By then the crowd was up on its feet, applauding and hollering as Slim was introduced. Mr. Hodges glanced at me for a moment, sizing me up with a flat look, as though he knew all about me and considered me just another unpleasant piece of business to be dealt with in a world where nothing could surprise him anymore. I wondered what he knew about me.

Then Slim came up to the podium, and suddenly his face was the only one worth thinking about. He smiled automatically, as though he knew it was expected of him, and lowered the microphone so he could speak comfortably into it. For a moment he stood still, just to let everyone get a good look. The sight of him took my breath away. He was still so handsome. He stood tall, acknowledging the cheers of the crowd with good grace, not as if he deserved them or even as if he didn't, just accepting it all, the way other people say grace for the blessing of food they receive every day of their lives, grateful but not surprised, never imagining a day when the bounty will cease, because it has always been there. He was so sure of himself, so straight and open and earnest. I loved him all over again, despite the life I'd lived without him. How could I not love him? He was so much more alone than I'd ever been.

He began his address. In the shadow of a frown that creased his brow, I saw a tiny crack in the mask he covered himself with. He was afraid, too. I'd walked in on the pivotal scene. He'd already lost the battle for peace, peace for the country and for himself, and so this was the day he'd chosen to show them what he was, and dare these last loyal few to cheer him if they could. He already knew the outcome, so he was afraid. It was written on his face. If I could have, I would have stopped him, but I was what I had always been, a spectator. It was too late to choose another role.

His words, carefully rehearsed, rang out clear and sharp. The audience clapped and acclaimed his statements as though they'd written the text themselves. "England's position is desperate," he boomed. "She cannot win the war by aviation regardless of how many planes we send her. Even if America enters the war, it is highly improbable that the Allied armies could invade Europe and overcome the might of the Axis forces."

The assembly applauded again. Slim paused to let the noise die down before continuing. "If it were not for her hope that she can make the United States responsible for the war, financially as well as militarily, I believe England would have negotiated a peace in Europe many months ago, and be better off for doing so."

More cheers followed that. Cries of, "That's right!" echoed in the hall. Nobody but me seemed to wonder why handing half of Europe over to the Nazis would leave England more secure than she was now. *If we were English,* I thought, *we'd fight to the death, even if winning was "highly improbable." If he were English, Slim would be leading the battle cry.*

I half wanted to whisper this into the ear of the woman sitting next to me but decided there was no point. Everyone in that room had already made up their minds what to think; they'd just come tonight to have their own opinions confirmed. The audience grew quiet again as Slim continued.

"I can understand why the Jewish people wish to overthrow the Nazis," he said more softly. "The persecution they have suffered in Germany would be sufficient to make bitter enemies of any race." He paused to let his words sink in. "No person with a sense of the dignity of mankind condones the persecution of the Jewish race in Germany. Certainly I and my friends do not."

For a moment, relief flooded through me. So many papers around the country had accused Slim and the America First supporters of hating Jews. Maybe this would quiet their criticism. I'd never actually heard or read anything by Slim that mentioned Jews by name, but plenty of people had speculated about his opinions.

It was hard for me to precisely understand anti-Semitism. In my entire life, I'd never met anyone Jewish. But I knew all about feeling like an alien in my own land and how people were capable of ostracizing, even demonizing, people who didn't fit into an accepted mold. Every day of my life I'd seen how ignorance and cruelty walked hand in hand. The papers never talked much about what was happening to Jews in Europe, not in a direct way. The reports talked about confiscated businesses and freedoms denied, but that was all. The rest was just implied and hinted at, but I knew from Nils's letters to Paul that these weren't just rumors. Something terrible was happening, but no one would talk about it.

I couldn't bear for people to think Slim condoned such evil. He had looked past my lameness and seen to the inside of me. People who tried to label him an anti-Semite didn't know him like I did. Hearing him denounce the Nazi persecution, seeing his eyes cast down in sorrow and sympathy, no one could dare to pin such an ugly name on him. For a moment, I thought I'd been wrong to be so worried. Maybe everything would be all right.

If he'd stopped right there, that would have been the moment everyone remembered about Des Moines, everything would have turned out differently for him, but he didn't. That speech changed his life. No amount of explanation would soften its meaning. Sometimes I still try, but no matter how I rearrange the words or use the times to justify them, the phrases are still there, black and white and red. They mean what they mean.

"But though I sympathize with the Jews, let me add a word of warning. No person of honesty and vision can look on their prowar policy here today without seeing the dangers involved in such a policy, both for us"—he looked up from his notes and stared into the eyes of the audience—"and for them."

"Instead of agitating for war, the Jewish groups in this country should be opposing it in every possible way, for they will be among the first to feel its consequences. Tolerance is a virtue that depends upon peace and strength. History shows that it cannot survive war and devastation. A few farsighted Jewish people realize this and stand opposed to intervention. But the majority still do not. Their greatest danger to this country lies in their large ownership and influence on our motion pictures, our press, our radio, and our government. We cannot blame them for looking out for what they believe to be their own interests, but we must also look out for ours. We cannot allow the natural passions and prejudices of other people to lead our country to destruction."

Even after he said this, many people were still cheering, but a few were frowning and even booing. Still more were whispering among themselves, shaking their heads as though they couldn't quite believe that "Lucky Lindy," the hero of all their childhood dreams, could actually say such things. It was as if Lindbergh, much like the despots he claimed to deplore, had declared Jews a foreign nation within our borders, to be tolerated only if they kept to themselves, made no noise, demanded no rights. It sounded almost as though he was issuing a threat. They could hardly believe their ears.

I didn't blame them. Neither could I.

Chapter 18

"Miss? Miss, your ticket?"

"Oh, I'm sorry. I know it's here somewhere." I fumbled in my pocket for the ticket stub. "Here it is." I tried to smooth out the wrinkles before handing it over, but it was no use. I had unthinkingly crushed the little slip in my pocket over and over, until it was so creased the conductor had to squint just to read the destination.

"Oklahoma, eh?" He smiled and rubbed his nose thoughtfully. "I got a cousin used to live in Oklahoma, but she and her family moved off to Utah when the dust came. Can't see where that was much improvement. I been through to see her a time or two. Just as barren as Oklahoma was. A regular desert. Can't think why anybody'd live there to begin with." He spoke cheerfully, but then his cheeks reddened as he remembered where I was headed.

"Sorry," he sputtered. "No offense intended, miss. I'm sure Oklahoma must have its good points, same as anywhere," he added seriously.

"No offense taken. Every place looks like heaven to someone, I suppose. Though you're right about it being flat, and the dust was terrible. But if you live somewhere long enough, flat starts to feel like coming home."

"Well," he said with a laugh, "at least can't nobody sneak up on you there. You can always see what's coming."

"I guess so. Anyway, that's what we tell ourselves."

He laughed again as he punched my ticket. "You have a nice trip now. You'll probably be glad to get home. Looks like you didn't get too much sleep in the big city."

I smoothed a hand over my hair, thinking how awful I must look. "Not used to all the city noises, I guess."

"You just close your eyes and we'll be there in no time." He winked and held out my ticket. As he moved on to the next passenger, he looked back once more. "No place like a train for a nap. Those wheels thump so regular, you'll sleep like a baby."

I was looking forward to that sleep the conductor promised, for I hadn't slept at all the previous night, and when morning came, I looked for the first train back to Dillon. There was no reason to stay longer, not after what had happened.

Slim had been waiting for me in a small office near the auditorium. The room looked sterile and unused, housing only a gray metal desk and two folding chairs that faced each other straight on, as though they were ready to square off for battle. Slim stood near the desk with his back turned, his hands shoved in his pockets, tapping his foot nervously on the mottled linoleum, his impatience echoing through the empty space like a drum cadence. He cleared his throat when I came in and took care to make sure the door was closed after Mr. Hodges excused himself. Neither of us sat down or moved toward the other. It seemed safer to stand at a distance. I clutched the soft paper-wrapped package to my breast like a shield.

After an uneasy hesitation, Slim spoke first. "You've caught me by surprise, Evangeline. You should have let me know you were coming." He sounded uncomfortable.

"And just how would I have done that?" I said, more archly than I'd intended. "Contacted Mr. Ashton? Who would have contacted some faceless lawyers in New York, who would have sent me a carefully worded letter suggesting that I stay home?" I checked myself and murmured an apology. This wasn't how I wanted to start off. "How are you? How are your children?"

"They're fine. Growing like weeds, of course. I can't think where the time has gone." He paused for a moment. "How is Morgan?"

I couldn't help but smile. I would have made the trip again, just to hear him say Morgan's name. "He's away at college. University of Oklahoma. He almost quit before he got started, though. He wants to fly more than anything. I guess he got that from you."

"And did his valedictory speech go well?" he asked. "I was proud to hear he was first in his class. He's obviously a much better student than I was. He must get that from you." He smiled, and for a moment I was stunned into silence.

"My letters . . ." I faltered, uncertain of what to say next, but my heart beat a little faster.

"I read them all," he said. "Even before you began writing I had people check up on him from time to time—anonymously, of course. Though I much prefer your letters. I'm sorry I can't answer them, Evangeline, but you understand."

"No, of course. You couldn't risk . . ." I agreed, but, truthfully, I couldn't see that the risk was so very great. If he could anonymously make inquiries about Morgan, couldn't he have anonymously responded to my letters? Still, I was pleased to know he'd read them at all, I didn't want to push the issue. "It's good to see you."

"You too," he said. His face seemed to relax a bit. "Do you want to sit down or anything? At least take off your coat." He came nearer and held my coat while I extracted my arms from the bulky sleeves. I put the package on the desk and covered it with my coat and handbag. We turned and leaned side by side against the edge of the desk. "I meant that, about it being good to see you. You were about the only friendly face in the crowd."

"That's not so. They cheered you like the star quarterback of the high school football team."

He snorted derisively. "The ones who weren't booing, you mean. Government plants, most of them. Roosevelt is out to label me as a coward and an anti-Semite. The crowd cheered me because that's what crowds do. They act like one big, mindless mass and follow the guy in front because it's easier than actually thinking for themselves. They cheered, but they didn't understand. Not a one of them."

He shoved his fist into his palm and ground it as if he were milling pepper, working hard at a task with no purpose. I wanted to take his hands in mine and let them rest, cool and soothing on my cheek, forgetting all about the speech, bathing him in comfortable words and assurance, but I couldn't.

"Neither do I," I confessed. "I can't imagine you really believe those things you said. Even if you do, how could you say them? You had to have known how people would react."

"You sound just like Anne," he said, pushing himself up off the desk and beginning to pace the room nervously. "She begged me to leave out the last part. Said it was 'like lighting a match near a pile of excelsior.' She even rewrote it, but I changed it back." He ran his fingers through his hair, that old, unconscious gesture that had always seemed so boyish and appealing. Now it just spoke of age and fatigue.

"That's why Anne didn't come. She said she couldn't bear to watch, so here I am alone." He stopped his pacing, and for a moment I thought he was going to reach for my hand, but then he stepped back, shoved his fists in his pockets, and resumed his restless pacing.

"It felt pretty lonely walking into that hall, knowing no one was truly on my side. All the reporters were circling like vultures, waiting to catch me out, hoping I'd trip, or have a heart attack at the microphone. Or better yet, walk in wearing a swastika on my sleeve. Anything so they'd have a good headline in the morning. Well"—he laughed ruefully—"I guess I gave them one: 'Lindbergh Attacks Jews!' That's how the morning editions will read. Never mind what I actually intended. None of that matters. Even if there were a reporter who would explain what I said in logical, rational terms, no one reads past the headlines, anyway. People always want to believe what's worst about other people."

"I don't," I said plainly. "Ever since I met you, I wanted to believe the best about you. I confess, listening to you today makes it harder. Slim, you want people to understand you? Start with me."

He was silent for a moment. Then he took a step back, pulled up a desk chair, and perched himself on the back of it. Though his arms were crossed casually across his chest, I could tell that underneath his palms were clenched defensively, ready for a fight. "All right." he said coldly. "Ask me anything you want."

I took a step closer to him, hoping to break through the wall of suspicion that divided us. "Slim, I'm not here to attack you. I'm not a reporter looking for a headline. There was a time when I understood everything you thought before you said a word, but things are more complicated now. If you knew that saying these things would make people think you were anti-Semitic, why did you say them? You made it sound like the Jews who live here aren't real Americans, as though they are some isolated group of foreigners who are with us, but not of us."

A picture I'd seen flashed in my mind: a German street, a rainy day, a black and gray sea of overcoats, each like another, but here and there a glimpse of yellow star, the space that opened in the crowd between stars and sea. It seemed a strangely familiar scene, as though I'd walked there myself and knew it all well, especially the empty spaces.

Slim growled, obviously irritated at my lack of understanding. "Of course they're Americans, but they ought to start acting like it! Anyone who has America's best interests at heart can see that we should stay out of this war. Germany has air power that we can't even begin to match. If we get into this fight, a fight that isn't ours to begin with, it will cost of millions of dollars, tens of thousands of lives, and in the end, we will probably lose! Anyone with an ounce of sense and loyalty to *this* country should see that."

"And you don't think American Jews are loyal to this country?" I asked slowly, not really certain I understood his meaning, hoping I didn't.

"Don't put words in my mouth," he snarled. "Awful things are happening in Europe. I'll be the first to admit that Hitler has abused his power. War inevitably brings terrible consequences, but when I weigh the cost of a war that's happening an ocean away against the potential cost in American lives, it's just not worth the price."

"But, Slim," I said dubiously, "you click your tongue and say, 'What a pity,' as though we were talking about a little feud between disinterested parties. How can you dismiss Hitler's tyranny as a mere abuse of power? Slim, the man is a murderer! He's crowned himself a god and filled the foundation of his temple with bodies! We can't just stand by as though it doesn't concern us."

Slim thumped his fist impatiently against wooden chair, "Now, this is just the sort of hysterical rhetoric I'm talking about, Evangeline.

A few people, putting their ancestral loyalties before the interests of their adopted country, start these terrible rumors about wholesale murder of Jews. They prey on the emotions of the American people."

"But," I insisted, "these aren't just rumors—"

"No, you're wrong!" He nearly shouted and was back on both feet again, stabbing the air with his finger at the beginning of every sentence, a static punctuation to underscore the experience which was his alone. "I have been to Germany. I have met the German people and men high up in their government. They are not the barbarians you are describing!

"I fled this country, running for my son's life, the only son I had left, because the press hounded us like a pack of wild dogs! They showed no respect for our privacy. They sold our suffering for a nickel in the early edition and made it so dangerous for my family that we had to escape to Europe. Even there, I was always looking over my shoulder. I've never slept through the night again, always lying awake, listening for the scrape of a ladder against the wall of the house, or the creak of a window opening in the nursery." His voice broke for just a moment. I looked into his eyes, expecting to see tears, but all I could see was rage. He continued speaking, more softly, but with smoldering intensity.

"In all those years, in all those countries, the only place I felt safe was Germany. No reporters hounded us, no one asked questions they shouldn't. We were treated with respect. Everyone knew his business and kept to it. The government wouldn't have tolerated anything less. If the war tensions hadn't been so high, we probably would have stayed. I'd asked Anne to look for a house. It was the only peace I've had since . . ."

My heart melted for him. The pain, the terrible, unimaginable pain I'd felt come upon him the night Baby Charles was taken had scarred him even more than I'd feared. It had left him blind.

"Oh, Slim," I mourned, wanting to cry, if only because he couldn't cry for himself. "I am sorry, so very sorry for all that you've been through. I'm glad you found some healing in Germany, even if it didn't last. Maybe you were right about Germans at that moment in time. Maybe they were a civilized society before the war. Maybe Hitler has been only recently corrupted by power. But maybe not. Has it occurred to you that they may have been using you, filtering what you saw and manipulating you so you would go back to America and say just what you did—that Germany was too strong to be contained so we should just stay out of it?"

For an instant I thought I saw a flicker of doubt in his eye, but I don't know for sure. If I did he quickly extinguished it and left my question unanswered. The implacable mask was back.

"Slim," I said urgently, pleading for him to listen, "these rumors about what is going on in Europe aren't just stories. A friend of mine has a brother who lives in Holland, and he writes the most awful letters. He has seen it with his own eyes. Thousands of people have disappeared! When Hitler's army conquers a city, it brings soldiers, tanks, guns, and boxcars. Mile after mile of freight cars roll into the stations, and the soldiers fill them with whoever they consider undesirable, mostly Jews. They stuff them in like so many cattle going to the slaughterhouse. Then the trains pull away, and no one ever hears from the passengers again. Their names are removed from the mailboxes and painted over on the shop windows. New people move in: good, loyal members of the Nazi party. They live in empty Jewish houses and sit in chairs that don't belong to them, and people forget who used to live there, just like they never existed. No one knows how many. No one even bothers to count."

Slim stood, silent and unmoved as I spoke, the same maddeningly blank expression on his face. I couldn't help myself. I shouted at him. He had to acknowledge me. He had to hear me. "Thousands of them, Slim! Whole villages! Don't you wonder where they went?"

The door opened, and Mr. Hodges, who had been standing guard outside, peered in and glared at me.

"Do you need anything in here, Colonel?"

Slim shook his head. "No, Ben," he said gruffly. "Thank you. I'll be out in a minute." The door closed again, and he turned to me and frowned. "For God's sake, Evangeline! Lower your voice. You're not being reasonable. I'm sure your friend repeats all sorts of third-hand stories in his letters, but I doubt there is more than a grain of truth to it. Of course there are terrible things happening to Jews, terrible, but it's nothing as bad as you say. The German people couldn't be willing to engage in such barbarity."

"Would they be willing to look aside while someone else did it for them?" I asked archly, wanting to wound him with doubt and, if only for a moment, pierce the wall of self-righteous certainty that he wore like a coat of armor. But it was an impossible task. My questions ricocheted unanswered off him and bounced back to me, echoing starkly through the room, leaving me as bewildered as ever.

"I can see there is no point in discussing this further," he said stiffly and picked his hat up off the desk, preparing to leave. The interview was over. "You're obviously not willing to listen to reason and are taking this all too personally."

"You're right," I answered more softly. "I do take it personally. I've got reason to. It could just as well be me, you know.

"How would I fare in Germany, Slim? Where does Hitler stand on the question of cripples? Would someone as twisted as me qualify for membership in the Master Race? Or would I be loaded into a boxcar, too? What about Morgan? Of course, he is *your* son, so his lineage is impeccable, at least on his father's side. Do you think that would be reason enough to overlook his unfortunate maternal heritage?" My voice dripped with sarcasm, and I knew I was being cruel, but I couldn't stop myself.

"On the other hand, he might never have been born in the first place. That's what they do with the genetically undesirable in Germany today. They take them to the hospital against their will and perform operations so they can't reproduce and pollute the populace."

"Stop it, Evangeline!" he barked, the impenetrable mask finally pierced. He was furious, and I was glad. I wanted us to share one honest emotion, even if it was only anger. "They don't do any such thing," he hissed defensively. "All this emotional drivel obscures the truth! You're not looking at the facts."

I cut off his argument with an emphatic shake of my head. "The Slim Lindbergh I know never used to be bothered by the facts; he worked on instinct. If you'd looked at the facts you'd never have landed in Paris."

"You're wrong," he said. "I made that flight because I did the calculations and they worked. The facts supported it. It was science. Just like what you're talking about—excuse me, what you're dramatizing—is a science. It's known as eugenics."

"Yes, I know all about it," I countered and snorted. "Even in Dillon we still hear about a few things. That Dr. Carrel, the French researcher you worked with on the artificial heart pump, is a big proponent of eugenics."

Slim's eyebrows lifted slightly, and he seemed taken aback, surprised, I suppose, that I followed his activities so closely. "*Voluntary* eugenics," he said more calmly. "It is a simple fact that if you can control reproduction, making sure that only the strongest bloodlines are joined, you can create a people who are physically superior, more intelligent, and unplagued by feeblemindedness or criminal tendencies. What is so awful about that?" he asked simply, seeming certain I would agree with his position once he laid it out so logically.

"A tidy argument, but it seems that in Germany they are having trouble finding enough volunteers." Slim's brow creased into a frown again at my words. "Slim," I continued, "who is going to willingly chop down their own family tree? Who do you suppose would despise themselves so much?"

"Anyone with any sense," he retorted incredulously. "Wouldn't the world be a better place if children weren't born disabled or mentally slow? If you could have planned it that way, Evangeline, wouldn't you prefer to have been born with two straight limbs?"

I stared at him, shocked to realize that the man I'd lived my entire life for knew so little about me. His eyes were the same grey-blue, his skin as tanned and healthy as it had always been, if slightly more lined near his eyes. He looked as he always had, and yet the man I had known was dead inside. I had been worshiping a ghost.

The realization so stupefied me that it was impossible to speak. He mistook my silence for assent. "You see, Evangeline"—he took a step closer and spoke softly, almost enticingly—"you've got to look at all the facts. You've been oversimplifying things."

"No." I shook my head and whispered, "No, Slim, it's just the opposite. I've overcomplicated things, and for a long time. For months—no, make that years—I've been trying to piece together who you are instead of asking the one question that matters, though I didn't realize it until just now." I took a deep breath and plunged ahead.

"If you were to meet me today, would you still want me?" I locked eyes with him, ready to see him full-faced and unfiltered. "Would you turn off your mind and listen only to your heart, lay down next to me on the new wheat, and forget yourself inside me?"

The air was dead between us, the silence long and eloquent.

He couldn't deny the accusation in my eyes, and his gaze shifted uncomfortably away from mine. "I'm not that optimistic anymore, Eva. I'm not that careless. I can't afford to be. Be honest; neither can you."

I grabbed my coat and threw it over my arm, my emotions so thick and foggy I forgot about the package lying underneath. "*My name is Evangeline*," I whispered, blinking back tears. "I don't know who you are. Maybe I never did." I walked to the door and closed it behind me.

Chapter 19

Ruby was a caterpillar puffing sagely on a hookah, smoking and listening as we sat on the porch waiting for the kitchen floor to dry. A bowl half full of unshelled peas we were supposedly cleaning for supper sat forgotten between us. The floor had actually been dry for some time, but we paid no mind. Supper would be late. After keeping everything bottled up inside for three days, I was finally ready to talk. Ruby listened without moving a muscle.

"It was awful," I said softly, looking down and watching my bare left hand. "I was in such a hurry to get out of town I didn't even realize I'd left the quilt behind until a good hour after the train pulled out of the depot. Who knows," I said with a shrug, "maybe he never even saw it. Maybe it's still there. Maybe someone else found it and took it home." The idea of abandoning my best work in an empty office for the janitor to find was distressing, but I couldn't help but wonder what would happen if Slim found the package himself and opened it, fingered the stitching curiously, trying to decipher the message I'd left behind. Did he know enough of me to read that private code, the one I'd meant for us to share?

"Well, whoever has it is sure lucky," Ruby said, taking another pull from what was left of her cigarette and exhaling thoughtfully. "It was beautiful work, Eva. Your best ever."

I didn't argue. Ruby was right. She had watched me work on the quilt in the weeks before I boarded the train to Des Moines. It was exquisite. All the colors of the prairie were in it, the colors you never know are there until you fly high over the uneven ground and see how everything works together so richly, a palette that exists beyond your imagination yet somehow, when you see it laid out below you, seems like an integral part of your instinct and memory. That quilt was my masterpiece—the landscape, the sky, perfectly real but better than reality. Up close the quilt was lovely, but it wasn't until you stepped back that it truly took your breath away. The colors blended and blurred into a vision mysteriously made more focused and honest by the clarity of distance.

Over the years, all my quilts had aimed for that tender impression more true than a photograph. I had finally captured it. A silvery wingtip cut across the quilt's upper corner at an acrobatic angle and seemed to glint in the bright sunlight while the white fringe of the flyer's scarf fluttered on a breeze of minuscule silver stitches. Beyond that the sky sang in a hundred brilliant gradations from diamond white to the color of a jay's cap until it melted into the dark, waiting earth and the outline of roofs and trees below, where a woman and boy stood in silhouette, tiny and patient, five hundred feet below, faces upturned and hopeful.

Ruby had gasped when she'd seen it. "Oh, Eva! It's the most beautiful thing I've ever seen! You're an artist, Eva. There's no other word for it."

I had brushed aside her praise as extravagant, but I was proud of my work. After so many years, so many quilts that were merely pretty, my diverse collection of threads and scraps finally said what I could never patch together in words. Running my hand over the quilted surface had felt like touching flight itself. When I'd wrapped it for the trip to Des Moines it had made my heart smile to think of Slim opening the gift, touching the work of my hands and understanding all the things that were too hard for me to say.

"So stupid," I berated myself, "so incredibly stupid of me to leave it behind. He'll have thought I was . . . I don't know, asking for something. That's how it will look to him, and that's not what I meant. I always wanted to be the one person who never asked him for anything."

Ruby raised her eyebrows and, with her cigarette butt still wedged between the fingers of her left hand, folded her arms across her chest in a pose of utter disdain. "Well, pardon me for saying so, but that's about the dumbest thing I ever heard. Really, Eva," she scoffed, "who do you think you are? Some kind of marble statue? You're a flesh and blood woman and you have a right . . ." She growled in exasperation. "Good Lord, Eva, you have an obligation to expect something, just the tiniest crumb of recognition from the father of your child!"

Ruby took a last puff, reached for the ashtray with unusual vehemence, and blew out a final, irritable column of smoke. "So, now that it's all over, do you wish you'd stayed home?"

I chewed on the question for a moment, letting my legs dangle over the edge of the porch and swinging them in small orderly circles while I sorted out my feelings. "No," I said finally. "I'm glad I went. Maybe I should have done it differently, or sooner, but in the end I had to find out the truth."

"Well, then, that's that." Ruby smacked her palm against the sagging porch smartly, announcing a change of subject. "Now what are you going to do?"

"About what?"

"Your life, you goose!" She groaned impatiently. "Eva, you can really be hard work sometimes. What's going to be different now that you've finally exorcised that ghost from your life?"

I knew she wanted me to say I was going to put on a new dress and knock on the door of the parsonage and tell Paul that I was finally over Slim, but I couldn't. I picked up the bowl of peas and started shelling them distractedly. Nothing was as simple as Ruby made it sound. Though I'd never told her what happened between me and Paul, I knew she'd noticed how things had changed between us. Paul never came by the house anymore, not even to see Mama.

Even if I did decide to invite Paul back into my life, it seemed I'd waited too long. The word around Dillon was that he'd been seen walking with Jolene Bergen after services. I'd heard Mrs. Dwyer share the news with Mrs. Linden as she cut and wrapped six yards of hideous moss-colored chintz intended as new dresses for the Linden girls, a matched set of pale, washed-out looking six-year-old twins nearly as ugly as the yardage their mother was buying.

Mrs. Dwyer, like everyone else in town, knew Paul used to come by our house pretty frequently. Though she never said so to my face (Mrs. Dwyer never said anything to me if she didn't have to), I knew she disapproved of the pastor keeping company with a woman of such questionable reputation. She leaned over the counter toward Mrs. Linden and hissed the news of Paul's outings with Jolene in a stage whisper that made certain I wouldn't miss a word as I stood near the wall, fingering a piece of machine-made lace. It infuriated me, hearing her toss Paul's name around like that, lobbing her gossip archly in my direction and hoping to wound me with it, but I didn't lift an eyebrow. I would have died before giving her the satisfaction of eliciting a reaction. Besides, I told myself, what right did I have to be jealous of anything Paul did. He was free to walk with anyone he liked, even the horse-faced Jolene. After all, I was the one who had pushed him away.

Ruby leaned over and bumped my shoulder with her own, knocking me out of my reverie. "Eva, when are you going to quit wasting time? He's not interested in Jolene Bergen, if that's what you're thinking."

"It's no concern of mine who he's interested in," I shot back, shelling peas more vigorously, nearly throwing them into the bowl.

Inexplicably, Ruby burst into laughter.

"What's so funny?"

"You are! You get any more jealous and you're going to bruise those peas." She laughed at her own joke. "Eva, I thought you never paid attention to gossip? Well, the old bats in town have gotten it wrong this time. Jolene and Paul have been seen together quite a bit lately, but there is nothing juicy going on. In three weeks' time, Jolene is going to have a big white wedding and become Mrs. Elmer Olinger. She been talking to Paul because she wanted him to officiate."

"Bud Olinger and Jolene?" I gasped in disbelief. "He must be twice her age!"

"More than that," Ruby reported gleefully. "He's sixty-three, same age as my dad. But, I guess he's still, well . . . let's just say he's as much of a man as he ever was." Ruby winked slyly.

Her expression was so knowing and comical that I couldn't help but laugh. "How come you know so much? Ruby, you are making this up. You should be ashamed," I scolded her halfheartedly.

Her eyes widened, and she held up her right hand Boy Scout fashion. "I swear it's true. Clara Johnson is remaking Mrs. Bergen's old wedding dress to fit Jolene. She's putting lots and lots of tiny tucks in front so nobody will notice the little surprise underneath the lace."

"Oh, now you're just being mean," I scoffed, returning my attention to the unshelled peas. "If she was really going to have a baby, why would she want to attract attention to the fact with a fancy wedding?"

"I believe it is known as a diversion." Again Ruby winked knowingly, reaching into the bowl to snatch a handful of peas and pop them into her mouth before I could slap her hand. "Maybe they think a big ceremony will distract everyone. Besides, Mrs. Bergen has always counted on her baby having a beautiful white wedding with flowers and cake and everything. Something she can show off about for years to come." I still had my doubts about the whole thing, but Ruby seemed sure of her facts.

"Clara told me that Jolene told her they are going on a long honeymoon tour all over the country," Ruby added through a mouthful of raw peas. "They'll drive off in a cloud of rice, and in a few months' time Bud and his bride will motor back into Dillon with a trunk full of souvenirs and a precious bundle that looks real big and healthy for a seven-month baby."

"Ruby, you're terrible." I grinned despite myself. "That's an awful story to tell."

"What's so awful about it?" Ruby retorted. "Jolene will end up with a baby and, before too many years go by, all the money Bud's been hoarding by living cheap as a bachelor farmer. Bud will get a young wife and a reputation as a rogue that will win him the jealous respect of every man in town. On top of that, I think they really care for each other. Seems like a nice arrangement to me."

"I can't decide if you are being romantic or practical," I said.

"It's a good balance," she answered pointedly. "You should try it sometime."

Jolene and Bud were married on a Saturday in late September. Practically the whole town came to watch. By Dillon standards, where weddings were generally buttoned up in five minutes without benefit of bridesmaids or organ accompaniment, and the bride usually spent the morning after the wedding night frying eggs for the groom's breakfast, it was a really elegant affair. The invitations were printed on white paper so thick it seemed more like shirt cardboard than stationery. I couldn't help but be impressed. Practically the whole town was invited. However, Mama refused to go. She said she couldn't imagine what Bud was thinking and that it was bad enough, a man his age marrying a little snit young enough to be his daughter, but having the nerve to dress up in a suit and invite half the town to eat cake and watch while he made a fool of himself was beyond her understanding.

"I'd just as soon get an invitation to see him and Jolene parade down Main Street buck naked. Anyway, I never liked the Bergens much. They're a snooty bunch. Always thought they were better than everybody else, and this proves it. I suppose you're going to go, Eva?"

"Well, it would be rude not to have at least one of us go, don't you think?" Mama grunted disapprovingly but didn't disagree with me.

Mama was right about people not liking the Bergens. They owned the hardware and feed store in town, which meant they were better off than most, and Mr. Bergen was always happy to share exactly how much better off that might be. Mrs. Bergen was the kind who was always pushing herself into some committee where she wasn't wanted to begin with and then lobbying to get herself elected chair. I had been five years ahead of Jolene in school, but that didn't stop her from once lobbing a green apple at my head so hard it nearly knocked me unconscious. All the Bergen kids were mean like that.

However, none of that stopped folks less hypocritical than Mama from showing up to see the spectacle. People who wouldn't have invited a Bergen onto the front porch for a glass of tea if it had been two hundred degrees in the shade dressed up and brought presents to the church because they'd never seen a fancy wedding, except at the picture show, and didn't know when they'd get another chance.

Despite what I'd said, good manners and curiosity weren't the only reasons I wanted to go. Paul would be there, and I wanted to see him. Ruby said she couldn't see any good reason why I didn't fall in love with him, and sometimes I thought she must be right, but it was too soon. I was not ready to love anyone, though I missed Paul's friendship very much. Maybe meeting up with him on a fine day, a happy wedding day where we could talk about the weather and the bride's dress, would give us a way to begin talking again without being too serious. Maybe we could pick up where we left off without needing to discuss painful things. It seemed worth a try.

As it turned out, Ruby had a cold the day of the wedding and couldn't come, but I put her name on the card of the gift along with mine and promised to tell her about every detail of the ceremony. There hadn't been much time, but I had run up a quilt on the machine in Jolene's wedding colors, peach and green. It was nice, but for sheer spite I made it a crib size, just to hint to Jolene that she wasn't fooling anybody. Considering my own past, I suppose I was the last one who could throw stones, but I'd never completely forgiven her for the apple-throwing incident. Besides, as I sat in the third pew of the church and studied the bride's middle under the folds of delicate white lace, it seemed to me that Jolene would be needing that baby quilt in only five months, not six like Ruby had calculated.

Paul officiated, wearing his best white lace and linen vestment, the one his Aunt Cornelia had made for his ordination, that he jokingly referred to as his "party frock." Jolene had chosen a full church service, complete with sermon, instead of the short recitation of vows that was usually performed at Dillon weddings. I guess it gave more of a chance to show off the dress, flowers, and scene her mama had spent so much money and effort orchestrating. Paul took his text from First Corinthians, Chapter 13, the part about the qualities of love, and read the verses in a strong, clear voice while the wedding guests squirmed uneasily in their pews; I knew why. It seemed awfully sentimental and slightly ridiculous to read something so romantic aloud, especially in reference to this slightly comic May-December coupling. Actually, I considered Jolene to be more in the July or August of her life than the spring, but no matter. People in Dillon looked on marriage as a desirable and practical necessity of survival. Of course, if affection and attraction or even love entered into the arrangement, so much the better, but it wasn't something you expected.

Riley Jenson, who was sitting next to me, leaned over to his wife, Velma, and whispered, "Well, one good thing. Least now Bud's got a himself a suit as is fit to be buried in. Looks like he might need it soon." Velma elbowed him to hush but grinned at him for having the sass to say what everyone in the church was already thinking.

It really was a lovely wedding. The bride looked beautiful, everyone agreed on that, as they have at every wedding since time began. People discussed the service briefly as they ate cake and drank punch in the side garden of the church, and then, as always at that time of year, the talk turned to weather and crop yields. It had been a good year, wet in spring, warm in summer, and everybody had gotten their wheat in unharmed by sun or hail. If a person never read the newspaper, you'd never know that the country was on the brink of war. I mentioned this to Riley, who was standing, eating a second piece of cake and looking uncomfortable in a new pair of shoes Velma must have made him buy for the occasion.

"Never read the papers myself," he said with his mouth full of cake. "All the news that matters is in the Almanac, anyway." If I hadn't been from Dillon, I'd have smiled at his humor, but being a resident, I knew he wasn't joking.

I drifted away, looking for a place to sit down. My leg was beginning to ache from standing so long. As though reading my thoughts, Paul came to the rescue carrying two folding chairs. He opened them under the lacy shade of a tree and invited me to sit down. "I heard you were back," he said. "Was it a good trip?"

"It was fine. Thanks. I must be getting old." I groaned, easing myself into the chair. "I used to be able to stand all day and it never bothered me."

"Oh no," he said gently, "not you. Not yet. It's just when you're standing in a crowd of people like this, doing nothing, talking about nothing, your mind has to keep occupied so it takes inventory and notices all the little pains that you don't take time to consider when you're working." He smiled broadly. "That's what I tell myself, anyway, and I'm already past forty. How old are you, Eva?"

I laughed. "Didn't anyone ever tell you that women don't like to talk about their age?"

"Yes, I think I heard that somewhere, but what a silly notion. We should be proud of our age. Each year we survive is a testament to personal initiative."

"Or stubbornness. You don't sound much like a pastor," I said with smiling disapproval. "I thought we owed each day to Providence."

"Just so, but it doesn't hurt to have something to say for yourself," he reasoned. "God says if we're lukewarm, He spews us out of his mouth. I interpret that to mean we are meant to stir things up a little, change things, hopefully for the better. That's what my father always preached. You see, I come from a long line of troublemakers." For a moment a cloud passed over his gaze, and he was far away; then he shivered as though suddenly chilled. He quickly shook off the mood and, smiling again, leaned toward me and whispered conspiratorially, "So, how old *are* you?"

"Thirty-five, but I feel forty-five," I said with a sigh.

Paul nodded in mock solemnity. "Well, you have lived through a lot in a short lifetime."

"Oh, I don't know," I surveyed the wedding guests, poor and shabby in carefully ironed best dresses and shoes polished to brilliance in an attempt to camouflage any worn spots of leather. "Everybody has, if you think about it."

"Yes," he said and sat silent. I knew he was waiting for me to tell him about my trip to Des Moines, but I couldn't. The subject was still too raw.

"Your sermon was nice," I commented.

Paul chuckled sardonically, "Ah, yes. I could see how riveted everyone was." He smiled and stretched his legs out to their full length, closed his eyes, and tipped his face skyward, enjoying the warmth of the afternoon sun. The full light of the day revealed the creases around his eyes and face, and I couldn't help but think that his age looked well on him.

"No," I protested sincerely. "I think they liked it just fine, but it's not the sort of thing we discuss in Dillon. You should know that by now, Paul. We feel things as deeply as anyone else, I guess. We just don't talk about them, that's all."

"Really?" he said facetiously, keeping his eyes closed against the afternoon sun but raising his eyebrows in feigned surprise. "Actually, I've noticed that. Still, I think everybody would be better off if they talked about love before they slip and find themselves falling into it without knowing what it is—or worse yet," he said, squinting through one opened eye and training it on me, "mistaking it for something it's not. I think Saint Paul's definition is very nearly perfect: 'love is patient, kind, is not jealous, or self-seeking, or easily provoked; love bears all things, believes all things, endures all things.' There is hardly anything missing."

"My mama and papa were like that," I murmured understandingly. "There wasn't anything fancy or poetic about the way my folks loved each other, but it was very complete. Something you could count on."

Paul pulled in his legs and sat up straight again. "But there is one thing the apostle didn't mention specifically, perhaps because it seems so obvious." He hesitated for a moment and turned his gaze toward me. "Real love is requited, Eva. You cannot love someone so completely, so selflessly, as you have tried to, unless the other person is as giving as you. Anything less isn't love; it's obsession. It's waste."

"Paul, I really don't want to talk about this right now." I shifted uncomfortably in my chair, noticing the dull ache had returned to my leg.

"Did you see him?" he asked, his voice lowering to an irritated whisper.

"Yes," I hissed in annoyance. "And I am back, so I think that should tell you all you need to know. Please don't ask me any more questions."

He angled his chair to face mine more fully and leaned in toward me. For a moment I thought he was going to reach out and take my hand, but he held himself back. "Eva, I *know* what love is, what it costs. It's a price I'd be glad to pay, if only you'd let me. We could be so happy together. Even though you won't talk about it, I can see it in your face, that you finally know the truth. Lindbergh doesn't love you. But I do."

My heart sparked in anger at him, furious partly that he wouldn't leave me alone but more because he knew me too well. The cruelest thing I could have said sprang thoughtlessly from my mouth. "You said it yourself, Paul. Love isn't enough. It has to be returned; anything less is a waste."

Paul face went so pale, so quickly, he looked as though he'd had a bucket of ice water thrown on him. I was instantly ashamed of myself.

"Oh," he fumbled awkwardly and shifted away from me in his chair. "I am sorry. I feel very foolish. All this time I thought it was him, and that you and I . . ." He rose from the chair. "Forgive me, Eva. I hadn't realized how you felt."

I was absolutely mortified by my behavior. With all my heart I wanted to say something that would erase all the hurt I'd caused him, but that was impossible. The best I could manage was an blundering apology. "Paul, I'm sorry. Please. Please, sit down. I didn't mean that I don't care for you. I honestly don't know how I feel right now. You made me so mad, I wanted to say something to hurt you. Don't leave," I pleaded. "We are friends. Can't we leave it at that?"

He stared at me for a long moment and then finally took his seat. "All right," he said, his voice filled with resignation. "We are friends. I'm sorry about the other. I won't mention it again."

A silence settled between us, gaping and clumsy, as though we had suddenly become strangers. I racked my brain to think of some small talk that would break the tension and remembered Nils. "How is your brother and his work? Have you had another letter from him?"

The distant looked passed across his face again, cold and close and resigned. His mind was far across the ocean where his questions lay unanswered. "No, not for a long time. Weeks and weeks." The muscles on his cheek twitched, and I could see his jaw tighten as though he were chewing on something tough. "I think he must be dead." He spoke dully, flatly, as a man in shock.

"Paul, don't say that!" I insisted. "Don't even think a thing like that. You know how slow the mails are now. His letter could be lost, or he could be traveling. There are a million things that could have happened."

"Yes," Paul said, nodding, "a million things could have happened, but I don't think they did. Sometimes, when you are very, very close to someone, you can sense their presence, even across an ocean, and once they are gone there is a hole. You can't explain it exactly, but you feel it, inside. A hole." Paul pressed his hand to his chest and left it lying there, still as a man taking an oath. "You understand what I mean?"

I nodded.

"I have this hole here for Nils. For some weeks. I've tried to explain it away, wish it away, but there it is." Slowly, his hand dropped down to his side, as though he was suddenly overcome by weakness. "There is just me now."

A million things could have happened to Nils, but Paul believed his brother was dead, and while he might have been wrong, believing it was just as painful as knowing for sure. As long as I had known Paul, I had never seen him less than certain of every word, gesture, and of God's ultimate justice. But now, looking at his face, creased with despair, I knew that he was as human as I, vulnerable and struggling with seeds of doubt. A tenderness I hadn't known I felt for him pooled inside me and left me feeling confused and inept. I weighed and measured words that might bring him some relief, but the phrases all sounded trite in my mind.

His eyes focused a long way off, as though the guests were all gone and it was just him, sitting alone on a chair under a tree, spilling his worst fears on a deaf wind. I could see the crowd, the bride, the members of the Naomi Circle standing with heads together, occasionally glancing disapprovingly toward our corner, wondering why the pastor and the cripple of tarnished reputation stayed squirreled away together for so long. *To hell with them all,* I thought.

Hiding my hand behind my skirt, I dropped it down to meet his and pressed it in my own, hoping to bring him some measure of warmth and comfort in a solitary place, but he drew back from my touch, and I knew, no matter what Paul said, we were not friends anymore, we couldn't be. We had passed the point where such common definitions would suffice. Paul refused to make it easier for me by pretending.

The sun was near setting when I got back from the wedding. The house was silent. Mama was napping in her rocker, and Ruby was nowhere to be seen, probably in bed out in the caboose nursing her cold. Someone had left a brown cardboard box addressed to me sitting on the kitchen table. I opened it right away but didn't have to tear back the wrappings to know what I'd find inside. My quilt, the story I'd stitched for Slim, lay new and untouched under three layers of white tissue. That was all. There was no return address.

The next day I started a fire in the trash-burning barrel out near the chicken yard. I opened each of the manilla envelopes I'd collected over the years and, one by one, fed Slim's clippings into the flames, then stepped back and watched the ash rise on a cloud of warm air and disappear into the four winds.

Chapter 20

Morgan got his pilot's license on December 3rd, 1941. The country went to war within the week, and without asking my opinion, Morgan joined the Marines. He was among the first to be shipped out. Since he was already a pilot, the U.S. Armed Forces were especially happy to welcome him into their ranks. When he wired me the news, I was angry. "He might have at least asked me," I fumed to Ruby.

"He might have," she replied, "but if he had, he wouldn't be Morgan. Besides, he'd never have thought for a moment you'd want him to hesitate in doing the right thing. All the boys are joining up. Did you raise Morgan to be less courageous than they are?"

"Of course not, it's just that . . . What if something happens to him?" I whispered. "I couldn't bear it."

Ruby's voice softened. "I know, but we can't show our feelings. It won't help anything if we let him see we're worried." When I saw my friend wipe a tear on the corner of her apron, I wondered if she would be able to heed her own advice. Then she took a deep breath, smiled, and we both laughed through our tears.

"All right, now." Ruby said. "Enough of that. He's going to be fine. Let's forget all this foolishness and get back to work."

Morgan stayed at school long enough to finish his exams, no point in losing a whole semester's work, and came home flying his own plane just three days before he had to report to boot camp.

It was a strange visit, all joy and apprehension and silver tinsel; Morgan was filled with excitement and fear and feigned bravado; Mama and Ruby and I were trying to pretend it was a normal holiday, but knowing it was much more precious than that. Ruby must have given him a dozen pairs of socks. "I hear it gets cold in Germany," she said.

Mama gave him a pair of leather gloves and Papa's gold watch, the one she'd been saving for him until he graduated college. We were all in a hurry to show him how we felt. It seemed urgent not to hold back anything in those days. I gave him the quilt I had carried to Des Moines. "I don't know if they'll let you keep it on your bed in the army," I said, "but maybe you can hide it under your regular blanket, and it'll remind you of home a little. Be careful with it, now. If you take care, it should last a lifetime."

"It's beautiful, Mama. Look, there's you and me, standing next to the house." He smiled at the tiny figures. "But who is flying the plane?"

"Well, that's you, too," I lied. "It's a dream quilt, the boy you were and the man you've become."

"Mama, you are some kind of artist." He leaned down and gave me a smacking kiss on the forehead. He was now grown so tall that kissing me on the cheek required a deep bend at the waist. "Don't you worry, Mama. I'll bring it back all in one piece, I promise."

We took special pains with Christmas dinner, but the food tasted like chaff in my mouth. Before I could blink it was time for Morgan to leave.

I drove him out to the airfield the next day to say good-bye to the plane before he had to rush off and catch the southbound train. Whitey had agreed to keep an eye on it for him until he got back.

Morgan walked around and around the plane, kicking the tires affectionately, checking the struts, and stroking the wings. "She sure is a beauty." He sighed, patting the fuselage lovingly. "Thank you, Mama, for getting her for me. I'm just sorry I didn't get to take you up in her. As soon as I get back, we'll go for a ride. I want you to know your money wasn't wasted."

"It's a date," I answered as cheerfully as I could manage. "I'm saving all my dances for you."

"How about just one," he said seriously. "It'd be all right with me if you had somebody besides me to dance with. You deserve to have someone around who appreciates you, Mama. Know what I mean?"

"I know." I nodded my understanding. "Maybe someday." I felt how the scales between us were changing a bit and knew the weight of worry was no longer tipped all on my side.

Morgan sighed deeply, took a last look around, and slapped his hand hard against his thigh with cheery finality. "Well, I guess we'd better be going if I'm going to make my train. Don't want to be late and catch hell from the drill sergeant the very first day." He made sounds of leaving, but still he waited. "Funny, all my life I wanted to get away from Dillon and go out into the world, but just now I'd give anything to stay." I didn't have to tell him I felt the same way.

It was cold, standing on the platform waiting for the train. So cold. I couldn't even feel my feet. Couldn't feel anything. As the train pulled slowly out of the station, Morgan leaned out a window and shouted above the whoosh of steam and squeaking metal, "Don't forget, Mama! As soon as I get back we're going flying. Wait till you see Dillon from the air. It's beautiful!"

"I know! I love you!" I shouted back. I tried to run alongside the car to keep him in sight a moment longer, but my cane slowed me down and the platform ran out much too soon. There was no way to keep up with him.

Chapter 21

April 1943

"That'll be a dollar forty with the oil, Miz Eva."

I dug the coins out of my purse while Mr. Cheevers, his lips pursed with distaste, tried vainly to wipe his hands clean on a red flannel oil rag. With most of the men gone to war, Mr. Cheevers had to pump gas himself instead of hiring boys to do it, and though he'd owned the filling station for as long as I could remember, it was plain he still hated the smell of gasoline on his hands. Not that he'd ever complain. Everybody had to do their part. When we thought of our sons and brothers, husbands and fathers, so far from home, maybe in danger, maybe even . . .

Well, in those days that was a sentence we never allowed ourselves to finish, not even in our minds. Let's just say that Mr. Cheevers would have pumped gas twenty-four hours a day for the rest of his life if it could have brought the war to an end even one hour sooner. That's why I'd planted more wheat and corn than ever that year. Ruby and I and a few high school boys too young for the draft were working the fields by ourselves.

"Where you off to today, Miz Eva?"

"Ellen Carson's house," I said. "Thought I'd drop off a gelatin and see if there is anything I can do. Maybe help with the children."

"Oh." The old man clucked his tongue sympathetically. "I heard about that. Too bad for her with all those little ones."

"Mr. Cheevers"—I smiled sweetly—"I don't suppose you could sell me an extra gallon next time? I wouldn't ask, but it's my mama's birthday in three weeks; she'll be seventy. I've been saving up sugar coupons for a month to make her a cake, and I want to drive up to the lake for a picnic."

Cheevers twisted up his nose and rubbed it with the back of his hand, whether in thought or annoyance I couldn't say for sure. "Now, Miz Eva. That wouldn't be right. You got an "A" sticker, and that entitles you to four gallons of gas. Wouldn't be right for me to sell you more and not do the same for everybody." He frowned as though scolding a child caught hoarding cookies instead of passing the plate. "No, I couldn't sell you an extra gallon. But"—he smiled—"I'll be happy to give you one out of my own ration."

"Oh no, Mr. Cheevers. I couldn't ask you to do that."

"You didn't. I'm volunteering. Shoot, I don't need it anyways. I live right up the road, and the only place me and the missus ever goes is to our daughter Louella's on Sunday for dinner, and we walk there. After one of Louella's Sunday dinners I need the exercise anyways." I blushed and continued protesting, embarrassed by his generosity, but Mr. Cheevers paid no attention.

"Here," he said, "you might as well take it now. I'll put it in a can for you. Tell your mama it was from me and the missus and we hope she has a happy birthday. Maybe you'd better take two. Wouldn't do to have you running out on the way home."

I assured him that one gallon would do just fine, but he wouldn't hear of me not taking a second, so I thanked him and said I'd save him a piece of the cake.

"Don't mention it. Say, how's Morgan doing? I saw in the paper where he'd made lieutenant." I nodded and grinned with pride. "Well, that's fine." He beamed at me. "How's he like it over there in the Pacific? Lots of pretty girls, I'll bet."

"Probably, but he never writes me about them," I said knowingly. "Some things you don't share with your mother. Mostly he says it's hot and sticky. He puts on a clean shirt in the morning and it's a wet rag by lunchtime. Funny, we never figured on him getting sent to there. When I think about Ruby and Mama and me, sending him off with all those pairs of wool socks and then him going to the tropics, it makes me laugh. He must have thought we'd lost our minds, trying to bundle him up like a three-year-old going out in a blizzard."

The old man laughed, showing a mouthful of straight white teeth—which made me realize he wasn't old at all. Only a decade older than me. I'd forgotten how young he'd seemed only a year ago, before the news had come that his only son had been blown apart by a hand grenade at El Alamein. Just one year before, he'd been young, with an optimistic bounce in his step and fingernails that were always trimmed and clean. Now his feet dragged and his nails looked ragged and stained.

"My missus did the same thing with Wally," Mr. Cheevers said, nodding sagely, "and then off they shipped him to Africa. Warm clothes was the last thing he needed. Of course, seems like no matter where you are or what you're doing, a fellow can find a way to complain about the weather. Wally was the same. Always complaining about the heat." We both smiled indulgently at the dissatisfactions of youth. "He didn't mention a thing about girls. You know, I was in Paris during the first war, and I remember how beautiful those French girls were. Pretty, pretty girls," he mused. "I hope Wally met up with a girl like that before he died. He didn't get much time, but I hope he took advantage of what he had. He deserved at least one nice memory."

"I'm sure he did," I said. "He was such a good-looking boy."

"Smart, too," his father agreed. He looked around at the peeling paint on the station front and the pile of old tires that nobody had time to haul away or even stack straight and added, "Wally would have made something of this place. I was going to retire and give it all to him when he got back. Don't know who I'm saving it for now." He shrugged. "Who'd buy it? Takes a young fella to keep up with a business. 'Nother year of this war and there won't be no young fellas left." Without thinking, he blew his nose on the smelly oil rag and then looked stricken as the odor reminded him it wasn't a handkerchief—at about the same moment he realized what he'd just said to a woman with a son away at war.

"I'm sorry, Miz Eva. Don't listen to me. I just . . . Well, I just miss Wally still. Makes me forgetful. Seems like I can't get away from it. No matter how I try to keep it in. I'm sorry. I just want this damned war to be over before we lose any more of our boys."

"So do I, Mr. Cheevers. I'm just sorry it wasn't over soon enough for Wally," I said sincerely.

Cheevers sniffed and nodded. "Thank you. I appreciate that. I do. Does me good just to hear somebody say his name sometimes. Seems like nobody will ever talk about him straight out anymore. Like he never existed. I know they're trying to spare my feelings, but it's too late for that, ain't it."

I shook my head in agreement, and Cheevers forced a brave smile back to his face.

"Anyways, you give your mama our regards. Hope she has a happy birthday."

"Thank you again for the gas, Mr. Cheevers."

The dust boiled up behind the car as I drove toward town. In the rearview mirror I could see Wally's father standing next to the gas pump, unconsciously rubbing his hands together, staring upward as though what he was looking for might be coming straight at him out of the shimmering heat of a summer sky.

Despite the heat, a shiver ran up my spine, and I drove a little faster.

The aspic salad I'd made for Ellen Carson was beginning to melt by the time I reached her front door. I was annoyed at myself for not taking the heat into account when I'd decided what to bring, but it probably wouldn't matter anyway. I couldn't imagine she'd feel like eating anything.

Word had spread quickly about Ellen's husband, Jim, being captured and sent to a Japanese prisoner-of-war camp. The rumors that circulated about how the Japanese treated captured Americans were pretty grim. Ellen would no doubt be imagining the worst, and who was to say her fears weren't well founded? I wasn't sure what I'd say when I saw her, but maybe knowing people cared enough to stop by would be comforting. At least the children, who were too young to understand what was going on, would enjoy the way the gelatin jiggled on their spoons.

I turned the bell twice. No one answered. Maybe no one was home. I thought for a moment of leaving the salad on the front porch with a note, but if I did that, Ellen might come home to a bowl of peaches and cherries puddling in pool of globby liquid. Just as I was turning to leave, the door opened to reveal Paul, wearing an apron over his shirt and clerical collar and balancing two-year-old Alice Carson on his left hip. I blushed in embarrassment and surprise at seeing him after so long, but it was impossible not to smile at the picture he made.

"Am I speaking to the lady of the house?" I asked seriously, and he smiled self-consciously. I was so glad to see him.

"You've caught me out of uniform, I'm afraid," he said, sheepishly holding out the embroidered edge of the clearly feminine apron. "Ellen was feeling tired with so many visitors stopping by. I told her to take a nap and I'd watch the children. The older ones are playing in the backyard, but as long as I was here I thought Alice and I could do the washing up."

"That was thoughtful of you. Not many men would have thought of it."

"Entirely selfish, I assure you. I long to be of some real use, but I fear that most of the time I'm just in the way. When you think of it, at times like these waking up to clean dishes is probably more consoling than listening to all the sermons I could preach. Anyway, it's something."

It was awkward with just the two of us. We had seen each other at church, of course, but that was all. A few of months after our conversation at the wedding, he had gotten word that his brother had been arrested and shot as a member of the Dutch Resistance. Nils was the last family member Paul had in the world; it broke my heart to think how alone he must have felt. I wrote him a sincere letter of sympathy, hoping to console him and break the ice that had formed between us, but the stilted, formal note of thanks he'd sent back let me know that my overtures were unwelcome. Once or twice he stopped by the house to bring mama a precious bag of coffee or some flowers, but he always came when he knew I would be gone and left before I returned. I couldn't blame him. Why would he want to see me? I'd been so cruel.

Without thinking, I blurted out, "I've missed you," and blushed a deep red, realizing it was true.

"Good," Paul answered seriously. "I had hoped you would."

His face looked so stern that I couldn't help but laugh. "You always say just what you think, don't you?"

"It is a flaw of mine."

"Maybe that's what I've missed about you."

"Well, it's something at least," he said, shifting Alice to a more comfortable position on his hip. "Why don't you come in out of the heat? There are people who say I make a really wonderful glass of iced tea. You could have one, and after you leave it would give you something else to miss about me. Besides, one more moment out in this heat and we'll be able to drink whatever you've got in there," he nodded toward my bowl, squinting doubtfully at the melting gelatin.

"It looks pretty awful, doesn't it?" I sighed, examining my ruined salad.

"Yes," he conceded. "Maybe if we put it in the icebox, it will resurrect itself. Come on in." He held open the screen door and stepped aside to let me pass.

Ellen's icebox was already stuffed with casseroles and cakes. Obviously I was not the first to drop by with condolences. I wedged my dish in with the others. The kitchen was cool and tidy. Newly washed glasses sat on the counter in sparkling rows. Paul had lined them up like columns of shiny soldiers. He saw me looking at them.

"Too fussy, I know," Paul said as he sat Baby Alice down at the table with a bowl of gelatin and a spoon. "I hate to admit it, but I've started lining up my spice bottles in alphabetical order. The rigidity of old age."

"You're just organized," I reasoned. "There's nothing wrong with that. Most of life is so unpredictable, it's nice to know exactly where the cinnamon is when you want it. There isn't much else we can count on."

"Especially in times like these," he agreed, rubbing his tired face with his hand, as though trying to rub out the lines of worry written there. "Sometimes," he admitted, "I think I can't go on, that if I have to bury one more mother's son or comfort one more widow I will just give up, take a walk out of town, and keep walking until I reach a place where they've never heard of war."

"But you'd never do that," I assured him.

"No." He sighed as he stirred a cloud of sugar into a pitcher of tea. "I only fantasize about it. As little as I have to offer, people look to me for answers. They think I know so much more than I really do. I can't let them down, so I just mumble my little prayers and hold their hands. I do what I can and rely on God for the rest, but I can't help wishing He'd made me more equal to the task."

"In what way?" I asked.

"To begin with," he said thoughtfully. "I'd like to be a better speaker, or a more agile one. I think too much. People want answers, but for me, every answer begets ten more questions. I'd also like to be more spontaneous. Then maybe I'd be have the courage to stop dreaming about things and just do them."

"Such as what? Walking out of town and never coming back?" I teased.

"Oh, but that's not really a dream, more an indulgence. Lately, I have a favorite story I tell myself." He stopped stirring the tea and closed his eyes, as though conjuring a vision in his mind. "I dress up in a suit, shoes very shiny and hair neatly combed, then I walk to your house and rap my knuckles firmly on the door. You answer, looking surprised to see me and without a moment's hesitation I say something like, 'Eva, you are a fool. You say you don't love me, and for a long time I believed it. At first I was embarrassed and I kept my distance. Then I was angry. But the more I thought about it, the more I realized the truth. You said you didn't love me, but that isn't quite right, is it?'" He opened his eyes again and looked at me directly, pulling me into the scene, making the dream real.

"'You don't know if you love me or not because you've never given me a chance. You're afraid that if I got too close you might find out if you really do care for me, and that terrifies you. I don't completely understand why. I don't think you do, either, but I know Lindbergh is part of it. To hell with him. He's not here. I am, and I'm not giving up. I'm coming to your house every week to call, whether you want me to or not, until you know me well enough to tell me truthfully whether you could love me.'"

His face was flushed, and his voice was strong, filling the room, demanding an answer. Baby Alice sat transfixed as he spoke, as though he were an actor in a play, her spoon frozen midway between the bowl and her mouth.

I was as drawn in as Alice. Twin flames of uncertainty and pleasure rose inside me. I was surprised to realize that pleasure was the stronger of the two.

Paul paused for a moment, and his breathing became more settled. "That's what I would say," he continued gently, "if I were the heroic, noble orator I'd like to be, but I'm not. Instead, I've been waiting, hoping that somehow we'd run across each other in a private moment. I'm not eloquent, Eva, or heroic, but if you'll give me a chance, you might come to care for me as I do you." He straightened his shoulders and spoke in a formal, measured voice. "Miss Eva, may I come to call?"

I felt a little embarrassed. It was silly, at my age, to think of opening the door to romance. Then a picture of Mr. Cheevers punctured my thoughts, and I saw him as I'd left him, as though he stood there still, alone and staring into the sky. *If I had only remembered how short life is,* he seemed to say. *How unsure. If I had only realized, what would I have done differently?*

But did I love Paul? I had loved Slim completely, instantaneously, helplessly. Our love was large and torrential, a river that swept me along with it, no use resisting or trying to swim in another direction. That was what I knew of love. What I felt for Paul was so different, a cool drink instead of a raging flood, the comfort of a fireside instead of a blazing inferno. Paul was sincere and present and left no doubt as to how he felt about me. He made me laugh and think about things more deeply than I would have alone. This tenderness I felt for Paul, was that really love? I cared for him too much to offer him a counterfeit affection. Then Papa's voice spoke in my mind, as clearly as it had on that summer night a lifetime before when I'd eavesdropped through the open window. *Real love is with someone who'll be there when the crop fails or your sight grows weak. You can count on it, like the earth under your feet.*

That was Paul. How I missed him, his steadiness, his honesty, his humor, and his kind, kind heart. Paul, trying so hard to make things a little better, polishing glasses to comfort a widow, sharing books and time with a fatherless boy, being my friend, seeing more in me than a checkered past and a cane.

Paul's eyes, so sad, searched my face for an answer. "Please, Eva. I know you don't love me now, but you like me, don't you? It's something to start with. Let's give it a chance, shall we? Just to see how it works out?"

"Oh, Paul, I'm so sorry," I whispered. "What I've put you through. You don't have to come courting." I didn't have to think any longer. The words came pouring from me, without explanation or act of will, and when I spoke them they were as much a surprise to me as they were to Paul. "I don't need to wait anymore. I love you. Will you marry me?"

Paul's face was shocked, and he literally stammered, searching for something to say, but before he could, Baby Alice dropped her spoon. It clattered metallically onto the table, spilling bright globs of gelatin everywhere while she clapped her chubby hands together and chortled with laughter.

The noise startled us both. Instinctively, I jumped up to find a rag to clean up the mess, but Paul grabbed my wrist. "Leave it," he whispered. He pulled me close and kissed me. I kissed him back while the baby giggled merrily, squishing wiggling lumps of gelatin though her finger and rubbing them into her hair as the distant sound of happy children's games floated in from outside and rested on us like a blessing.

When we stepped back from that first perfect kiss, any remaining doubts popped and vanished like transparent, trifling soap bubbles on a summer breeze. I loved Paul. How simple, how absolute. I wanted us to be married right that minute.

"A justice of the peace could perform the ceremony today," I babbled. "We could go to the house and you could tell Mama and Ruby while I change into my Sunday dress. You remember, the blue one? It's a few years old, but it still looks nice. We could drive to Liberal and be married before the sun goes down. Oh, Paul!" I stopped short, suddenly plagued with worry. "What about the deacons? Do you think they'll let you get married? To me, I mean. There's bound to be talk about me and Morgan. . . ." I could feel heat and color rising again in my cheeks.

Paul smiled indulgently and silenced my worries with his lips, kissing me slowly and gently but with a patient intensity that made me feel I might disappear into the perfect curve of his body. Still holding me in his arms, he lifted his lips softly from mine.

"Don't think so much just now, Eva. We'll work it out. I'm not letting anything get in our way." He spoke with such utter confidence it was impossible not to believe him.

"We will drive to the farm and tell your family today," he continued. "Then we'll send Morgan a telegram. It wouldn't be right to go forward without his blessing. I want to marry you as soon as possible, but in front of a minister, not a judge. And you must have a bouquet of flowers and a new dress. A *white* dress." He spoke firmly, his eyes square on mine as though to say that no matter what shame people in town might try to heap on my head, any sins I may have committed were long forgiven and truly forgotten. And suddenly, in the time it took for a look to pass between us, something changed inside me forever. I *felt* forgiven, by Paul, by God, by myself. I smiled, but it was impossible to keep a tear from running down my cheek.

Paul reached out, caught the droplet on his fingertip, and studied it for a moment, as though it were something more precious than a simple teardrop. "Eva, I love you more than my life. We are going to have a beautiful wedding. After waiting for you so long, I want there to be no question but that we are properly joined by God. One flesh, forever."

He pulled me again into the long arc of his body. Did I have any objections to his plans? I don't remember. If I did they were forgotten in the warmth of his embrace.

Chapter 22

As the station clock struck midnight, the hulking engine pulled up like an enormous black dragon and, with an exhausted shudder, expelled a cloud of steam, enveloping the platform in mist. I felt like a character in a fairy tale, joyful but slightly befuddled. Even with the pressure of Paul's hand supporting me as I climbed into the passenger coach and the sound of the conductor's cheery welcome, I kept thinking it was all too wonderful to be real, but when I looked out the window of the compartment, Mama and Ruby were there, beaming and mouthing, "Good-bye Mrs. Van Dyver!" as they tapped on the window, as though to remind me of my new name. It was all true.

Our beautiful wedding had been performed a short two hours before. Paul asked a fellow minister from Liberal, the kindly Reverend Doctor Horton, to marry us in the tiny chapel of his church. Dr. Horton's twinkling eyes and ready smile reminded me of Papa. When he wrapped Paul's and my right hand in the silken bonds of his clerical stole and declared that "those whom God has joined, let no man put asunder," I couldn't help but feel that Papa himself was present and giving us his blessing.

Though the ceremony included only the four of us, with Mama and Ruby as witnesses, Paul had insisted that we "do it properly." He put aside his clerical collar for the occasion, looking more handsome than ever in a new charcoal gray suit, a shirt with a soft collar, and a blue silk necktie. I carried a bouquet of purple lilacs and white roses and wore a new white traveling suit. Mama had made it herself, though Ruby and I helped with the cutting and sewing of the trim because Mama's arthritis was bothering her. Ruby thought we should sew a veil onto the hat, but I wasn't so sure.

Mama was on my side. "Nonsense," she said. "Eva doesn't need to hide behind any veil." She put aside the skirt she was hemming, took my hand in hers, and said, "You look him in the eye when you're saying those vows, Eva. Let him see you just as you are. It's the only honest way to begin."

Dr. Horton had kindly left out the huge sprays of flowers that had been used for a big wedding that had taken place earlier that day and had thought to bring all the candelabras out of storage for the occasion. The chapel glowed with the light from dozens of white pillared candles. Mrs. Horton played the wedding march on the organ as Paul and I walked up the aisle together, and I leaned on him lightly for support, my cane made unnecessary in his presence. Even Jolene Bergen could not have dreamed of a wedding half so elegant as ours.

We knelt down together, and the benevolent old minister breathed his blessing over our union while Ruby and Mama sniffed back tears. We recited our vows: love . . . honor . . . cherish . . . forever . . . with eyes locked, promising ourselves to each another with no reservations. When I looked into Paul's eyes I saw what I had seen there from the first moment I'd met him, honesty, and I knew I could trust that every vow he made to me was true and would last. I felt the same about my vows to him. It could not have been more perfect.

Now we were traveling all the way to California, where Morgan would be waiting for us, on leave for the first time in nearly two years. The Pacific was so far away to begin with, we didn't want to waste more of Morgan's precious leave time in traveling to Oklahoma, so San Diego seemed the perfect meeting place. On top of that, it was a marvelous excuse to take a honeymoon trip. As we boarded the train, I wasn't sure which pleased me more, being Paul's wife or seeing my son. Then it occurred to me there was no need to choose between the two, and I laughed with pleasure.

I was so busy waving to Mama and Ruby that I didn't notice the compartment until we were well out of the station. It was beautiful, all polished wood and chrome trim, with a paneled closet to store our clothes, two soft, upholstered seats facing each other across a tiny table, and a not quite double bed built right into the wall. "It's lovely! " I exclaimed. "Can we afford it?"

"On a minister's salary? Of course not," Paul said in mock serious-ness as he came up behind me, wrapping his arms around my waist, and kissed my neck playfully. "I don't care what it cost. All that mat-ters is that you are happy. I've waited too long to allow for any in-terruptions. I don't intend to let you leave this room or this bed for the entire trip."

I turned toward him, placed one hand on his chest and loosened his tie with the other. "Not even for meals?" I asked coyly.

"I don't know," he breathed, reaching over to turn off the light. "Let's decide when we get hungry."

But we weren't hungry for a long, long time. In some sense, I've never been hungry again. That night I discovered that Paul's touch, so gentle, so adoring and unhurried, filled all the empty caverns of my soul and made me want to do the same for him. When morning came, my heart stirred at the sight of his head sleeping peacefully on the pillow next to mine, and I wanted him again, even more than before, but I didn't wake him. There was no hurry. I knew he would be there that day and the next and the next; we had our entire lives to love one another. We could count on it, like the earth under our feet.

Morgan's sparkling eyes and ready grin were the same, but the thin, lanky frame of his boyhood had been layered over with muscles, topped with broad, powerful shoulders—he had the body of a soldier. Handsome and confident in his dress uniform, he scooped me off the station platform and squeezed me tight. We were neither of us too proud to cry a little.

My eyes were still full as I held him at arm's length for a better look. "When did you get so good-looking, Morgan? Were you always this tall?" I covered my mouth with my hand and took in a deep breath to stop myself from crying again. "I can't believe you're actually here. I didn't think I'd see you for another six months at least!"

"I know! We were lucky. Your letter came at a good time. I've been assigned to a new unit, the 475th fighter group, but it won't be activated for a few days yet. I convinced the C.O. it was better to let me take my leave now when there's nothing going on." He flashed that genuine, winning smile of his, so like Papa's, and it made me think that even battle-hardened commanders might not be immune to Irish charm. "The bad news is, I've got to leave to report to my new group in Australia in three days. I'm sorry there's not more time."

"Oh, never mind about that." I squeezed him again, to make sure he was real. "It's just so good to be together." I rested my hand on my son's muscled forearm at the same time as I reached for my husband's hand, pulling us into a circle. "We're going to have the best honeymoon in the world! Just the three of us," I said. We all laughed.

"Australia!" Paul shook his head in amazement. "That's half a world away."

"Oh, that's just where we're training." There was a little edge of pride in Morgan's voice. "Once we're ready we'll get a base in the islands, probably New Guinea. The Allies just got it back, and Uncle Sam wants to make sure we keep it." The determined look on Morgan's face convinced me they would.

I tried to calculate the distance in my mind but couldn't. Like Paul said, half a world away. Beating back the Japanese. Tiny planes tossed out like so much confetti over an infinite and unforgiving ocean.

The conversation lagged for a moment, but Morgan leaped in to lighten the mood before the atmosphere became too chill. "I almost forgot!" he exclaimed, grabbing Paul's hand and priming it like a pump handle. "Congratulations! When I got the telegram that you two wanted to get married, I let out such a whoop other guys heard me all the way in the mess hall! I think it's great, Paul, I really do. You and Mama are meant to be together. I've thought so for a long time."

Paul smiled and murmured his thanks. It was so wonderful to see the two men I loved getting on so well, I wasn't even bothered that they were talking about me as though I weren't there.

"I'd just about given up hope of her ever giving me the time of day," Paul said.

"Well, she's stubborn." Morgan nodded understandingly. "Always was. Won't budge an inch until she's made up her mind, yes or no, but once she knows what she wants nobody better get in her way."

"I've noticed that," Paul said slyly. "For years she held me at bay, and then, boom! Out of the blue she shows up and proposes marriage. Well, what could I do?" He held his palms out helplessly. "Imagine how embarrassing it would have been for her if I'd refused." He blinked innocently, as if the whole thing had been beyond his control. "So, here I am, the noose tied round my neck good and tight."

I slapped Paul playfully on the arm. "That's enough of that."

"Ouch! You see how she treats me?" Paul rolled his eyes toward Morgan and winked. "Admit it, Eva. You proposed to me."

"Don't be ridiculous. I have no recollection of any such unladylike event," I lied.

Morgan laughed and looped his arm through mine, picking up our suitcase easily with the other. "Come on, you two, we can continue this argument in the taxi."

Paul took my other arm, and we walked off together, my heart full of the complete picture we made. People walking past would think we were a family. Maybe we were.

Three days flew like an hour. We were so anxious to take advantage of every minute together that we barely slept. We spent a whole day at the zoo. I'd seen pictures of some of the animals in books, of course, but no encyclopedic reference could make you understand the sheer size of an elephant or just how elegant the arc of a giraffe's neck really is. There was a feeling of breathtaking intimacy in watching those beautiful animals just being themselves, like peeking through the window of a stranger's house. I felt a little guilty looking in on their private world, yet I couldn't tear myself away. If a zookeeper hadn't come up and tapped me on the shoulder to remind me it was five minutes till closing, I suppose I never would have left.

The zoo was my favorite, but we also went to the amusement park at Belmont Park, a museum, and took a ferry to Coronado. We had tea in the Hotel Del Coronado, which was so beautiful! I just had to buy a picture postcard to send Mama and Ruby. We went swimming in the ocean, and that was wonderful, too, though I'll admit to being a little scared. I never imagined the pull of the tide could be so powerful. Even after Morgan walked us by the base to impress us with the size of the ships that were in port, it frightened me to think of him sailing to Australia on the vast, uncontrollable sea, but I kept my fears to myself. When I had looked at San Diego on a map, I'd thought that we'd be just a hop, skip, and jump away from Hollywood. Morgan explained it would take hours and hours to get there by bus, so I never did get to see the handprints at Grauman's Chinese Theatre, but that was all right. I did see a woman crossing the street who looked exactly like Claudette Colbert! Of course, it was hard to know for sure from so far away, but I didn't want to get so close that we'd know if it wasn't. Why risk ruining a good story? Papa would have agreed with me.

It was a wonderful trip. I'm convinced that no tourist in California saw more than we did in those three days—but more than anything else, we just enjoyed being together. And how we talked! Walking down the street, riding a bus, through mouths full of hamburgers in diners, shopping for souvenirs, we talked without taking a breath. Morgan wanted to know everything about Mama and Ruby and Dillon. Funny, I had always thought of our lives there as being so dull and predictable that there were no stories to tell, but it wasn't true. We were as small and insignificant as any village on earth, but when I thought about it, there were little dramas unfolding every day in Dillon. Of course, if you weren't from Dillon none of it mattered, but Morgan was hungry for stories from home. He had a million questions. How was Mr. Dwyer's gout? How many bushels to the acre had there been last year? What had everyone said when Tommy Franks rescued his little brother Joey from drowning in an irrigation ditch? We laughed and talked and laughed some more, trying to crowd a year's worth of conversation into a few precious hours. Three days flew by like three minutes.

The last night before Morgan had to report for duty, we didn't get back to our hotel room until after midnight. The hot water ran out during my shower. I was cold and tired and dreading saying good-bye to Morgan in the morning. Paul and I had our first argument.

Paul was already in bed when I came out of the bathroom. "Do you want to get up with me at five and say good-bye to Morgan?" I asked.

"No, the two of you need some time alone. He's been good to include me, but I'm sure there are things you have to say to each other that will be easier if I'm not there."

"Nothing that you couldn't listen in on, I'm sure, but I wouldn't blame you for staying in a warm bed at that hour." I shivered as I did up the last buttons on my nightgown. "It's freezing in here! I thought California was supposed to be warm," I grumbled.

"It is. It's just the water that's cold." He pulled back the covers and made a space for me next to him. "Get in here. It's warm under the blankets."

He wrapped his arms around me, and soon my teeth stopped chattering. Paul yawned, and I echoed him. "Fine pair of newly-weds we are," he said, groaning with exhaustion and rubbing his eyes. "Less than a week after the wedding and so exhausted all we can do is yawn."

"Hmmm," I muttered with my eyes closed. "Most newlyweds are a lot younger than we are, my love. Also, they don't spend their honeymoon trying to see every sight in the state of California and then sitting in a diner and talking to their son until it's so late the waitress tells them they have to leave so she can close up."

"That's true," Paul said.

His voice sounded a little troubled, and I opened my eyes and studied his face.

"You don't mind Morgan being here, do you? I never really asked if this was the way you wanted to spend our trip. Maybe you'd have preferred having just the two of us?"

Paul dismissed that idea with a shake of his head. "Of course not. We've got a lifetime to be alone together."

"Oh, right," I said sarcastically. "Just you and me and Mama and Ruby." I couldn't help but chuckle at my own joke, and Paul joined in.

"And don't forget the entire congregation of the church," he said. "They're always watching us one way or the other."

"Oh, well, that's just Dillon. Everybody watches everybody; everybody talks about everybody. It's our main form of recreation."

Paul smiled and tried to stifle another yawn. "You and Morgan certainly did some talking these last three days. I never knew my wife was so well informed about local gossip."

I snuggled closer in his embrace. The word "wife" still sounded new and wonderful in my ears. "Having Ruby as a best friend helps," I mumbled sleepily. I kissed him good night, rolled over, and spooned myself into the warmth of his chest as I closed my eyes Everything was quiet. In another minute I'd have been dreaming, but Paul wasn't ready to sleep.

"Do you and Morgan ever talk about him?" he said quietly but pointedly. There was no doubt in my mind that the "him" in question was Charles Lindbergh.

I was suddenly wide awake and shifted slightly to the colder side of the bed, my back still turned to Paul. "When he was younger, I always said I would when he was older. Now he is older, I don't see any point to it."

"Don't you think Morgan would like to know?"

"He's never asked me about it." I tried to answer casually, but even I could hear the edge in my voice.

"Of course he's never asked, Eva," Paul said. "You're all he's got. He'd never risk hurting you by asking you about painful things, things that might embarrass you to talk about, but that doesn't mean he doesn't want to know."

"What is there about Charles Lindbergh that's worth knowing? You've said it yourself: the man's a coward and an anti-Semite." I rolled over to face him, daring him to deny my accusation.

Paul sat up. "Eva, there are a lot of things I don't like about the man, but I'm not blind to his accomplishments. Morgan is a lot like him, adventurous, brave, optimistic, and more at home in the air than on the earth. All those wonderful qualities are the legacy his father has left him. I think he deserves to know it." I didn't answer, just stared stonily, but Paul refused to be intimidated by silence.

"I swear, sometimes I don't understand you, Eva," he said, shaking his head. "You kept Lindbergh on a pedestal for years, building him up into something that no one could ever be, hoping that one day, finally, he'd glide into town and claim his son and you. Then, just like that, the adoration is over! You take out your sledgehammer and smash your creation into a million pieces and grind the shards into the dirt."

"Don't you dare lecture me about Charles Lindbergh!" I said. "I was just about the only person on earth who didn't idolize him. Everyone wanted to make him into the Lone Eagle, some mythic creature. I accepted him for what he was, or at least for what I thought he was. Now I see how lucky we were that he left Morgan alone. I'm just protecting my son. He's been through enough already." I lay down and pulled the covers up to my chin, signaling that the subject was closed.

Paul scooted across the bed and settled in next to me, pushing himself up on one elbow. His voice was infuriatingly reasonable but firm. I could see he had no intention of minding his own business. "This isn't about protecting Morgan, Eva. You're furious with Lindbergh, and not even because he abandoned you and Morgan. That at least would make some sense. You're angry because you thought you knew him and you were wrong. You were willing to give him everything in exchange for the honor of being the one person who truly understood him because you thought that meant he loved you. Now you know the truth; the man is an enigma to you, to everyone, and he doesn't love you. Possibly he never did, but that doesn't make him a monster." The hard line of his mouth softened, and he reached out to pull me closer. "No matter what he is or isn't to you, he's still Morgan's father."

I rolled away and sat up on the edge of the bed with my back to him. "Paul, I don't want to talk about this anymore."

"Well, I do." He pushed off the blanket, strode around the bed, and knelt down in front of me, making it impossible to avoid his eyes. "Eva, I won't let you shut me out. When you love someone you share the truth, even the painful parts. You've made it very clear to Morgan where the forbidden zones are. Soon he'll start building up walls of his own to go with the ones he's inherited from you and from Lindbergh. Give him a little time and he'll have constructed such a fortress of secrets that no one will be able to get close. Is that what you want for him?"

I tried to pull away again, but Paul held me fast. There was no getting away from those deep, piercing eyes, and the absence of cover filled me with panic. "This doesn't concern you, Paul!" I cried. "What I tell or don't tell my son about his father is between us. It's a family matter, so just stay out of it!" The ugly words spilled out of my mouth unbidden. Paul's face fell, clearly stung by my attack. His mouth twitched, and for a moment I could see him struggling within himself, fighting off the bitterness and resentment; he won that battle. Without saying a word, he got to his feet, pulled me to mine, and held me in his embrace, tight and close, as though he would never let go.

Anger, punishing silence, even a slammed door would have been easy for me to handle. I could have summoned a controlled response to any of those reactions. Paul's tender retort caught me completely off guard. I felt helpless in the face of his unyielding love. I sobbed in his arms.

We stood that way, wrapped up in each other for the longest

time, until finally my tears were spent and I leaned against him, more in love with this man than ever. He kissed me gently and wiped away the last traces of my tears.

"We are family now, Eva," he said softly. "We both hold the keys to all the doors in our lives; there are no locks between us. I love you, Eva. That won't change no matter what you say to me or to Morgan, but I think you owe him the truth. That's my opinion. You can do with it what you will."

I lifted my hand to his face, pulling it toward mine, finding his lips, pulling him back down onto the bed. As he eagerly followed my lead, I opened myself to him with no restraint, no boundaries, each of us at once yielding and demanding, one flesh forever.

I knew him . . . and he me.

Later, exhausted but unable to sleep, I laid awake for what was left of the night, puzzling over what I would say to Morgan but reaching no conclusion. The night sky began fading from black to misty gray. Taking care not to waken him, I lifted Paul's arm from where it rested on my hip, slid silently from the warmth of the bed, dressed in darkness, and left to meet Morgan in the coffee shop.

Morgan had gotten there first. He waved to me from a booth upholstered in a candy-apple red that gleamed artificially bright and cheerful in the dull dawn light. Morgan's wide, fixed grin told me he was determined to ignore the specter of farewell that stood just outside the door. We ordered breakfast, though when the waitress put the food in front of me I could do little more than pick at the scrambled eggs and push the potatoes from one side of the plate to the other.

We talked about Mama and her birthday picnic at the lake. I told Morgan how Mr. Cheevers had pressed the extra gallons of gas on me, taking care to paint a picture of that kind man that was more amusing than poignant. Morgan said again what a great guy Paul was. I smiled and agreed, but then the conversation lagged. Our silence was tight and uncomfortable, and I could see Paul was right. There were too many things unsaid between us. It was time for Morgan and me to quit protecting each other. I took a deep breath and resolved to tell him everything—but Morgan cleared his throat before I could speak.

"Mama, have you seen Virginia Pratt lately?" He dunked a donut in his coffee with a deliberately casual air.

"Why, no," I answered. "Not recently. I guess she's about ready to graduate, isn't she?"

"Yeah. Next month. She made salutatorian. Oh, damn it!" A soggy crumb from the coffee-soaked donut dropped on his shirt as he took a bite.

"Don't curse," I said automatically in my "mother" voice, handing him a napkin to blot the stain. Morgan grinned.

"Still trying to turn me into a gentleman, Mama?" He dabbed at the spot, but it wasn't helping.

"No. Trying to remind you that you already *are* a gentleman. Here. Give me that." I took the napkin from him, dipped it in my water glass, and gave it back. "See if that works any better." It did. "How do you know so much about Virginia Pratt?"

"She writes me sometimes," he said as he returned his attention to the coffee stain.

"You write back?"

"Sometimes." He shrugged.

This news surprised me, though it shouldn't have. Every mother of an adoring little boy knows there will come a day when she is no longer the most important female in her son's world, but when the moment actually arrives it's a shock. I couldn't help but wonder where the time had gone.

Today was not the day, I realized, to talk about the past, to tell him where he'd gotten those deep gray-blue eyes, so different from mine. Morgan was grown up and living his life, living it in uncertain times. He didn't care about yesterday. His mind was set on today and tomorrow and another pair of eyes, hazel, I remembered, and sparkling with curiosity, placed evenly in a heart-shaped face that bore a delicate pink-and-white complexion, translucent as fine china with the sun shining through it, framed with long red curls. Virginia Pratt. I didn't know her well, but I recalled her as a quiet girl who read a lot—shy, but not painfully so. She'd liked to hide behind her mother's skirts when she was little but would come out and greet adults with a solemn handshake when prompted. A pretty girl. That was the picture imprinted on Morgan's mind. That was the way it should be. Mr. Cheevers would agree, I was certain. I decided then that, no matter what Paul said, today was not the day to tell my son about his real father. Someday, I silently promised myself, when the war was over and Morgan was home for good, there would be no secrets between us. He would know everything. In the meantime all he needed to know was the face of a pretty girl and that I supported his choice.

"She's seems like a sweet girl," I said approvingly. "Must be smart to stand second in the class. Always had real nice manners, I remember." Morgan nodded in agreement and continued blotting the spot that had already completely disappeared. I cleared my throat uncertainly. "Anything you want to tell me?" I asked.

He put down the napkin, took another long drink of coffee, and shook his head. "Not right now. We've talked about . . . you know . . . things," he admitted as a blush of color rose in his cheeks. "She's always wanted to be a teacher. It'd be a shame if she didn't go to college while she has the chance. Besides, she's young yet. It'd be selfish to ask her to wait. It's a long war, and, well . . ." His voice trailed off, and he brushed his hair out of his eyes. "I'm a pilot," he said simply. "You know, the odds aren't good for me, Mama."

"I know," I whispered. My hand rose unbidden to cover my mouth. "So many times I've thought I should have insisted you stay in college. Maybe I shouldn't have let you learn to fly in the first place."

"Mama, you couldn't have stopped me. No one could have. It's just part of me." He leaned in toward me, and his eyes became brighter, as they always had when talking about flight. "When I joined up all I thought about was flying, just me and the plane and blue sky that doesn't end. I never really thought about *why* I would be flying. Not that I didn't understand that there was a war and that I would be in it, but I didn't really know what war was. The newsreels clean it up and make it seem so simple and straight, but there's no color in those pictures. There's no spewing red of blood, or ravenous orange flame that eats tail sections alive, or blue-black ocean that sucks downed planes into the depths and hides them where they'll never be found. A battle reported in black and white is just an outline of the real thing."

"You've grown up fast, haven't you?"

"Eighteen months are like ten years when there's a war on," he said matter-of-factly. "I thought I'd ship out, wrap a white scarf around my neck, shoot down a few zeros from far enough away so I couldn't see the pilots' faces, and win a medal or two. Maybe dance with some fast girls from the USO in my spare time." He raised and lowered his eyebrows meaningfully, and we both chuckled, but then he suddenly became serious. "I never pictured myself being afraid.

"Mama, do you remember Mrs. Hutchinson from church?" Of course I remembered her. She'd been Mama's fourth-grade Sunday school teacher before she'd been mine and Morgan's in turn. She didn't teach anymore, but she was still chair of the altar guild and exerted a lot of influence in the church; for that reason, she was one of the many people I was dreading facing when I returned to Dillon. I doubted she would approve of me as a pastor's wife.

"Well," he continued, "she wrote me a letter after I'd made first lieutenant congratulating me on my promotion and saying how everybody was so proud to have a real live war hero who'd come from Dillon."

"Mrs. Hutchinson is right," I replied. "Everybody in town is proud of you. You're Dillon's first pilot."

Morgan shook his head emphatically, and I could see that he was truly bothered by the idea of people thinking he was something more than he was. "Mama, I'm no hero. I just love to fly, that's all. When I climb into the cockpit and feel the engine hum it's like feeling my own heart beating, and when I lift off from the runway and rise up toward the sun it's like reaching out to touch the door to heaven. As soon as I look down and see the airfield fading off in the distance, I'm afraid, because I know there's a good chance of me or one of my friends not making it back. With all my heart I want to turn back at that moment, but I keep the plane on course because I know I have to. Somebody has to."

"Morgan!" I clucked my tongue in mock distress, careful to keep my tone light. "I think maybe I let you read too many books when you were little. That's the only place where people aren't afraid. Real people are scared every day. Some of them climb under a rock and hide, and others, the good ones, the ones like you"—I smiled—"stuff their fears into a sack and do what they have to do. That might not be too courageous, but it's enough to get the job done, and it takes a lot of heart. So you just let Mrs. Hutchinson send her letters, all right?" Morgan nodded mutely.

"Besides," I joked. "Remember, she's head of the altar guild, and if she didn't spend some of her time writing to GIs she'd probably decide it was time to embroider new altar cloths and start nagging at me to help." I shuddered theatrically at the idea, and we both laughed.

It was getting late. Morgan glanced at his watch, but we already knew he had to go. There was so much more I wanted to say. Instead I smiled and reached across the table to take his hand. "Morgan, how do you suppose that out of the whole world, I got the best young man on the planet as my son?"

He sat a little taller in his seat and impulsively pulled my hand to his lips and gave it a smacking kiss. "I'm glad you came, Mama."

"Nothing in the world could have kept me from it."

Standing outside the door of the coffee shop, unembarrassed by the waitress' obvious and teary-eyed interest in the farewell of a mother and a soldier-son, we hugged and held each other as long as we could. I watched until Morgan turned the corner toward the bus stop that would take him back to the base, then walked quickly in the opposite direction toward the motel, head down, my heels clicking evenly against the sidewalk while I dug in my coat pocket for my handkerchief.

Paul was shaved and dressed when I got back to the room. He was already packing our suitcases. "You don't mind, do you?" he asked. "I thought this way we'd have time for a last walk on the beach before we have to leave for the station. Who knows when we'll get another chance."

Something in that sentence seemed to sum up all the uncertainties of the world. My lip trembled, and Paul dropped the shirt he was folding onto the bed to reach for me, crossing the room in three big steps of his long legs. Grateful for his arms around me, I held back the tears. If Morgan could be brave, so could I.

"I miss him so much already, even worse than before. When he left the last time he was so young, so innocent and confident, almost magical in a way, like nothing bad could ever happen to him. Now, I don't know." I dabbed at my eyes with the handkerchief I held clutched in my hand; it was already quite damp. "He's grown, and he's afraid. It's like he's suddenly become aware of his own mortality and just the knowledge makes him vulnerable. If anything happened to him, what would I do?"

Paul held me tighter and rubbed his hands up and down my back as though trying to warm me after I'd come in out of the cold. "He's going to be fine," he said soothingly, and I could feel the deep bass of his voice rumbling confidently from his chest. "You were right the first time. Nothing will touch him."

"What makes you think so?"

"Because I believe in God and happy endings. Besides he's an eagle's offspring, at home in the sky. Surely that's a lucky talisman for a pilot."

I couldn't help but smile a little. "Are you a pastor or a pagan? Lucky talismans? What kind of creed do you subscribe to?"

"The kind that embraces hope in all its forms and trusts God for all grace," he said sincerely. "How else are we to go on?"

Later, as we walked on the beach, Paul spotted the silhouette of a destroyer slipping silently toward the open sea. It was probably too early in the day to be Morgan's transport; there was no way to know for certain. Standing ankle-deep in a temperate surf, Paul and I held hands and prayed for the safe and rapid return of every mother's son aboard the nameless vessel while the tide teased and swirled gently around our feet with a playfulness that seemed to mock my apprehension. For that moment at least, I felt at peace.

Chapter 23

Of all the things I've ever had to do, forcing myself to walk down the aisle past the gauntlet of staring eyes to take a seat in the front pew, where the minister's wife should sit, on that first Sunday after we got back from San Diego, was the hardest. A week before we left, Paul had informed Mr. Dwyer, who was head of the deacons' board, of our intention to marry and asked him to lead the Sunday service during our honeymoon. According to Paul's report, Mr. Dwyer had been flabbergasted by this seemingly impetuous decision on the part of his normally staid and predictable pastor.

"He sputtered quite a bit and then said he thought we'd better convene an 'emergency meeting of the elders' to discuss the wisdom of such a move and its impact on the congregation. I told him there was only one person I needed to discuss marriage with and that you'd said yes. Then I turned on my heel and left him standing there with his mouth open." When Paul told me the story as we were cocooned in the perfect, tiny world of our train compartment, the bombastic deacon's meddling seemed trivial, a good joke between the two of us. On that Sunday in Dillon I wasn't so sure.

It was impossible to face breakfast that morning, which was

probably just as well. My stomach was so full of butterflies I'm not sure I could have kept anything down, and wouldn't that have made a lovely impression on the congregation? Nothing in Ruby's jokes or Mama's stolid encouragement eased my fears. I was certain Paul would have been able to say something to me that would help, but he'd gotten up and gone to the church before dawn. It was surprising for me to realize how quickly I'd come to value his advice and support. He molded himself into the family easily and immediately, as though we'd been married twenty years instead of two weeks. When we'd moved a full-sized bed into my room and scooted the quilting frame a bit farther into the southwest window corner to make room for Paul's desk and books, his things looked as though they'd always been there. The room seemed suddenly cozier and more welcoming, not crowded at all, and I wondered how I hadn't felt naked in all that empty space for all those years.

Naked was the perfect way to describe my feelings as I pulled myself over the threshold of the church door and through the vestibule to the sanctuary. Mama and Ruby were right behind me, but even so I felt terribly alone. I could feel the heat on my face as I limped toward my seat. Maybe it was my imagination, but the pews seemed full to bursting with curious saints that day, and I suddenly had a horrifying vision of myself tripping and falling in front of everyone. My cane thumped more loudly than it ever had on the worn wooden floorboards, and I was reminded of what a poor congregation we were, not a pane of stained glass or an inch of carpet in the whole place, just simple white walls and woodwork that Paul had painted himself.

Paul smiled encouragingly from his seat near the altar. I sighed in relief when I finally reached the front pew without incident and took my place while the ancient organ groaned out the opening bars

of "Savior, Like a Shepherd Lead Us." I sang along, grateful that
people were watching their hymnals now instead of me.

The choir sang on key, mostly, and Paul preached a good sermon, one of his best, I thought, even squeezing in a couple of jokes
relevant to the text. That was not normally his style, but I had suggested he try adding a little humor to his messages, not by way of
being entertaining, but more to help people translate the lofty-
sounding words and acts of the biblical fathers into terms they
could relate to. It pleased me to see how much more engaged the
congregation became after they'd laughed a bit, leaning in closer toward the pulpit and thoughtfully nodding their agreement when
Paul exhorted them on the urgency of not giving up before the race
had been won. For the first time I thought that even with all my
faults, I might be more of an asset than liability to my husband. As
Paul finished leading the closing hymn and prepared to give the
benediction, to my surprise, Mr. Dwyer stood up, grasped his coat
lapels with both hands, and cleared his throat. Paul was clearly
taken aback by the interruption and shot me a worried glance.

"Pardon me for breaking in, Pastor," the deacon boomed in his
best oratorical style, "but I have something to say on behalf of the
board and the congregation as a whole." My heart pounded appre-
hensively. Disapproving of our marriage, even to the point of calling
a deacons' meeting was one thing, but calling Paul on the carpet because of me, especially in front of the whole church, was too shame-
ful to imagine. What had I gotten him into?

Mr. Dwyer cleared his throat again and furrowed his brow omi-
nously. "We were all of us surprised by our pastor's sudden announcement of his intention to marry, especially without consulting
the board on his plans. To add insult to injury, he failed to invite a
single member here present to the wedding." He paused impor-

282 • *Marie Bostwick*

tantly before going on. "However, we are all good Christians here, and mindful of our Lord's teaching, we have decided to forgive and forget. So, Pastor Van Dyver and"—he nodded in my direction, his eyes twinkling just a bit—"Mrs. Van Dyver, please accept our congratulations on the celebration of your nuptials. Since we couldn't join you at the ceremony, we thought we'd at least better come to the reception, which we decided to throw for you ourselves. It will commence immediately following the service in my store!" At this triumphant finish, the congregation burst into applause. Paul still looked a bit stunned and seemed unsure of how to respond.

"Well, come on, Paul," Mr. Dwyer boomed. "Say the benediction! My missus made a huge cake, and it's over at the store drying out!"

The entire gathering laughed, and Paul joined in before raising his hands wide, as though reaching out to touch every member there present as he spoke the familiar, comforting words of blessing: "And now, may the Lord bless thee and keep thee. The Lord make His face shine upon thee and be gracious unto thee. The Lord lift up his countenance upon thee and give thee peace." With the organ's triumphant fanfare, Paul stepped down and away from the altar to join me, and we were suddenly surrounded by a throng of people, all wanting to shake our hands and wish us well.

Mrs. Dwyer had indeed made an enormous wedding cake, with pink and white rosettes and a doll-sized bride and groom on top. She'd even thought to paint a tiny clerical collar around the groom's neck. Everyone laughed at that. The other ladies of church had provided a fizzy pink punch, trays loaded with sandwiches, and bowls of salted nuts. Plus, they'd taken up a collection to buy us a beautiful gift, an entire set of blue willow china, eight settings. Mama was especially impressed with that. "Imagine," she breathed in wonder while running a cautious finger around a plate rim, "everything matching everything else and not a chip anywhere! I never saw anything so pretty. Do you dare use them?"

Paul winked at me from across the room where he was trapped with several stacks of canned baby peas on one side and Mr. Dwyer and Emmit Smalley, who were arguing about predestination, as usual, on the other. There was no hope of escape, but Paul didn't seem to mind. In fact, he appeared to be enjoying himself. I was, too. Everyone was so kind—though I found all the compliments and sudden attention overwhelming and a bit bewildering.

I saw Mrs. Hutchinson standing alone manning the punch bowl. She waved me over, and I worked my way through the throng to talk with her. She had always been a sweet woman, plump and pink with snow white hair, always smelling faintly of lavender and new bread. Even so, I was a little nervous greeting her. Her approval or disapproval of Paul's choice of wife could influence the entire congregation. She had been chair of the altar guild for as long anybody could remember—even when I was a little girl she seemed about as elderly as she was right now, which I suppose was about eighty. When she saw me squeezing through the crowd toward her, she smiled and filled a glass with punch.

"Thirsty?" she asked, offering me a cup. "It's warm in here with all these people." I thanked her and took a sip of the punch. It was too sweet, but I drank it anyway.

"Morgan wanted me to thank you for your letters to him. It means so much to get mail from home," I said.

"Oh, I'm glad to do it," she said with a dismissive wave of her hand. "It's my way of helping with the war effort. I try to write every serviceman from Dillon at least once a month. It's not much, but at my age"—she added with a wink—"it's about all I can manage." Then she asked, "How is Morgan? It must have been wonderful to see him."

"It was," I said sincerely. "I feel so lucky, which I guess is a strange thing to say when the whole world is at war, but so many people haven't seen their boys since they signed up and others will never see them again. Then here I am. I got to spend three whole days with my son. I'm married to a wonderful man, and now this." I spread my arm out to indicate the room and the warm welcome home. "I just don't know what to say. It's all a little—"

"Unsettling?" she interrupted, looking at me with her wise old eyes that seemed to see right inside my thoughts. They were eyes to trust.

"Yes," I admitted in a whisper and leaned closer to make sure no one else could hear. "Mrs. Hutchinson, when I was a little girl all the people in town either pitied me or mocked me because of my leg. Then I had Morgan, and nobody would speak to me at all. After Papa died, people softened up a little, but they still held me at arm's length. Folks tolerated me, but just barely. Now, overnight, people are talking to me, shaking my hand, asking me over for coffee. . . . It's nice, but I know it's just because of Paul. People in Dillon don't like me; they never have."

As I spoke, Mrs. Hutchinson's tranquil countenance clouded over. "Evangeline Glennon Van Dyver, that is a bunch of hooey!" she scolded, and I nearly smiled at her reproach, as though by invoking my full name she'd get my full attention, exactly the way Mama did to me when I was little—and exactly as I'd done when Morgan was a boy. A mother's instinct and a mother's care.

"When you were little, yes," she agreed, "there were people who pitied you, but mostly they were concerned about you. It's a small town, Eva; every child here belongs to all of us, and when they aren't well, we all worry. And, yes, there were children who taunted you, but that's what children do!" She pointed a gnarled finger at me and shook it admonishingly, then sighed with exasperation and continued on, more gently.

"If you'd had two legs straight as sticks, they'd have teased you about the length of your hair or the freckles on your nose or something else. But, you were so self-conscious! I remember how shy you were in my class, never even tried to talk with the other girls, always off by yourself, reading. You never let anyone get close." Just then two little girls in pigtails with matching ribbons, the Robins girls, approached the table. Shyly, they asked Mrs. Hutchinson if they could have more punch. She ladled the fizzy pink potion into their waiting glasses, gave them a smile, and cautioned them not to drink too much or they'd upset their stomachs. They thanked her and scooted off toward the food table, looking for a second slice of cake. Mrs. Hutchinson shook her head disapprovingly.

"They'll ruin their supper, that's all. Oh well"—she shrugged in defeat—"I suppose it's a special occasion. Now, what were we talking about?" She answered her own question before I could say a word. "That's right, you. Yes, when you had your baby and no husband to go with it, people were shocked. A lot of folks avoided you, and I'm ashamed to say that I was one of them. Others cut you cold. Well," she said uncertainly, "I don't know if that's right or wrong, but that's the way it's always been. I guess we think that sort of treatment will make girls think twice before they . . ." She lowered her voice, and I thought I detected just a hint of a blush on her well-lined cheeks. "Well, you know what I mean," she whispered.

"Over time, though, people saw what you were made of. People in this town respect you, Eva. They have for a long time."

"If that's true," I said, "they did an awfully good job of keeping it to themselves until today." Even as I spoke I felt a little ashamed of the bitter edge in my voice.

Mrs. Hutchinson nodded sagely. "You're right, Eva, but you've got to forgive them. It's hard for people to come right out and say what they think if they're not sure everyone else will feel the same way. Sometimes they need a little nudge.

"The day you left on your honeymoon, Mr. Dwyer called a special meeting of the church just to plan this party for you and Paul. I will admit, there were one or two hateful old busybodies (don't ask me to tell you who, that'd be gossiping) who wanted to turn the meeting into a vote on whether or not we should keep a pastor who would marry a 'woman of questionable character,' as they put it." I felt my face flush with embarrassment, ashamed to think of my past being discussed in public and mortified to imagine my actions casting a shadow on Paul. Mrs. Hutchinson eyed me sympathetically.

"Now, Eva, don't go upsetting yourself. Mr. Dwyer may be a little too fond of the sound of his own voice, but he's a good man deep down. He told the old biddies to sit down before somebody started telling tales on them! Then," she reported with a satisfied nod, "Charley Cheevers, of all people! I don't think I've ever known him to speak in public! Charley got to his feet and said you had more character than any woman he'd ever met. 'Look at the way she's raised her boy,' he said, 'and how she took care of her folks and ran her business. Good as any man! And she lives clean, too, never been seen to smoke or drink or chase after men. Sure, she made one mistake when she was young, and she got caught, but as near as I can tell, that's the only one. That's a damn sight less than most people. Hell, we ought to be proud to have a woman like that as our pastor's wife!'"

"Mr. Cheevers has always been kind to me." I smiled.

"Yes," Mrs. Hutchinson agreed, "Charley Cheevers is the salt of the earth, and everybody in town knows it. Once he spoke up for you, seems like it gave everyone permission to voice their agree-

ment. They meant it, too. At my age I can tell the difference between sincerity and the need to go along with the crowd." Again
there was a mischievous wink.

I could have hugged the old lady right then and there, but I still
had my doubts. "But really, Paul is the one who—" I started.

Mrs. Hutchinson scowled again and waggled a warning finger in
my face. "Don't go doing that to yourself. It's not like people in
town took to Reverend Van Dyver right off, you know. He was
awful different, and it made them nervous. He was good-looking,
but he had a strange accent and manner. He preached long, serious
sermons full of big words that hit a little too close to home for most
folks. Of course, we're supposed to come to church because we
want to find out where and how we need to change, but most people really come to service wanting to hear about how the other fellow needs to change." She chuckled, pleased with her own joke.

"People had a hard time warming up to Paul," she continued,
"but he seems more accessible since you came into his life, more
human. Make no mistake, Eva, this party is for both of you, and it's
more an apology than a wedding celebration. It's the church's way
of saying we're sorry for the way we've treated you both in the past;
and, Eva," she said hoarsely, raising her chin and looking me in the
eye, as though determined to face the music square on, "I include
myself on the list of those needing your forgiveness. We were wrong.
But there's no one we'd rather have lead our church than you and
Paul. The only question is, will you accept our apology?"

For a second I was moved beyond words; then I said, "Of course
I will," and somehow just saying those words filled me with a light-
ness I'd been waiting for all my life. For the first time, I felt like I
was in exactly the right place: home. Without thinking, I embraced
Mrs. Hutchinson. Hugging her was like wrapping my arms around
a pile of sweet, warm bread dough. When she squeezed me back,

we lost our balance for a moment and nearly tipped over the punch bowl. With a joint gasp, we broke apart just in time to grab the bowl before it spilled. Then, looking at each other and realizing how close we'd come to unleashing a pink, sticky flood all over the pristine white tablecloth, we broke into a tide of laughter that attracted the attention of Mrs. Dwyer, who was working nearby refilling the sandwich trays.

"What are you two up to?" she asked cheerily.

"Isn't it wonderful?" Mrs. Hutchinson grinned and patted me on the arm. "Mrs. Van Dyver has just agreed to make a quilt for the raffle at the church bazaar this year, haven't you, Eva? " Her eyes twinkled, as she was clearly enjoying the look of confusion on my face.

My jaw had dropped in surprise, but Mrs. Dwyer's expectant face showed me there was only one thing I could say.

"Of course, I'd be happy to."

"Well, that is good news!" Mrs. Dwyer exclaimed. "Your quilts are so beautiful, Eva, I'm sure we'll raise more money than ever before. We'll be halfway to a new organ before you know it. How kind of you. But making a quilt is so much work, and the bazaar is in September. Is there enough time?"

"Well, perhaps some of the ladies would be willing to help me with the cutting and quilting?" I asked.

Mrs. Dwyer was enthusiastic about the plan. "I'm sure we could find at least a dozen ladies who would love to help," she twittered, "if only for the chance to see your work and learn from it."

"Wonderful idea," Mrs. Hutchinson agreed. "And after the quilt, Eva, we can start embroidering new altar cloths!" the elderly woman chirped, as Mrs. Dwyer led me away by the arm, eager to spread the word.

Chapter 24

July 1944

"Maybe staying here was a mistake," I said to Mama as we stood together at the kitchen sink, washing and drying a mountain of teacups left behind by the ladies of the Tuesday Sacred Sewing Circle. "The parsonage has a good-sized parlor. If Paul and I had moved there instead of telling the church they could rent it out, you wouldn't have to put up with all this noise and mess. Seems like someone is here every minute! If I'd known being a pastor's wife was such a big job, I'd have asked for a salary."

"Ha!" Mama snorted. "As though they'd give you one. Darling, every married woman unwittingly signs up for some sort of job she never counted on doing—none of it comes with a pay packet."

"Still," I argued, "I feel badly crowding you in your own home, Mama, surrounding you with chattering women every minute of the day. It's like living in a henhouse, and I know how much you like your peace and quiet."

"Actually," Mama reflected, seeming genuinely surprised by her own revelation, "I don't mind. It's true I've always kept to myself, but I think that may have been as much from circumstance as from choice. We lived out so far, people never came to visit much, and with your Papa around I never wanted for conversation. At my age it's nice to have people around, gossiping and laughing. It keeps me interested."

"So you wouldn't rather Paul and I moved to town?"

"Certainly not!" she exclaimed, "I'd be too lonely. Besides, if Paul wasn't here, who'd take care of the farm? I'd much rather have him around than a hired man. Luther Krebs never had two words to say for himself, and I never saw him that he didn't have dirt under his fingernails, not even on Sunday. The man made my skin crawl." She wrinkled her nose in disgust and scrubbed the teacups with renewed vigor.

"Well, Paul's not much of a farmer," I said, laughing. "He still can't milk a cow without spilling half the milk when Flower kicks the pail over."

"I heard that!" Paul shouted good-naturedly as the screen door slammed, announcing his arrival. He took off his hat, hung up his coat, and spied the pile of dirty teacups. "Shall I grab a towel and help you dry?"

"No," Mama demurred, "we're almost done here. Sit down and relax. You shouldn't let Eva tease you so much, Paul," she scolded. "You're a fine farmer, for a beginner. You brought in a perfectly respectable crop."

"I don't call two acres, tilled and tended on Saturdays and spare evenings, farming; it's more like a hobby." He fished a donut out of the jar before I could tell him he'd spoil his appetite for dinner, which would have been ridiculous, anyway. Paul was always hungry. He took a bite of the donut and then kissed me hello, getting powdered sugar all over my lips. Laughing, I wiped it off and kissed him back. Mama pretended not to see, but I noticed the trace of a smile on her lips.

"Eva's right, Mother Glennon," he continued, "I'm no good at all with cows. I always preferred sheep. They seem smarter, or more contemplative, anyway."

"Sheep are not smarter than cows," I retorted. "Just so dull-witted they can stand still for hours at a time." I poured him a glass of milk to go with the donut and set it on the kitchen table. "You're home early."

"My meeting with Mr. Dwyer was canceled. He has a toothache." Paul sat down at the table, loosened his tie, took a deep drink of milk, and sighed with satisfaction. "I thought I'd come home early and plant those rosebushes I bought in Liberal. I want to get them in before the weather turns too cold. Where is Ruby? I thought she might want a couple of bushes out near the caboose."

"Peter Norman came by earlier to take her for a ride in his new car. Smelled of shaving cream and bay rum." I nodded meaningfully. " And last week he took her to the pictures."

Paul raised his eyebrows in interest. "Is that so? Well, good for Ruby. Pete seems a nice enough fellow."

"I suppose so," I said begrudgingly, "but I have to admit I don't like the idea of anyone marrying her and taking her away. It wouldn't be the same if I couldn't talk to Ruby every day."

"We could always buy another caboose and make room for Pete," Paul teased.

"Very funny," I said, flicking a bit of dishwater in Paul's direction while Mama fussed that I'd get water all over the clean floor. I started to ask what harm water could do to a clean floor, but Paul very sensibly interrupted.

"Eva, Mrs. Waters is going to take over the Christmas pageant this year, and she wanted to know if you'd be in charge of the costumes."

I groaned at the thought. "Goodness, Paul, between making the raffle quilt, embroidering altar cloths, going to meetings of the WCTU, the Naomi Circle, and the Sunday school curriculum committee, I'm just about worn out. I hardly have a moment to work on my own quilts." I dried the last saucer and sat down next to him. Mama said she was tired and wanted to lie down before dinner, as she did most days when Paul came home. She'd never been tired in the afternoons before Paul and I were married. It was kind of her to give us some private time.

"I'll just tell Mrs. Waters you don't have time." He shrugged as though it were a matter of complete indifference to him.

"But I hate telling people no," I mumbled through a bite of donut I'd stolen from him.

"Well, you'd better learn how to pretty quickly or you'll die of overwork. Pastors' wives are always in demand, especially if they are beautiful"—he reached over, took my hand, and kissed it on each adjective, like punctuation—"and lovely"—*smack*—"and kind—*smack*—"and talented—*smack*.

"They admire your accomplishments," he continued. Just be grateful you never learned to play the piano." He grinned. "You'd never have a moment's peace."

"You don't think she'll be upset with me?" I asked doubtfully.

Paul shook his head. "Disappointed, but not upset. I'll explain it to her. She'll understand. With four young children and another on the way, she knows about being too busy."

"Lydia's having another? Does she have time to run the pageant?"

"Probably not, but I bet you Joseph and Mary will both be played by little Waters. She'd probably cast this latest addition as Baby Jesus if she could, but I understand he or she will not arrive until spring. Ah, well. Maybe next year." He grinned impishly, and I smacked him on the hand.

"You're terrible. But thank you for handling Lydia. Did you stop by the post office today?"

"I did," he said and drew a small packet of envelopes from the breast pocket of his jacket. "There is a letter here addressed to you with many exotic-looking stamps on it."

"Morgan! Why didn't you tell me?" I snatched the letter from his hand and tore it open before giving him a chance to answer. I unfolded the pages and cleared my throat before beginning.

Dear Mama and Paul,

Finally, after so many months of you enduring the 'small town' gossip and foibles of life in McDonald's 475th Fighter Group I finally have some real news to report! You won't believe it because I half don't believe it myself, but somebody pretty famous has come to visit us and give us some special flight training. I can't tell you who and I can't even tell you what he's showing us how to do, but I know you'll understand who I'm talking about.

Remember the picture I've had on my wall since forever? That's right! It's him in the flesh! I sure never thought I'd see him again in person. You can imagine how excited all the fellows are. Everybody has been asking for his autograph. Of course, I already have one!'

"Oh, my Lord! It's Slim!" I whispered to myself.

I spoke to him after one of the training sessions and said he probably didn't remember me, but I'd met him when I was five years old and it had been the biggest thrill of my life. He got this real funny look on his face, like I'd caught him out and he was embarrassed that he couldn't remember, even though he

*said he did. But, shoot, why would he? I was just one kid out
of the millions that thought he was the greatest. I was just the
one lucky enough that day to get picked out to meet him personally. Boy, I'll never forget it. And it seems my luck is holding out because he asked if he could take me out for a beer on
Friday! Can you believe it? There's a million things I want to
ask him! After all, he's the reason I wanted to fly in the first
place and I'm convinced there's still nobody on earth who
knows more about aviation than he does.*

*He's still got his stuff too! Just yesterday he was flying with
my wing and we ran up against the enemy and darned if he
didn't take out a zero that was dead set on doing the same to
him. Sent the other plane right into the drink! It was a sight to
see, I can tell you that!*

*Well, I have a million other things I'd like to write, but if I
don't stop now I'll be at the end of the chow line and there's a
rumor we've got steak tonight. I'll believe it when I see it, but
still, I'd better get over there, just in case. I'll write again soon.
Give my love to Grandma and Ruby.*

> *Love,*
> *Morgan*

My stomach felt hollow and sick all at once, like it had when I
was little and got the wind knocked out of me while learning to ride
Ranger. "It's not possible!" I cried. "How could Slim be flying a
combat mission? I thought the government wouldn't let him serve,
and now he just turns up in New Guinea? Even if they did, what are
the chances that he'd just happen to end up in the same unit as his
own son? Do you think he went looking for him?"

"I don't know." Paul said incredulously. He was clearly as confounded as I. "Maybe, despite all Roosevelt's rhetoric, Lindbergh's

just too valuable to leave sitting on the sidelines. Whatever he's doing there, it must be a very big secret. The papers haven't said a word. It's amazing that Morgan's letter got through intact. The censors must have missed it."

"And Slim is out there with Morgan," I murmured disbelievingly. It was all to much to take in. "Do you think he's going to talk to Morgan about . . ."

"It's time someone did, Eva."

"I know," I admitted. "After you and I quarreled that day in California, I was going to tell him, but I lost heart. It just didn't seem like the right moment. Now he's going to hear it from the father he barely knows, a stranger. It should have been me. Do you think he'll hate me for keeping it from him?"

"Don't be silly." He dismissed the very idea with a wave of his hand. "Morgan could never hate you. You've been everything to each other. He'll understand that whatever you've done, you've done from love."

"I hope you're right," I said doubtfully. "Whether I was right or wrong, it's too late to change now, isn't it? I suppose I should feel relieved, but something just doesn't feel right. Oh!" I shook my head, exasperated with myself. "Why do I have to think so much? Always four emotions at once! Why can't I just feel one way about things?"

Paul grinned. "If you did, you'd be very dull company indeed. You're complicated, Eva, but you're never boring. Cheer up." Paul thumped the table with conviction. "Everything will work out for the best. You'll see."

"Hmm," I murmured, unconvinced. "I guess I'd better tell Mama and Ruby."

"All right. Then come back and I'll help you cook dinner. It will keep your hands and mind busy with something else."

"You're right, "I agreed, but a warning bell knelled within me. There was no point in arguing about intuition with a man as practical as Paul, but I knew my heart wouldn't rest easy until I heard from Morgan again.

Sleep came at a price that night. All my dreams were of water, not cheery, babbling brooks or peaceful ponds, but water stretching on all sides, heaving and contracting like the breath of some terrible giant. I was afraid to move in case the giant remembered my name and swallowed me whole.

No matter how dreadful and real the omens, there is no way to prepare your mind for the moment when the Western Union man arrives at your front door with the message you've been dreading.

REGRET TO INFORM YOU YOUR SON LT. MORGAN GLENNON'S PLANE SHOT DOWN OVER PACIFIC JULY 27. SEARCH IN PROGRESS. WILL KEEP YOU INFORMED.

Cold ebony letters swam stupidly over the yellow paper sea, swelling and joining, shutting out the light until there was nothing left in the world but black, and my knees refused to support me any longer.

When I woke, Paul was sitting next to me on our bed, holding my hand, while Ruby mopped my forehead with a cool cloth and Mama peered anxiously at me from over the footboard.

"That's better," Ruby said soothingly. "You'll be all right now. You sure scared us, though. You've been out for a good half hour. Paul caught you before you hit the floor, but when you didn't wake up we called for Dr. Townsend. He's on his way. "

I looked up into Paul's troubled eyes. "I'm sorry . . ." I started to apologize, but the words wouldn't form in my mind. There was only one word left in my vocabulary. "Morgan," I whispered searchingly.

In the face of a crisis, Mama rallied her strength and took charge. Her voice sounded as firm as it had in the old days, as though Papa were standing right next to her. Maybe he was. "Don't worry, Eva," she commanded. "It's bad, but its not the worst news. They're looking for him. You've got to keep your mind on that and not give in to despair. There's reason to hope. Tell her, Paul. "

Paul nodded and reached into his pocket. "There were two telegrams, Eva. You fainted before we had a chance to open the other. Here." He handed me the second message, which was already rumpled and creased from handling. They must all have read it several times.

I'LL FIND HIM.
SLIM

Time slowed to a tenth of its normal pace. I tried to keep on a brave face, think positive thoughts, do normal things. Paul went into the church to work as usual, but not until I insisted, convincing him that I was fine and promising to call him if I heard anything. Still, he was home early every night, sitting next to me and holding my hand while we all pretended to listen to the radio.

Mama decided that we should keep busy and prodded me into cutting out fabric for several Churn Dash blocks with the idea that the three of us, Mama, Ruby, and I, would piece it together and have it finished to give to Morgan once we got word he'd been found. Despite Mama's prodding, I could tell she was just as worried as the rest of us. More than once, she sewed the pieces with the wrong sides facing each other and had to take out the whole seam and start over.

Ruby fidgeted in her chair and got up from her seat every five minutes, peering out from behind the calico curtains to see if the Western Union man was coming up the road. That whole week, she didn't finish a single quilt block. Cooking would probably have been a better choice than sewing as a distraction, but the minute news of Morgan's disappearance got around town, the ladies of the church had descended on us with casseroles and fried chicken and an assortment of pies. There was no need to make anything ourselves, and most of what people brought got thrown out anyway; worry dulls the appetite.

Though I had begun the project only to appease Mama, working on the quilt helped more than I can say. After a time, I found a rhythm of rocking and stitching and thinking, every stab of the needle a plea, a prayer, a supplication to God, to Slim, to the winds that blew over my head and halfway round the world to wherever Morgan might be.

On Sunday Paul said it would be all right if I preferred to stay home from church. "People will understand if you aren't feeling up to it," he said. I went anyway. I worried about Paul worrying about me. I sat in my regular seat and prayed without words, with groans and aches rising from the deep places in my soul until there was no way to contain them and tears ran silently down my face, so many I didn't even bother trying to stop them with my handkerchief.

I was grateful that people didn't try to talk to me much after the service, though many of them squeezed my hands tenderly and said they were praying for us. I thanked them sincerely. Mrs. Hutchinson found me and gave me a little bookmark with lace edging and an embroidery of a dove and olive branch she'd made herself. "I meant to save it for you for a Christmas present, but then I thought, why wait? At my age, it doesn't pay to put things off." Everyone was very kind and very careful with what they said. When I got home I'd never felt more exhausted.

As long as the days were, nights were longer. The house had never seemed so still and quiet, and my mind couldn't help filling the void with doubt. Lying in bed, the curve of my shoulders spooned tightly against his chest, Paul and I spoke in whispers, the same conversation every night.

"What if he didn't make it?"

"You mustn't think like that. You and Morgan were so connected, if he were gone, I think you would already know."

"Ruby didn't know when Clay died. Her own husband had been dead for days and she never knew it until the telegram came."

"Morgan is your child, your own flesh. It's different."

"What if they can't find him?"

"Slim said he would. He promised."

"He's said a lot of things before. Why should I believe him?"

"Because he's your best hope. Because he's the best flier in the world. Because he's a father who's seen his child face to face. He's already lost one son. He won't let it happen again. Only death could keep him from it."

Only death could keep him from it. I repeated that sentence over and over in my mind and twisted it in new directions; only Slim could keep Morgan from death, only death could keep Slim from Morgan, a poem to chant to the darkness. When the moon rose so high that no more light cut through the black, I felt the muscles in Paul's arm soften and go slack with sleep. I waited out the night alone, relieved when the clock finally ticked off the million minutes to morning and I could rise and use my hands instead of my mind.

Finally, late Wednesday afternoon, more than a week after the telegrams had arrived, Ruby got up from her chair to go look out the window for the hundredth time, but before she could pull back the curtain, I heard the tinkling of a bicycle bell. I dropped my sewing to the floor and went running out and down the road without even thinking to bring my cane, flying faster than I'd ever done before. Paul came running after me. I snatched the telegram away before the delivery boy could even ask if I was Eva Van Dyver. My hands trembled as I read.

MORGAN FOUND SAFE. BROKEN LEG, BRUISES, NO MAJOR INJURIES. HOME IN SIX WEEKS.
SLIM

Chapter 25

Dear Slim

Thank you for your letter and your good wishes to Paul and me, though I assure you I'm the lucky one, not Paul. But the deed has been done and now he's stuck with me for good! We really are very happy together and every day I marvel at my good fortune.

It is truly so good to hear from you and know you are well too. We should have handled it this way all along. Morgan says thanks for your most recent letter. He'll be answering it soon, but in the meantime sends his love. Thanks to you, he is recovering quickly and will be his old self in no time.

It bothers me too when you say that even though you are now so happy to know Morgan and want to find where you fit in his life, you are still filled with remorse about not doing it sooner. Please, don't punish yourself that way. It took great courage, greater courage than I have, to sit down with a son who was a stranger to you and introduce yourself as his father. If there is blame to be handed out, I certainly must claim a share of it.

Oh, we have been through so much, together and sepa-
rately, made so many mistakes and changed so much in the
past twenty-odd years! It's a wonder we bear any resemblance
at all to what we were; two children, innocent and trusting,
heedless and hopeful, walking hand and hand through a sea of
wheat, ripe for harvest. Slim and Evangeline. I had begun to
think of them as just shadows, memories or myths long dead,
but now I think I was wrong. They are buried in us somewhere
still. Perhaps the peace and the wisdom of years will yet wipe
out some of our mistakes and bring those two innocents back
to the surface. That is my hope for us all.

Sincerely,
Evangeline

The propeller sputters and hums quick and smart, as though it had been cranked only yesterday instead of sitting in mothballs for three years. It's almost as if the old girl has been expecting him all this time and now wants to show him she's fit and lively, as good as any fancy plane he'd flown for the military. Watching him grin and yell, "Atta girl!" as the engine comes to life, talking to her encouragingly as he checks the tires and struts, leaning against her body and smiling with pleasure as he feels the purring vibration within, it's clear Morgan sees his plane as more human than machine.

He hobbles carefully but confidently over to inspect the wing. He needs only one crutch now, more for balance than strength. Dr. Townsend sawed the heavy plaster cast off his right leg this morning. A beige-colored bandage is still wrapped around his foot where the two small toes were amputated because of gangrene. The doctor says once he gets the feel of walking without those toes, he'll be right as rain, probably won't even need a cane, though I've joked about lending him one of mine. Still, because of the injury, he's classified 4-F for combat and is entitled to a discharge. So he's pursued, and gotten, a position as a flight instructor at the new training base right up the road in Liberal.

He will start training P-38 pilots in a month, showing them how to mix their fuel the way Slim taught him, stretching their range another three or four hundred miles. It was that extra range that gave Morgan time to find an island where he could ditch his plane and wait for help. He was farther out than anyone thought possible, but Slim insisted the search area be expanded, knowing that Morgan would remember what he had been taught. Now Morgan will pass that knowledge on, and maybe another life will be saved. It makes me proud that after all he's been through, he's more determined than ever to keep flying.

Still, my heart beats a bit faster when I think of him flying again and all the things that can happen if a person is not careful.

"Now, Mama," he hollers over the roar of the propeller, which has become a spinning blur, seemingly as anxious as Morgan himself is to be up and off, free of the weary earth. "I've got a box set up on that side for you to climb on after I'm in. Paul will give you a hand. If you'll just let me steady myself on your shoulder, I think I can boost myself up."

He lays a big hand on my shoulder and pushes himself backward onto the wing while I stand as still as I can, worried that one wobble will send us both tumbling to the ground, a tangle of weakened legs, crutch, and cane.

"Are you sure you're up to this, Morgan?" I have to shout to make myself heard. "We've hardly got one good set of legs between us. Maybe we should wait until you're stronger."

"Mama, I've waited three years and I'm not waiting any longer! I feel better than ever. I'm young, I'm strong, and the wind's behind me!" He yells even louder with the sheer joy of being alive, a wolf howling at the moon. "Look up there, Mama! This is my sky! I own it! Now, get up here, old woman, or I'm taking off without you!"

After climbing aboard I turn and wave at Paul, who smiles and waves back, his hat blown off and his hair standing on end in the bluster. "I'll be right back," I shout as we begin to pull away.

"I'll be waiting right here!" His smile breaks into laughter, and I laugh with him, filled to bursting with the surprise and joy of that special knowledge that the man I love will be waiting for me.

We shudder down the landing strip, working and hopping and straining to break loose of the ribbon of runway that lies beneath us and upward into the cool, limitless edge of heaven. I see how right he is.

Everything is just as I left it, perfect. The view from above is unchanged, as miraculous as it was twenty years before, fresh and humbling as seeing it for the first time. I can barely make out Paul standing next to the car below, his face turned skyward, scanning the clouds for a look at me as I search the ground for a glimpse of him.

We fly southeast toward the farm. I see the house and barn outlined in shadow against the rich red and gold of the earth, just as I remember it from years before. I see Ruby run out of the house, alerted by the noise of the engine, and Mama following more slowly behind. Their faces aren't clear from so far away, but their silhouettes are as dear and familiar to me as if touching their hands. I would know them perfectly were I standing on the surface of the moon.

I stitch my quilt from memory. People it with those I love. Ruby and Mama. Morgan, a boy with his father's eyes. Papa, young again, his purple work shirt like a flag of courage. And Slim. And Paul. And me. Room enough for everyone, and the work not finished if even one is left out.

I reach out my hand to touch the wind, and the splendor of the skies reaches back, cool and welcoming, as though it had all been imagined for us and sits waiting patiently, rich and deep, waiting for those with hunger enough to journey on and heart enough to rise up, those who love life enough to be ready to lose it in the barest hope of seeing things from God's perspective, the world new and unblemished, without war, or malice, or boundaries, or blame. Things as they might be.

Slim's sky. Morgan's sky. Mine, too.

Acknowledgments

There are probably few things more presumptuous than sitting down in front of a blank sheet of paper and saying, "I think I'll start writing a novel today." This is why books have acknowledgment pages, because every writer knows they never write alone.

Dozens of people were with me on this bold, exciting, frightening journey from idea to printed page. I wish to take a few lines to thank those who helped me reach the destination.

Many thanks to David Milofsky who first told me I was a writer and helped me to become a better one; to my husband, Brad, whose unseemly optimism helps me believe that anything is possible and truly believes, however wrongly, that everything I write is the best thing he ever read; to my mother, Margaret, and my sisters Betty, Donna, and Lori, who never hang up the phone without asking me if I wrote today and scolding if the answer is no; to my gallant sons, Alex, Trey, and Jackson, whose humor and zest for living bring me joy and endless inspiration; to my many encouraging friends who endured the reading of early drafts, especially Susan Witkow, Raynor Cunningham, Jane Burke, and Julie Naughton.

Thanks to the warm, welcoming, and generous people of the Oklahoma panhandle region; to the curators and volunteers of the Mid-America Air Museum and the Seward County Historical Museum; to librarians in towns big and small, especially those at the University of Oklahoma Library and the Liberal Memorial Library; to the nice people at the Bluebird Inn in Liberal, Kansas, who make the best breakfast in town.

Thanks to those who showed me the path through the no-man's land that lies between finished manuscript and printed page; to my agent who has become my friend, Jill Grosjean, the patron saint of first-time novelists; to my editor, Audrey LaFehr, whose unfailingly kind and courteous manner always brings the word "lady" to my mind; to the good people at Kensington Books—publishers, editors, artists, copy editors, administrators, and support staff—who work so hard to put good books into reader's hands.

Finally and foremost, thanks to the God of creation, my Heavenly Father, who gives me, and every writer, a world worth writing about.

A Special Chat with Marie Bostwick

I love to read almost as much as I love to write. If you came to visit me at my house in Connecticut, the first thing you'd notice is books: books on shelves, piled on desktops and nightstands, stacked on floors, with more arriving every week. It is impossible for me to walk by a bookstore without going inside, and once inside I'm sure to find just one more volume I can't live without. One of the best things about reading is discussing a story with friends. I love that moment when someone says, "I really like the part when . . ." and everyone gasps because that was their favorite part, too, and they all start talking at once, throwing out questions and observations, arguing over character choices, delighted to discover that someone else understands exactly how they feel.

One of the most satisfying things about writing FIELDS OF GOLD was finding that my reading friends were so eager to discuss the book. Though I have fielded a wide variety of questions about the book, readers do seem to have some common enquiries. I thought this might be a good place to address some of them, just in case you've had some of the same questions as my other reading friends.

Whenever I read a book that is historically based, I always want to know which of the events really happened and which were the author's invention. Many readers have wondered the same thing about this story so, first things first.

Charles Lindbergh did barnstorm in Texas and parts of Oklahoma for a couple of years in the early twenties. There's no evidence that he had any romantic liaisons with any young women during that time; in fact, he seems to have been reserved and even a bit prudish as a young man. However, he was very good-looking, and it is not hard to imagine that the sight of the dashing young aviator may have brought a flutter to the heart of many a small town girl. Surely they tried to flirt with him, but did he respond? Who is to say? This is absolutely a work of fiction, though I have tried not to take literary license beyond the point of the believable. My historical standard was not so much what did happen as what could have happened. Lindbergh did go on a victory tour after his flight to Paris, and he did make a stop in Oklahoma City; who is to say that he couldn't have stopped off to see Eva on the way? Of course, the conversations between Eva and Slim were invented, and my attempts to explain some of his less admirable actions and character traits are purely personal conjecture. However, in the arena of actual events such as the kidnapping, Lindbergh's interest in eugenics, his work on developing an artificial heart, his involvement with the America First organization, and unofficial contributions to the war effort, including flying combat missions as a non-uniformed civilian and teaching pilots how to stretch their flight range, I tried to stay true to the historic record. The reality of his life was so fascinating that there was little need for imaginative embellishment.

Many people want to know where I got the idea for FIELDS OF GOLD. For me, every story idea begins with a question, a "what if" or "why not?" Usually those questions arise because of something I've read, but in this case, it was provoked because of something I'd seen: that wonderful old movie *The Spirit of St. Louis* starring Jimmy Stewart as Charles Lindbergh. In the film, Lindbergh is brave, shy, humble, determined, and seemingly a perfect human being. At that time I knew very little about him. As I watched the movie I kept wondering if he really could have been so flawless and if he wasn't, would that have made his accomplishments less heroic? This started me thinking about heroism in general, what it is and why we have such a need to pretend that people who do heroic deeds are perfect. To me, heroism lies in the fact that we sometimes exhibit traces of nobility and selflessness in spite of our flaws. It is in overcoming our fears, our circumstances, and the imperfections of our character, or in giving in to them, that we show what we are made of.

That is where my story began, with questions. My research showed Lindbergh was just as human as the rest of us, subject to the same weaknesses we all face, but I didn't want to write about Lindbergh himself. Historians have done a far better job with that than I could ever hope to. Also, I wasn't really interested in examining him as an individual. I was more intrigued by what he represented, the questions we all face in choosing whether or not to be the heroes of our own life story. Will we fulfill our early promise or allow the hurts, disappointments and tragedies of life overwhelm us? That's where Eva comes in. She is shy, fearful, bitter, cautious; in many ways she is just as flawed as Slim and began life with far fewer advantages, yet she chooses the better part. She is what gives the story hope and focus. This is Eva's story. Lindbergh was the catalyst for the story, and the events of his life added structure to the book, but by the time I was finished writing, I was much more interested in Eva than I'd ever been in Slim.

Sometimes people want to know if I see myself in my characters or if they are modeled after real people. The answer is yes and no. All the characters reflect pieces of my own experience, but they tend to be compilations of people I've known rather than specific personalities. For example, the relationship between Eva and Ruby is not based on any one relationship I've had but is reflective of the many strong, supportive relationships I've experienced with my women friends and family. What makes Eva and Ruby's relationship so special (and so familiar to those who are fortunate enough to have a true friend) is their ability to accept one another just as they are, in spite of their differences. They are there for each other through life's joys and sorrows, and are unswervingly loyal to each other and their friendship even when they disapprove of each other's choices.

One of the things that is so interesting about the writing process is the way in which the characters and places come to life. The fictional town of Dillon, Oklahoma, is a very real place in my mind. All the characters, even the more minor ones, are very dear to me because even in their worst, most gossipy moments, their care for one another is apparent. Still, aside from Eva, I think Ruby is my favorite. Her chattiness, energy, and no-nonsense approach to life balance out Eva's quieter, more thoughtful, and sometimes less confident personality. They really do need each other.

More than anything else, it is the relationships among the characters that drive the plot and the choices Eva makes. This is especially evident in the book's marriage relationships. It wasn't intentional but as the story developed, a pattern emerged among the successful marriages in Dillon. They may not have been flashy or wildly romantic, but the partners were comfortable with each other, accepting, committed, self-sacrificing, with shared common dreams and goals. This is true of Mama and Papa's marriage, Ruby's and Clayton's and, eventually, of Eva's marriage to Paul. In fact, it is only when Eva understands Papa's

312 • *Marie Bostwick*

assertion that love is shown not in temporary passion, but in sticking by each other through the difficult days and she is able to recognize and accept her feeling for Paul as true love.

It seems that growing up in such a loving home with such caring parents ought to have made Eva into a woman who could easily give and receive love, but that is not the case. Certainly her disability contributed to this, but it wasn't the only factor. In some ways, I think Mama and Papa may have loved Eva too much. Papa refused to see Eva's disability and, at some level, his unwillingness to acknowledge her as she truly was made Eva feel that her true self was not worthy of love. On the other hand, Mama prides herself on her realistic approach to life. In her determination to deal with Eva's disability head-on, she sometimes neglects to see how much more there is to Eva than a crippled leg. She fails to see Eva's strength, faith, courage, beauty of face and spirit, and to believe that someone could truly love her daughter in spite of her physical limitations. When Slim comes to town, Mama is happy that her daughter has had a romance, even if it is only for a night, because she believes that is the most Eva can hope for. Sadly, Eva believes it too. She settles too soon for a pale imitation of love and fights with everything she has to hold on to it because she can't imagine that she will ever deserve more. In Paul, Eva finds the perfect partner for love and life because he sees her clearly without the filter of fantasy and values her for her virtues as well as her flaws.

Of course, the compensating joy of Eva's painful relationship with Slim is her son. As a single mother, it would have been easy for Eva to allow Morgan to become the center of her universe, saddling him with the terrible but unspoken responsibility of bringing happiness and meaning into his mother's life. One of the things I like best about Eva is that she avoids her parents' mistake of loving her child too much. She is a good mother, devoted, though somewhat overly protective. She delights in her child and yet he is not her whole reason for being. She has her own friendships, her own voice and a strong artistic sensibility, which is so beautifully expressed in her quilts. She had dreams for her son, but when he shows her how small those dreams are in comparison to his potential, she alters her plans for him, points him in the right direction and lovingly releases him from her embrace. As a mother of three boys, I know the most difficult, loving thing a mother can do is let her children go, telling them she has absolute confidence in them when what she really wants to say is, "Hold my hand and don't let go." Eva's bravery in releasing Morgan to his future sets her up to take the even bolder step of confronting Slim and finding out the truth; he doesn't love her anymore, if he ever did. To me, Eva's willingness to face the truth about herself and her ultimate refusal to continue believing the fiction she has made of her own life is an act of courage that is simply breathtaking.

There are many, many more things I could tell about Eva, Slim, Paul, Ruby, and all the good people of Dillon, Oklahoma, and how they came to life on the pages you have just read, but there probably isn't paper enough in the world to write it all down. Thank you for allowing me to share their story with you.

Years ago, when I set out to learn to write, I dreamt my stories would fuel a few of those same animated, curious, thought-provoking discussions I have so loved taking part in as a reader. I hope that has been your experience in reading FIELDS OF GOLD and that my comments have added to your enjoyment of the story. If you have any other questions or observations, I would love to hear from you. Please take a look at my website, www.MarieBostwick.com, where you can find more information about FIELDS OF GOLD, book signings and upcoming releases. Feel free to e-mail your comments and questions to Marie@MarieBostwick.com.

Blessings,
Marie Bostwick